Sebek moved toward Daniel with his easy predatory grace and stepped into his space, as if Daniel was a thing he owned. He was too close. If they made their move, and Daniel wasn't quick enough…Daniel was standing as straight and stiff as he could, trying to match Sebek's height; for a moment, neither moved.

Teal'c's grip on Jack's arm tightened before his hand dropped away. As soon as the opportunity came, they were going to take it.

"Your threats are meaningless," Sebek said, and waved at the Jaffa, who leveled their weapons at SG-1. "If your friends mean anything to you, your choice is simple."

Daniel didn't look at any of them. His chin came up, and he pointed to the Ancient inscription. "Do you see this? Do you have the slightest understanding of what it means? It's a warning. It means whatever's in there is dangerous. A warning from the Ancients is incredibly rare." He leaned forward, nostrils flaring, gaze still locked with Sebek's, and said, "Only a very, very foolish person would ignore it. Whatever's in there is causing…this." Daniel swept one hand around in a circle, indicating all of them. "None of us are immune to its power."

Sebek threw back his head and laughed with typical Goa'uld condescension. "Why should a warning from a long-dead race mean anything to us?" he said. He gripped Daniel by the neck, long fingers sliding around his throat like steel talons. "It is that power we must harness. So now you will choose, or we will choose for you."

# STARGATE

## SG·1

### SIREN SONG

# STARGÅTE
## SG·1™

## SIREN SONG

### JAIMIE DUNCAN AND
### HOLLY SCOTT

FANDEMONIUM BOOKS

An original publication of Fandemonium Ltd, produced under license from MGM Consumer Products.

Fandemonium Books
PO Box 795A
Surbiton
Surrey KT5 8YB
United Kingdom
Visit our website: www.stargatenovels.com

# STARGATE
## SG·1

METRO-GOLDWYN-MAYER Presents
RICHARD DEAN ANDERSON
in
STARGATE SG-1™
AMANDA TAPPING   CHRISTOPHER JUDGE   and MICHAEL SHANKS as Daniel Jackson
Executive Producers ROBERT C. COOPER   BRAD WRIGHT   MICHAEL GREENBURG
RICHARD DEAN ANDERSON
Developed for Television by BRAD WRIGHT & JONATHAN GLASSNER

WWW.MGM.COM

ISBN: 0-9547343-6-X
Printed in the United Kingdom by Bookmarque Ltd, Croydon, Surrey

For our mothers

Jaimie and Holly would like to thank: Katie and MLHull for their valuable insight and suggestions; Lori Goldman for offering encouragement at a critical time; Sally Malcolm and Tom Reeve at Fandemonium Books for giving us the opportunity to publish the book; and Sabine Bauer for her assistance during the editing process. Special thanks to our fellow *Stargate* fans (especially the LJ crew), who share our love of the show and the team, and who have brought us both so much joy over the last few years.

# CHAPTER ONE

Colonel Jack O'Neill staked out his vantage point beside the meeting hall and eased down onto a strategically located bench. The village nearest P43-912's Stargate was pretty enough, with lots of tidy homes and flower gardens, and friendly folks everywhere. So far, this had been a completely uneventful mission: meet, greet, smile, exchange pleasantries, ignore the Relosians' awed and frightened stares at Teal'c, send Major Samantha Carter off in search of valuable things like trinium and technology, and let Dr. Daniel Jackson get busy with the negotiating.

In fact, it was always like this lately. A new planet, peaceful exploration, mundane trade stuff, and then SG-1 was on its way to the next mission. It was all so…routine. Which explained why Jack was bored out of his skull. This struck him as being pretty ironic, given the fact that many times in the past year, he'd wanted nothing more than a few hours of down time for a hot shower and a nap. But even so, a spectacularly loud explosion or a few firing matches with Jaffa wouldn't be completely unwelcome.

There were days he didn't mind the slow pace – days when they sat around drinking homemade barley wine, eating stews full of unidentified meat and vegetables, and accepting the gratitude of people they'd actually been able to help. On those days, Jack could forget that everything had changed around him while he was standing still and that his equilibrium was not yet restored. Daniel's return from the ascended state had removed that awkward off-kilter feeling he'd had the entire time Jonas had been with them, and now they were finding their old rhythm again as a team. The thought made Jack smile; their rhythm was a combination of staccato call-and-response, with a dash of shout-and-pointed-silence. It worked for them.

The missions were coming faster now that Daniel was back to his old self – almost at the pace of the second year the team had been together, after they'd figured out enough destinations to keep everyone busy and still have some left over. Jack reminded himself that he had the universe for a workplace. A little boredom was a small price to pay for that.

"Sir, there's enough trinium here to justify setting up a mining operation. Not a huge amount, but my preliminary guess would be two deposits, maybe three." Carter sat down on the bench next to him and handed him a hunk of unrefined ore. Her face was smeared with dirt, as though she'd been down there clawing it up with her own hands. He wouldn't put it past her. "It's a quality vein, extending about one mile beneath the surface."

Jack took the rock and tossed it in the air a few times, like a lumpy baseball. It was so light it might as well have been hollow. "Daniel thinks they'll give this to us for free."

"Really?" Carter snatched the rock mid-toss and began waving a scanner over it. "Maybe they've got no use for it."

"Or any interest in why it's useful to us." Jack tilted his head and watched Daniel in animated conversation with two of the Relosians, whose purple robes shimmered in the sunlight. They were wearing some of the craziest headgear Jack had ever seen, puffy red towers with rows of shiny beads dangling off the ends. Daniel accepted yet another ceremonial cup full of what passed for beer in the village. It wasn't bad stuff, although it made Jack's eyeballs burn whenever he inhaled too close to the cup. "Doesn't that seem odd?"

"Not really. They're pre-industrial, so it wouldn't occur to them that we plan to make weapons with this."

"Lucky us." Jack flipped open his chronometer and glanced at the time. Teal'c had left for the 'gate to report in to Hammond half an hour ago, and it was less than a ten minute walk. "Carter, did you pass Teal'c on your way in from the quarry?"

"No, sir." She stopped fiddling with the rock.

Wrapping his fingers around the watch, Jack tapped the wristband a couple of times. He had seven years of experience with this team, and Teal'c always reported back to him when he returned from completing a task.

Unless something was wrong.

Jack keyed the radio. "Teal'c." A short burst of static, then silence. "Teal'c, do you read me?" After a moment, he nodded to Carter, who gave it a try on her own radio. Still nothing. Jack straightened and shifted the weight of his vest around, to make it sit more comfortably on his shoulders. "I'm going to take a walk," he said quietly. "Stay here with Daniel."

"You think something has happened to Teal'c?"

He looked out toward the forest, then back at the cluster of huts near the center of the village. "Just keep an eye out."

"Yes, sir," she answered, as one hand came up to cover her P90.

Jack rose from the bench and moved off toward Daniel, who was surrounded by a group of elders and two pretty young women serving drinks. They were still talking. Amazingly, Daniel never seemed to run out of alien conversation starters. Sometimes Jack could barely think of subjects for small talk with people of his own planet; he supposed Daniel's fluency was a gift. Or a curse, for the person on the receiving end of all that curiosity.

"Jack!" Daniel gestured to the Relosians, some kind of interstellar sign language for 'hang on a second,' and said, "I've made some progress. They want to trade us for these beans."

"Beans?" Jack looked down at the shriveled grey things Daniel was holding in the palm of his hand.

"Not just any beans, Jack." Daniel curled his hand closed to protect his prize. "These are sacred ancestral beans, handed down by their forefathers. Each year at planting, these are buried in the first row plowed."

"And then a beanstalk grows, and they live happily ever after."

Daniel narrowed his eyes. "Jack, be serious. They are offering these to us as a gesture of lasting friendship."

"Right," Jack said. "Of course they are." He fluttered three fingers at the Relosians, a halfhearted 'be right with you' wave. They nodded their approval and turned to each other, their conversation escalating in a wave of excited chatter as their red-beaded hats clattered with movement. "Wrap it up, then."

"There's still some points to work out, and I don't—"

"SG-9 can do the detail work, like always."

Daniel nodded, though a troubled frown briefly appeared on

his face. Jack knew this was one of those moments – the missing details of Daniel's life that were hiding in the cracks of his post-descension memory, rising to the surface one by one. SG-9 would come in to clean up the offworld bargains and treaties; as a member of Stargate Command's flagship team, Daniel wouldn't have the time to spend weeks hammering out interstellar trade agreements. Now that he'd been reminded, he wouldn't forget again. Jack was never sure whether these kinds of details were recovered memories or something learned all over again. It didn't really matter, since Daniel was a quick learner.

"Start packing," he said, watching as Carter took up a position near the head of the trail. Without waiting for Daniel to pepper him with questions, Jack turned and set out toward the valley path.

The village sat atop a small green hill overlooking the forested valley below. The Stargate was hidden deep in the forest and invisible from the settlement. Jack followed the trail to the edge of the cultivated gardens and stood in the middle of the path, his gaze tracing its faint edges down the hill, across a short stretch of open plain, and right to the forest perimeter. He pulled open his front jacket pocket and withdrew field binoculars, then enhanced the focus and scanned quickly over the area. No sign of Teal'c.

After a moment, he lowered the binoculars, but his sense of alarm notched up a peg. He reached for his radio, and after a moment's hesitation, he keyed it. "Daniel, Carter."

"Yes, sir," Carter said, followed by Daniel's static-overlaid, "Go ahead, Jack."

"Gather up anything you don't want to leave behind – day packs only – and meet me on the trail."

"Jack, I need to—"

"Daniel, that's an order. Do it now."

"Trouble, sir?"

"Not yet," Jack said. There was no reply from Daniel; Jack knew Daniel's thousand-yard glare was currently burning a hole in the back of his vest, but he also knew Daniel was already three-quarters packed. There were some things Daniel didn't question – very few, but a direct order was one of them. That, at least, hadn't changed at all.

It took less than a minute for Carter and Daniel to make their way up the hill. Daniel was stuffing items into his pack as they approached, but he stopped long enough to hoist it on. Carter fastened the straps for him. "Did you say our goodbyes?" Jack asked Daniel over his shoulder.

"Not exactly, no. But I gave the beans back, until we could seal the agreement. Are we leaving?" Daniel asked.

"Maybe. Keep your eyes on the trail," Jack said. Carter raised her weapon in tandem with his own.

"I don't think these people are any threat to us," Daniel protested.

"Teal'c is late," Jack said, and that was all he needed to say; Daniel cut the commentary.

The canopy of trees shielded an unsettling kind of gloom, broken randomly by shafts of sunlight shooting through the thick overgrowth of leaves and moss. Too much contrast, and the light seemed as impenetrable as the darkness. It made Jack wary; too many ghosts in his peripheral vision, which wasn't quite as sharp or discerning as it used to be. He reached out with one hand and signaled quickly – *fan out, keep a watchful eye forward, quiet.* Carter and Daniel immediately dropped behind him to obey. With a distance of only a few paces between them, they continued moving down the faint trail.

Jack listened to the sounds around them, even as his gaze swept across the trail looking for shapes, dark masses, things that were out of place. They could have used Teal'c's tracking skills. His own couldn't compare. Anyway, it was possible he was wrong, that nothing had happened, that Teal'c had simply encountered a friendly local and—

"Ouch," Daniel said behind him.

Jack whipped around, his P90 leveled in the direction of that mild complaint. Daniel was holding his nose with one hand, looking pissed off, and Carter's face registered sharp wariness. Daniel reached out with one finger and touched the air in front of him. It shimmered red for a moment before the color died away.

"Force field," Carter said. She moved to the side, testing the boundaries; Jack moved with her, a mirror image. It took six paces for him to reach a firm barrier, but Carter continued on past that point. Carter met his eyes. "You're inside, sir; we're outside."

"I gathered that," Jack said tightly. All around him, the forest was alive with sound. He turned slowly, tracking stray noises he couldn't identify, and asked, "Doesn't this feel a little familiar?"

"Déjà vu," Daniel murmured, rubbing his nose. "We've seen this before."

"Several times," Sam said, poking experimentally at it. "Goa'uld design."

"Last time we saw it in a forest, though..." Daniel met Jack's eyes. "It was because of Aris Boch."

Jack's face twisted into a grimace. Four years had passed since their last encounter, but for Jack, the capture of his entire team by the bounty hunter, Aris Boch, had been a memorable event. All the details were fresh in his mind, from the force field Boch initially used to contain them, to the shield-penetrating weapons, to the way he'd held them all hostage to ensure each would cooperate for fear he'd harm the others.

*Can you take him?* Jack had asked Teal'c, because he really wasn't sure himself, and because he'd needed to know if they had a chance of rescuing Carter by force.

*I can.* Teal'c had seemed certain. Maybe he'd been wrong.

Jack backed away from the force field. Carter and Daniel didn't even need to be told what was coming next. They crouched and waited out of the line of fire as he raised his weapon and loosed a few experimental, useless bursts toward the shield. He didn't want to assume anything – some version of force field technology was available on half the planets they'd explored to date. That didn't mean Aris Boch was behind it. What were the odds?

The voice came from the edge of the woods, to Jack's left. "I see you've learned nothing since the last time we met. The mighty SG-1, trapped by the greatest hunter in the galaxy." A pause, and then, as if he couldn't resist pointing it out: "Again."

With a sigh, Jack turned and faced Aris Boch. It really was

déjà vu – same armor, if a bit more battle-scarred than the last time they'd seen it; same nasty-looking weapon, like the mother of all pistols, heavy, deadly and looking like it was a part of him as he casually aimed it in their direction. Cocky bastard. Although he knew it wouldn't work, Jack leveled his weapon at Aris, who only smirked at him, hazel eyes sparkling with self-satisfied amusement in the rugged face. Bad enough to be caught by a bounty hunter, but twice by the same bounty hunter was…well…

As if Aris could read his thoughts, he smiled broadly and said, "Embarrassing, isn't it? Don't feel too bad, Colonel. I've tricked aliens with brains twice the size of yours."

"Yes, that makes me feel much better," Jack said testily. "Where's Teal'c?"

Aris moved his free hand to his wrist. Teal'c's suddenly winked into view, sprawled unconscious in the middle of the path and proving that Aris wasn't aiming at the dirt. On instinct, Jack moved toward Teal'c and with a muttered curse jerked back from the forgotten force field.

Aris looked down at Teal'c and prodded him with the toe of his boot. "He's fine. You should already know I'm not in the business of damaging valuable merchandise," he said, adding after a beat, "If I don't have to." Teal'c stirred, but didn't wake. "If I had known he would be this easy, I would have gone for hand-to-hand."

Jack sighed. When Teal'c was on his feet, this was going to be ammunition for weeks' worth of ribbing. If they lived that long. Jack asked, "How did you find us? And what the hell do you want?"

"Good questions, Colonel. They're the questions I would ask, if I were in your place." Aris looked over at Daniel, then at Carter, his smile widening in response to their identical frowns. After a moment, he put his foot squarely on Teal'c's chest and pushed. Teal'c's eyes flew open, and Aris stepped back in a smooth motion, out of reach of Teal'c's long arms. "As for how I found you – blame your Relosian friends for that. One of them was only too happy to sell you out. But I'm afraid you won't get an answer to the second question yet."

Jack yanked his cap down, frustrated. Of course the Relosians had sold them out. The planet was too peaceful. Nothing that looked this peaceful was ever as good beneath the pretty painted surface. He should know by now not to trust people who wore fancy hats. Jack leveled the P90 at Aris's chest again – never mind that it wouldn't do any good; it made him feel better – then asked Teal'c, "You okay?"

"I am uninjured." Teal'c's murderous scowl indicated only his pride was bruised. Aris pointed his weapon directly at Teal'c's head. Teal'c pushed up off the ground to stand beside Daniel.

Jack gave Teal'c a long look. Wordless understanding passed between them. His team was outside the shield, and Jack was inside, effectively cut off from them.

"How touching. Everyone all together again." Aris smiled his cynical smile. "Especially you, Dr Jackson. The last anyone heard about you, you were…" He raised his eyebrows and circled a finger above his head. "A glowing cloud."

"Your intelligence really isn't that reliable, is it?" Daniel said mildly.

Carter stepped forward, drawing Aris's attention. "Look, we should be past playing games. We know what you do, and how you operate, so – just tell us what you want."

"Very bold, Major!" Aris squinted at her, his expression amused. "You've been getting used to taking charge, haven't you? Getting ready to lead a team of your own, perhaps?" When Carter didn't answer, Aris chuckled and went on, "What I want, Major, is for you and Dr Jackson to come with me. I need your expertise. And of course, I'll need the Colonel here and Teal'c as bargaining chips."

"We won't go with you," Daniel said immediately. Jack stepped as close to the force field as he dared while avoiding another jolt. His fists clenched; he forced them to relax. Daniel could say the words, but without some way of breaking through Jack couldn't stop Aris from taking them and he couldn't help Teal'c.

"Now, now. Dr Jackson, haven't we been through this already? I tell you what you're going to do, and you do it."

"Or…not," Jack said with more bravado than he could back up.

Aris regarded him pensively. "Colonel, I really don't have time to play nice. And I don't think you want me to force them, do you?"

"What kind of expertise do you need?" Daniel said. Jack watched him; Daniel was in full negotiation mode, all sensors on. Good for Daniel. "Because there's no reason you need all of us."

Uh-oh. Wrong turn. "Daniel," Jack said sharply.

Aris looked over at Jack, a smile twisting his face. There was a new scar on his forehead, curving angrily down past the corner of his left eye, which drooped a bit. "That may be true, Doctor. Why don't we ask the Colonel here how he feels about that?"

Jack set his jaw. There was no right answer, though it didn't matter what he said; Aris wasn't stupid, and there was no way he'd leave either Jack or Teal'c behind as long as he held two of their teammates prisoner. He wouldn't want them on his trail. "Looks like we're all taking a ride."

"Sir," Carter began, but Jack cut her off with a look.

Aris watched the exchange, then said, "Colonel O'Neill, I'm wounded that you don't trust me with the safety of your people."

"Trust?" Jack echoed. His finger twitched on the trigger of the P90, itching for a viable target. "You've never given us a reason to trust you."

"How quickly your people forget." Aris pointed at Teal'c. "I let a Tok'ra go, and I saved his life."

"I have not forgotten," Teal'c said, in a low growl. "But this is a new day."

A fleeting look of remorse crossed Aris's face. "Sorry about the knock on the head, Teal'c. It's business. Nothing personal."

Teal'c inclined his head in that stiff way that told Jack he was going to get his payback, eventually.

"Anyway," Jack said impatiently, "you didn't do it for Teal'c. You did it because you hate the Goa'uld."

"You know, that's right," Aris said as if it had just occurred to him. He smiled again. "It's irrelevant, though. Right now, you don't have a choice. You are, in fact – say it with me, now – choice-less."

"I hate that word," Jack muttered.

"Sorry to cut short the small talk, but now you're all going to march to my ship like good, obedient little soldiers," Aris said. Although he still had his weapon trained on Teal'c, Jack knew he could as easily point it at any one of them and ensure compliance. "Drop your gear here – I'll ring it up later." A few feet from Jack's face, a shimmer of red as the shield dissolved and fell in front of them. Aris stood patiently by, waiting.

Starting with Daniel and ending with Teal'c, Jack met the eyes of each of his team in turn as they stripped off their weapons and gear. No way in hell were they boarding that ship. Once they were inside the hold, there was no guarantee they'd be able to make it out again before it was too late. Besides, they still had no idea what the bounty hunter wanted them for, and all of Jack's instincts screamed that this was a disaster in the making. He motioned to Carter and Daniel to move out, then followed with Teal'c at his side. Aris was behind them, not too close, but close enough.

He couldn't shoot them both in time.

Jack and Teal'c moved apart a few steps. At Jack's unspoken signal, they made their move. A turn and a leap…and Jack found his nerve endings on fire. All his limbs stopped cooperating; he sprawled on the ground, shaking and twitching. It was ten times worse than being zatted. He gasped and gritted his teeth, trying to ride out the pain.

Somewhere nearby rose the muffled thud of a body hitting a personal shield – *that would be Teal'c*, Jack's brain helpfully supplied – and then Teal'c was on the ground next to him, flat on his back. Jack's hands and arms spasmed, and his spine was melting. After a moment, the white fire racing around his body died down to intermittent sparking, and he took a deep breath. So much for the brilliant escape.

"Teal'c. I'm disappointed in you," Aris said, leaning over him.

"It is, as you say, business," Teal'c replied. He sat up and reached out to Jack, who waved away his concern.

"I'm all right," Jack breathed, though his muscles were still trembling.

Aris leaned in and wagged the point of his blaster at Jack. "Just so you know, I'm trading you first."

Jack lay on his back on the floor and looked up at the ceiling. He drummed his fingers against his chest, tapping out the opening bars of 'Smoke on the Water.' "Slo-ow motion Wa-alter," he sang under his breath. The ceiling looked familiar. Just like the ceilings of all the *tel'taks* in his life, swirly brushed metal and random intersecting arcs. He pretty much hated *tel'taks*, he decided, slapped his hands down on the floor beside him and ended with a loud, "That fire engine gu-uy!"

Daniel's head jerked up from his chest. Teal'c raised an eyebrow. Carter glanced over her shoulder and went back to futzing with the door controls.

After unhooking his glasses from the collar of his shirt, Daniel slipped them on one-handed and peered at him. "Who?"

"Slow motion Walter," Jack answered. Lifting his head, he waved a hand. "You know, the fire engine guy." When Daniel's lips pursed and his eyes narrowed, Jack sighed and let his head fall back against the floor. "Are you telling me you never listened to Deep Purple?"

"Smoke on the water," Teal'c said. "Fire in the sky."

Jack rolled his head to look at Daniel and aimed a finger at Teal'c. "See? The *alien* knows Deep Purple."

A self-satisfied expression crept over Teal'c's features as he closed his eyes and went back to being a statue.

Carter's yelp and a shower of sparks cut off whatever Daniel had been about to say. "Damnit!" she hissed and sucked the ends of her fingers while she walked in a tight circle, ending up back at the door panel.

"You okay?" Jack craned his neck to look at her.

She took her fingers out of her mouth long enough to say "Yes, sir," and went back to glaring at the panel.

Through the door they could hear Aris Boch laughing. The intercom switched on with a click, and Aris's laughter was in the aft cargo space with them. "You break it, you're going to owe me.

These things aren't cheap, you know."

"If you open the door and let us hit you on the head with something heavy, we won't have to break anything at all," Jack pointed out reasonably.

"Except his head," Daniel corrected him.

"Yeah, except that."

After a pause, Aris gave a rumbling chuckle. "You aren't going to get through the door until I let you, and the only other way out of there is the rings. You'll want to hold your breath, though, if you go that route."

"You first," Carter grumbled as she leaned close to the open panel again and started pulling out crystals and putting them in her pockets for safe-keeping.

"I heard that," Aris responded, sounding wounded. "And you'd better put those crystals back like you found them. Since I *am* going to have to let you out of there eventually."

Jack rolled to his feet, looking in the general direction of Aris's voice. "And why is that? What the hell do you want with us this time?"

"With you? Nothing. But Dr. Jackson there is going to be useful. As is Major Carter."

Jack leaned closer to the com panel and said, "Nobody's doing *squat* for you, so forget it."

"Maybe," Aris conceded. "Or maybe…" This time his pause lasted so long that, by the time he took up the thought again, they were all looking at the ceiling and the hidden intercom speaker, waiting. "Maybe I'll appeal to your nobility." Somehow he made the word sound nasty. "You like to be heroes, right?" When none of them bothered to answer, he snorted, half-amused, half-disgusted. "Or maybe I'll shoot off your fingers or something, Colonel, until Dr. Jackson does his job. Either way, I'm going to get what I need."

With a frown, Daniel got slowly to his feet. He chewed his lip for a moment, staring at the floor. His hands found their way into his pockets as he assumed the casual, thinky pose that invariably made Jack nervous, and said, "What, exactly, do you need?"

"Daniel," Jack warned.

"Just tell me," Daniel said, holding up a hand to silence Jack.

Jack wasn't sure, but he thought he heard Aris sigh. "Nothing much. Do some reading. Keep the Goa'uld from killing everybody."

"Oh," Daniel said, ducking his head and then looking up at Jack, a little grin giving him crinkles around his eyes. "That again."

Carter smiled, not quite showing teeth.

Jack sat down next to Teal'c and laced his fingers over his knees. "You remember how to do it?" he asked Daniel.

Daniel shrugged. "Like riding a bike, right?"

"A little, only usually with more—"

"Gunfire," Teal'c said.

"And yelling," Carter added.

"And insolence," Jack said. "You remember your insolence?"

Daniel patted his pockets. "I know I've got it here somewhere."

"You are all very amusing." Aris didn't sound all that amused. "Sebek is going to laugh the whole time he's killing you."

"Sebek?" Jack looked the question at Daniel, whose face had already lit with puzzled recognition.

Daniel shook his head. "According to Tok'ra intelligence, Sebek – also known as Sobek – is dead. Bastet and Kali the Destroyer allied against him and killed him. Bastet took his head as her trophy."

"Or not," Jack said.

"No, that was reliable intelligence," Daniel said. "In fact, other Goa'uld believed it to be true. Yu didn't contradict me, when I mentioned it."

"While you were his slave?" Jack raised his eyebrows. "You and Yu had a lot of these little conversations?"

"A few," Daniel said, raising his eyebrows back. "Sebek was never one of the big players, I don't think. But I could be wrong. There's still stuff—" He fluttered his fingers next to his temple. "—missing."

"That's inconvenient," Jack observed and, ignoring Daniel's half-pained, half-pissed expression, turned to Teal'c. "T? You heard of this one?"

"There are many minor Goa'uld in service to the system lords, and many planets to be administered."

"Administered." Aris's voice crackled over the intercom, brittle with irony and anger. "Right. That's what he's doing, administering." The intercom clicked off.

Slumping down next to Jack, Daniel leaned his head back against the wall and stared into the middle distance. The brain was working. Jack could practically see him feel around the edges of the gaps in his memory. He looked away.

More sparks showered out of the control panel, and Carter jumped back and did a few more tight circles before shifting crystals around again.

Teal'c closed his eyes and was quiet, resting while somehow remaining alert, waiting for opportunities to present themselves. Not for the first time, he reminded Jack of fire, banked low and hot in the centre.

Jack drummed on his knees. "Slo-ow motion Wa-alter," he sang under his breath. "That fire engine gu-uy."

By Sam's watch, they'd been in the cargo hold for a little over eighteen hours. The Colonel and Daniel had 'I-spied' every single item in the room – which wasn't much, besides a couple of empty storage cases and themselves – but when Daniel had started with "I spy with my little eye something that means 'gift of the Nile,'" the Colonel had gotten testy and made a new rule outlawing the hieroglyphics in Goa'uld *tel'tak* wallpaper. After that, the game had deteriorated into an argument regarding the relative cultural value of Hammurabi's Code and *The Simpsons*, and she exchanged a quick glance with Teal'c to make sure he'd be ready to move if they had to intervene and wrestle the two of them to their separate corners. Eventually a remarkable detente was forged over the structural similarities of strip comics and petroglyphs, and Sam dropped her head against Teal'c's shoulder and let herself slip into a shallow doze. In her dream, the stars were stretched in long, solid bars, rainbowed as their light passed through the prism of hyperspace, and the *tel'tak* rode along those rails toward some distant point of blackness.

Falling into the gravity well, she woke with a jerk. Daniel was watching her.

"Bad dream?"

She shook her head, then rolled her shoulders, wincing as her spine crackled. Beside her, Teal'c was asleep sitting up. The Colonel was over next to Daniel, on his back, his cap over his eyes.

She braced a hand against the wall and levered herself up. One step over Daniel's legs took her to the tiny bathroom – at least Aris had left them with facilities, and she even had some water in her canteen. Their kits and all of their gear, including the rest of the water and the MREs, were in the forward compartment with him. The toilet had no tank and used some kind of chemicals in any case, and there was no sink in there, either. No use in thinking about their out-of-reach canteens, so she returned to the cargo hold and, with a pat on Daniel's shoulder, went back to fiddling with the door control panel.

After a few minutes, Daniel came and stood next to Sam, arms folded across his chest. He leaned forward to look around the panel door. "Not making much progress here," he observed quietly.

"Actually, I think he's got the system completely cut off from this side," she said.

"But the sparks—"

"Mostly for show, to string me along." She switched a blue crystal for a red one with the same lack of results she got the last time she'd tried that. "And to tick me off."

"If you know he's got it rigged so it can't be accessed at all from in here, why have you spent the last day working on it?"

With another shrug, she pulled out the red chip and replaced it with a clear one. "Because if he rigged it, he must have rigged it *somehow,* and if I can figure that out, maybe I can get around it." A little more fruitless twiddling, and she added, "And besides—"

"It gives you something to do."

"I never was good at 'I Spy.'"

"Nor was I," Teal'c said softly. He rose and rolled his shoulders. Then he stepped to the middle of the room and began to work his way through the fluid poses of a training exercise, loosening muscles stiff with waiting. Sam paused in her work for a little while to watch him and marveled at how deadliness could look so beautiful. Daniel watched, too, his face falling into lines of concentration, his eyes becoming more and more distant, as though Teal'c's orderly gestures were a part Daniel's own mental exercise, a physical mantra that led Daniel inward. Sam watched him watch Teal'c and resisted the urge to smooth the frown from his forehead.

Finally, as Teal'c came to the end of the sequence and began again, she turned back to the crystals with a sigh. Blue, clear, red, green. If she had a screwdriver she could pull the whole housing out of the wall, and then she'd be getting somewhere, maybe. Over the hum of the hyperspace engines, she could hear Teal'c's measured breathing. Blue, clear, red, green. The Colonel slept, rationing resources. Daniel explored the inside of his head, on the trail of details about Sebek, things he'd known in another life. The cargo hold seemed charged with potential energy, stored up, going nowhere. Or somewhere.

When Daniel spoke, his soft voice made her jump. "You know," he ventured tentatively, "we *could* let him take us where he wants and maybe see if we actually *can* help."

"Go where Aris Boch wants us to go? I don't think that will sit well with the Colonel."

"Aris said that there are people in danger. Keeping the Goa'uld from killing people isn't such a bad thing."

"You're assuming we can believe a single thing he says." She was tempted to start prying at the housing again, but her fingertips were still a little numb from the last time, so she settled for glaring at the panel. "I'm not sure I want to stake my life on it."

He looked at his boots, his jaw set. "We know his people are oppressed."

"Most of the galaxy is oppressed."

"That's the tricky part, isn't it?"

She fumbled the crystal she was holding and caught it against her stomach. In the center of the room, Teal'c stopped moving and became an attentive stroke of darker space at the fringes of her vision.

Daniel went on, "How do you decide what...who...is worth dying for?"

"You tell me," she demanded before she could stop herself. Sam felt a sudden anger expanding inside her chest, making her throat burn.

Daniel's wince put the fire out fast. More than a little appalled at herself, she closed her eyes and tried not to think of First Minister Dreylock and her denial of Kelownan culpability in the accident that had taken Daniel's life. Dreylock had made Daniel into a criminal. And *that* was a crime.

As if he were the rebellious voice in her head, Teal'c said, "Some neither appreciate nor seem to deserve such sacrifice."

Daniel looked at him, and, after a moment of consideration, straightened from the wall. "People are people. Appreciation isn't the point. You don't ask for the appreciation of the Jaffa when you fight for them. You don't ignore their oppression because they're undeserving. You believe in their freedom, even if some of *them* don't."

Sam looked from Teal'c to Daniel and back again. Teal'c had a point; the smaller, meaner part of her came back to Dreylock, her insufferable, arrogant self-righteousness as she'd accepted Daniel's gift while simultaneously insisting it was valueless. The anger flared again. The Colonel had fought until the moment of Daniel's death to prove that his sacrifice *meant something*. The thought of Aris *selling* that kind of sacrifice for his own gain made her sick. But Daniel was right, too; even Teal'c acknowledged it. The conflict between the two positions made an irritating noise in her brain, like the grinding of gears that failed to mesh. She rubbed her temple with her knuckles as if she could get in there and fix that. Now, Sam tried not to see Daniel in the infirmary bed, held together by bandages, dissolving into light. Gone. Instead, she looked at him standing two feet away from her, miraculously remade, completely new, still himself. All the same, anger glowed under the ashes.

She plucked at his sleeve to make him look at her. "Sorry," she said earnestly. She could see him reading her thoughts in her expression. "I'm not blaming you. I don't."

"Yes you do," he said with a brief smile that held no irony, only affection. "It's okay. I get it." He gave his own original question serious consideration. "On Kelowna, I don't think I actually made a choice. I think circumstances made the choice for me."

"You would have died in any case," Teal'c said. "But you died saving them. That is a choice."

After considering that argument for a few moments, Daniel finally nodded. "Then Aris Boch isn't as right as he thinks, is he?" He looked past Teal'c to the far side of the hold.

"About what?" Sam asked.

"About us. Even if we do what he wants, we're not choiceless. Not in the way that counts."

Sam turned to follow his gaze as he spoke and found the Colonel watching them with dark, unreadable eyes.

One year after Jack O'Neill had rejoined the Stargate program and formed SG-1, General George Hammond's staff aide had given him a doomsday clock as a gag gift, a gentle poke in the ribs because of the program's naysayers. It stuck up from his desk like a ticking time bomb, and Hammond had hated it, from the screaming red of the digital display to the way the numbers flashed once a second. Whenever he'd had teams offworld, he found himself staring at the numbers, thinking about casualty reports and the letters he'd written to the families of soldiers he'd sent through the 'gate. It hadn't been long before the clock went into the drawer and the aide was dismissed.

Even so, Hammond often thought about that clock. Especially when his people were late reporting in.

Hours inside the mountain never seemed to match up with the hours worked in the normal world above, especially when there were several teams offworld operating on the local time of their destination planets. It wasn't unusual for teams to return in the wee hours of the morning. Hammond carried a list of all the away missions in his head and, as if that bright red alarm were flashing in the back of his brain, he knew when a team was even a few minutes overdue.

This time, it was SG-1.

2300 hours came and went, but he waited a few extra minutes to be sure. "Anything?" he asked Sergeant Harriman, who was haunting the control room with him, two ghosts augmenting the skeleton nightshift crew.

"No, sir." Harriman checked his watch against the 'gate system's internal clock. "Ten minutes overdue."

Hammond looked through the heavy bulletproof glass at the silent grey mass of the 'gate. "Dial it up," he said. "There might be a problem on the other end."

"Yes, sir," Harriman said. A moment later, the floor shuddered as the 'gate slowly came to life. Even after all these years, they still had those initial tremors during the massive energy draw. The Stargate was a marvel to Hammond. He understood its purpose, its function, but the fact of its existence still provoked wonder in him, from time to time. He watched the wormhole blossom and settle into a calm event horizon.

Harriman wasted no time. "SG-1, Stargate Command. Do you copy?"

They waited. Moments like these, the tension in Hammond's gut tightened until he felt twisted into knots. He narrowed his eyes against the glare from the event horizon while Harriman tried again. "SG-one-niner, do you copy? Colonel O'Neill, please respond."

Hammond listened to a few seconds of silence, then said, "Keep trying to raise them, Sergeant. And let me know if you do."

"Right away, sir." Harriman glanced up at him. "Should I call in any additional teams?"

"SG-14 is already prepping for their departure in three hours. If need be, we'll scrub it and move to rescue operations."

"Understood, sir." Harriman went back to calling every thirty seconds on the mark. Hammond stood behind him, mentally running down the personnel roster and ticking off available teams. No routine mission was a priority when his people were missing.

It was shaping up to be a long night.

# CHAPTER TWO

Aris Boch dropped his ship out of hyperspace beyond the defense perimeter. The planet that floated in the middle of the forward viewscreen was a thin crescent of light, not much bigger than his thumbnail. The orbiting *ha'tak* was closer, an oblique pentagram, the central pyramid gleaming gold like a tooth. The mothership looked no bigger than Aris's palm, and he couldn't help covering it with his hand and closing his fingers into a fist around it. When the voice of the duty officer growled out of the com demanding Aris identify himself, Aris dropped his hand and thought of replying with a few well-placed volleys. But modest little cargo ships like his *tel'tak* didn't *have* weapons, did they? And if they did, the Goa'uld must never know. He dutifully recited his pass-codes while letting his ship drift closer, riding the momentum he'd picked up before jumping to hyperspace above Relos.

As the numbers and letters rolled off his tongue, he let his gaze scan the outer ring of the *ha'tak*, a familiar game, picking his targets. The mothership seemed worse for wear – although in better shape than its counterpart on the planet's landing platform – and in a number of places the shielding was patchy and the interior decks were exposed to hard vacuum. He could make out the tiny, insect-like flitting of repair drones swarming around a new breach and snorted out a laugh. One dead-on plasma burst would tear open that whole section and cripple the ship, if anyone wanted to take the planet. But that was just it: nobody did. The *ha'tak* bristled at nothing, defended the planet from nothing but the galaxy's indifference. Aris drifted on.

His authorization received, he goosed the sublight engines and vectored toward the planet. For a moment, the ship shuddered and Aris was pushed back in his seat while the inertial dampeners struggled lamely to realign forces. The hyperspace drive gave a hiccup, and a hyperspace window partially formed ahead of the ship only to collapse again, sending a wave of distortion out in all directions.

Over the com, the duty officer barked a query, and Aris grumbled a reply, the last bit about trashy Goa'uld workmanship prudently kept under his breath.

He couldn't afford to be too picky. After destroying the last one, he'd been lucky to get a ship out of Sebek at all. It was bad enough to have pissed off Sokar by ditching not only his Tok'ra target but the consolation prize – Teal'c – as well. That had been nothing, however, compared to coming home by Stargate empty-handed: no *tel'tak*, no payment, no useful intel to sell to Sebek, and hoping he wouldn't be killed the moment he stepped through the 'gate. Two-and-a-half years was long enough to go without transportation, to play nice with a Goa'uld and trade without a position of strength, to have to travel by 'gate and by paying passage or, more often, by stealing transportation offworld lest he lose the independence of his income. But Aris was a patient man, and if the *tel'tak* he'd been given was barely spaceworthy, well, it was still spaceworthy, and that was enough. He'd had time to build up Sebek's trust, such as it was, and to pay attention to what was going on in the galaxy.

If all went well, he wouldn't be forced to serve the Goa'uld much longer.

That thought brought him back to the planet, which was now a half-circle as the *tel'tak* traced its slow arc dayward. Nightside, there were no lights visible at all – not that he expected any – although he could imagine that, back when that first Goa'uld *ha'tak* had lunged into orbit from hyperspace, there had been at least a hint, something tantalizing, a glitter of occupation. Now there was only the rumple of cloud cover – and darkness. Today, as usual, a storm was spinning in the southern hemisphere, on the edge of the terminator, its arms outflung across a quarter of the world, its eye blankly staring upward. From here, though, he could smooth it with his thumb. But he kept his hands on the controls and squinted as the sun flared on the curved edge of darkness, flooded the cockpit with hard, white light, and blotted out the stars.

From space, his planet was beautiful again. He could imagine it as it was before the Goa'uld had come, before his people had been slaughtered and the young ones enslaved. The sight of *ha'taks* settling down to the ground, the screams of terror and the death that surrounded them all, were fresh in his memory. It had been hard to overcome his hatred, to smile and joke and deal with the Goa'uld, to find ways to flatter them and nurture their greed, increasing his value to them. He'd long ago traded his integrity for the sake of his life and the lives of those he had a duty to protect. But he hadn't been able to protect them, in the end, and the life of a hunter was much the same as that of a slave. He had no options, no way out, no true freedom. It was simply a form of servitude more pleasant than the choking death in the bowels of the mines.

Aris adjusted the velocity and let the ship fall into the planet's gravity well, angling toward the northern hemisphere where the storm's tattered edges meant wind and rain and numbing cold. The heat shielding held up against reentry, but warnings flared in red on the holographic readout on the viewscreen. Goa'uld script made everything – even good wishes, he suspected – look nasty. He turned off the alarms and hung on while the ship bucked down through the churning atmosphere. The pilot interface translated into mere numbers the hazards of wind sheer and gravity and all kinds of resistance, so his struggle to keep the ship from spinning was more mental than physical. Still, the muscles of his arms tensed anyway, corded with the effort even though his touch remained light and nimble on the controls. Overtaxed, the inertial dampeners went offline, and for a second Aris was pulled in two directions at once when the ship barrel-rolled and the internal gravity fought with the planet's. He shut the ship's gravity plating down, got the *tel'tak* flying straight and upright again, skimming a ceiling of roiling clouds and buffeted by sheets of rain.

There had been a moment in his youth, a day when he'd had to make a choice. The risk had been great when he'd snapped the neck of a faithless Jaffa whose fear of his god was not enough to keep him honest. His prize could have earned him instant death, but it impressed Sokar enough to give him the tools he needed: access to the Stargate, and basic weapons. From there Aris had built his reputation, first with Sokar, and then with other Goa'uld who understood the value of barter for things they couldn't obtain without drawing too much attention to their activities. He was indiscriminate in the jobs he took. He couldn't afford a conscience, even when it kept him awake at night.

He leaned forward a little and peered down at familiar territory. From this altitude, the mountain ranges, one for each finger on his right hand, were parallel creases running north to south, divided by bands of snow and, in one vast valley, the black snake of a river. Dayward, there was an angled cage of white and grey, shafts of sunlight spearing between banks of clouds and setting a distant ocean on fire. But the clouds closed ranks and the scintillation of water dulled to steel once he turned the *tel'tak* inland, gliding downward until it seemed to scrape the bare peaks with its belly. Here, the turbulence was worse, tossing the *tel'tak* like a die in a cup, so he slipped into the widest of the valleys and followed its curving path into the shelter of the cliffs, lower and lower, until he could make out individual trees on the valley floor and the rubble of the moraine that lay scattered behind the retreating glaciers.

It was a circuitous route, but from down here he didn't have to see the scars in each of the two valleys on either side, dayward, nightward, where the cities used to be. Now there were only fields of tumbled stone below the mountains, the black scoring of orbital bombardment still visible above the treeline.

At the end of this valley, the glacier hung precariously from the edge of a cliff, spilling itself in a waterfall that, even in the early morning light, was brilliantly turquoise. Aris leveled off at the next plateau and then plummeted again, pulling up at the river's surface and shooting out the end of the valley, through a notch between sheer rock faces and over the open plain below.

Here, the darkness lay at the feet of the mountains like a panting dog, heavier, dirtier. The cargo ship slipped between layers of smog. Below it the river fell away, blackened and sickly, sliding over the last of the plateaus into the city. There were a few lights here, haloed in the sooty air. Someone was home.

"Home," he said out loud, with a twisted smile. The word tasted like acid on his tongue. He circled around the golden apex of the pyramid that rose from the black clouds like a parody of the mountains around it, and aimed the ship at a landing pad obscured by banks of steam belching from valley floor.

Inertial dampeners, Jack decided, were overrated, or maybe Aris Boch hadn't bothered with them when he went for the upgrade package on the *tel'tak*. Either way, Jack was happy he had a pilot's stomach, because the ship was bouncing around like a cork on a stormy sea, and the green cast of Daniel's face meant he was taking the metaphor a little too seriously. After a moment of complete weightlessness the floor rose up under them, only to fall away again. Jack hooked his fingers into the strap of Daniel's empty holster and yanked him down onto the floor before he could fall on top of Jack and break something important.

Teal'c was braced with one wide hand and one foot on either side of the frame, his shoulders hunched. The ship lurched one way and then overcorrected, throwing Carter into Jack and sandwiching him between her and Daniel. Jack slumped even lower against the wall, gasping against the weight of his own bones.

Once he managed to lift his head a little, he found Teal'c on his knees. "Aris Boch has increased the internal gravity," Teal'c said between gritted teeth. He collapsed onto the floor and rolled laboriously onto his back.

"No kidding," Jack managed, before the world telescoped to a bright prick of light and winked out.

When he opened his eyes, he was still on the floor, feeling like his limbs were being held down by sandbags. It took a second for him to register that he was half right. Carter had fallen onto his left leg and still lay draped face-down over him, her spiky blond hair hiding part of his boot.

"Heavy," Daniel said and after a beat drawled, "Man."

"Very funny," Jack replied with a grimace as he got his elbows under himself and levered himself up. The weight was easing a little now. Daniel's face started to go green again. "Don't you dare," Jack warned him and wiggled his foot next to Carter's head. "C'mon, Major. My leg's asleep."

With a groan she managed to get to her hands and knees.

"What the hell was that?" Jack demanded. He pulled his leg out from under her and circled his ankle. Pins and needles stabbed all the way to his hip. He flipped open his watch. Twenty minutes.

"Maybe malfunction in the gravity plates, sir," she suggested to the floor. "Or maybe a black hole too close to the hyperspace window—"

"Or maybe I like to see you flopping around like brentle fish, all disoriented and easy to handle," Aris Boch said from the doorway. With a swift kick, he deflected Teal'c's off-balanced lunge and, slamming him into the deck, stood on his spine and rammed the muzzle of his gun into the back of Teal'c's neck. "Stand up," he ordered, jerking his head toward the door. "Play nice and I won't kill anybody. Yet."

Daniel heaved himself to his feet and, steadying himself against the wall, said in a low, steady tone, "I'm not going to help you if you hurt them."

"I'm going to hurt them if you don't help me," Aris replied, mimicking Daniel exactly.

"Oh, please," Jack growled. The two men – Aris broad-shouldered in his armor, Daniel in rumpled BDUs – stood on opposite sides of the cargo bay and stared each other down. Jack resisted whistling the opening bars of *Rawhide*. All they needed was some blowing tumbleweed and a lurid sunset to give them dramatic shadows. Jack shifted his weight impatiently. After a day of sitting on his ass, it was time to move. "Can we take the standoff outside? This place is giving me a headache."

And it was. Whatever Aris had done to the gravity plates, being on the ground wasn't helping, and Jack still felt like there were lead weights around his ankles. When they filed out ahead of Aris and his gun, Jack was pretty disappointed to discover that the problem wasn't with the ship but with the planet.

"Oh great," he muttered. "One of those."

Carter stumbled across the threshold into the grey light and said, "Gravity's substantially higher than Earth's."

"Yeah, got that." Jack tried not to drag his feet. It was undignified.

"Welcome to Atropos," Aris said, and swung his free arm expansively to take in the whole landscape.

Suddenly, the gaudy golden interior of the *tel'tak* didn't look so bad.

Atropos wasn't exactly a pretty planet. Once upon a time it might have been a lovely vacation spot; Jack could see the appeal of the sweeping mountains and waterfalls. But now even the water seemed depressed by the place and fell with sluggish oiliness, made heavy by silt. The sun was a bleary eye peering between two peaks, and the mountains cast cold shadows into the valley beneath them.

From their vantage point on the landing above the valley, Jack followed the biggest of the rivers as it made its tortured way between its banks and into the city below. Its black gleam was visible between the tumbled angles of buildings designed, it seemed, after the school of ramshackle. There were a few crooked spires still standing. One tower in particular curved up above the rest like the fin of a shark and glowed dully, silver edged with sunrise-red. Jack wondered what kind of sea monster was cruising under the chop. The rest of the city, though, looked like it had been kicked over by a bratty kid on the beach, whole sections flattened around the familiar footprints of orbital bombardment. The craters' edges were probably still black, their bottoms still crackling glass, but it was hard to tell because the city had sort of scabbed over, and a motley collection of tents and lean-tos and makeshift structures encrusted the blasted spaces.

On its landing platform in the middle of the city, dwarfing even the shark's fin tower, the mothership caught the light, honey and red, the only patch of real color in the valley. It could only be described as smug. Pretentious. Jewelled. Squatting in the rubble of a civilization. In short: Goa'uld.

Jack took stock. Pretty as it looked at first glance, the *ha'tak*, in his estimation, was actually not in great shape. There was some serious scoring on the central pyramid, and there was a lot of heavy equipment hunkered down at the edge of the platform. He couldn't make out much detail, but there was definitely a sizable hole in the outer ring. He filed all this away. Sebek: discount bin Goa'uld.

Check. But even a crappy Goa'uld was still a Goa'uld. And Jaffa by any other name would still shoot on command. Most of the time. He exchanged a glance with Teal'c and got a raised eyebrow in reply.

Down below, lights were coming on here and there, winking tentatively as the sun blinked, clouds closing the valley in, and the world got a little darker and suddenly colder. Jack zipped his jacket up to his chin and coughed out a plume of breath.

"Atropos. Greek," Daniel recited to no one in particular. "Along with Clothos and Lachesis, one of the Fates who spin, measure, and cut a human being's thread of life."

"Short thread, I'm guessing," Jack added.

Aris scowled. "That's what the Goa'uld call it. We have another name."

"Of course," Daniel said, looking interested. "What is it?"

"Doesn't matter. It's not ours anymore."

Daniel's expression bordered on sympathetic. Jack kicked him in the ankle.

It was clear what the Goa'uld saw in the place. In the flank of the mountain on the opposite side of the valley gaped the entrance to the mine, dark, toothless, drooling a steady stream of workers and wagons heaped with black rock. On the next plateau down, the refinery groaned and belched fire, and the steady thumping of the crushers stomped through Jack's chest and made his heart stumble. How long, he wondered, would it take for that sound to grind a guy's bones to dust? If he were lucky, he reasoned, the stench would kill him first.

"Nice," Jack said sourly. The air was acrid and tasted a lot like rotten eggs, if the eggs had been soaked in gasoline. The back of Jack's throat was worn raw after only a few breaths.

Beside him, Carter had a hand over her mouth and nose. "Is that sulphur?"

"It is not," Teal'c answered. "But it is a by-product of the smelting. Extremely toxic with long exposure." His scowl was eloquent. "I have seen many naquada operations, but none on this scale," he went on, his eyes roaming the valley. "The devastation is extensive."

"Your capacity for understatement never ceases to amaze," Jack said and turned to Aris. "Tell me again why you want to save this place?"

Aris said nothing, but as he turned to look at the city, his controlled expression opened for a second, long enough to bring that sympathetic look back to Daniel's face. This time, though, Daniel had moved out of kicking range.

"It's not the place that matters," Aris answered finally. Jack waited for the zinger, but it never came. Instead, Aris waved his weapon toward the mine. "That way."

"Great. Another mine," Jack said. He glanced in Daniel's direction, but Daniel was busily looking elsewhere. Jack turned his attention Carter's way. "You ever get the feeling we've really done it all?"

"So much talking," Aris said. "And yet, there's nothing I want to hear you say." The tip of his blaster against Jack's ribs underlined his point. It took all Jack had not to turn around and try to rip the thing out of Aris's hand. Instead he set his jaw and started moving.

None of the people would meet Daniel's eyes.

This was the first thing he noticed; the second was the fact that all of them looked hungry. Not starved, but not well-fed. As he made his way down through the dark mine shaft beside Teal'c, pebbles slipped out from beneath their feet like a rolling carpet, making each step uncertain. He stuck his arms out for balance, but didn't take his eyes off the endless stream of workers filing out of the mine.

"Teal'c," he said, under his breath. Teal'c turned his head slightly, but didn't speak. "Are they all slaves?"

"It would appear so," Teal'c answered. He watched the parade of men, women, and children in threadbare clothes for a moment, then said, "It is clear the Goa'uld do not care if these people die in the mines. They do not intend to take them as hosts."

Daniel skidded to a stop; Sam crashed into him, nearly knocking him headlong down the hill. Teal'c's hand on his arm steadied him. He looked back at Aris. "You said it isn't the place that matters. You mean it's the people that matter, don't you? It's not about profit."

"Still talking," Aris said.

"I stop when I hear answers," Daniel said.

"You'll stop when I say stop."

"Good luck with that," Jack said to Aris. "Threatening to shoot him doesn't work, either."

"Nice," Daniel said. Jack ignored him. Daniel directed another question to Aris. "But what do you need us for? We can't do anything for you."

"That's where you're wrong." Aris took a long, appraising look at Daniel. "You and Major Carter over there have what I need."

Daniel glanced back at Jack, whose face was closed, his lips pressed hard together. "Care to elaborate?" Daniel asked. Jack moved a little closer, and Aris twisted sideways so Jack was in front of him rather than behind.

"You're a linguist, Doctor. A translator. Major Carter here knows math. But none of this will be of any use to you if I have to kill you for not shutting up. Now move."

"You won't kill us if you need us," Daniel began, but as soon as he said it, he realized his mistake.

Aris pointed the gun at Jack, then at Teal'c. Eyes on Daniel, he agreed, "True."

"Right." Daniel nodded slowly and turned back toward the path down into the mountain. He didn't look at Jack, but said in a low voice, "Maybe Sebek was exiled here. That would explain why Yu was so quiet about it." Ahead, a bedraggled woman raised her eyes to his, and curiosity compelled him to hold her gaze until she looked away.

"Perhaps Yu considered death too good for his enemies," Teal'c said. "It is not unusual for a minor Goa'uld to be sent to a world of living death for punishment."

"Indentured and sent off to a crappy planet," Jack said. "Sounds about right."

'Crappy planet' was really a bit of an understatement, Daniel decided. 'Hellhole' was maybe more accurate. They left the main tunnel for a narrower branch that angled, if anything, even more steeply downward, then another and another, until Daniel could feel the whole weight of the mountain on his head. The acrid air inside the mine was thick and heavy with dust that dimmed the lanterns and coated all exposed surfaces. The workers who labored upward past them were shadowed with it, their eyes dull white and the round circles of panting mouths shockingly pink in dust-dark faces. It was even colder in there than it was outside, as though all the winters since the mine was opened had settled into the stone. Bones would *feel* like stone before long in there. A mind could die before a body did, with nothing to stare at but black stone and dust, or the back of the person ahead, or one's own feet pacing the same path over and over.

A contingent of six Jaffa came up behind Daniel and the team, and the straggle of slaves shrank back against the wall, all eyes averted. After they'd passed, Daniel caught one or two of the slaves making a sharp, snapping gesture with their fingers, but seeing him, they dropped their hands and their expressions of hatred fell away, replaced by that blank dullness, empty despair. Somehow, he was encouraged. A glance over his shoulder showed him that Aris kept his own eyes straight ahead or on his own prisoners as if the slaves weren't there, three feet away from him. He paid no attention when one bowed old woman trailed her fingers across his armored thigh as he passed.

They trudged on. And on. After a few more turnings, there were no more slaves. The air was a bit clearer here, but the darkness between the light sconces seemed more oppressive. Daniel shortened his pace a little to come closer to Jack.

Finally, Aris stopped before a poorly lit chamber. "In here."

Daniel ducked his head and moved down a short ramp into the large open room. Three walls were the same dark rock as the rest of the mine, but directly ahead, a single slab of metal rose from the floor of the cave to the ceiling. Man-made, definitely, and covered with symbols – simple glyphs. In spite of himself, a thrill of anticipation rose in his gut. Something new, something he hadn't seen before, or looked for; something he hadn't known existed. He stared, fascinated, at the tiny symbols.

"Do you know what it is?" Aris asked him.

Daniel could feel the others moving closer behind him, but he had eyes only for the glyphs. "I have no idea," he said and smiled a little. It was another way of saying that he'd know soon enough. All translations were puzzles, made just for him. Jack's hand on his shoulder interrupted that thought, and he turned away, reluctantly. "It's…obscure," he said, in response to Jack's telegraphed warning. Of course he wasn't going to give anything away. "I don't recognize it."

"That's too bad, because the price of your freedom is an open door." Aris settled himself on a rock beside the door, one hand resting casually on his weapon. At his feet were signs of excavation, like someone had been digging around and later refilled the hole.

"Why is it so important?" Sam asked.

Aris leaned back, opened his mouth to answer. Then, as if he thought better of it, he paused. He glanced up at the door, and his expression changed subtly before he said, "If you can't open that door, my people are going to die. All of them."

"Why?" Daniel asked softly.

"Sebek wants whatever is in there. But," Aris indicated the door with the muzzle of his blaster, "he can't get to it."

"And he's taking it out on your people," Jack said sourly.

"Yes." There were shadows in Aris's eyes, and for a brief moment Daniel felt sorry for him.

Aris took a breath, then reached to his belt for a tiny packet of blue roshna. He emptied it into his canteen. "Major Carter, I don't suppose you found a way to break the cycle with this. Did you?"

Sam's face was pale. "We worked on the sample you gave me but didn't have much luck."

With a shrug, Aris said. "Fair enough. At least you tried." Still, in spite of his response, his eyes were shrewd when he shifted them to Daniel.

Daniel knew he didn't have to point out that their focus had not been on helping Aris but on figuring out if the roshna he and his people were addicted to also was responsible for their resistance to Goa'uld implantation. Thinking about it gave him a vaguely bitter taste in the back of his mouth. One more compromise they'd made over the years, one more opportunity they'd seized.

Aris upended the canteen and downed the contents, then wiped his mouth with the back of his hand. "Sebek doesn't like it when things don't go his way. It's making him crazy."

"How can you tell?" Jack said. "Is it the bombastic ranting or the penchant for gold loincloths?"

"None of his scientists could break into it, so he had them all killed. Ripped their hearts out, right here on the floor."

Daniel glanced down. Nothing under his feet but black rock. "That's...not comforting," he said.

With the canteen, Aris tapped the metal door, producing a hollow ring that echoed through the chamber. "Either you'll get into this thing for me, or I'll find another use for you."

The symmetrical patterns seemed vaguely familiar to Daniel – matched figures stretching the length of the door, slightly off-center – but he couldn't make a connection. "There are still some gaps in my memory. Without my translation tools, I may not be able to help."

"Oh, you'll be of use to me." Aris leaned forward, his brown-golden eyes black in the dimness. "You'll open the door, or I'll trade you for roshna. Either way, you'll serve a purpose."

Daniel nodded, but he looked to Jack, who was the final decision-maker in this arena, no matter whose gun was on them or what options Daniel might think they needed to pursue. They couldn't speak freely, at this point, and he had no alternatives in mind. Jack might, but he'd have to wait for his opportunity to arise. Jack was staring at Aris with a thinly veiled hatred, bold enough to make Daniel clear his throat for attention. Even with that unspoken signal, it took several more seconds for Jack to shift his gaze to Daniel. "I might be able to help," Daniel offered, not at all certain it was true.

Without a word, Jack gestured up at the door with one hand, then dropped his arm to his side in disgust. Tacit permission to proceed.

All the way across the door, lines of glyphs repeated, dancing and taunting Daniel. He traced them with his fingertips, waiting for them to tell him what he needed to know to identify them. Deep imprints, stamped into metal, uniform and strong. It was a bold language. He followed the line of symbols to the right, letting touch lead him.

"There's a mechanism here," Sam said. She was scouting around on the right edge of the door. "Maybe some way to open the door, with this."

"We've tried that," Aris said. "If it ever worked, it doesn't now."

Daniel's fingers ran off the edge of his canvas and into something more familiar. He pointed at the inscription in front of his face. "I don't know what the rest of this is, but that's Ancient."

"Great," Jack muttered.

"Are you able to translate this, Daniel Jackson?" Teal'c asked.

"More or less." Daniel turned to them. "It says, 'He who is locked in here shall die.'"

"I'm guessing that means 'do not open'," Jack said.

When Daniel met Jack's eyes, he read the change of plan clearly: *No more. Shut up.*

Apparently Aris saw it too, because he growled, "I don't need a genius linguist to tell me that a locked door means 'keep out.'" In one fluid movement he rose and grabbed Jack by the wrist. The gun to the side of Jack's head, he twisted Jack's arm behind him, straight out, and bent Jack's wrist with his thumb in the middle of his hand so that Jack's fingers splayed and he sank to his knees. Dexterously shifting his grip, he pinned a little finger and started to bend it back. Jack winced once before his expression went stony.

Daniel made his face settle into a determined but reasonable cast. "I'm telling you what I see, that's all."

"You have to see more than the obvious. Maybe the concept of the death of thousands is too abstract for you. Maybe I need to put this in concrete terms." Aris pressed harder on Jack's finger. "For instance, this finger is the morning shift in the mine." Jack's expression didn't change, but he hunched forward a little more.

Holding out a placating hand, Daniel licked his lips. From the corner of his eye, he saw Sam and Teal'c were poised in a way that suggested they were already plotting their moves. "I get it," Daniel told Aris levelly. "I get the concept, believe me. I don't need any demonstrations." The concept was all too clear, embodied by an empty planet that had once been his home, and a people who no longer existed.

"Daniel," Jack warned through gritted teeth.

"Jack." He waved behind him at the door. "The *Ancients*, Jack."

"The *Goa'uld*, Daniel." Jack clamped his teeth shut when Aris twisted a little harder.

"Start reading," Aris ordered.

"Don't," Jack said.

"Start reading," Aris repeated.

"Jack—"

Aris twisted again, and even from where he stood Daniel could hear the pop of Jack's finger breaking. Opening his mouth wide, Jack let out a gasp that didn't become a shout. Then he locked his jaws again.

Under Daniel's feet, the floor lurched. He was aware of Sam yelling something, of Teal'c pulling her back with a hand on her arm, but it suddenly seemed like they were on television, separate, flattened, unreal. His ears started ringing. He leaned his back heavily against the door and, spreading a hand out beside his waist, let his fingers fall into the lines and angles of the strange script. He could feel the meaning in them vibrating through his fingertips. A memory stirred – a silver-backed fish darting under black water – and faded. He let go of the wall and rubbed his temple with his knuckles. He'd seen this script before. Behind his eyes, he could feel the pressure of wind blowing up from an ocean, the smell of salt, warm grass. The Ancient words seemed to bruise his backbone and the pain anchored him. His fingers found their way back to the alien script. Still on his knees in Aris's grip, Jack glared into the space in front of him, breathing hard.

"Easter," Daniel whispered. He rolled onto his shoulder and pushed himself away from the door with one hand. He let his head fall back, and his eyes trailed the script from right to left, from left to right, drifting downward until they fell on the familiar shapes of the Ancient letters. They were layered on top of the original incised writing, as incongruous as graffiti on the Parthenon.

Behind him, Jack grunted and there was a muffled thud as he fell forward onto the stone floor. Outside the crushers on the plateau pounded their unrelenting rhythm and sent their vibrations deep into the mountain, through bedrock, into Daniel's bones, a shuddering like music you can't dance to. The Ancient letters seemed to float in front of the cryptic text, fuzzed around the edges as they jittered a little in front of Daniel's eyes, keeping time with the pounding in the mountain or maybe the pounding of his heart – he couldn't tell. He heard a gust of breath as Jack sat up and cradled his hand against his chest. Aris's boots scraped the floor. The sounds were too bright, and in Daniel's mind's eye there was a transitory gleam of fish scattering, memory dispersing, coming together – the smell of ocean, warm grass bending away from a salt-wind. Beneath the rumble and the shiver of the mountain, beyond his breathing, beyond the blocky, interlocking segments of the Ancient warning, he could see blank-eyed faces turned away from the sea.

"Easter," Daniel said again, more firmly, nodding.

"Easter," Jack repeated, his voice thin and breathy with not shouting. "As in bunny?"

Daniel turned to him, smiling, but the smile faded when he saw Jack's face. The hiss of wind in grass was lost to the grinding of the mine, the mass of the planet bearing down on them. Daniel leaned against the door again, let it take his weight. "As in Island," he said.

# CHAPTER THREE

"I'm sorry, sir. We should've tried to take him." Sam winced as she made a final turn with the strip torn from the hem of Teal'c's t-shirt and pulled the knot gently, binding the Colonel's little finger to the next one.

"Ow," he said dully, as though by rote. Then: "It's only a broken finger, Major. Save the heroics for the big stuff."

Sam looked up from her task and nodded toward the faint shimmer of the force field. Beyond it, Daniel was standing like he had been for the last twenty minutes: head thrown back, lips moving around unvoiced words, eyes roaming the text on the door. "If we'd acted then, maybe we wouldn't be here now," she said. "Tactically, this position is way worse."

"Thanks," the Colonel answered and pushed her hands away as she made some final adjustments. "Insightful analysis."

"I'm just saying—"

"I got it, Major. Things suck. Pretty much par for the course." He started to rub the back of his neck with his damaged hand but grimaced at the sting of pain and stopped. "Any minute now some Jaffa's going to come in here and be totally humorless and make us kneel." He got up, walked a few paces and flicked the field experimentally, then sucked on his tingling finger. "I hate kneeling."

"As do I," Teal'c said. He was sitting against the rock wall with his eyes closed. One of his hands rested on his stomach above his pouch, fingers kneading it slowly. There was a faint crease between his eyebrows.

"Well, it's not like you had to do it a lot in your former life," Jack said, and Teal'c smiled at him, ever so slightly.

Sam wasn't too enthralled by the idea of another audience with a Goa'uld either. Taking the Colonel's cue, she rubbed her neck and rolled her shoulders. There was a whopper of a headache looming at the back of her skull, and the pulsing shudder of the mine wasn't helping. Probably dehydration, she told herself, or low blood sugar.

The single MRE packet Aris had thrown into the makeshift cell with them lay beside her, open and empty.

For his part, Aris was finishing his second MRE and starting on the third. He tapped Daniel on the shoulder and asked, "What's this one?"

Daniel gave it a distracted glance. "Uh, macaroni."

"Is that good?"

He nodded, his eyes fixed on the text. "If you like chicken."

Sighing a little wistfully, Sam pressed her index finger onto empty foil and picked up a crumb of granola.

When it was halfway to her mouth, the Colonel said, "Are you going to share that with the rest of us?"

She met his eyes and put her finger on her tongue. He turned away with a small frown, and she felt a tremor of satisfaction, even though her brain was throbbing and too big for her head. The nice little fantasy about daiquiris and nachos she started to build was interrupted by a kick to the side of her boot.

"What?" she snapped.

"What, *sir*," he corrected.

"Whatever," she muttered under her breath and went back to cleaning crumbs off of the wrapper.

"Excuse me?"

"Whatever, *sir*."

The Colonel was scowling down at her. "What's behind that door?" he demanded.

She looked up at him and shrugged with one shoulder. "I don't know." *I don't have X-ray vision,* she added to herself. "Something the Ancients don't want anybody to get at, obviously." There was a sort of sickly pulsing in her eyeballs, and her mouth tasted like bright copper.

"Like what?"

Another shrug. "I don't know. Maybe it's quarantined. Maybe there's a really nasty bug in there. Like the one that killed them off."

"A weapon," Teal'c said, without opening his eyes. "Something of great power that they wish to safeguard for their return."

O'Neill aimed his finger at him. "Yeah. I like Teal'c's idea."

"You would," she said, this time not quite far enough under her breath and the Colonel's scowl came back to the power of ten.

On the other side of the force field, Aris was choking down his stolen macaroni and cheese while watching his prisoners. Daniel was oblivious, still in the same pose, only now one of his hands was following his eyes across the text, like he was trying to snatch the meaning out of the air in front of him. The rumbling vibration of the crushers was making her butt numb, but the Colonel was standing up near the shield and Teal'c's legs were sticking out and she had no space at all for her own legs and everyone else had dibs on space and good ideas and she was empty, full of nothing but 'yes, sirs' and 'I don't knows,'" like somebody else lived in her head, their orders, their intentions—

"You *would*?" Another kick on the side of her boot.

She glared up at him. *His* orders, *his* plans, *his* intentions. "Maybe it's not a weapon. Who knows why the Ancients would lock something up? Maybe it's somebody's garage for all we know." She was tired of saluting by reflex like her arms didn't even belong to her, like somebody inside was pulling strings, like Jolinar was using her voice and looking at Sam in the mirror and thinking 'me'—

Rolling onto her hip, she leaned over low and retched up one third of an MRE.

The Colonel crouched in the narrow space and brushed her hair back with the good fingers of his left hand.

"Don't feel so good, sir," she gasped. When he pressed the canteen against her arm she took it and allowed herself a small sip. It was mostly empty.

"That makes two of us," he said, giving her neck a pat.

"Three of us," Teal'c added.

She raised her head and gave the Colonel a thin smile of apology. Aris was still watching.

"Better pick up the pace, doctor," he suggested to Daniel, and finished the last of the MRE.

Daniel's eyes were starting to throb with the force of the headache

STARGATE SG-1: SIREN SONG

twisting through his brain. He pulled his glasses off and rubbed his eyes. The intertwined glyphs had taken on a uniformity he couldn't unravel, and they marched behind his eyelids even when his eyes were closed. He was acutely aware of his teammates a few feet away; his fingers twitched with sympathetic pain for Jack's injury. He would have to think faster, or make a convincing argument as to why he hadn't made more progress. Lying might work, if he knew what lie to dish out or what Jack had in mind from this point forward. Options were nonexistent, it seemed, but his perspective was limited to the wall, and the Ancients' warning, and his fear for his teammates.

He squinted up at the silent message, then pressed his palms flat against the cool metal. The glyphs were similar to the *rongo rongo* of Easter Island, but it made no sense – Easter Island had been populated a mere 1500 years, a drop in the bucket compared to the Ancients and the Goa'uld. He sighed. Polynesian culture was not a specialty he'd ever cared to pursue in more than a superficial way, and he had no reference tools at all to consult. "Maybe what's there developed independently on and offworld from something much older," he said out loud.

"Talking to yourself?" Aris asked. Daniel slipped his glasses back on, ignoring the twinge of pain that shot through his temples, and took a long look at Aris's face.

"Sometimes it helps to solve a puzzle if I trace the parts out loud," he said, without any expectation that Aris would understand. "I need a few minutes rest. To think it over."

"Rest standing up," Aris said, and pointed to the wall. "Feel free to lean."

Daniel shifted his glance across the chamber, to Sam's pale face, then to Teal'c, whose eyes were closed. Finally he met Jack's eyes. Somehow he was going to have to find out if Jack had a plan to get them out of this. Even an attempt at escape was better than nothing, and he knew at this point Jack's focus was on that and nothing else. To Aris, he said, "Just a few minutes."

"You humans are so needy," Aris said, as he rose from his perch at Daniel's side. "It's amazing you ever figured out the Stargate system in the first place."

"Yes, isn't it," Daniel said, pushing back a flare of personal irritation.

Jack stood as they approached, his bandaged hand dangling at his side. "Daniel?" he said, eyeing Aris. "Everything all right?"

"Peachy," Daniel said. Aris hovered right behind him. "I'm not making much progress." He glanced at Jack's hand. "How're you guys doing?"

"The sooner we get out of here, the better," Jack said, nodding toward Teal'c, who sat sweaty and still in the corner. "I don't like this place," he added, adding a tight smile to punctuate the understatement.

"Is there anything I can do to help, Daniel?" Sam pushed up from the ground and brushed her hands off on her BDUs.

Jack shot her an annoyed look. "How about if you wait until I give you the go-ahead, there, Carter?"

"Just trying to help, sir," she said, but the frown that creased her forehead matched her clipped tone.

"Guys?" Daniel said, looking from one to the other. The tension ratcheted up tenfold as they stared at one another. "What's going on?"

"Carter here thinks she's running her own show," Jack said. "She's been at it all day."

"She has not." From behind Daniel, Teal'c's voice rose, and they turned to see him watching them. "You are mistaken, O'Neill. Major Carter only offered her assistance."

Jack turned to him. "You haven't been *right* since Apophis brainwashed you, have you? How many times have you switched sides? How do we know that you won't turn on us again?"

"Jack!" Daniel said. He reached out a hand to grip Jack's arm, to get his attention, but the force field flared red between them and sent a sizzling jolt up Daniel's arm. Daniel stepped back, knocking into Aris, who shoved him away and retreated a few paces, all the better to hold weapons on them.

"Sir...sir." Sam lifted her hand in an appeasing gesture and then scrubbed it over her tired face. "I'm sorry, sir. I should have waited for your order."

"You have done nothing wrong," Teal'c said, still staring at Jack. They were toe to toe now, eye to eye. "Nor have I."

"They're all in my head," Carter said haltingly. She squeezed her eyes shut. "All of them. Every one she took as host."

"What are you talking about?" Jack said, his voice rising. "Make sense, Carter!"

"Do not raise your voice to us in this manner," Teal'c said, tensing with readiness. Daniel glanced at Aris, who was paying rapt attention to the little tableau, and then over at Sam, whose features were contorted into a mask of horror.

"It's happening again," Sam whispered. She backed away from Jack and Teal'c until she hit the wall and could go no farther. "I don't want your memories!"

In that moment, it clicked for Daniel – Sam was talking about Jolinar. Not her memories, but the memories from Jolinar's blending. He leaned as close to the force field as he could and said their names sharply, breaking their focus on each other. "Whatever's happening here, it's not about us. Do you hear me? Stop this."

Jack blinked at him, then turned toward Sam, who was sinking toward the ground, curling inward in a fetal position. "Carter," he said sharply. He took a couple of steps in her direction, then stopped suddenly and raised his hands to his head. "What the…" He staggered backwards and Teal'c stopped him, holding him up with one hand on his elbow. "Okay, that's…" Jack sat down abruptly; it looked more like a fall, to Daniel, but Teal'c eased the way. "I know *that's* not real," he said, and his hands went to the back of his neck, scrabbling down the back of his collar and over his bare skin there, and then to his throat, to smooth the unblemished skin. "Yeah," he said, as if confirming something the rest of them weren't privy to.

Daniel looked up to find Aris watching them. He didn't seem nearly as wary as he should; this was obviously not a new experience for him. "What the hell is happening to us? You know, don't you?"

Aris wavered under Daniel's direct, furious gaze, then admitted, "I've seen it before."

"And you didn't think you needed to warn us?"

"What good would it have done?" Aris shrugged. "The effects are temporary. I didn't think it would take you long to get this thing open."

"Well, you were wrong."

"Obviously. My faith in your abilities was clearly misplaced," Aris said.

"You need to take the others back to the surface," Daniel said. "I'll keep working on this, as long as you want. Just—"

"Not a good idea," Jack said. He was pale as a ghost. Teal'c helped him up from the ground; Jack patted Teal'c on the arm, a wordless apology, and Teal'c released him. The tension between them dissolved as quickly as it had risen. "We're not leaving you down here."

"Jack, I don't need you here." Daniel hated to say it, but if the brutal truth would convince Aris, then he didn't care. "I don't need any of you. Not even Sam."

"You do need me," Sam said. She made no attempt to get up, but her eyes were like laser points, focused on Daniel's shaky argument. "Maybe if you can't get the thing open with words, I can do it with science. That device…" She pointed to the small indentation in the wall to the left of the door and then let her hand fall to her lap. "I should stay."

"I don't need you," Daniel said again, a bit more desperately, but he could tell from Jack's expression it was a losing battle.

"With what just went through my head…or, didn't…" Jack cleared his throat, but didn't elaborate. "We all stay. Or we all go. I vote for 'go.'"

"What gave you the idea your vote counted?" Aris said.

"Then tell me what's happening to us, so we can use it to help," Daniel said.

"Would if I could." Aris crooked a finger at him, and Daniel reluctantly moved away from his friends until he was back before the door. "I've seen it in Sebek's Jaffa. Even in Sebek himself. It's been getting worse lately, but he keeps coming down here. It's like he can't stay away."

"I can't believe you didn't think this was information I might need to know," Daniel muttered.

"Is that enough of a 'reference' for you?" Aris taunted.

"Every piece of information is part of the key," Daniel snapped. "*You* don't seem to be affected by whatever this is."

"Very perceptive," Aris said. Daniel waited for an explanation, but of course Aris had nothing else to say on the matter; it was ridiculous to expect him to give up anything that wasn't pried out of him.

"Listen." Jack rubbed the back of his neck slowly. "Why can't Daniel work on this up top? Take a few notes, maybe…work from them…"

Aris tilted his head to the side, then said, "Too late." A moment later, the sound of Jaffa stomping down the corridor came to Daniel faintly, growing closer.

Jack sighed. "This day just gets better and better."

Jack wondered if Jaffa did something special to their boots to get that extra stomping, ringing sound when they marched. It was all about the intimidation and the rib-cracking, which, admittedly, was pretty intimidating. He figured it wasn't a coincidence that the Jaffa stomped in precisely the same rhythm as the throbbing in his finger and the pounding in his head. A conspiracy all over.

He rubbed his neck and listened to the stomping and the syncopated thudding of the crushers and pictured Aris Boch on the receiving end of some Jaffa intimidation. Then he remembered that Aris had probably been there and done that, thus their current predicament. So, he decided to multitask, turning part of his attention to actively hating the Goa'uld. Oh, and because they were so lucky, an apparently obsessive and possibly crazy Goa'uld.

"Is there any other kind?" Daniel asked.

Startled, Jack looked at him through the field. "Did I say that out loud?"

"Yeah."

"The part about the boots?"

"No," Daniel answered. "Not the part about the boots."

"This place sucks."

Teal'c glowered through the force field at Aris. "I concur."

Jack was going to respond with something snarky about how nice it was that Teal'c was such a team player, but Jaffa-shadows were looming, and the stomping was getting closer, and Jack was too busy counting the shadows to deal with Teal'c at that moment. Four of them. Two front, two back, Sebek probably in the middle. And, of course, Aris Boch with his blaster, and the force field, and the fact that Carter was still hunched over her knees against the wall, staring blankly, and that Teal'c was standing down but still scowling his most dissatisfied and scary scowl. There was a crawling in Jack's skin his rubbing fingers couldn't scour away. He saw kneeling and possibly rib-cracking intimidation in his future.

"What are those? Lizards?" Jack aimed his chin at the helmets of the honor guard that swept out of the narrow tunnel mouth and down the ramp into the antechamber. They were in the standard cowls and grieves, two of them in skull caps and the other two in helmets thick in the neck and extending out into long, toothy snouts. Red, beady eyes glowed as the Jaffa took up positions in a row behind their god.

"Crocodiles," Daniel corrected. "It's a symbol of rebirth."

Jack's smile was thin and bitter. "I love their sense of irony, don't you?"

Daniel nodded and turned resignedly to face the nemesis du jour. "Funny," he said.

Coming as close to the field as he could get without numbing his face, Jack cocked his head and studied the Goa'uld. "Funny?"

"The tattoos." Daniel pointed at the forehead of the nearest Jaffa. "That's Lord Yu's mark."

"Huh," Jack said. He wasn't sure whether to celebrate about that or not, but he didn't have time to think on it too much, since the Goa'uld was stepping forward and looking down his nose at them.

As anyone who knew the Goa'uld would expect, Sebek was wearing a fine specimen of a host, easily six-two-and-a-bit without the elaborate King Tut headdress. He tipped the scales at two-twenty give-or-take, but was fine-boned, full of lean muscles, like a gymnast or a diver. His eyes, traced out in dark kohl, were pale grey and too direct, aimed at Jack like they could flay him, turn him inside out. Even though his own eyes were burning and his vision was a little foggy at the edges, Jack looked back and didn't blink, and Sebek's full lips curled upward at the corners in a coy grin, part condescension, part admiration. His skin was dusted with gold all the way down his neck to the gilded crocodile cowl that encircled his shoulders and gripped the ends of his linen cloak in sharp ruby teeth. Jack wondered if any Goa'uld would be able to fight at all in that short linen skirt and delicate gold-wire sandals. Then again, the ribbon device on Sebek's right hand meant that he wouldn't have to. Rib-cracking intimidation was going to be the least of Jack's worries.

Sebek's smile widened as he leaned forward to run a gold-capped finger across Daniel's cheek, grip his chin, and lift his head so he could delve into him with those eyes. Jack couldn't stop his hands from clenching and was rewarded with a flaring stab of pain from his broken finger.

"So," Sebek said. Actually, it was more like a purr, his voice low and insinuating and confident, the voice of somebody who was used to never having to raise it or repeat anything. He had perfect teeth and showed them all as he turned Daniel's head this way and that. "You are going to unlock our treasure chest."

The voice crawled up Jack's spine and slithered into his head. Things stirred somewhere at the back of his brain, sibilant.

"Aris Boch tells us many things about your people. He has promised us that you are intelligent, talented in unique ways, and that you will be useful to us." Sebek smiled again and let Daniel go. "In addition to being sturdy and rather beautiful."

Daniel's face was taking on that clenched-jawed resistance, his brow notched in a frown. He met Sebek's eyes directly, and Jack pretended he didn't notice how similar their stares were. Behind him, he could hear Carter getting to her feet, the faint whisper of her jacket against the stone as she dragged herself up the wall. Sebek's eyes slid away from Daniel and looked over Jack's shoulder at her, frankly interested and assessing. The slithering at the back of Jack's skull was making his flesh crawl.

Sebek turned his attention to Teal'c. "*Shol'va*," Sebek murmured, drawing out the epithet like it was a term of endearment. The smile thinned and became satisfied, cruel. "A prize. There are many who would offer great rewards for your return. There will be a demonstration of our power, and you will remind your brethren what it means to defy a god."

"I will not."

Shrugging Teal'c's assertion away, Sebek addressed Aris. "You."

Aris stepped forward, his blaster angled toward the ground. Jack had to flinch a little inwardly when Aris bowed his head; he could feel the muscles protesting. His own neck twinged in sympathy and he added that to the list of things to hate the Goa'uld for, since sympathy for Aris Boch was the last thing Jack wanted to feel.

"If you are correct about these," Sebek waved a golden hand in the team's direction. "Perhaps your—"

He stopped, and the hand came up to his temple as his eyes rolled up for a second, showing white. Jack could hear Carter breathing hard behind him and a sound that might have been, "Oh, God," but he didn't turn to look; he focused on the Jaffa who shifted nervously, hunching their shoulders. The ones in the skull caps exchanged quick glances; the other two were like machines in their helmets, but still they seemed to crumple for a moment under the weight of their armor before recovering. Jack felt like he could crumple a little, too, curl away from the winding slither along his spine, and he reached out to steady himself on Daniel's shoulder, only to yelp out in pain when his hand grazed the field between them. Not that Daniel would have been able to do much, anyway, since he was swaying on his feet, eyes wide, unseeing.

Teal'c caught Jack, kept him upright while his vision grayed out and the hissing in his head tried to resolve into words. When Jack opened his eyes, confused as hell, Sebek had recovered and was watching him with that same unwavering gaze. Inwardly, Jack cursed missed opportunities.

The snake angled his head toward Aris, then pointed to Daniel.

"Bring him," he ordered.

Hopping to it like a well-trained dog, Aris grabbed Daniel and dragged him after the Goa'uld toward the vault. Daniel's feet were slow, his body boneless, and he stumbled in Aris's grip with both hands cupped over his glasses, his head hanging low.

"You will open this door," Sebek said with imperturbable assurance. There was a faint clatter as his capped fingers ran across the incised writing and then over the raised Ancient warning. "You will open it, and we will claim our rightful prize."

Daniel straightened and looked up at the door, his own fingers reaching out and sweeping reverently across the writing. "So…you actually know what's in there?" he asked faintly.

*Oh, no. No way,* Jack thought. He knew that tone of voice. That was the sound of Daniel disappearing into a question, sliding into that place where all that mattered was the script and the dead voices. "Hey!" he shouted. "If you're so interested in getting in there, why don't you do it yourself? You're the *god* here, right?"

Sebek turned his full attention on Jack, and Jack steeled himself for whatever was going to come next. As so many snakes did, Sebek stared him down, as if unable to believe the level of insolence that was being shoved in his face. Jack got some satisfaction out of that. Even if it was the last he was likely to have for a while. "Release them," Sebek ordered, and Aris's hand went to his wrist, where the controls were. The force field separating them from the Jaffa fell.

*This is the chance,* Jack thought. His muscles tensed, ready for action. Sebek's eyes were bright, and they were narrowed at Jack, and a moment later, when Sebek's hand came up and leveled the ribbon device at him, Jack could feel his grimace of pain beginning even before the actual sensation hit. Daniel was shouting as Jack hit his knees, saying formless words that were lost in the haze of agony…and then the pain stopped.

Jack pitched forward and caught himself on his hands, panting heavily. That had been too easy. He'd had worse. Much worse. It wasn't a good sign; there was more to come. He shook his head, trying to clear it, and listened to Daniel's voice.

"If you do that again, I'll never help you," Daniel said, in such a quiet, firm voice that Jack felt enormous pride in him. Even if it was incredibly unlikely his threat would work. So much for Daniel's curiosity.

In the silence that followed, Jack got himself together and his legs under him, and Teal'c's arm looped under his and hauled him up. He hated himself for showing such obvious weakness, even if it was out of his control. "Thanks," he muttered, and Teal'c squeezed his arm, a silent signal. Jack followed the direction of Teal'c's gaze, then met his eyes and Carter's, who nodded her understanding. Four Jaffa, one Goa'uld. The odds were even, more or less. There would never be a better chance.

Sebek moved toward Daniel with his easy predatory grace and stepped into his space, as if Daniel was a thing he owned. He was too close. If they made their move, and Daniel wasn't quick enough…Daniel was standing as straight and stiff as he could, trying to match Sebek's height; for a moment, neither moved.

Teal'c's grip on Jack's arm tightened before his hand dropped away. As soon as the opportunity came, they were going to take it.

"Your threats are meaningless," Sebek said, and waved at the Jaffa, who leveled their weapons at SG-1. "If your friends mean anything to you, your choice is simple."

Daniel didn't look at any of them. His chin came up, and he pointed to the Ancient inscription. "Do you see this? Do you have the slightest understanding of what it means? It's a warning. It means whatever's in there is dangerous. A warning from the Ancients is incredibly rare." He leaned forward, nostrils flaring, gaze still locked with Sebek's, and said, "Only a very, very foolish person would ignore it. Whatever's in there is causing…this." Daniel swept one hand around in a circle, indicating all of them. "None of us are immune to its power."

Sebek threw back his head and laughed with typical Goa'uld condescension. "Why should a warning from a long-dead race mean anything to us?" he asked. He gripped Daniel by the neck, long fingers sliding around his throat like steel talons. "It is that power we must harness. So now you will choose, or we will choose for you."

"Don't do it, Daniel. That's an order." It didn't need to be said, or so Jack hoped, but the words burst out of him anyway. Daniel's eyes shifted his direction, the whites pink with blood from bursting capillaries, and then Sebek raised him off the ground until the tips of his boots skimmed the dirt beneath him. Daniel made a strangled sound, words caught up and jumbled in the void of air.

Jack made his move.

Two steps, one punch, and he knocked the nearest Jaffa on the ground. Their body armor couldn't protect their faces, and Jack was on top of him in a split second, beating, punching, drawing blood with his fist. He heard the commotion behind him, *zat* fire, a shout, the thump of fists on flesh and a harsh cry of pain, but no time to stop to see who was coming out ahead. He knew his team's abilities; if it could be done, they'd do it. He got to his feet and turned in Sebek's direction, but the blinding pain hit him again, so fast it lifted all the breath from his body. He gasped and fell to his knees, and a hand landed on his shoulder. Sebek. The stream of light from the ribbon device blinded him, and the roaring in his ears grew louder as his muscles contracted, as his body tried to fight the invasion of fire in every cell.

"Sir!" Carter's voice, from somewhere behind him, but he couldn't move, couldn't fight, couldn't do anything at all but gasp and breathe and wait for it to be over. Blackness encroached on the edges of Jack's vision, a cool darkness that wanted him, and he wanted to fall into it.

And then he was on the ground, and the light was gone, and there was a sound so awful he couldn't process it. Someone was shrieking. Carter? No. Too shrill. Not Teal'c, or Daniel. Jack struggled to place the noise, but his thoughts were too jumbled to be any good. Nothing made sense.

"No!" Teal'c shouted, and the distress in his voice brought Jack back from the edge of unconsciousness.

"God, no, oh, God," Carter cried, and Jack rolled to his side, afraid for her.

When his vision cleared, he saw her. With a look of stricken horror on her face, Carter was frozen, one hand still on the throat of the Jaffa she had overpowered, all her attention on Daniel, who was on his hands and knees, rising carefully, a little uncoordinated but intact. Teal'c, who held a *zat* in his hand, taken from the Jaffa he had just killed, was unharmed. Confused, Jack looked back at Daniel, then – it had to be Daniel, though he seemed fine, he seemed—

On the ground next to Jack, Sebek was sprawled, eyes open. Dead. Daniel must have killed him. For this, Jack was going to forego the standard ribbing when Daniel said he didn't really want beer with his thank-yous. He looked up, the start of a grateful smile on his face…and then he stopped. Daniel was leaning on the wall, one hand splayed across the writing, oblivious to it, and he was staring at Jack. Slowly, a smile spread over his features and narrowed his eyes, a smile that was unlike Daniel. Not Daniel. But Jack had seen that smile before.

"Daniel," he whispered, and the smile widened.

"No," Daniel said, in a voice that was not his own, a voice corrupted by the thing inside him. A sick horror flooded through Jack as Daniel's eyes flashed the terrible yellow-white of possession. Sebek smiled out at him, using Daniel's body. "Now your friend will tell us what we wish to know."

Jack's entire being rebelled. His stomach turned over and he squeezed his eyes shut. He couldn't look. Not Daniel. God, not Daniel. But it was too late. There was a hand at his collar, and he let it haul him to his feet without protest; his body was barely under his control anyway. He was no use to Carter and Teal'c this way.

Or Daniel.

"Be smart," a voice whispered in his ear, and it took him a moment to register it: Aris. Fury surged up within Jack; this was Aris Boch's fault. If Aris hadn't brought them there, Daniel wouldn't be lost to them. Jack pulled away with a snarl, but Aris snapped him back with little effort. "Be smart," he said again, shoving his weapon into Jack's back.

"Take them," Sebek said to Aris, and it was Daniel's voice, on purpose, to taunt them. Jack heard a small sound that might have been a sob from Carter. He raised his head, locking eyes with Sebek to see Daniel's light blue gaze subsumed by the snake's will.

Jack turned to check the remainder of his team. Carter's face was contorted with her misery, and Teal'c seemed ready to snap Sebek's neck, even if that neck just happened to be Daniel's, too. Aris jabbed Jack in the back again, and Jack threw his hands out to the side.

"Okay," he said, and at the sound of his voice, Carter and Teal'c looked to him, seeking something to hold on to. He nodded to them both. Best he could do. They'd talk it over later. If there was time.

He caught a last sideways glimpse of Daniel as Aris herded them through the tunnels and back up to the surface, the remaining Jaffa trailing behind. Daniel's hands were running over the writing on the wall; Daniel's smile was filled with joy.

No. Not Daniel anymore, Jack reminded himself. Next time he saw the thing that used to be his friend, he might have to kill it. When the bile rose in his throat, he pushed it down, merciless.

That thing wasn't Daniel anymore.

# CHAPTER FOUR

It was good to be away from the pounding in the mine. Sam's head felt a little clearer already, except for a roaring in her ears that came from the inside. It was hard to see through it, think through it. She resisted pressing her fists against her ears or rubbing them across her eyes. Instead, she counted intersecting hallways, left turns, right turns. Modeled after the *ha'tak*, whose shadow sliced across the city and blocked out the light of twin moons, the complex seemed reassuringly familiar. The Goa'uld weren't innovative. They organized their space predictably. It wouldn't be hard to find their way out again, after they'd taken care of the Jaffa. After they'd taken care of Aris Boch.

Up ahead of her, the Colonel's fingers tapped out an uneven rhythm on his thigh as he walked; he was counting, too. When he turned his head to look down a passageway, she could see him in profile. His face was expressionless. Behind her, Teal'c was probably making a similar survey of the complex, although for him it would be more of a refresher course than anything else. A hundred years following prisoners through the corridors of Goa'uld motherships and bunkers would leave their mark in his memory, indelible as the lines in his palm. Even though she knew from experience where the brig was within the rectangular base of the structure, she counted hallways anyway. Her mind was still a little unruly and not counting meant thinking about Daniel.

He would be conscious, she knew. He'd watch his hands move, and the gestures would be all wrong. When Daniel was Daniel, he would read the writing on the vault door and his fingers would spread out, steepled and stiff above the incised figures – all those dancing human forms and intersecting curves that looked like animals balanced on mountains or wave crests – and he'd follow along each line like the physical movement of his hand through the air could restrain his brain a little, keep it from rushing ahead. Sebek wouldn't know this. Sebek would use Daniel's hands all wrong.

Sam balled her fists. The Colonel's hands hung open at his sides. She took a few deep breaths and made her fingers uncurl.

"Here," Aris said. The entourage stopped, two Jaffa on either side of the cell door.

The brig was a little different from the ones she'd been in on the motherships. The same exterior wall of horizontal bars, a door set into a solid wall, activated by a code on a touchpad. There were two other cells, one on either side, both empty. Sam thought of the people she'd seen scrabbling up the piles in the mine, following the carts, stumbling back down again into the black-rock darkness, or the ones sleeping huddled up against the fractured walls of the city, trying to absorb some of the dissipating heat of the day from the stone. They were rags and angles, and when they watched the Jaffa pass with their prisoners, there was nothing in their eyes, not even fear. Aris didn't even turn his head to look at them. The whole planet was a prison. Sebek didn't have much to be worried about.

She couldn't think of Sebek without the image of Daniel's face invading her mind. Sebek would carry Daniel's weight wrong. He wouldn't tilt his head back and let his mouth fall open while he was thinking; 'the genius guppy look' the Colonel called it sometimes, when he was pretending to be annoyed. Daniel would feel the wrongness of Sebek's gestures, the horror of them. She shuddered. Sebek had smiled. He'd raised Daniel's head, and there had been blood on his lips, and he'd looked at her.

The roaring in her ears made her feel sick. She followed the Colonel into the cell, stepped aside to let Teal'c in after her. They all turned to face Aris.

"You son of a bitch," the Colonel said, matter-of-factly, like he was noting how old Aris was, or that it was raining outside.

"I told him to work faster," Aris answered. "Now, he'll work faster." He slapped the panel on the wall. "On the bright side, maybe now I won't have to break any more of your fingers," he added as the door slid shut.

"Well, there's that," the Colonel replied with a bitter half-smile. He walked to the open bars of the exterior wall so that he could watch Aris walk away, taking three of the Jaffa with him. His jaw worked for a moment, then he turned to face Sam and Teal'c. "Options, people. Let's hear it."

"Sebek knows what Daniel knows," Sam said. "Codes, everything."

Teal'c added, "If Sebek is in service to Lord Yu, he will be able to earn much favor in return for this knowledge. The System Lords will make good use of it."

She nodded her agreement. "Especially if we can't warn the SGC that security has been compromised."

This wasn't news to Jack. "I asked for options."

Sam frowned and went to the door. There was no control panel on this side. Reluctantly, she faced him. "Escape. Get Daniel. Steal a ship or find the Stargate, if there is one. Remove the Goa'uld."

"That's what I like about your plans, Carter. They're elegant in their simplicity." He reached to pull his hat off, and remembering that he'd lost it, scrubbed at his hair instead, his face pulled into a scowl that made the notch between his eyebrows deeper under the livid red mark from the ribbon device. He leaned back and angled his face closer to the bars to get a look out into the hall, where the Jaffa was watching them. He waggled his fingers at him. "How ya doin'?" After a moment of getting nothing on that front, he shuffled stiffly to the far side of the cell, slid down the wall and pressed the heels of his hands into his eyes. His broken finger stuck out at an angle.

"You okay, sir?" Sam asked, coming to crouch beside him. When he dropped his hands, she peered closely at the burns on his forehead. There were a few small blisters starting. It had been close.

"My brain feels like scrambled eggs, but I don't have a snake in my head, so I'm doing better than some." As she sat back on her heels, he pinned her with a gaze that was sharper than it had a right to be after what Sebek had done to him. "What the hell happened?"

Teal'c disengaged from his staring contest with the Jaffa guard and settled onto one knee in front of them. He looked over his shoulder in the direction of the guard before turning back and speaking in a low rumble. "We were disabled, as were Sebek's Jaffa. Sebek himself was in distress."

"Or the host was," Sam speculated.

The Colonel's gaze sharpened even more. "Disabled how?"

She could tell he had an idea but was still gathering the pieces.

"You felt it, too, sir, in the antechamber. Pain, headache, nausea, um…paranoia." She winced an unvoiced apology in the Colonel's direction. "And—" She faltered a little as she tried to grope for words to describe it.

"Memory," Teal'c finished for her.

That was it. The word seemed to snap the disorientation, the disjointed images, the wild swings of emotion into context. She nodded and settled back against the wall next to the Colonel. It was difficult to pin down: a memory, but not just pictures. "I could feel it," she said. "I wasn't just remembering. I was *feeling* it."

"What?" the Colonel asked.

She pressed her lips shut for a moment. "Jolinar. But not just her." Shaking her head in frustration, she tried to sort it out. "Her memories, but…not her point of view."

Involuntarily, her hands clenched into fists on her knees. There was a sickening lurch inside as she thought about the antechamber, Sebek aiming the ribbon device at the Colonel. Daniel had been so still, his glasses reflecting the killing red. She'd been facing off against a Jaffa, and he'd been coming at her, but he'd stopped, clutched at his stomach, fingers scrabbling at his pouch. She'd been able to hear the squeaking scream of the symbiote inside him. Of course she couldn't have; the sound had been in her head, but it had been more than that. It had been coming at her from outside, and it had been inside her, winding around her spine, a voice hissing in her brain.

"Hosts," she whispered. Her fingernails were making tiny crescent cuts in her palms. How many millennia were encoded in Jolinar's DNA? Generations. The Nascian man she took had been terrified. The memory twisting at the base of her skull, she opened her eyes, focused on Teal'c's stony face.

She'd fallen and the pain in her knees when she'd hit the stone floor of the antechamber had shocked her back to herself again.

When she'd looked up, Daniel was raising his head and there was blood on his lips, and he'd smiled.

Her voice was thick. "I'm sorry, sir. I tried to get to him, I swear."

Teal'c's expression didn't change, but he managed to convey sympathy anyway. "I, too, was overcome with sensations." Now his scowl deepened. "Adoration for the god, Sebek," he clarified, like he was confessing crimes. "It was most unpleasant."

"False god," O'Neill said.

"False god," Teal'c agreed.

Tilting her head so she could see the Colonel's face better, Sam asked, "You, sir?"

One eye closed in a wince as he looked into the middle distance and then down at his hands in his lap. "Kanan," he said finally.

"Oh," Sam said, and that was totally inadequate and also way too much. She averted her gaze, accidentally caught Teal'c doing the same, his eyes on the floor in front of him like he was observing a moment of silence or waiting for someone to hit him, and that wasn't good to see, either. The ghost memory twisted at the back of her head, and she lifted a hand to rub at it, just as the Colonel was doing the same, their elbows bumping. He flicked a look sidelong at her, a stiletto blade of warning and a taut wire of connection. When she dropped her hand, he raised his to his neck, fingers digging into the spaces between his vertebrae.

She watched his fingers grinding into his neck and the roaring seethed up in her ears like foam on boiling water. As noisy as it was in her head, the silence in the cell was heavy, the kind that dust settles in, disturbed only by the infrasound vibration of the distant crushers and the even thud of pacing Jaffa boots. Still on one knee, Teal'c was motionless except for his eyes, which followed the guard as he passed slowly back and forth outside the bars. When he was beginning his fifth circuit, Teal'c turned back to Sam and the Colonel and raised his eyebrow.

"Kind of lively for a stationary picket, don't you think?" O'Neill said.

Sam mirrored Teal'c's nod. "Not exactly palace guard, sir," she said.

The speculative expression on the Colonel's face faltered for just a second, and she knew that, like her, he was thinking of Teal'c back in the early days, standing motionless for all the hours of his watch at the doorway of their quarters on one of their first missions. Daniel had been observing him the entire time. He and Teal'c had spent the rest of the long night discussing Jaffa discipline and total commitment to assigned duties. Daniel had filled up half his field journal with notes.

"They remain agitated," Teal'c said. "This could be exploited."

Nodding, the Colonel watched the guard with eyes narrowed in thought.

"Goa'uld," Sam said, as the idea began to form, still drifting and shadowy but coming clearer.

"What about them, besides the 'they suck'?" O'Neill asked, without shifting his attention.

Again, Sam groped in her mind, waiting for the picture, the relationships to coalesce a little. After a moment, she gave it a shot. "The Jaffa and Sebek were obviously affected."

"It must have been a severe disruption for the Goa'uld to risk leaving his host," Teal'c added.

"Right, so the host is affected, too, like we all were."

"Which means?" O'Neill made a 'move along' gesture with his good hand. Outside the cell, the Jaffa paused to gaze impassively at them, and the Colonel smiled tightly. "Still here. Thanks for checking."

When the guard moved on again, Sam continued, "Well, there's a common thread, isn't there? We all experienced memories, or... well, something, anyway, that involved the Goa'uld. Jolinar, Sebek, Kanan. Why?" He gave her a 'you're asking me?' face, and she had to smile a little. "The point is, there's something, I don't know, *directed* about this disturbance. It's not just the fumes or the gravity or the fact that we haven't eaten in two days."

"And the effects are alleviated now," Teal'c said.

"Right. So it's got to do with the mine. With what's behind that door."

"That door Daniel is going to be opening any minute now." The Colonel looked at her steadily, and Sam shook her head.

"If it were so easy, he'd already have done it."

"Unless Daniel Jackson was stalling for time," Teal'c said.

"Oh, he wasn't stalling," the Colonel said. "Lots of writing, nifty puzzle. Daniel was doing his best. You know it, I know it." He leaned forward to look into the hallway again before letting his head fall back against the wall. "But Daniel figures everything out, eventually."

Sam pictured Daniel's hands, thought of him pressing the IDC and stepping through the Stargate and into the 'gate room, and of the look of relief that would be on the General's face right before Sebek snapped his neck. Goosebumps rose on her arms; she shivered and rubbed her bare skin, pushing away the feeling. "If he can't get into the mine, he still has one place he *can* go," she said softly. "One code he *does* know."

The Colonel turned his gaze toward the back wall, so she couldn't see his face. After a long moment, he said, "We can't let it get that far."

Sam's heart thudded in her chest. She'd thought about it before – after Jolinar's death years ago, and again when the Colonel had been implanted by Hathor. She'd imagined the moment when she would have to kill her friends – quickly, to spare them the unending torture of possession by a Goa'uld. Her hands had been covered in the blood of friends before, but never like this. A part of her had believed it would never happen.

But they'd been lucky, and Daniel's luck had apparently run out. After all his narrow escapes, all the times he'd been close to death and survived or come back from things even worse than death – to die at the hands of his friends…

Sam looked at the Colonel's face, the thin line of his lips and the set of his jaw, and knew she would not be the one to deliver the fatal wound. She would bear the same guilt, though. There was no relief in it, for her.

"I do not believe Sebek wishes to separate himself from the technology inside the vault," Teal'c said. "He could easily have left this world in the hands of his First Prime, but he has not."

"No." The Colonel's fingers twitched in his lap. "He's staying right here. Where we can get our hands on him."

Sam flinched at the explicit reminder.

"We are vastly outnumbered. We will not be able to get close to him." Teal'c's voice was low and even, but Sam knew it was not that easy.

"We've been outnumbered since this started," O'Neill said. "Nothing's different now."

"He may move on to someone else," Sam suggested, a little desperate. The Colonel didn't look at her.

Teal'c's slight hesitation was more telling than the quietness of his voice. "And if he does, he will leave this host in the same condition as his previous host."

"There's always a chance, Teal'c," she snapped. He inclined his head, deferring the argument. There was no point, and she was ashamed of herself the moment he looked away. "Teal'c," she began, but just then the guard wheeled around in front of the door as another joined them.

"Move to the rear," one of the Jaffa ordered, as he maneuvered into their space, holding a staff weapon on them. The end of the weapon bumped against the side wall. Slowly, Sam got to her feet and backed away, hands half-raised.

A young boy came stumbling into the cell, prodded along at the end of a staff weapon. His face was covered with dirt, and his clothes hung from his body like tatters from a scarecrow. Sam frowned; the bones of his wrists jutted out at sharp angles, and he looked as though he had not eaten well in a long time. One of the Jaffa shoved him hard enough to knock him down, and next to her, the Colonel tensed. He got up and took one step forward. "Leave the kid alone."

"Mind your business, Tauri," the Jaffa snarled, and raised the staff weapon a little higher, right to chest-level. The Colonel held up one hand, a gesture of understanding, but he was still rigid with anger. They watched as the guards threw the boy down against the wall, then backed away. "Do not speak to him," the Jaffa ordered them. "He is none of your concern."

"Right," the Colonel said, and Sam knew without looking at him that he had no intention of following that command.

She didn't, either.

It took a few minutes for the guard to resume his normal patrols, back and forth at five times the regular rate. As soon as it happened, Jack dropped to one knee and edged closer to the boy, who was curled against the wall, his head lowered onto his grubby arms.

"Hey," O'Neill whispered. "Kid. We're not going to hurt you."

Refusing to look up, the boy shrank away as though he could dissolve into the brick.

"Sir. He has no reason to trust us."

"Perceptive," he replied. She gave him a look that should have withered his sarcasm, but she was off her game and the Colonel was focused on the boy.

"We are prisoners," Teal'c said, "like you."

The boy lifted his head and fixed Teal'c with a startling blue gaze full of hate. "You're nothing like me." He looked from Teal'c to the Colonel to Sam, but his expression never changed. No curiosity, no softness; just a blazing anger. "You want to trick me." His eyes darted toward the shadow of the passing guard. "I'm not stupid, and I don't *have* anything," he protested, his voice cracking. He pressed his lips into a thin line.

Crouching next to the Colonel, Teal'c answered, "We want nothing from you."

"You *always* want something," the boy growled. "Jaffa take."

"Not all Jaffa."

The boy made a noise of disgust. He glared at the tattoo on Teal'c's forehead, gathered a mouthful of spit and aimed it at Teal'c's face.

"Hey!" the Colonel snapped. The boy's head whipped around, and he stared at the Colonel without remorse, then looked away again.

Teal'c rose and wiped the spittle from his forehead with the back of his hand. He stared at it for a long moment, then said finally, "Do not admonish him, O'Neill. There are many who have the right to do as he has done."

Sam shook her head wearily. "Teal'c, you can't take the blame for all Jaffa everywhere in the galaxy." She turned to the boy, whose brow was furrowed, for once something other than anger showing in his eyes. "We don't want to trick you. And we don't want to hurt you. We want to get out of here, just like you do. And Teal'c isn't what you think."

His eyes shifting from her to the Colonel to Teal'c, the boy leaned forward a little. "Teal'c?" he asked. His eyes narrowed to suspicious slits again.

"Yes," Teal'c confirmed.

The Colonel hooked his thumb in Teal'c's direction. "You know him?"

"*Shol'va*," he answered, without the edge of derision the word usually carried. He shifted his gaze to O'Neill. "You're SG-1, aren't you?"

The Colonel let a thin smile warm his face a little. "Our reputation precedes us. I'm Jack. That's Carter."

"Where's the other one?"

The smile faded. "He's in the mine, with Sebek."

For a moment the kid's gaunt face held no expression at all, but slowly his mouth hardened and the anger was back. "He lied," he said, finally, through clenched teeth.

"Who lied?" Sam asked.

"If *you're* here, I should be free. He *promised*."

"Sebek?"

He turned his blazing eyes on her. "My *father*."

O'Neill raised an eyebrow in Sam's direction. She stared at the kid as it all began to make sense – lies, truths, bits of information, all coalescing.

"You are the son of Aris Boch," Teal'c stated, confirming out loud what Sam was thinking.

Other than dropping his head to his knees again, the boy made no reply.

"Wait a minute," the Colonel objected. "The Tok'ra said he didn't *have* a son."

Sam could remember quite vividly the Colonel's account of the conversation he'd had with the rescued Tok'ra and his grudging respect for Aris's powers of manipulation. Not that it had worked on them at the time, but Aris was good at spinning the occasional compelling yarn to get what he wanted.

"They lied," Aris's son answered, his voice muffled by his arms. "Everybody lies."

It took the President half an hour to call Hammond back on the red phone, and when he did, he seemed entirely too patient. Too used to hearing that a member of SG-1 was missing; too confident things would work out fine. Hammond knew it wasn't intentional. The man had been nothing but supportive of the program over the last years of his presidency. But that was coming to an end now, and SG-1 was the team with more than their share of close calls. If they weren't so good at getting themselves out of the enormous trouble they got into, the President might have called back in five minutes. It didn't really matter. Hammond already had his plan in place. Briefing the President was the smallest part of it.

Around three hours after SG-1's report-back time had come and gone, Hammond had sent SG teams 14 and 17 after them, loaded to the gills with protective gear and heavily armed. He'd looked straight into Major Harper's eyes and told him, "Find them, Major," and Harper had nodded and stepped through the 'gate as though he had every confidence in the world that he could carry out those orders. There was no other way to go about it, or so Hammond had always believed. Fake it until you make it, Jack O'Neill would have said.

Harper's recon squad was now just a shade over two minutes late.

Hammond had a comfortable chair for occasions just like this one, but he never actually slept in it. It was as if he had an innate ability that enabled him to keep his head on straight through the long hours, no matter how many days those hours stretched into. The coffee helped, too, Air Force dark, strong enough to hold the spoon upright when he stirred in his sugar. He pored over files, worked on overdue performance evaluations for his direct reports, went over inventory and requisition forms, cracked open budget files. Anything to keep him from composing letters of condolence in the back of his brain, tiny squares of white paper that loomed larger as the hours went on and were filled with lines of imaginary black scrawl. Last words, about the fallen. He hated everything about condolence letters, even the taste of the glue on the envelope flaps. The visceral memory plagued him.

Harriman didn't need to page him when the gate activated. He was out the door and down the stairs, into the control room even before Harriman could get to the com. SG-14 straggled down the ramp after SG-17, dragging a handcuffed Relosian with them, his eyes as big around as the 'gate. No matter the reason they'd brought him back to Earth, this couldn't be a good sign.

Hammond met Major Harper at the end of the ramp, looked into his eyes again, and saw nothing but bone-deep exhaustion and disappointment. The Relosian looked like he might dart for cover any moment, but one of Harper's men had a big hand on his shoulder, anchoring him to the spot.

"Report, Major," Hammond ordered.

Harper threw off the slump of weariness in his shoulders, drawing himself to attention. "Sir, we've been over every inch of that village. There's no sign SG-1 is still in the vicinity. They left behind some of their equipment, including some books and the laptop Dr. Jackson was using for the negotiations."

"You've searched the quadrant nearest the 'gate?"

"Yes, sir." Harper glanced at his men, then said, "Sir, we double-timed it over that entire area. There's nothing there. This one, though, tried to sell us a load of bull about how there were evil demons in the woods that lure in travelers and eat them. Not what I'd call a sophisticated cover story." He gestured toward the native, who flinched.

"Have you managed to find out what he does actually know?" Hammond asked, looking not all that closely at the bruise on the young man's cheek and the corresponding redness of Harper's knuckles.

"We think he sold their whereabouts to someone, but he won't tell us who, or what they wanted with SG-1. Maybe he doesn't know, but we haven't had enough time yet to find that out."

"Did you capture him by force?" Hammond asked.

"No, sir. The Relosians seemed to want to cooperate, and their leaders looked pretty shocked that he might be in on this. They offered him up on a silver platter."

"You're certain they're telling the truth?" Hammond had dealt with enough duplicitous offworld governments to know that the wide-eyed innocent ones were often the ones most likely to torture his people until they gave up their codes.

"Reasonably so, sir, yes." Harper fished in his pocket and pulled out a handful of small objects. He let them tumble into Hammond's palm.

"What are these?"

"These are what they were trying to give Dr. Jackson when he left in the middle of negotiations. They were concerned that we were backing out of the deal."

Hammond sighed and handed the beans back to Harper. "Major, I'll waive the debrief. Put together a comprehensive search of the planet using UAV and any other means you deem necessary. I'm sending SG-9 back to complete the negotiations."

"Yes, sir," Harper said. "Sir, time is of the essence. I don't know what's happened to them, but—"

Hammond stared hard at the Relosian, who stepped back a pace, only to run into his keeper. Allowing himself a bitter smile, Hammond was gratified to see he still had the power of intimidation. He turned to Harper. "Find out, Major. Use any approved methods at your disposal. We'll send a coded message to the Tok'ra, to tell them we have a problem that requires their assistance, and request a meeting."

"Yes, sir!" Harper turned and tilted his head to his lieutenant. Between them they pulled their reluctant captive off the ramp and headed toward the interrogation rooms.

When Hammond turned the corner toward the control room, he found his way blocked by Dr. Fraiser. "Doctor?" he said.

"Something I can do for you?"

Janet smiled; she looked as wiped out as he felt. "I just thought it'd be best to be nearby, in case my staff were needed."

"Wise thinking," he said, glad as hell her staff weren't needed. Yet.

"General, can I buy you a cup of coffee?" she asked.

He smiled at her. "No more coffee for me tonight. But I could do with some breakfast. Just as soon as I send this message to the Tok'ra." He followed her into the corridor, still focused on the problem at hand.

No matter what they found on that planet, or what the Relosian prisoner coughed up, it likely wouldn't lead directly to SG-1. He'd have to find another way, and the Tok'ra were going to help him find it, like it or not.

# CHAPTER FIVE

"**O**ur—" His lips closed, and the sentence became a bemused hum instead. Still, though, the thought continued on with its own momentum inside his head, undulating outward like an unfurling ribbon – *empire* – and dividing, options fluttering toward the horizon, each with its own arcing trajectory: *self, hopes, right, doom.* Even after they'd fallen still there was the smear of a ghostly afterglow, rumination on possible futures dissipating like jet trails against a blue sky.

He took a moment to learn what a "jet" was before he went back to staring at the writing on the vault door. For a second, he could feel the gaze inside shift with his and roam briefly across the text. But it slid quickly, if reluctantly, back to him again. His host was appalled. That, Sebek was used to. It was the undisguised curiosity that was new. Slaves bowed their heads – *kneel* expanded outward and faded – or their eyes flickered across him with fear; the passing touch of their attention was the breathless, unworthy tribute of adulation. Slaves spoke to his feet because of his brightness; he could sear them with his godhead if he chose.

Watching this one become privy to his thinking, though, and mirror him back at himself through alien metaphors, this was unsettling. Now, Sebek found himself hunching his shoulders and turning this body away, sheltering, before he remembered, straightened, and raised his chin. "Our glory," he said, and then said it again to hear the voice, to sharpen its softer edges to an appropriate blade of – *arrogance* – authority. The gaze within didn't waver. No matter; soon there would be no need for this one, and Sebek would push it under the dark water and be alone again in his new royal seat.

But today there was a need for this one. Numb for a second, until he extended a ganglion and released the required protein, Sebek's fingers followed the regular, precise edges of the script in the middle of the door. He smiled. Before, the words had been mere shapes, blocks and dashes without relationship to sound. Now, they were embedded in layers of voices, *his* voice in many languages, repeating, the same message whispered and shouted by many simultaneously, cacophony contained within the parameters of the text the way echoes are trapped in a room. With little effort he could focus on one, force the others into the background, but they continued to buzz at the periphery of his attention, blurred the way many voices speaking together were blurred, slightly desynchronized. It was a mystery how the host endured it, this sloppy overlapping. He could feel the pleasure the host took in this plurality and shook his head, disdainful. This one was Greek, this one Berber, this, Abydonian, here, English. Their names came to him easily. The Ancient symbols slipped into one frame or the other, but fit none precisely.

There were gaps and excesses, divergences, failings and silences, and each deviation or inexact translation was itself surrounded by a half-actualized halo of information: this people never developed private property; for that, death was not a state but a transition. It was an almost overwhelming density of context. The blue sky was not clear or empty at all, but full of swirling currents of activity.

Sebek had all the information he needed. But he didn't know *which* information he needed. The overlapping, contradictory, complexly related contexts threatened to dissolve into an incomprehensible babble. He went deeper, seeking fundamentals. It was somewhat familiar, this delving, not so different from his own genetic recall where long-dead knowing stirred under his attention, lost its separateness, and became his own. But unlike his genetic memory, the organization of this mind, its system of relation and association, was chaotic, tangled and winding and likely to make sudden shifts that turned out sometimes to be shortcuts, often to be dead-ends. Sebek was used to dredging a mind for information, but the hosts of the past had been suppressed immediately, husk-hollow and nothing left of them but the whistling wind-sound of despair he could choose not to hear. But he didn't just need what this one knew; he needed *how* he knew it. Not just vocabulary, but grammar. Not just the wine, but the bottle that gave it shape. He required this one's presence. It was distasteful.

He wiped his fingers on his thigh as though they were sticky with the residue of the host's presence. He forced himself to stop.

Behind him, Aris Boch's boots scraped the stone, and his sigh of boredom, or possibly impatience, buffeted Sebek's concentration.

"Leave us," Sebek ordered them. He could feel the Jaffa exchanging glances. Aris's soft snort of derision was aimed at their reluctance. Turning to face him, Sebek raised his eyebrow. "And you."

"My lord," his First Prime, Ankh'et said. "Your guard—"

"Knows better than to question our orders." Sebek slid his gaze in Ankh'et's direction. "If we repeat ourselves now, it will be the last thing you hear." Sebek looked down and nudged the corpse at his feet with the tip of his boot. Its eyes were open and opaque with cataracts. Blood was caked around its slack, gaping mouth, its eyes and its ears. It looked like it could disintegrate like ancient parchment, and he had not used the host for long enough to make it into such a husk. He felt a tremor of consternation and quickly crushed it. "Take this. Burn it."

After touching his knee to the floor, Ankh'et rose to attention. A flick of his fingers summoned the other Jaffa, and the two pulled the dead host up to its feet. One held it upright while the other stripped the ribbon device from its stiff fingers. Sebek held his new hand out to receive it, watching Aris while Ankh'et carefully put the golden caps into place. This host's hands were bigger than the other's, and the finger-caps were tight. The fingers were swollen a little, too, a residue of the trauma of blending. Sebek hadn't been gentle. He reduced water retention and blood flow to the fingertips just a fraction, and the caps became more comfortable.

When the device was seated and the Jaffa had dragged the corpse up the incline into the tunnel, Sebek turned his palm upward and gazed at the crystal there. It took only a second for the glow to warm his skin with the prickle of deadly energy. *Die* pulsed, once, twice in his mind, and the crystal pulsed, too. He spread his hand wide and aimed the device at Aris. Aris was impassive, his face neither expectant nor defiant as he met Sebek's eyes. Inside Sebek, the blue attention watched. Sebek could have allowed the pulsing command to translate itself into action, but instead he smiled. Aris betrayed no relief.

"And you," Sebek repeated.

Aris was slow to respond to the order, his stare verging on openly insolent as he swung his blaster up – pausing as the muzzle passed Sebek's chest – to rest on his shoulder. He backed up the slope to the tunnel entrance.

"Your usefulness is waning, my friend," Sebek warned him. There was a flash of comprehension in Aris's eyes. He surely had to know, now, that he was but a tool for use by his god.

"Then how 'bout you follow through on the deal, and I'll be out of your hair? My lord." The pause between demand and honorific was slight.

Sebek let his smile thin, more cruel than amused. "We will decide when you have fully fulfilled your obligations. *We* are obliged to do nothing." *Die* pulsed again, throbbing behind his eyes, and he closed his mailed hand into a fist, lowered it to his side.

Aris looked like he was going to say more, but then his face hardened into a still mask. Instead of speaking, he took another backward step into the gloom of the tunnel and disappeared. Sebek dismissed him from thought and turned back to the door.

The silent script was more familiar now. It was oddly primitive-looking, as though the vaguely human figures dancing in an evocative, simplistic landscape had been scraped out with a crude tool. But the refined material of the impenetrable door belied that notion. Neither obviously metal and not quite stone, the substance was one that Sebek had never seen before, and a quick skim through the sea of past knowledge suggested that no Goa'uld in his line had, either. As simple as the figures appeared when taken one at a time, their overall arrangement, the way they seemed to interlock and mirror and parody each other, suggested that there was something sophisticated about them, something more than mere pictographic or even developed ideographic logic at work. "Ideographic," he murmured aloud, testing the new word.

His fingers were numb again when he ran them over the carvings. *Loss* hissed for a second in his blood and was gone. Adjustments were made and then there was tingling and a settling in; his hands became his hands. The edges of the figures were still sharp. In all the eons that this door had remained closed, no one had caressed its message into smoothness, nor had the corrosive air within the mine dulled it. It had remained in this pristine state for him. It would whisper its secrets only to him. *If.*

He leaned forward and rested his forehead, then his cheek, against the words. He could sense it now, the secret purring against his eardrum, ready to resolve into speech. Somewhere in the clutter and whirl of the host's stolen memories there was a key. But although the script was familiar and clearly *waiting* for Sebek, it was still opaque, and although Sebek closed his eyes and felt the secret leaving its mark on his skin, although he followed the host's memory into the centre of this knot where dog-eared books fell open on loose spines, where the images of inscribed tablets and the staring stone faces of Easter Island were overlaid with the sharp-stale smell of fermented beer and the past-ripe scent of pink blossoms outside a window, there was no understanding there, nothing to unfold. What the host knew was that it didn't know.

Sebek growled. Next to his cheek, the undeciphered writing seemed to hum through his bones. Inside, the blue gaze sharpened, attentive, and Sebek's fingers were numb when he raised them and used them to rub at his eyes. He could still smell pink flowers and their cloying sweetness, brown-edged petals falling, past their prime – *unbearable* – Sebek pushed away from the wall, his empty hand outstretched toward the drifting memory – there, somehow at the center of the knot, something else. In the spring there were flowers in the trees, and Sebek felt *grief* bloom outward, a dark flower wilting against the blue, a vine knotted. He followed it backward, inward, downward. The host resisted, but there was no resisting now. The book in the memory, the images of staring stone sentinels and dancing human forms, blocky Ancient script, a bed with crumpled sheets and the shadows of branches, another bed, stained with seeping, blood, a knot of bandages around softening bone…experience lying in layers, connected not in time, but in sense. The smell of blossoms, brown, falling. *Rot.*

The pain in the memory was intense, and the host's body jerked so that Sebek's head struck the door sharply. He staggered a bit before he contained the response, created distance between himself and the memory and the host. In his mind's eye he held them at bay, one in each hand, present and past, body and mind balanced across the fulcrum of his own perfect control. He turned his attention to the left hand where the memory throbbed. In it, this one, this host, was dying. His body was dissolving, and the petals of the flowers curled inward, brown, unanchored, drifted downward. Sebek was familiar with the sensation of dying – Bastet and Yu had taught him that – and with the miracle of awakening in the sarcophagus. This host knew that miracle, too; Sebek found the memory close by, the next page in the book. But this, this dying was different. Beyond the dying there was – *fear, yearning* – there was – *escape, elation* – beyond dying there was not death, and not the return to the heaviness of flesh. There was something more…wondrous.

This one had resisted, but there was no resistance now. Sebek breathed in the scent of flowers and around him vastness opened, embracing, fathomless plenitude. The stone faces stared up from the book, the figures paced their way through their dance from margin to margin, and beneath and beyond there was meaning, a slowly flowing ocean where this language was not unknown. The pictures in the book were mute, but the flowers outside the window were a doorway to something else. *No.* The memory in his hand was water in a broken bowl, and soon it would drain away. The body in his other hand thrashed.

When Sebek turned his head to look at the writing on the door, the blocky regularity of the Ancient script no longer spoke itself in twenty imperfect languages, but spoke in its own. And the second script behind it leaned so close, so close to Sebek's ear he could practically feel it breathing. In the memory there was no flesh, no flesh at all, only release, expansion. *No. No, no, no.* In Sebek's body, here and now, the host's heart stumbled, recovered, began to race. Sebek strained to hear the voice, the secret. His breath came in heaving, sour gusts. The hands that braced him against the door were perfectly without feeling. *No. No.* The alien script had a voice that was sweet, promising, and the Ancient sea rocked back and forth speaking, speaking everything. And everything was there, just there, so vast and full it was like nothingness, and his body made a noise, a howl of pain.

"No!"

The word filled the room, leaving a hole inside him where it tore itself free. His throat hurt. "My—" he began, but, disoriented by contradiction, the sentence wouldn't form. He felt himself lowered to the floor and his knees pulled up, as his arms hugged them and he rested his forehead on them. "My throat hurts," the host rasped, his voice echoing thinly in the vault. "Mine, you son of a bitch."

The first thing Daniel did was to thrash. His legs kicked out and his head cracked backward into the vault door, and it wasn't enough. Sebek was still in there. After a long time, Daniel unclamped his hands from the back of his neck. The fingernails of the left one were red crescents. The sight of the ribbon device on the other hand made him thrash again. *Murder* pulsed behind his eyes and the crystal in his palm glowed lividly. He scrambled away from it, away, anywhere. When he came back to himself he found he'd worked his way across the floor into the corner where the vault door met the black stone of the mine. He lay on his side, curled up tight, and his breath was hot and sickly with fear and anger. His hands were on the back of his neck again. The slick touch of the gold caps on his fingers made him retch, and he pulled at the ribbon device, abandoning the effort after a moment; it seemed too difficult. There was nothing in his stomach to come up, so he rolled onto his knees and spat onto the stone between his hands, then sat down, leaning against the wall.

"O-oh-kay," he told himself shakily. "What say we get a grip?" He looked around the chamber. He was alone. "I'm Daniel…" Eyes roaming the empty room, he waited as though for someone to contradict him. "I'm Daniel Jackson and I have a snake in my head." The matter-of-fact tone of it seemed to help a little, except that his hand started clawing at the skin at the nape of his neck again, and he had to physically restrain it with the other. "And I'm…talking." Again, he waited, blinking into the relative silence. "And that's strange, considering."

Using his mailed hand to brace himself against the door, he

slipped on the metal surface, fell, and had to try again with the other. When he'd gotten to his feet, he leaned heavily on the door, his hand with the ribbon device held away from him like it was contaminated.

"Sha're," he blurted suddenly and nodded. "Yes. She was able to speak when Amaunet was dormant…" His voice trailed away as he shook his head. "But you aren't pregnant, Dr. Jackson. So what makes you so special?" He realized belatedly that the question was directed as much at the Goa'uld in his head as it was at himself. The idea that the snake might answer threatened thrashing again, but he breathed hard through his nose and stared at a spot on the far wall until the panic settled into reasonably manageable background noise.

He could feel Sebek. There was a coiling at the base of his skull, not a physical sensation, really, but something like bad news coming, a dark, heavy, cold-water tension. Having a Goa'uld in his head, it turned out, felt an awful lot like dread. On that bizarre level where Daniel spent more time than was strictly healthy these days, that was comforting. He'd had lots of practice dealing with dread. And it wasn't like Sebek was the first house-guest who'd arrived uninvited and refused to leave. One snake couldn't be that much more horrible than the voices of Ma'chello's ghostly-schizo Goa'uld-crazymaker. Of course, the Linvris had never really been there. Now, Daniel was awake, and Sebek was definitely there.

"Why do I always have to do the pep talks?" he wondered aloud. "I'm clearly very, very bad at them."

As he stood there for what felt like a long time, long enough for his tailbone to get sore from leaning against the door, it occurred to him that he didn't seem to be running away, even though running away, maybe finding his team and springing them from detention and going home and getting the snake out of his head all seemed to be a good plan on the face of it. He rubbed his hand across his mouth and stood there in the vault, realizing eventually that he was pretty much waiting for the Jaffa to come and haul him off to jail. That's how it went, wasn't it? SG-1 either got away or thrown in jail. Daniel had obviously not gotten away. But there were no Jaffa, because Sebek had dismissed them. The dread at the base of his skull seemed to draw itself up, uncoiling and humming like a high-voltage wire. *Power*. His own spine straightened with it. *Assurance*.

Of course the Jaffa wouldn't arrest him. They wouldn't do a damn thing to him.

He was their god.

The thought felt good, and the good feeling made him sick again, but the plan seemed a little more manageable. He could simply order his team's release. Nobody was going to question their god. And that thrumming in his spine that was Sebek and his arrogance, he could take advantage of that. He could play Goa'uld.

He stood, unmoving, in the vault.

His neck itched. Absently, he fingered the scrapes and cuts he'd left with his fingernails. His hand came away flaked with dried blood, but there were no scrapes or cuts anymore.

It was this that tipped him off the edge of himself. Sebek was under the skin. His tusked head was buried in Daniel's brainstem. The snake's body, infinitely divided into finer and finer ganglia, insinuated itself into every function, controlled every secretion and every prickling of nerves. He was *everywhere*. What was left was this small, floating island called Daniel. Under the surface, Sebek was Leviathan, dark-backed and looming, waiting. And Daniel found himself staring down into the depths. Rubbing his fingers together, feeling the disintegrating flakes of his own dried blood, Daniel felt the elegant, sinuous power of it, of this *thing* that could smooth away the evidence of Daniel's panic, just like that, the *control* it represented, the absolute awareness and engrossment. Unlike Daniel, who daily skirted the edges of what his own mind refused to show him, Sebek had no subconscious. Everything was surface in him, exposed. And it was so close, Daniel could feel Sebek inside.

The dark shape rose up under him, and with it came eons of memory, like a cold current lifting darkness into the light. *Run away,* he thought. *Play Goa'uld.* He stood still and stared into the rising shadow under his feet. Answers, thousands of years there, just there. Weaknesses. Failures. Strategies. Hatred. *Desire.* More, more, more. The generations of Sebek's line flung themselves into the future, carried themselves forward in the DNA, remembering what they wanted, what had been unfulfilled, each one hungrier than the last, every disappointment tabulated, every revenge calculated. Daniel clutched at his stomach as Sebek's desire coursed along nerve endings, became a hollowness in Daniel's body. *Don't look*, Daniel said, and kept looking. Sebek was a pure desire. He was pure focus. Pure. He was beautiful.

Daniel's fingers were numb…and then they weren't. Sebek was inside, in the blood. All the answers to all the questions Daniel had ever asked were in the blood.

He stood in the vault and didn't run away.

He could smell flowers. Cloying and sweet, the scent was sharpened by Sebek's attention, filled up all the space around them. *Don't go there*. Daniel turned away, but it was everywhere. *Desire* smelled like flowers, was curled at the edges, brown, floating downward. The memory was a translucent scrim stretched taut over nothingness. But it wasn't nothingness. It was his death, but it was impossible because no one could remember his own death, no one except, maybe, the members of SG-1, and Daniel had a few to choose from and this one in particular was as compelling as it was terrifying. He was suspended between horror and fascination, and he could feel Sebek inside. Beyond the ripe-rot smell of it, his time among the ascended was blank. Except that Sebek, with his pure desire and absolute control, had touched it, and it had spoken to him; it was in Sebek's memory. Some attenuated version of Daniel's Ancient memory was folded into Sebek's somehow; Daniel could see it, obliquely, like he was looking at his own reflection in someone else's eye. Disoriented, Daniel clutched at the wall, the gold caps on his fingers rattling against the script. *No*, he thought and closed his eyes tightly. But he didn't look away. The Leviathan yawned open and swallowed him.

When Sebek opened Daniel's eyes again, he was on the floor, head on his knees. He was tapping his capped thumb and forefinger together in an uneven staccato that matched his heartbeat. After awhile, both slowed and steadied to an even rhythm.

He lifted his head and craned his neck to look up at the door.

"We require Jack O'Neill," Sebek said.

# CHAPTER SIX

The crazy thing about Goa'uld holding cells was how cold they always were. With his eyes closed, Jack could conjure the memory of being held prisoner on Apophis's ship, headed for Earth. The floor was as unforgiving here as it had been there. His tailbone was starting to ache.

Once, Daniel had said he thought the snakes made the cells cold on purpose – a kind of mental torture, a subtle thing to set their prisoners on edge. As psychological torture went, Jack could think of a dozen things that might have been more effective, and half of them he hadn't had to leave Earth to learn about first hand.

Daniel's comment always stuck with him, though. Especially now, when Daniel wasn't around to say it again. So many things Daniel had repeated a hundred times over the years, from bad puns to information dumps. Jack had gone through stages with it – annoyance, resigned expectation, acceptance – and then Daniel had ascended, and Jack had realized he'd taken it for granted that Daniel would be around to annoy him forever. Daniel always did have a hard time dying.

With a grunt, Jack shifted and turned on his side. He folded his arm beneath his head, but the hard floor bit into his hip. Teal'c had taken last watch, but that was a formality, since neither of them had slept much. In Teal'c's case, he was still having some trouble adjusting to the act of sleeping, and in a strange place he had a tendency to meditate instead. Jack wished he could teach Teal'c the art of dropping into a light doze whenever the opportunity arose, but he wasn't having such great luck with that himself. Some role model he was. Besides, Teal'c had over one hundred years of habit to unlearn, and his brain trumped his body.

Or maybe it was more than that. Whenever Jack closed his eyes, he could feel something pushing at his consciousness – and whatever it was, he didn't want it coming in. Carter had been tossing and turning since she'd bedded down, and Jack had no desire to

join her in dreamland. Even when he was wide awake, there were
things running through his head that he was having trouble clamp-
ing down on. For all his internal grumbling about the cold, it was
warmth he shied away from when he closed his eyes. The light
there in that place between real things and dreams was mellow and
golden, and beyond that was a whole lot of pain.

He didn't remember all of what had happened to him in Ba'al's
fortress, but his body remembered the light, the warmth of the
place, and the gentleness of that feeling was the definition of cruel
joke. His conscious mind didn't *remember*, but he *knew*. Ba'al was
Goa'uld, and Kanan was Tok'ra, but it was a difference in degree,
and not much degree at that. The tiny cell in Ba'al's fortress had
been a bigger version of Jack's own body. Trapped was trapped was
trapped, but although he was a sadistic son of a bitch, at least Ba'al
was honest, and *his* prison had had a door.

Jack pulled up his legs to ease the small of his back and concen-
trated on the cold.

He'd been sick, mostly absent, when he'd been hijacked. Daniel
wasn't absent at all. Knowing Daniel, he was front and center, talking himself hoarse – or whatever the silent in-the-head equivalent
was – the way Jack knew he himself had beat his fists raw against
the cage of his own bones, in the memory of Kanan he couldn't
quite reach. Jack didn't feel a bit sorry for Sebek.

With a growling sort of sigh, Jack sat up and opened his eyes.
This cell, if anything, seemed even smaller than the spaces inside
his head. He stretched out his arms, making space, and considered
pacing, but that wouldn't do anything but tell him exactly how
much space he didn't have. Teal'c turned to meet his eyes, a question there, but Jack shook his head. When Carter woke up, she'd
make it her business to tear everything down and examine every
part of the dreams he wasn't having. It was all about the clues. The
cell was like every cell they'd ever been in. The clues were in their
heads. Carter would make diagrams. He could already picture her,
hunched over her laptop, categorizing ghosts. Teal'c, though, simply nodded and closed his eyes.

The fourth occupant of the cell hadn't slept either, as far as Jack could tell. The boy hadn't moved, but he was as tense and wary as he had been when he was brought in. Although his head was down, his posture was a dead giveaway, and Jack wasn't at all surprised that he didn't trust them, despite his knowledge of who they were. Like father, like son.

The kid looked like he hadn't eaten a square meal in weeks. His hands were too big for his narrow frame, awkward-looking even as they clutched his elbows. Adolescent. He was gawky, bigger than he seemed, and probably bigger than he realized. Jack guessed that the kid would stand taller than Carter if he ever straightened his spine. He should have been playing kid games, growing out of his clothes and making the girls gawk. Instead, his fingers moved restlessly across his flaky skin, and his breath wheezed a little in his chest, while he curled his toes under and tried not to take up space. Suddenly, the room seemed even smaller.

Looking at the kid, at the slouch of his shoulders and the pale grey of his skin – the way the kid was thwarted, closed down, shrunken muscles, collapsed potential – Jack knew why Aris had no qualms about offering up Daniel, or any of them, as sacrifice for his son's life. He was pretty sure Daniel wouldn't have had any qualms offering up his own life, if he'd known. But that wasn't the point.

Jack squeezed the pockets of his pants, looking for a power bar. Aris had left them with whatever food they were carrying, not out of kindness, but out of practicality. It wasn't much, anyway. He drew the last one out of his pocket and tossed it to Teal'c, then nodded toward the kid. Teal'c inclined his head.

"Young man," Teal'c said. The boy twitched at the sound of Teal'c's voice, but didn't look up. "You must eat something."

"They only feed us once a day," the boy answered, his voice muffled through his arms.

Teal'c tore open the wrapper and held it out toward the boy. "Take this."

The kid lifted his head and zeroed in on the power bar. His nostrils flared, and his fist opened involuntarily. Jack frowned. He'd been that hungry – more so – at least once. And just as proud, too. The boy's gaze shifted to Jack, assessing.

As if it was of no concern to him at all, Jack lay back down and stared at the ceiling. "We don't need it," he said. A moment later, he heard the crinkle of paper as the bar was ripped out of its wrapping. One small victory.

In the silence that followed, Jack ran back through all the scenarios he'd been building in his head over the course of the short night. Option A: they'd overpower the guards. So far they'd been spectacularly unsuccessful so far in every attempt they'd made. To get to Daniel, it'd take better luck than that. On the heels of option A came the big decision: to drag Daniel away with the snake still in him, try to make an escape and pray the Tok'ra could get it out, or…not.

It was the 'not' part of the equation that was difficult. The snake was going to slow them down, and they might all die anyway. Jack kept taking that piece of the puzzle out, turning it over in his hands and feeling the shape of it; he kept looking at it until it didn't cause him such immediate pain. Beside him, Carter groaned softly, her foot kicking out before she pulled her knees up, curling tightly. Teal'c watched the kid stuff the power bar into his mouth and swallow without even chewing. A faint smile made a crease at the side of Teal'c's mouth.

If the snake had to be killed – and removal wasn't an option – Jack would be the one to do it. Daniel was his responsibility. Carefully, he set that thought aside again. Limited exposure was all that made it bearable.

Jailbreak or no jailbreak, they had to deal with Aris; with his son at stake, he wasn't going to be giving them any unexpected breaks. Not like last time.

Too many variables. Math always did make his head hurt.

Jack turned his head so he could see Teal'c and the kid. Teal'c had moved closer, and the boy was unfolding by degrees, a little less cautious in their presence.

"How long have you been a prisoner in this place?" Teal'c asked.

The boy shrugged and glanced at the door, then back at Teal'c. "They don't like prisoners to talk. But you know that already," he added, gaze fixed on the golden tattoo on Teal'c's forehead.

"Yes." Teal'c sat down beside him, with his back to the wall. "But we will hear them approaching."

"They sneak up, sometimes," the boy said. Jack wondered when Jaffa had become stealthy, or if that was a new trick they'd added to their repertoire under this particular snake.

"Then we will be cautious." Teal'c's expression was gentle, but Jack knew half of his attention was focused on listening for anyone in the corridor. "Where did they keep you before bringing you here?"

"Why do you care?" The boy folded the power bar wrapper carefully against his knees, making it smaller and smaller. When he couldn't fold it any more, he closed his hand around it like he was afraid Teal'c would snatch it away. When he looked at Teal'c, his expression dared Teal'c to try.

"We must make a plan of escape," Teal'c said, which was more than Jack would have told him. After all, it was Aris Boch's kid. But Teal'c knew what he was doing.

Another shrug from the kid. "That's your business."

"We would not leave you here," Teal'c began, but the boy was shaking his head.

"They're coming."

Jack looked at Teal'c, who gave a curt nod of confirmation. "Jaffa approach."

"I wish I could do that," Jack muttered. He still didn't hear anything. He reached over and shook Carter's shoulder once, twice, until she sat bolt upright, ready to swing. "Easy, tiger," he said. "Time to put on your fighting face."

The wild-eyed look eased away after a moment, and she combed her hands through her messy hair. "Sorry, sir," she said. "Bad dreams."

"I figured," he said, getting to his feet. He gave her a hand up.

She jerked her head around to glance at the boy, then asked, "How's…?"

"He and Teal'c've been getting acquainted."

"Well, that's good," Carter said, and began patting down her pockets. Jack waved her hands away.

"Thought of that already."

"Oh." She squared up her shoulders. She looked like she hadn't slept a wink. Plus, she'd puked up the last thing she'd eaten. Jack noticed the tremor in her hands before she caught him looking and put her hands in her pockets.

"You might want to fish one out for yourself," he told her, without actually pointing out that she looked like hell.

She met his eyes for a long moment, then said, "I'm fine, sir."

He nodded, completely unconvinced, but there was no time to get into the finer details of Carter's psyche. Two Jaffa had appeared at their doorway, not quietly, but without the usual fanfare. Maybe that was what the kid considered 'sneaking up,' from his kid-perspective. Jack could've backed away from the door without needing to be told, but it was more satisfying to make them work for it.

"Step away," the Jaffa ordered. Teal'c positioned himself in front of the boy, for all the good it would do.

"Must be room service with our breakfast," Jack said. "Hope they got the eggs right."

With a hiss, the lock released and the door slid open. When Aris Boch stepped between the guards into the room, his weapon holstered, the kid gasped but said nothing. Jack could practically feel the kid's muscles twanging as the boy scrambled to his feet behind Teal'c. Anger, or excitement; hard to say. Aris didn't look at his son.

"I hope the three of you managed to get some rest," Aris said. "You'll have a busy day ahead of you."

"Great accommodations," Jack said. "Nice beds."

"It's the best you're going to get, under the circumstances," Aris said. "But you won't be needing one tonight."

"No?" Jack said. "Do tell."

"Sebek has ordered me to bring you back to the vault."

There it was. Not unexpected. "You mean, *Daniel*," Jack said, putting a nice sharp point on his friend's name.

"No, I mean Sebek," Aris said, just as sharply. "Better get used to it."

"Not likely," Jack said.

Carter bent down to pick up her jacket, but Aris waved her off. "Won't be needing you today, Major. Just the Colonel here."

"Why?" Carter said, then caught herself. "Er, I mean…not that the Colonel's not useful, but you might need my help. That device by the door may be an access panel."

"Sebek's got that taken care of. With Dr. Jackson's help, of course." The idea that Daniel would help Sebek in any way made Jack's blood pressure notch up ten points, but this wasn't the time to start a battle. There'd be plenty of chances for that later. Aris crooked a finger at Jack. "Let's go."

"Thanks so much for the vote of confidence," Jack said to Carter, unable to resist.

"You know what I meant, sir," she said, face wrinkling up into an apologetic grimace.

"Father?" From behind Teal'c, the kid's voice seemed much smaller, more unsure, than it was before, and he looked a lot more like a boy now, less like a teenager. The expression on Aris's face didn't change, but his eyes went toward the sound, and toward Teal'c standing watch over him. Teal'c didn't seem to see a difference between the Jaffa and the bounty hunter, where the kid was concerned.

Aris moved toward his son. Teal'c, who had been a wall of resistance until that moment, began to step aside but even so Aris shouldered into him, staggering him off-balance. His face stony, eyes fierce, Teal'c righted himself and stepped smoothly back into Aris's path. When Jack twitched forward, one of the Jaffa shoved the tip of a staff weapon into his back. Teal'c raised a warning hand, but Aris caught it and knocked it aside.

"Don't interfere," Aris said, in a low voice. He and Teal'c stared at each other for a long moment. Behind Jack, one of the Jaffa chuckled softly, anticipating blood like a dog waiting for the kill.

Teal'c glanced up and met Jack's eyes. There was a message in that direct stare, but Jack had the frustrating feeling that he wasn't catching on. He dropped his gaze to Teal'c's hand, the one Aris had pushed away; Teal'c's fingers were curled under, protecting something from view. Not enough time to get a good look, because Teal'c clasped his hands behind his back, like he was giving up the field.

Now Jack's eyebrow rose. Whatever Aris was up to, Teal'c was playing along. Teal'c moved one shoulder aside, a minute gesture, and allowed Aris to pass.

Aris dropped to one knee beside the boy and briefly laid a hand on his hair, not quite ruffling it. With his thumb, he rubbed smudges of dirt off the boy's face, but he said nothing. When he stood and returned to Jack's side, he ignored Teal'c. "Let's go," he said, and headed off down the corridor without looking back.

With a last glance at Carter and Teal'c, Jack followed.

Sam leaned into the bars and peered into the hallway. It wasn't getting darker – the lights were glowing as steadily as ever – but it felt that way. As she stared, the hallway seemed to get narrower and longer and grey around the edges. Her knees were wobbly, and she had to curl her fingers around one of the vertical struts and breathe slowly with her head down until the dizziness passed. If something was going to happen, it had to be soon.

"What does Sebek want with him?" she wondered aloud, her forehead resting on the bars while she watched the remaining Jaffa pace his way to the far end of the corridor, pause, turn rather less than smartly and come toward her. He held her gaze for a long moment, his mouth slanted up in a leer. She rolled her eyes and leaned her back on the bars instead. "He's got Daniel. What can the Colonel offer him?"

The passing guard leaned closer than necessary, made a low noise that had to be the Jaffa equivalent of "how *you* doin'?" which was so not right, she didn't even have a category for it. She stepped away from the support of the bars and aimed a warning scowl in his direction. It got her a growling laugh in return.

"Hands off," she muttered, not quite loud enough for the Jaffa to hear.

Over by the wall, the kid was watching her. After a moment he smiled thinly, shook his head and looked at the floor. Teal'c was following the guard with his eyes, and for brief moment, the look on his face reminded her of her brother, way back in the Dark Ages before she'd joined the Air Force, when he thought she was the one who needed protecting. She was gratified to see Teal'c's expression shift immediately to a sort of smug warning, not of what he'd do, but what she could. She smiled tightly at the Jaffa, asking him to try his luck. The guard's laughter died abruptly. Teal'c kept staring until the guard moved on out of sight.

Sam shrugged it off and went on, "You don't think Sebek needs a new host already, do you?"

She looked the question at the kid, but he was picking at his toenails and clearly not interested in what the Goa'uld might want with Colonel O'Neill. Not that he'd know anything, anyway, except maybe about how to die in a mine before he turned fifteen. His reddish hair was thinning at the crown, she noticed, and his scabby scalp showed through. She wondered if he'd seen protein in the last year.

"Maybe you're next," the kid said without looking up, and Sam's sympathy got a little harder to hang on to.

"Perhaps not," Teal'c said, drawing her attention.

He was holding something between his finger and thumb, a wafer about the size and thickness of a credit card. He flipped it over and angled it into the light cast through the bars from the corridor. It gleamed dully for a second before he palmed it as the guard made his slow progress past them again.

When the guard was gone, Sam stepped closer and Teal'c held the contraband out to her. It felt like a credit card, too, except that instead of embossed with numbers it was a featureless grey. She raised her eyebrows at Teal'c. "Aris slipped you this?"

"He did."

"Did he include a note telling you what it is?"

"He did not."

She turned to the kid. "Hey." He didn't look up. "Can you tell me your name?"

He raised his eyes slowly and looked at her from under lowered brows.

"Fine. We'll go with Mr. Boch Junior, for now." She held the card out for him to see. "Do you know what this is?"

The spark in his eyes said 'yes'; his shrug said he wouldn't tell her anyway. Sam wondered if teenage attitude was coded in the human genome, because the annoying body language seemed to be universal. Cassie could have brought this guy home to drive Janet nuts. Sam sighed. "Your dad slipped this to us. Maybe you've seen something like it before."

There was definitely something going on in that head, no doubt about it. His eyes didn't leave the card she flipped it over, ran her thumb along its edge. He shrugged again, as the guard appeared on his annoyingly regular drive-by. She followed Teal'c's example, hiding the card in her closed hand.

The kid started to scream.

Sam whirled to look at him and found him on his feet, his face inches from hers. The smell of rotten teeth and hunger assaulted her as he screamed out the last of his breath and sucked in another. He didn't look scared or angry. He was just screaming, long, raw-voiced howls, his fists clenched at his sides.

Before Sam could think of what to do in these perfectly bizarre circumstances, and before Teal'c could put his hand on the kid's skinny shoulder or ask what was wrong, the cell door slid open and the guard was inside, his staff aimed at a space somewhere between them as if he, too, were confused and more than a little unsure as to whom he should be threatening.

"Cease this noise!" he bellowed.

The boy sucked in another breath. Then, mid-howl, he snatched the card from Sam's hand and made a break for the door.

It was insane. The Jaffa was right there, but the kid was spider-fast and managed to make it a single step past him, just close enough to the door to grab the doorjamb with one hand. The guard didn't bother to wrestle with him. He simply clotheslined him with the staff and flipped him onto his back on the floor, finishing with the tip of the staff pressed into the kid's sternum. Teal'c lunged forward to get a hand on the guard's arm. The guard twisted his arm free, and in that moment, as Sam was pulling back a fist, she caught movement from the corner of her eye. A second guard outside the bars. The warning she tried to shout was chopped in half by her grinding teeth as the *zat* fire hit her, snapping her head back and whiting out her vision in a searing flare of pain.

"Dirt-crazy," someone said. And someone else was laughing.

With an effort, Sam managed to peel open an eye. Her bones were humming; she could hear it, the blue dance of residual energy crackling around inside her skull, and a ghostly skirling along her limbs. She was leaning up against the cell wall, the weight of a large, firm hand on her shoulder keeping her from dissolving altogether.

"They all go dirt-crazy," the second guard replied to the first. They watched through the bars, their faces twisted in identical sneers of distaste.

Beside her, the kid was in hysterics. In fact, he was laughing so hard he had his arms wrapped around his middle and was slowly sliding sideways until he was lying on the floor, curled up tight.

With a snort of disgust, the second guard walked away. Sam counted his footsteps. There had to be another room beyond the cells, one that she hadn't seen when they came in. Only one guard in there? More? She swallowed hard against the rising of her stomach and closed her eyes. The kid was winding down to hiccups, each one a hook catching in her brain. The first guard stared at them for a moment before returning to his pacing.

"What is amusing?" Teal'c asked.

The question must have been very funny, because it started the kid off again. Only, this time, the laughter thinned to a wheeze that ended in a suppressed sob. Sam could feel his bony body shaking next to hers. Her eyes on the empty hallway beyond the bars, she groped blindly for him and laid a hand on his shoulder but he shrugged her off, then pushed himself up so he could slouch a couple of feet away from her.

He scrubbed his eyes angrily on the backs of his wrists before answering. "Dirt-crazy," he said, wiping his nose on ragged sleeve of his tunic. "We all go dirt-crazy." Tapping the side of his head with a grubby finger, he crossed his eyes and let his tongue loll.

"Grit for brains. Corroded." His face fell again into its regular lines of resentment as he looked over Teal'c's shoulder at the bars. "So they say."

Teal'c thinned his lips in a frown of understanding tinged with disapproval. "It was imprudent to act as you did."

The kid watched the guard pass the cell, and then his eyes slid to Teal'c's and he lifted a hand from his lap to point at the door. "Perhaps not," he contradicted, perfectly mimicking Teal'c's earlier intonation.

Teal'c turned to look. Something was bubbling along the edge of the door. A thin, viscous grey line drooled down along the seam between the door and the wall. Sam could smell something like lemons. Flapping her hand against Teal'c's leg, she waited for him to stand and then lever her up to her feet. She peered first at the door, then at the kid.

"Some kind of acid?" she guessed. He shrugged, but the side of his mouth curled up for a second. "The card?" The other side of his mouth turned up too.

She braced herself against the bars near the door and tried to see if the solvent was visible from the outside. She couldn't tell. The guard was leaning against the wall at the end of the corridor, but he straightened up when she leaned out, so she pulled back again and listened for his approach. No footfalls. He seemed content to take a break from the pacing for a moment, having made his point about their chances of escape. Beside her, the drool had slithered its way to the floor. There was a faint hiss as the locking mechanism released.

She grinned at Teal'c, who came to stand in front of the door. "Hey, kid," she said.

"Aadi," he corrected her. He walked himself up the wall with his hands but didn't come to join them.

"Sorry. Aadi." She spared some of the grin for him. "You get ready to move when I say, okay? And stick close to us. Got it?"

He nodded.

She leaned her head against the bars again and caught the guard's eye. "Excuse me," she called. "Can we get some water?" It was only a gambit, but the word "water" made her already parched mouth even drier.

"Rations at dawn," the guard answered.

"Look, we haven't had any water for two days."

"Rations at dawn," he repeated.

Making a show of desperation that wasn't all that much of a show, Sam bowed her head and let out a little sob. Then, reluctantly, she raised her head and asked, "What do I have to do to get some now?" The cajoling drift of her voice made her feel way more than a little creepy.

At that, the guard shouldered himself away from the wall and strolled toward her. His smile showed perfect white teeth. When he shot a quick look down the hall, probably toward the guardroom, Sam caught a faint, milky glow in his right eye and noted the puckering of his eyelid. That must be why he was doing chump work guard duty instead of fighting with Yu's army: some old injury the larval Goa'uld couldn't fully heal. He was partially blind, maybe had some trouble with depth perception. Sliding a glance at Teal'c, she rubbed her finger next to her right eye and he nodded again.

Then she aimed her own smile at the guard as he leaned in closer. She licked her lips and went on, "I bet I could trade something. No one has to know."

As the guard was opening his mouth to speak, Teal'c – hidden by the door and the guard's blind spot – cracked the door open, snaked an arm through the gap and grabbed him by the neck. Teal'c stifled the guard's surprised yelp with his other hand, then stepped into the corridor. He spun the guard around so his back was against the bars and Teal'c's forearm was across his windpipe. From inside the cell, Sam held one of the guard's arms with one hand and caught his falling staff weapon with the other. The Jaffa thrashed silently for a moment and went limp. Teal'c let him slide to the floor, then took the staff from Sam. She came into the corridor and unclipped the *zat* from the guard's wrist.

Looking down at him she whispered, "Please tell me I'm no good at that seductress stuff."

"You are merely proficient," Teal'c answered. Sam grinned.

Only an alien male could've walked the line that effectively.

"Good," she answered. "Next time, you get to bat your eye-lashes, and I get to do the strangling." She stood and whispered to Aadi, who was hovering in the doorway, "Stay here." Then she sidled down the hall toward the guardroom, Teal'c close behind.

It was gloomier at this end, and a rectangle of light fell through the open door into the hallway. Sam crouched low to duck her head around and peek inside. She pulled back to lean against the wall beside the door, raising one finger at Teal'c. Then she took a deep breath, spun on her knee into the doorway and fired the *zat*.

A nice, clean shot. The second guard didn't even have time to turn his head from his console. He finally went slack, his head lolling backward as the energy arced and sizzled around him.

While she was collecting his *zat* and Teal'c was hooking the fallen staff with his foot and flipping it up to catch it, Sam called up the map of the complex she carried in her head. The route they'd taken in would be easy to retrace, but it wound through some high-traffic areas near the entrance. Plus, there was another problem.

She stepped back into the corridor to wave at Aadi, who looked suspiciously both ways before trotting up to her.

"How well do you know this place?" she asked. "Have you been in other sections?"

"Give me a weapon," he replied.

"We'll protect you," she answered. "Look, we need our gear. Would your dad have kept it with him or turned it over to the Jaffa?"

Aadi set his jaw and looked at the floor. Sam sighed.

"Do you even know how to work one of these?" She held up the second *zat*.

"I've watched."

"Are you going to follow my orders?"

He nodded. When she didn't hand the *zat* over, he met her eyes. "Yes, I'll follow orders," he said with exasperated formality.

Even though she'd always thought of herself as rather fond of children, Sam had to wonder if it were possible to keep kids while they were cute and then maybe send them someplace at puberty until they were human again. *Military academy*, she thought suddenly, and added, *Sorry, Dad*. She didn't bother to hide her reluctance as she gave Aadi the *zat* and showed him the firing key.

He grinned as he hefted the weapon, then looked up and down the hallway. "I know a better way out," he said, and pointed through the guardroom door. "That way."

"Okay," Sam agreed, and took point, Aadi behind her, and Teal'c on their six.

When she was at the door on the far side, a double burst of *zat* fire startled her. She turned in time to see the second guard's body disintegrate with a last blurring ripple. Aadi was standing with the *zat* still aimed at empty space, and his face was alight with feverish triumph.

"He wasn't a threat. You didn't need to do that," she snapped. Teal'c confiscated Aadi's *zat* and stuffed it into his waistband.

"One less Jaffa," Aadi said, his smile wide and defiant.


On the journey through the winding corridors, Aris was careful not to let O'Neill get too close. He had the upper hand and the advantage of having a plan, but O'Neill had a score to settle. Of all the things Aris had observed about O'Neill, his loyalty to his team, and theirs to him, was the most admirable. It was also the most likely to get Aris killed, now that Sebek had changed the game by taking Jackson as a host. He would have to stay constantly on his guard. With the rest of his team held as ransom to his cooperation, O'Neill might start to think there wasn't much left to lose. Aris couldn't let that thought take hold.

There was plenty to admire about O'Neill, but all those things made him dangerous. Nothing could be allowed to interfere with the plan. It had taken Aris too long, and he'd sacrificed too much, to get careless now.

The Jaffa followed them out of the bunker, making conversation impossible. O'Neill seemed unconcerned on the surface, but his sharp eyes took everything in, and Aris was certain he was making maps and catalogs of useful items in his head for future reference. It was what Aris would do, in the same situation. Near the exit, where the poisonous atmosphere the Goa'uld had given them was palpable, Aris waved a hand at them. "Sebek wants me to bring him alone."

The Jaffa exchanged glances. These were the dregs of Yu's army: old men whose time as warriors was coming to a close, young men disgraced in battle, and a few of the injured or crippled whose symbiotes couldn't make them completely right again. Aris had sized up their capabilities long ago – the same batch of castoffs had been here since Sebek's arrival – but he watched O'Neill make the same assessment, and knew he saw their weakness.

"Sebek has given me no such order," Na'tak said. He was the most unpleasant of the entire cadre. Aris had been looking forward to wringing his neck for a very long time.

"Your lord and master is not himself," Aris said, with a wry smile. The limp joke earned him a stone-faced stare from O'Neill. Aris made a note not to press that wound too hard. "*I* brought them here in the first place, remember? I think I can walk him to the mine."

"Very well," Na'tak said, doing exactly the wrong thing, as Aris had known he would. "But you are warned, hunter. Be quick."

Aris resisted the urge to shoot them both. It wouldn't be productive. "Oh, very quick," he said, unable to keep the amused scorn out of his voice. "We'll run all the way."

O'Neill watched them turn and go about their business, in opposite directions. Water leaked from his eyes – not tears, Aris knew, but a reaction to the fumes. It happened to all offworlders. Even the Jaffa were not immune to the poison from the mines. When the sound of the Jaffa's footsteps had faded, O'Neill turned back to Aris, waiting. "So," he said.

"You want to know what I passed to Teal'c, don't you?" Aris said. O'Neill's expression shifted subtly to curiosity, with a quick flash of surprise. Good. If Aris could keep him off guard, he'd have a better chance of keeping them all alive long enough to be of use.

"Like anything you say would be even close to the truth," O'Neill said. He rubbed his hands over his face and eyes, an irritated gesture, sweeping moisture away.

"That won't help," Aris said. "You'll get used to it."

"Not that we'll be here that long," O'Neill said, challenging Aris to contradict him. Aris didn't bother.

"I gave Teal'c a little something to make his stay shorter," Aris said. He waited for the expected reaction to play itself out, while O'Neill worked through his motivations, looking for the angle.

"So he can help your son," O'Neill said.

Aris inclined his head, let a small smile curve across his lips. "Let's hope the Jaffa were a little slower to pick it up than you were. Your people will need it, when the time comes."

"Uh-huh," O'Neill said, as skeptical as if someone had told him he was free to take his team and walk off this world forever. "And why isn't that time now?"

"That's not your concern."

O'Neill tensed. "Listen. Not to put too fine a point on this, but we don't have a lot of options here. And if you're trading us off for your kid, you'd better think twice about that. This snake is not going to let your kid go."

Aris kept his face neutral, but the words registered hard with him, confirmation of his own instincts. It didn't matter, though. The situation was as untenable as it had been even before he'd known for sure Sebek wasn't a fair trader. He unholstered his weapon, but let his arm drop to his side without pointing it at O'Neill. Subtle threats and intimidation wouldn't work on this man, but they had mutual experience of each other, and each had seen proof that the other would do whatever was necessary to gain the upper hand. He triggered the door and let it slide open so the planet's atmosphere could rise to meet them. He hated the sight of his planet now. His son's legacy, if he survived any of what was to come. The Goa'uld had a lot to pay for.

"Let me make it clear for you, Colonel. You're a means to an end. You will help me appease Sebek so I can get into that vault, and I'll free your friends."

"So they can free your son, and get themselves killed in the process," O'Neill said.

"Everything comes with a price," Aris said. Too close to the wound, again. Anger flashed in O'Neill's eyes, tamped down in the space of a heartbeat. O'Neill would never trust him. He was too smart to make that mistake.

"You think you know what's in that vault, don't you?" O'Neill was watching him, a little too closely. He was more perceptive than Aris had given him credit for.

"Sebek's not the only one who can benefit from what's down there. In case you hadn't noticed, something down there doesn't agree with the Goa'uld. If it hurts them, it has value to me." There it was – the spark of interest, in O'Neill's eyes. Now the groundwork for cooperation was laid. "My people have been enslaved by the Goa'uld for a long time, Colonel. What would you do, if this was your world?"

"You don't do subtle very well," O'Neill said impatiently. Blatant manipulation apparently had little effect on him. Not that Aris had expected anything else. "You know damn well what I'd do."

"Then we understand each other," Aris said. O'Neill didn't respond, but he would follow the path to its logical conclusion: if whatever was down there harmed the Goa'uld, it was worth finding. Who would ultimately use it against the Goa'uld, though…well, that was a question that would be answered later. Aris was going to make sure it was him. O'Neill would do the same. But Aris had a blaster and hostages. O'Neill's friends would have his son and a sense of duty and decency that meant they wouldn't use him against his father.

Aris smiled. He dug down into the breast pocket of his armor and withdrew Jackson's cracked glasses. "Take them," he said to O'Neill. "Sebek's too weak to heal Jackson's eyes, so he can't see very well. He might need these."

"*He* might?" O'Neill said, without moving to pick up the glasses. Any minute he was going to make a move to kill Aris; Aris could see it in his eyes.

"Dr. Jackson," Aris amended. "Sebek is weak. We can use that." He waited for O'Neill to accept the temporary treaty implicit in 'we,' and the peace offering, such as it was.

O'Neill took the glasses from Aris's hand and shoved them in his front pocket.

# CHAPTER SEVEN

The only thing worse than the stench of the planet's air was the stink of the mine – a wet, dank smell, like a hundred years' worth of mildew and rot trapped in the stifling darkness, and it made Jack sneeze. The irony wasn't lost on him; too bad Daniel wasn't there to rag him about it.

This time, as they descended into the mine, Jack went ahead with Aris right behind him. Jack counted his steps to focus his thinking; three hundred and seventy-seven steps, jagging ever downward in circular paths, through dimly lit passages and narrow, rough-hewn doorways. All the while, he steeled himself for dealing with Daniel...Sebek. He had to stop thinking of him as Daniel, or he would never be able to do what he had to do.

By the time they reached the vault chamber, he'd sealed every trace of worry and fear behind a wall of sarcastic indifference. All that remained was disgust and anger, because those might still come in handy. If things got too bad, if he lost control of the situation, he could always provoke the snake into killing him. Words were a handy weapon in the face of arrogance; smart remarks never failed to send most Goa'uld into a killing rage. Jack had always known insolence would serve a purpose one day.

They found Sebek standing in front of the vault doors, his face inches away from the surface as he ran both palms over the inscriptions. Such a familiar posture, one Jack had seen Daniel assume a thousand times when he was a hair's breadth away from working out a problem – but Jack had already slammed that door closed. Sebek might look like Daniel, he might even do the things Daniel had done once, but Daniel was as good as dead while that thing had control of him. Jack could imagine all too easily what it was like to move through the world without conscious thought, without control of his limbs or his voice, or even his memories and dreams. He could only hope Daniel was as unaware of the horror of it as Jack had been while Kanan was dragging him around the galaxy in search of a captive slave girl.

Even so, when Sebek turned to them, Jack caught himself searching for remnants of his friend. He couldn't help it; it was what he wanted to see, and he looked in spite of himself, careful not to give his intention away. Instead of Daniel's intense look of concentration, and the easy smile that usually followed it, he saw a creature staring out at him through Daniel's blue eyes, a calculating gaze that erased any lingering hope. Not that he'd expected anything different. In an awful way, it made things easier.

Sebek had stripped down to Daniel's military-issue black t-shirt and BDUs, and it was a jarring dissonance of the recognizable and the strange. Jack wished the snake had done something to make himself look less Daniel-like – changed into one of those wacky Goa'uld outfits, maybe – because seeing him wearing Daniel like a suit of clothes was unnerving. The only thing that made him not-Daniel, on the surface, was the tilt of his head, or the curving sneer that passed for a smile. That, and the ribbon device he wore on his right hand.

Sebek spoke first to Aris, ignoring Jack entirely. The sound of his voice was Daniel's voice, roughened and deepened, warped by Sebek's presence, but Jack could still hear Daniel beneath, if he let himself listen. "You will remain with us."

Aris looked steadily at him, as if trying to decide whether or not it was worth it to obey, then said, "I have business to do on your behalf. You don't need me here."

"You will do as we command!" Sebek shouted. Aris holstered his weapon and folded his arms across his chest, but he made no move to leave; it passed for obedience.

As soon as Sebek's miniature tantrum passed, it was as though Aris no longer existed. Sebek turned to Jack with a calculating stare, much as he had assessed him when he'd first seen him the day before – but this was different from before; he looked at Jack like he *knew* him, which made the hair stand up on Jack's arms. Of course, Sebek now had access to all Daniel's information, which was what scared Jack all the way around. There were a few things Daniel knew about Jack he'd prefer no snake ever find out, too many sore points like fresh, hidden bruises, waiting for someone to jam a finger into the right spot.

"You are the one called O'Neill," Sebek said, raising his chin and narrowing his eyes.

"We've met," Jack said, conscious of Aris moving away from him. He braced himself.

"Ah, but we have learned much more about you since our first encounter," Sebek said. He smiled, a twist of Daniel's lips that profaned the expression. "We have our host's memories to draw upon, and he has been most helpful in teaching us about you."

Jack could feel his jaw tighten. He clamped down on the denials he was about to spew. Too soon in this game to get ribboned to a crisp, so he shifted his gaze away from Sebek and toward a neutral corner of the room, but Sebek was already in motion. He moved closer to Jack, closer still, until his chest touched Jack's arm. A shiver of revulsion started at the base of Jack's spine, but he resisted the urge to pull away. Slowly, Sebek moved around him in a tight circle, behind Jack, then coming around to face him. "You are a great leader among the Tauri," Sebek said. "What a pitiful statement upon their armies, if you are the best they can produce."

"Oh, we do okay," Jack said, and forced his tone of voice into neutral.

"We could not think of a reason not to kill you," Sebek informed him, in a conspiratorial whisper. "We were looking forward to it. First you, then the woman, and the *shol'va* last – a special kind of death, for him. Something lingering. Something befitting a traitor."

"Time's a'wastin'," Jack said, and met Sebek's eyes with a calm born of long practice. "Or were you planning to talk me to death? 'Cause I've got to tell you, it's not very efficient."

"Our plans have changed. This one thinks you can be useful to us," Sebek said, tapping his belly, as if Daniel was the snake coiled inside. "He thinks you should be allowed to live."

"I thought nothing of the host survives," Jack said blandly, though a devastating certainty rose inside him: Daniel probably did want Jack to live, but he hadn't given that thought up willingly. The snake was *in there*, burrowing around inside Daniel, stealing everything that mattered to him. "Or have you finally given up on that old schtick?"

"Nothing important survives," Sebek said. "We take what we wish, when we wish to take it. It is unfortunate that you were not privileged to understand this for yourself, as your previous experiences as a host were sadly interrupted."

Jack straightened. This was what he'd hoped wouldn't happen: a snake who knew just where his wounds were, and how to apply maximum pressure. "A Tok'ra isn't a Goa'uld," Jack said, without any conviction whatsoever. Damn, even after all these years, he still didn't quite believe it. With Sebek less than a foot from his face, staring at him for any sign of a reaction, he couldn't sell it.

Sebek tilted his head, eyes narrowed again. "They are traitors, true, but they were once as we are. They refuse to wield the power that is their birthright." His gaze traveled significantly to Jack's neck, to his throat, then back to Jack's eyes. "But you were host to another, before Kanan."

Hard to forget that experience; Hathor's face loomed in his mind's eye, and her fist, with the mature symbiote squirming and screaming, waiting to dive right into him. His skin was crawling now, like a thousand ants marching over his body. "Right, that. But it didn't take," Jack said. He smiled self-deprecatingly. "I'm snake-resistant."

"Insolence," Sebek purred, though he didn't sound displeased. He sounded like a cat about to eat a mouse he'd been batting around for hours. "But you have something we must have." He reached up one hand and drew a line across Jack's forehead with his index finger; the touch was like acid. "You have stored the knowledge of the Ancients in your mind. We would not believe such a thing, were it not for our host's certainty that this is true."

"Daniel exaggerates," Jack said, and felt like a jerk for saying it, but it wasn't like Daniel was in a position to care about slurs to his character.

"No," Sebek said. "He does not. He cannot. His thoughts are open to us; he cannot hide them." Shoulder to shoulder with Jack, Sebek pointed at the vault door, then lowered his voice to say, "You will use this knowledge to open this vault for us."

"That's your big plan?" Jack said, incredulous. "Listen, if you really know what Daniel knows, then you know I don't know as much as you think I know." He paused for effect. "Or something like that."

"Your attempts to confuse the issue are not amusing to us," Sebek said. "You remember the language you learned, do you not? You have activated these devices before by your presence."

"No, I haven't," Jack said. There was a tiny fragment of memory pushing at the back of his head, a conversation with Daniel where Daniel had gone on and on about his theory that Jack was the one who activated the Ancient repository by stepping through the circle on the floor or some such nonsense. Daniel had even insisted that he was sure Jack remembered some of the Ancient he had learned, and the accompanying Latin, but Jack was quick to squash that notion, even though he really did remember a thing or two, or ten. Jack hadn't been listening closely enough when Daniel went on about the why and the how of activating the Ancient devices. It was all geek-speak to him, but now it appeared Daniel hadn't let go of that theory. Unfortunately for Jack. He hoped none of it had been right, because if it was, he was in a world of hurt.

"We shall soon discover the truth of the matter," Sebek said. "You are untainted by a Goa'uld presence. You do not possess the marker."

"Whatever," Jack muttered. He stuffed his hands in his pockets. "Find another volunteer."

"We do not need your cooperation," Sebek said, and gestured to Aris. "We do not even need you alive."

"Do your worst," Jack said. Sebek's face contorted with rage and his fingers closed around Jack's throat with a death grip. Daniel's hands, but with unnatural strength. Jack felt the breath in his throat die, strangled out of him, and he grabbed at Sebek's arm, twisting and prying. Like a solid piece of iron, his arm was locked in place. Jack's vision greyed. His lungs burned.

A moment later, the fingers at his throat began to tremble, and their grasp weakened, easing the pressure by degrees until Jack was able to gasp in a breath. Sebek's eyes were closed, and the rage on his face had changed to fear; sweat dotted his upper lip, and he turned pale. Jack wrenched Sebek's arm away and shoved him back. Nausea hit Jack then, followed by the sensation that something was crawling inside him, burrowing into his neck, winding around his spine. *Not again.* He slapped at the back of his neck, half-panicked, and the feeling faded away, as suddenly as it had arrived. On the heels of it came a slow, rolling flow of images: running through a sparse forest at night toward a Stargate; standing before the Tok'ra Council shouting down Selmak's latest ridiculous strategy; wrenching himself out of the body of the one called O'Neill before the Jaffa can arrive.

Jack pressed the heels of his hands into his closed eyes and growled with frustration. Not his memories. Not things he wanted in his head, and he would never be able to get rid of them. He hated Kanan with his whole *body.* Slowly, the tide of images pulled back, until he was able to breathe without them closing on him.

"Jack."

He shook his head to clear it, because he was hearing the impossible, his own wishful thinking. That voice didn't belong to Sebek. It was –

"Jack, it's me. It's really me. Listen. Please."

He raised his head and stared at Sebek – Daniel – *whoever* it was. Daniel leaned against the far wall, hunched over and panting, as if he couldn't stand under his own power. His words came out broken, raspy, as he said, "Jack, I don't have much time. It's too difficult to stay in control. You have to let us into that vault."

"Daniel?" Jack shook his head again. It was like he had cotton padding around his brain. He had to get clear of the fog in his head. This was too easy a trap to fall into; hope was the worst of all. "If you were really Daniel, you'd never ask me to give a snake a weapon."

"Jack, we don't have any choice. It serves our interests, believe me. The weapon disrupts the Goa'uld hold on the host. It could be incredibly valuable to us. If Sam were here, she'd tell you the same thing." Daniel – Sebek – stretched out a hand to him. "If you don't open that door, he'll kill you. He'll kill us all, and he'll still get in."

"Oh, he won't kill you," Jack said hoarsely, and pressed his back against the wall. He had his breath again, and it was getting easier to speak. "He pretty much has to keep you around."

"For now. But he can move to another host anytime." Daniel doubled over, grimacing, then raised his head and said, "He's weak, Jack. He's insane. He's one of Yu's subordinates – he's already contacted Yu. A mothership is coming to get the weapon, or destroy it, if we can't get in. But we can't let it be destroyed."

"Why the hell not?" Jack said. "You seriously expect me to open that door and hand him a weapon?"

"We can take it back to Stargate Command."

"Because that's always worked out so well for us in the past," Jack said, with all the sarcasm he could muster. He watched Daniel closely, watched his posture, as he clenched his fists and stared at Jack.

Daniel shook his head with that peculiarly frustrated look he sometimes got when Jack was being deliberately dense. "Think of all the knowledge I carry, things we don't want our enemies to know. Things Sebek has already picked through. If we can get in there, maybe the weapon will destroy him and free me."

"Oh, right," Jack said, and now he was sure of who he was talking to, and the last bit of hope died inside him. He pulled himself all the way upright and jammed his hands in his pockets, casually. "Because the only thing *Daniel* ever thinks about is himself."

A flash of gold in Daniel's eyes, confirming Jack's belief, and Sebek drew himself up to Daniel's full height. With feral speed, he grabbed Aris's knife from the holster at his thigh, shoved Aris away, and held the knife to Daniel's throat, blade against the tender exposed skin there. Jack lunged forward, but Sebek pressed the knifepoint deep, drawing blood. Jack stopped short at the sight of red streaks running down Daniel's neck. "We will end this now," Sebek said, using his own voice again, "and take you as host. This host will bleed out slowly until he is a lifeless husk, and we will still have what we desire."

Jack clenched his hands into fists and looked to Aris for any signal that he was ready to move – a nod of the head, a drawn weapon, *anything* to give Jack a reason to move on Sebek. But it wasn't going to happen. Aris moved his hand to the hilt of his weapon, but didn't unholster it. "You've got to be kidding me," Jack said, staring at Aris.

"Whether he takes you, or doesn't take you, I've got nothing left to lose," Aris said. His hand remained on the butt of the gun.

Jack shifted his gaze back to Sebek. The knife was dug in now, and there was a broad cut, creeping too close to Daniel's jugular. Daniel was going to die for nothing, here on this world none of them cared about, and Sebek was going to take him anyway, and there was not one damn thing he could do about it. "You son of a bitch," he said, through gritted teeth.

"Your insults are meaningless to us," Sebek said, pulling the knife another few millimeters over Daniel's skin. "Open the door."

"It might not work!" Jack said, desperate to stop the progress of the knife.

"We will soon see."

Without taking his eyes off Sebek, Jack made his way to the device on the right hand side of the vault door. *Here goes nothing.* He stuck his hand inside. Nothing happened. Relief hit all at once, but it was short-lived when Sebek ordered,

"Turn your hand."

Jack sighed. Slowly, he moved his hand until it was palm down, and a bright white light began to glow in the small space. Jack yanked his hand out and stepped back. "You got what you wanted. Put the knife down."

It seemed to take forever, but Sebek lowered the knife. He wiped its edge on his sleeve, smearing the t-shirt with Daniel's blood. "We are already healing," he said, with an ugly smirk. "But we are touched by your concern."

The light began to creep along the edges of the door, then toward the center, filling and illuminating each individual glyph. Brighter and brighter, until Jack had to use one hand to shield his eyes. At last it winked out. The ground rumbled, deep vibrations in the earth beneath their feet, and the vault door began to slide open, shedding dust and dirt as it rolled over a long-abandoned threshold.

When the tremors stopped and the door to the darkness beyond stood open, cold sweat beaded across Jack's face. Sebek was behind him now, and when he spoke, Jack could feel warm breath against the back of his neck. "Jack," Sebek said, and laughed, a low, menacing sound. "You will lead the way."

It took the Tok'ra less time than Hammond expected to send a representative, and when they did, it was Jacob Carter who stepped through the 'gate. Not alone, however: he had a second Tok'ra with him, someone Hammond didn't recognize, a young-looking man with curly hair and a grim expression on the sharp-featured face. The eyes were narrowed, like he was reserving judgment but was certain all suspicions would be confirmed. The expression wasn't unusual. In Hammond's experience, the Tok'ra often seemed grim and disapproving, like they were waiting to be proven right. He conceded that millennia of fighting Goa'uld would have the same effect on him, if he were ever unfortunate enough to live that long. Although he was pretty sure he wouldn't be quite so superior about it.

"George," Jacob said, with a warm smile and a handshake. "It's good to see you again, even under the circumstances."

"Good to see you too, Jacob." Hammond's friendship with Sam Carter's father had been one of the most enduring of his life. He'd known Jacob for twenty years, and symbiote notwithstanding, he was always pleased by Jacob's rare visits home.

Jacob scanned the room, looking for his daughter, as he always did. Chances for them to spend time together were few and far between. "Is Sam offworld?"

"That's why we've called you," Hammond said. Comprehension dawned at once in Jacob's eyes, but Hammond continued on with the details, since the scraps of information they had might be useful in some way, if only to ease Jacob's mind that they were doing all they could. "SG-1 is missing. Disappeared from P54-X3J during a routine meet-and-greet."

"Captured?" Jacob asked.

"That's the theory. We've got some intel to that effect."

"Right," Jacob said, processing the possibilities. He sighed, then nodded to the Tok'ra at his side. "This is Malek."

"Of course," Hammond said. "It's a pleasure to meet you." Pieces from various mission reports slid out of memory and into place, providing him with the information he needed to deal with this man: Malek, the Tok'ra who had helped to solidify the fragile alliance between the Jaffa and Tok'ra, and who had defended the Queen, Egeria. He was a known quantity now that SG-1 had encountered him several times over the past year, but his name had stuck in Hammond's mind because Teal'c's opinion of him had been less than complimentary. He'd stopped short of calling Malek a coward, but his mission report had been clear about how he didn't think Malek could be relied upon to assist in a close-quarters fight.

Malek inclined his head, a bit stiffly as was usual for the Tok'ra, and said, "It is an honor, General."

Jacob squinted at Hammond. "How long has it been since you've had any sleep, George?"

"You mean, a full night's worth?" Hammond answered, and a smile twisted Jacob's lips.

"You know damn well what I mean. You don't look so good."

"I've been a little busy," Hammond said. He gestured toward the door. "Let's adjourn to the briefing room, where we can talk."

Hammond found it comforting to have Jacob there as a sounding board, someone to run all the details by, to make sure he hadn't missed anything. He gave Jacob a copy of SG-14's mission report, but verbally summarized the high points to spare him the trouble of paging through it. Malek, however, began reading as soon as Hammond set the folder in front of him, and continued in tense silence throughout the briefing, his head bowed over the document.

"SG-14 brought back one of the natives, the Relosians." Hammond pointed at the file on the table in front of Jacob. "He tells us that a man paid him to lure one of the team members into a trap. We don't think that, beyond this one individual, the Relosians are to blame here. They haven't seen a Goa'uld in several generations, and we don't believe they had any reason to harm our people."

"You're completely certain about that?" Jacob looked skeptical. "At least one of them had reason."

"Internal politics. The man has some idea of becoming the leader, the…" Hammond thumbed the next page open in his file. "…the Princep of his people, and was interested in disrupting the incumbent's alliance with us. He doesn't seem to have had accomplices. He insists that SG-1 was taken offworld. Major Harper assured me that his team searched the area thoroughly. If SG-1 is still there, they're hidden from sight, but my gut tells me they aren't there."

"So does mine." Jacob folded his hands on the tabletop and was quiet for a moment. "If one of the System Lords has captured them, I think we might have heard about it by now. SG-1 is a big prize. Not something any glory-seeking System Lord would keep quiet, not the way the rivalries within their ranks are working these days."

"I was hoping you'd say that. Unfortunately, that doesn't leave many obvious options."

At that, Malek raised his head. "No. It does not." He glanced at Jacob. "And we do not have the resources to spare to locate them." Jacob met his eyes, and for a moment, a silent communication passed between the two of them. Clearly, there was some argument simmering here that had been put on hold before they'd set out for Earth.

"I'm not asking that you pull Tok'ra away from their assignments," Hammond said. "Just that you give us whatever intel you can. We'll take care of the rest."

"There's something else." Jacob's fingers tapped against each other, before he stilled his hands. "I know you're thinking about their personal safety – hell, I am, too. But I also know you're thinking about the threat they represent to your security here, if they've been captured."

"It's a threat we've faced before," Hammond said. The long list of security breaches unfurled itself in his mind's eye. This was not a new concern.

"Well, yes, but now there's more to it. Ever since you've allied with the Tok'ra, every capture of SGC personnel has the potential to cause damage to our network as well. This is a…growing problem…for the Tok'ra."

"Of course," Hammond said. Malek shifted in his chair impatiently, giving a hint of what he was thinking. Hammond added, "This is why it was agreed between us that the SGC would never need specific information as to the whereabouts of Tok'ra bases or the placement of Tok'ra operatives. Despite the fact that we have shared information of a sensitive nature with you." The pointed reminder wasn't meant for Jacob, but for Malek, who zeroed in on it immediately.

"What you ask of us is problematic at best," Malek said. "General, I am not unsympathetic to what you require, and I recognize you do not have the offworld resources to accomplish recovery of your team without our assistance. But you must realize, the Tok'ra nation is less than one quarter the strength it was when we first became your allies. The threat of infiltration and annihilation of the Tok'ra grows every day."

"Your point being?" Hammond asked. Jacob was looking down at his tightly clasped hands. Hammond's jaw set into a hard square, and his eyes narrowed. "Are you refusing to assist us? Jacob?"

"George…" Jacob looked up again, and when he spoke, Selmak had control of him, and spoke with the deep, distorted tones of the symbiote. "General Hammond, you must understand that it is not lack of willingness on our part. But there are those on the Tok'ra Council who would argue that if we were to locate Colonel O'Neill and the others, it would be more practical to quietly assassinate your personnel than to attempt a rescue that could expose an operative to suspicion."

So that was it. No wonder Jacob had had difficulty articulating it. It fell to Selmak to represent the Tok'ra's true concern. A flash of anger burned through Hammond – they'd sacrificed a hell of a lot to help the Tok'ra, the arrogant bastards, though the Tok'ra always seemed to think it was the other way around. He squashed the quick words of anger that rose to the surface, and instead said, "Selmak, I shouldn't have to tell you that this is not acceptable to us. If you take any step in that direction, our alliance will be immediately severed."

"Yes, General. I do understand. I have made this point to the others several times, but there are still many Tok'ra who believe we do not need this alliance – that the Tauri represent a greater hindrance than help to our cause." Selmak stopped speaking, and Jacob's head dropped down again.

This time, it was Jacob who spoke. "George, you already know I don't agree. Obviously. Selmak doesn't either."

"Nor do I," Malek said, though he still looked as though there was a great deal he was leaving unsaid. "However, I remain deeply concerned about the threat to our cause, and have been for some time."

"If I remember correctly, we've sheltered your people at some great risk to ourselves," Hammond said. "It would seem to me that the threat to your cause often comes from within your organization. Not from us."

Jacob nodded. "That may be true. But, much as I hate to say it, our operatives are spread pretty thin right now. We don't have a lot of leeway to spend time tracking down SG-1. Despite my personal connection to this…we can only do what we can do."

"General, I should add that the Tok'ra cannot be summoned this way every time your personnel turn up missing. It is an unfortunate fact of war that some will be lost." Malek paused, then said, "While I have the greatest respect for the members of SG-1, they cannot be held in higher esteem than the millions of others the Tok'ra fight to free."

Hammond met Malek's eyes and held that gaze for a long, long moment. Politics. Damn, he loathed the entire structure of threat, compromise, and rhetoric. When Malek finally looked away, Hammond said, "No disrespect intended, Malek, but I'm well aware of what's at stake. I'm afraid you don't understand our position here. The Tok'ra and the Tauri are allies. To us this means that when we make a request for assistance, we expect it to be answered in the affirmative."

"You speak of requests when what you truly make are demands,"

Malek said. He lifted his chin. "Is this the way the Tauri treat their supposed allies?"

Jacob held up a hand. "This isn't getting us anywhere. There's no reason for this to degenerate into a pissing contest." He tapped his copy of the mission report, still unopened in front of him. "Let's go with the assumption that they're not on P54-X3J and that, if they are, your people will handle it."

"I'm with you so far," Hammond said.

"And they probably haven't been captured by a System Lord, so if they've fallen into the hands of a Goa'uld, he's planning to use them for something else. Say, to get Earth's security information out of them."

"There are many other reasons SG-1 might prove useful to a Goa'uld," Malek said. "It may be that their chief use is to provide the pleasure of watching them die slowly."

Jacob winced. For a moment, Hammond could not stop the flood of images those words brought with them; he'd read Dr. Fraiser's reports after the Colonel's return from Ba'al's fortress, as well as Teal'c's report of torture by Heru'ur's guards. And those were only a couple of the instances that came to mind. He knew the risks, and the horror of it.

"The 'why' of their capture might tell us who has them," Jacob said. "Have they been working on anything in particular the Goa'uld might want them for? Pissed anyone off lately?"

"Hard to say," Hammond said. "This is SG-1 we're talking about. Over the years, they've accumulated a lot of enemies."

"Fortunately, most of the Goa'uld they have offended are dead now," Malek said. "Many by the hand of SG-1."

"There are still a few out there," Jacob said.

"It's a short list," Hammond answered. "However, I'll have my people go back through the mission reports, to see if there are any loose ends that might lead somewhere."

"We'll put the word out to our operatives, to be on the lookout," Jacob said.

Malek rose from the table and bowed. "I will see to it, Selmak. General, with your permission," he said.

Hammond nodded, then gestured one of the security personnel over. "Go with the airman. He'll give you whatever you need."

Jacob waited until Malek was out of sight on the staircase before he said, "George, don't overestimate what we can do. They could be anywhere. It's a big galaxy out there."

"I know that, Jacob." Hammond sat back in his chair. His back was aching and his stomach was growling, but at least he was feeling more hopeful than he had been before Jacob showed up. "Don't underestimate your daughter. Or Jack, or Teal'c, or Dr. Jackson."

"Wouldn't dream of it." Jacob stretched and sat back, mirroring Hammond's posture. "I don't suppose we could grab some coffee, could we?"

"I thought coffee didn't agree with Selmak," Hammond said.

Jacob's face fell, revealing the true depth of his weariness. "He's going to make an exception, in this case. 'Gate travel really takes it out of me these days."

"Maybe Selmak hasn't had good coffee."

"Maybe Air Force coffee is what convinced Selmak coffee was evil," Jacob said, and pushed back from his chair. "Come on. How about if you grab those mission files? We can go through some of them ourselves."

# CHAPTER EIGHT

The hallway on the other side of the door was empty. Sam nodded to Aadi, who stepped up beside her, Teal'c close behind.

"Which way?" she demanded.

He pointed left, and they set off at a jog. Although they stepped as lightly as possible on the stone floor, their footsteps still echoed in the narrow passage. The hallway was lit by recessed pot lights in the ceiling, which cast bright circles on the floor and left the spaces in between in darkness. Obviously they were outside the holding area; this kind of lighting would be counterproductive when it came to keeping an eye on prisoners.

"What is this place?" she asked Aadi as they slowed to a stop beside another door and he waved her past it toward the one at the end of the hall.

"Quarters, I think," he whispered.

That brought Sam up short again. "You're taking us through troop quarters?"

He flashed teeth in a smile that stopped just this side of mockery. "Slaves," he clarified. "From when Sebek used this building, before the landing station and the big ship."

"So, abandoned, then, right?" His answer was a shrug. Sam aimed a look over his head at Teal'c. "Hopefully."

The door at the end of the hall was locked. She pulled the panel off the wall beside it and got to work on the crystals, while Aadi chewed his thumb and Teal'c kept a wary eye on the corridor behind them. How long until dawn and somebody came with rations and found the guards? Guard, she corrected herself, as she wiggled a sticky crystal free. A part of her brain caught a wistful thread on the idea of rations.

"What is beyond this door?" Teal'c asked.

Aadi shrugged again. "I think laundry. Or kitchens. I was little when I was here."

Sam re-slotted the crystal. Nothing happened. She started over.

"Your father worked in the laundry?" That image started out as amusing, but didn't stay that way.

He must've seen it on her face, because he looked away. She was considering a 'sorry' when the door cracked open, and a wedge of light fell into the hallway.

"Well," she said, her eye to the opening. "Not abandoned."

It was definitely the laundry. The door opened onto a small landing that looked down on a long, well-lit room lined on one side by steaming vats as tall as Aadi, and on the other side with some kind of static driers. Down the middle, colorful linens and robes hung on wires, dripping into a drainage trough that ran the length of the room. At two of the driers, slaves were laying clothing out on racks, pulling them taut and sliding the racks into the open mouths of the machines. Other slaves stood ready to pull the racks out immediately, unclipping the now-dry material and dropping it in careful layers onto hand trucks, which were rolled down to the misty far end of the room for pressing. Discounting the *ha'tak*, this had to be the only good-smelling room on the whole planet, and she wondered if the scent of laundry soap was another one of those galactic constants, like fir trees and sullen teenagers.

Fortunately all fourteen slaves were too busy with their work to pay much attention to a doorway leading to an empty part of the complex, and she and Teal'c managed to slide the panels open far enough for them to squeeze through, Aadi first under Teal'c's arm, then Sam. The door sighed shut behind them as they crouched together on the landing. In the middle of the side wall beyond the driers, a good thirty, forty paces away, was the only other door. At the far end, next to the pressers, a single Jaffa was leaning on his staff, looking bored and unhappy in the thick humidity. Sam didn't envy him his chain mail and greaves.

Silently, Teal'c aimed the blade of his hand at the hand trucks collected at the bottom of the stairs, each one with a basket big enough to hold a person. Sam crept down the stairs, bent low to keep behind the inadequate cover of the meshing along the railing. From the bottom of the stairs, she waved at them to follow her. The humming of the machines covered the sound of their boots on the steps. Aadi's bare feet were silent.

Once at the bottom, Teal'c climbed into the basket and Sam, smaller and a little more agile, crouched behind it, helping Aadi get some momentum going before leaving him to push and half-crawling beside it. She kept an eye on their shadow as they went, to make sure that her own wasn't at all visible around that of the truck. They stuck close to the wall so that Sam was sandwiched in pretty tightly. Occasionally, when Aadi's steering got sloppy, or the truck jogged on the cracked concrete of the floor, she found herself pinned and had to shove with her shoulder to get Aadi back on track. Still, they made good progress.

About halfway to the door, someone spoke to Aadi, a low hiss of recognition and alarm, and the hair rose on the back of Sam's neck. She heard him murmur something that sounded like "Esa" and "Bren," and whoever it was moved away. A moment later, Sam could hear a man singing. Another, thin, wavering voice picked up the song, and another, farther off, until the song rose and fell around them, weaving its mournful way through the thrumming of the machinery. When they were even with the door, two men – she could make out the tops of their heads – rolled a wire rack hung with robes along beside them, blocking the guard's view of the open doorway. Someone else, a woman bowed in half like she had some kind of bone disease, came up beside Aadi and took the cart from him. Hidden behind the rack, Teal'c stood and stepped out of truck, while a third man heaped clothing into the now empty cart. Nodding their thanks the three of them quickly slipped out the door.

Sam took a moment to get her bearings and to stretch the tension from her legs. She wasn't feeling too steady. She glanced up at Teal'c, who was looking away down the corridor toward the next set of doors.

"Aadi," she said. "We have to find our gear. We need—" Teal'c's pointed look made her change her mind about mentioning the tretonin in Teal'c's pack. "There's equipment we'll need when we access the 'gate."

Aadi snorted in disbelief and then laughed. "You can't get to the 'gate. It's in Sebek's room, the place where he sits in his big chair and—"

"We can deal with that later," Sam interrupted him. "We need the gear. Do you have any idea where it might be?"

"It is likely that it will be stored near the armory," Teal'c answered, "which will be on the ground level, and carefully guarded." He didn't look too happy about that. "It may be more prudent to find Aris Boch and use his authority to gain us access."

Sam gazed blindly down the hallway. "Maybe." Then she looked earnestly at him. "How long?" He would've taken his dose of tretonin before leaving Earth, but she couldn't remember if he'd had one on Relos before they were captured.

Drawing himself up even straighter, if that were possible, Teal'c said, "I will be fine."

"How long?"

He answered reluctantly. "A day, perhaps two under good conditions."

"Right." And a planet with heavy gravity, and toxic atmosphere, two days already with minimum rations and practically no water, and the certainty of hand-to-hand combat. So much for 'good conditions.' She found herself wrinkling her nose the way the Colonel did. "Okay, we'll have a look at the ground floor. We have to pass through there, anyway. If it looks good, we go for the gear, and if not, we head for the mine and go with your plan."

"Agreed."

They started off again, and were a few paces away before Sam realized that Aadi wasn't with them. She stopped and looked back. He was standing in the middle of the hallway looking uncertainly first at them, and then back toward the doorway to the laundry.

"Aadi," Sam whispered as loudly as she dared. "Let's go. It's not safe here."

He shook his head. "I don't want to go there," he said in a low, scared voice. "You can get your own gear." He cast another longing look toward the laundry. "Esa can sneak me out in the linens."

Sam stole a glance through the doorway. The view was still blocked by the drying rack. "Can Esa take all of us?"

He hesitated and shook his head. "No. They won't take you. Him." He aimed his chin in Teal'c's direction as he came toward them. "Maybe they'll turn you in for favors." He took a step backward toward the door. "You go. Through that door and then around – there's a big room with windows in the roof, and then the doors out."

Teal'c leaned close to her ear to murmur, "He will betray us."

Inside the room, the rack rattled as someone moved it away from the door, and Sam pushed Aadi up against the wall out of sight. She could hear the Jaffa shouting something and the sudden hiss of escaping steam. Trucks rumbled by.

Her eyes close to Aadi's she asked, "Would you?"

He shook his head.

"Your father would."

"I won't."

He would. She knew he would. And if they let him go, they'd lose the only leverage they had with Aris. The idea of holding a kid hostage made her feel dirty and heavy, but the whole place made her feel dirty and a little extra weight on her conscience would be bearable if it got them – all of them – off this awful planet. Maybe.

"We can protect you."

"None of you can protect me."

"You trust this Esa person to protect you."

Aadi frowned. "He's different." He cast another nervous look over his shoulder and pushed her away. "They're changing shifts. If I don't go now—"

The rest of his sentence was drowned out by the sudden shrieking of an alarm.

"Our escape has been discovered," Teal'c said as he circled Aadi's arm with his hand and began to draw him down the hallway away from the door. "There is no time for this debate."

Aadi set his feet and struggled against Teal'c, but it was no use: Teal'c looped an arm around his waist and picked him up like a suitcase while Sam trotted along behind them. She caught up in time to clamp a hand over Aadi's mouth, preventing him from shouting out.

"You want to go back to that cell?" A shake of the head and wide eyes. "We aren't going to hurt you, but if you aren't quiet, the only ones who are going to come here to save you are Jaffa. Your choice."

The kid went slack in Teal'c's grip, resigned. She nodded to Teal'c, and he put the boy down. Aadi barely had his feet on the ground before they heard a shout behind them. The Jaffa was in the hallway with the bent woman, who was pointing at them.

"Oh crap," Sam said, and both she and Teal'c raised their *zats*. They were too far away still, so instead of shooting they turned to run. Aadi slammed into the door at the end of the hallway and curled himself into a ball at its foot while Teal'c returned fire. Sam yanked the panel off the wall. Two crystals in, two out, one here, the other there. The door snapped open, tumbling Aadi into the atrium beyond. Scooping him up with one arm, Teal'c continued to fire until Sam ducked through the doorway after them. When it closed, she shot the control panel with the *zat*, covering her face with her hand against the shower of sparks.

The atrium was huge, the length of a football field with an arched glass ceiling that revealed a roiling grey sky, lit in the east by a thin wash of red. They were standing on a mezzanine that circled the room on all four sides, a couple of stories above the main floor. Sam risked a peek over the edge. In the central space, a smattering of Jaffa met in the middle for instructions and then dispersed. One of them looked their way and pointed.

"The door!" Sam shouted at Aadi over the rising sound of pounding boots. "Where is it?"

He whirled in place to scan the room and finally pointed. "There. Down!"

Sam followed his outstretched arm. She couldn't see the doors themselves, but a ruddy light stained the main floor in a long rectangle at the far end of the atrium. "I don't think down is going to be an option."

There were two stairwells leading up to the mezzanine, one on either side of the room. Both were between the fugitives and the doors. Three Jaffa were storming up the stairs on the left, another four on the right. No chance of going either way.

"Here," Teal'c called, and waved them toward a narrow side hallway. Slipping into it, Sam counted five doors leading off of it, two on either side and one at the end. Teal'c slapped the control panel for the nearest door on the left, but before they could make it inside, the door at the end of the hall opened and a Jaffa stepped through. The staff blast cooked the air beside Sam's face. She threw herself against the wall, twisting away from it and toward Teal'c and Aadi. Teal'c turned away too, trapping Aadi behind the wall of his back, like she'd seen so many Jaffa do when they shielded their Goa'uld charges with their own armored bodies. Only Teal'c had no armor.

He fell heavily, smoke rising from his left side, his staff weapon spinning out onto the mezzanine. Sam didn't pause to assess the damage, but twisted around on her knee and *zatted* the Jaffa twice. A quick check over her shoulder showed her Teal'c rising to his hands and knees, then sitting back on his heels. He waved her on as Aadi bolted through the open side door. Five long steps took her to the end of the hall where she leaped over the dead Jaffa and stabbed the control panel. The door slid open. Another narrow hallway, this one dark. She reached an arm inside, pulled off the control panel, yanked out as many crystals as she could hold in one hand, and tossed them on the floor, where they shattered. Then, holding the door open with the toe of her boot, she pulled off her jacket and dropped that, too. She let the door close, the sleeve of her jacket showing at the seam where the two panels came together. Then she sprinted the few paces back down the hall and threw herself into the next room, past Teal'c who was holding the door open for her, and colliding spectacularly with Aadi. Somehow, he ended up in her lap on the floor, both of them facing the door, her hand clamped again over his mouth. Teal'c locked the door as footsteps stormed past them.

Sam held her breath and Aadi tightly until he started to struggle against her. She let him go. He scrambled into the corner and stared wide-eyed at the door as a Jaffa on the other side shouted orders. There was a staff blast, and another, and then the sound of footsteps receding down the next hallway.

Teal'c sank to his knees.

Sam crawled across the floor to him and gingerly pulled away the charred edges of his jacket. It had been a glancing blow, but it wasn't good. It was a long way from good. She slapped the side of his face, first gently, and then harder, until he opened his eyes. "We can't stay here," she whispered.

"I agree."

"Can you walk?" The question was a courtesy. He had to walk, or they were dead.

"I can."

While she was helping him to his feet, a noise behind her drew her attention and she craned her neck awkwardly to look. Up near the ceiling there was a ventilation grate, hanging open on its hinges. Aadi's feet were kicking and wriggling, and then they disappeared inside with the rest of him. Teal'c braced himself against the door, so Sam could hop up onto the packing crate Aadi had used and peer into the narrow space. She couldn't see a thing.

"Aadi!" she whispered and waited. Nothing. Damnit.

The shaft was a good size for an underfed thirteen-year-old boy, but there was no way a grown woman and muscular, wounded adult man were also going to fit in there.

She jumped down, sat on the crate and ran trembling hands through her hair. *Think.* Her brain obeyed, though as if playing in slow motion. Everything seemed stretched and ungainly. When she looked up at Teal'c, he seemed far away at the clear centre of a grey-edged circle.

"We could take the hallway," Teal'c suggested, angling his head toward the door Sam had disabled. "The Jaffa will not expect us to be behind them."

She nodded. "And there's got to be more stairs around here. Service entrance, maybe."

She gathered her strength and heaved herself to her feet, then went to lean on the door next to him. One ear pressed to the door, she listened carefully. Through the sound of Teal'c's labored breathing she could make out the steady pulsing of the alarm and a distant shout, but nothing else. There was no way to know if anyone stood guard outside the door. She drew back her head at the sudden sound of footsteps, coming from the small hallway and dwindling again in the direction of the mezzanine. Maybe their luck was improving.

After checking Teal'c to make sure he was ready, she keyed the control and stepped to the side as the door panel slid open. She checked the hall. It was empty, except for a single Jaffa past the doorway at the far end. Sam crept along the wall, pausing beside the fallen Jaffa to slide his knife out of his boot. She left the *zat* in her waistband, not wanting to alert the guard when she opened and charged the weapon. The knife was riskier but quieter. Fortunately for her, the other Jaffa wasn't wearing a helmet. She pulled herself to her full height and balanced on the balls of her feet – he was a little taller than she was – blew out a breath and lunged forward, circling his neck with one arm. She yanked his head back and sliced her knife across his throat. He slumped without a fight, and she lowered him to the ground, used his sleeve to wipe the blood off of her blade before tucking the knife into her waistband and nodding to Teal'c. He braced himself on the wall until he got to the doorway, and she looped his arm over her shoulders.

"Geez," she gasped, stepping around the dead Jaffa and into the dimness of the hallway beyond. "All that muscle is really heavy." He tried to pull away from her at that, but she held him firmly. "Joking, Teal'c. You're a—" She grunted as she got a toe under her discarded jacket and flipped it up to catch it with her free hand, grinning to feel the powerbar still in the pocket. "You're a feather-weight."

"I am not," he contradicted her softly. She handed him the jacket and they got moving again. She could feel the heat of his wound against her side, but he made no sound of pain or protest.

The hallway wasn't long – about thirty feet – and ended at an intersection. At one end of the new corridor was yet another inter-section, at the other a doorway, a regular, human-type door. A left turn would take them deeper into the complex, maybe toward the armory and their gear; a right turn would lead toward the outside wall of the building – always provided her geography wasn't too screwed up. Teal'c was already leaning right, so she let his momentum carry them in that direction.

"Door will be guarded," she said, as they eased along the hallway toward it. Teal'c was getting heavier, his legs starting to buckle a little every couple of steps. "Hang on, hang on, hang on," she chanted under her breath.

This door opened onto a stairwell and another door at the bottom, pale light showing through its grated window. Outside. She got Teal'c into the stairwell, where he leaned on the railing, and turned back to pull the door shut behind them.

She never saw the blow coming. It caught her on the side of her head and spun her away from her assailant, so that she hit the floor on her hands and knees at Teal'c's feet. She heard the crackling, springing sound of a *zat* firing and Teal'c's grunt of pain. The current discharged along the railing in blue arcs, and Teal'c tumbled after them, rolling heavily down the stairs and colliding with the wall at the bottom.

With a snarl, Sam lashed out, getting her foot between the Jaffa's legs. Twisting her body, she used her leg like a lever and threw him off balance. She only had time to register a blur of motion, then she was rolling, tangled in his limbs, and crashing down the stairs with him.

The fall knocked the wind out of her, even with the Jaffa as padding, and she lay on her back on top of him while the world whirled and canted and rocked back into its regular upright geometry. When she was able to breathe again, she craned her neck to look back up the stairs. There was no other pursuit, for now. Getting her elbows under her, she pushed herself up and rolled over onto her stomach. Nothing broken. Everything bruised.

The Jaffa was dead, his head twisted at an awkward angle.

"Teal'c," she whispered and spat a bit of blood onto the floor. She'd done a number on her tongue.

He'd hit the wall with his back, and, unlike the Jaffa guard, he wasn't lying akimbo. Everything seemed to be in its place. But he was out cold. Sam let her head fall onto his shoulder as she shuddered in a breath and let it out slowly.

"Teal'c," she said again, her mouth next to his ear. "Please, wake up. We're not safe here." She tried slapping him again, but with no luck. "Please, Teal'c. I can't lift you if you don't help." She managed to get to her knees and then unsteadily to her feet. She got a hand under his armpit and one on his arm and pulled. Getting him going was practically impossible. Her eyes were tearing up from exhaustion and hurt and fear and it made her furious. Heaving with all her might, she got him upright, stepped over his legs and braced him from the other side with her knee while she grabbed him under both arms and tried to drag him. He wouldn't budge. Too many days without food or water, and she was dizzy and too weak to pull him the stupid three feet to the door. "Damnit, Teal'c! *Wake up*! The door's right there! It's *right there*!"

She leaned away from his weight and pulled again, but her boots lost purchase on the concrete floor and she fell, cracking her elbow hard enough to send lightning up her arm. With a wince, she let out a hopeless little laugh. "You know, in other circumstances, this would be kind of funny." Except it wasn't.

She sat up. Teal'c's head was in her lap. She bowed as low over him as she could and patted the side of his face. "Okay, okay," she conceded. "We'll take a minute and regroup." She pulled the *zat* out of her waistband, wincing at the *zat*-shaped bruise against her spine, and put it on the floor beside her. "Next escape, you are so carrying *me*." Her ears were ringing and the floor was rising and falling under her like a rolling sea. She rested her head against the wall and thought of the Colonel and the look on his face when Daniel had lifted his head, blood on his lips…

Daniel was grinning at her when she opened her eyes. But it wasn't Daniel at all. She reached out for the *zat*. A hand grabbed her wrist to stop her and the face came closer, large, pale eyes peering at her through a curtain of dark, curly hair.

"My brother says you're worth something, Major Carter," the woman said with a faint twitching of the lips that might have been a skeptical smile. "I hope he's right."

If there was one thing Jack tended to lack on missions, it was healthy curiosity. He left that to Carter and Daniel, and spent his time worrying about other things. Like how to get out of a stroll into a yawning dark hole with a Goa'uld literally breathing down his neck. This whole adventure was taking on some ridiculously cliché overtones, the kind he was going to mock like crazy if he lived to tell anyone about it. Now was the moment he wanted to turn to Carter and ask her what she thought was down there and if there were any weird energy readings, but he knew that answer already. His body was telling him, via the slippery nausea and the creeping panic, that something down there was Very Bad. As he stood there alone with Aris and Sebek, he had a weird sensation of his limbs having been amputated: no Daniel, to bury his clear-cut objectives in moral quandaries and fascinating cultural details; no Teal'c, to exchange a knowing glance with; no Carter, to say, with respect, "I don't think so, sir" when he made a suggestion. No team, to order into position as they set about exploring.

Aris Boch stood at Jack's left elbow and stared into the darkness with him. "We'll need light," he said, and glanced at Jack. "Don't suppose you know how to turn those on?"

"Sorry," Jack said. "Can't read the instructions."

Behind him, Sebek huffed out a silent laugh, which raised the hair on Jack's neck again. "It is fortunate that you amuse us."

"Yeah," Jack said. "Fortunate." He shifted the focus of his attention to Aris, whose weapon was within grabbing distance. As if reading his intentions – and given the situation, it wasn't hard – Aris drew the weapon and secured it in his hand.

"Don't try it," he said softly. "I'd hate to have to kill you."

"And leave you without a tour guide?" Jack said. He and Aris exchanged a long, steady look. There wasn't any way out but in.

"Provide light," Sebek said.

"With what? Do you want me to glow?" Jack craned his neck to look over his shoulder at Sebek. "Seriously – no idea here."

"Then you may use your implements." Sebek's arm curved around Jack, holding out Jack's small flashlight. Jack took it from Sebek's hand and swayed to the left, away from that arm, bumping gently into Aris in the process. "And you also, hunter," Sebek said.

Jack clicked the light on, then off. "Okay," he said. Sebek shoved him from behind, not quite hard enough to knock Jack off balance, but enough for him to get the message.

Just past the threshold, the smell hit him: old, musty, like a stack of used books. Whatever was in there had been closed up too long. The dry air whispered past him like ghosts escaping as the pressure equalized. Jack squinted ahead and switched the flash on. The blackness seemed to swallow up the light, giving no comfort. Aris's version of the flashlight was a stick that stuttered to life, a soft blue, when he shook it, and it seemed to fare no better. Jack hesitated until Sebek jabbed him between the shoulder blades with one of his gold-capped fingers.

"Move forward!"

"Hey," Jack said, in pointless protest. He switched off the light, let the darkness press against him, close and cloying. "If you're in such a hurry, by all means, step right on by."

"Do not try our patience, human." The snake hung back in the doorway, framed by the dim orange of guttering torches in the antechamber.

Aris fiddled with his stick until the blue flared brighter. "That's better," he said, and charged past Jack as though he had no fear of what might await them inside. Jack's instincts were screaming a warning, but he felt no obligation to give it to Aris. If Aris went down, it meant one less obstacle to overcome on his way out.

"Come on," Aris said, a disembodied voice in the dark.

Jack sighed and followed the sound and the intermittent wink of blue. He could hear Sebek behind him, but didn't bother to look.

A few paces in, he smacked into Aris, who was broad and unmoving in his path. "What?" Jack said. Aris turned and pushed him aside.

"Step carefully," Aris said. "There's something strange about this place."

"You just now figured that out?" Jack said. A low ambient glow rose in their space, gathering intensity like a bulb on a dimmer switch until he could make out shapes, and then distinct images. On either side of them, walls of solid stone stretched to a low ceiling, rough-carved, perhaps two feet overhead – close enough for

Jack to feel a little cramped. Aris was already stooping, even though he had plenty of clearance. Each wall was covered with writing, floor to ceiling, the same little picto-do-dads that had been etched on the vault door. Jack resisted the urge to touch them. Probably not a good idea. The light extended about ten feet ahead of them, and at its edge the engravings were interrupted by plain, flat pillars that flanked the hall. If he squinted a little, Jack could see the writing start up again on the far side of the pillars and fade into blackness.

"Look at this," Aris said, striding to the edge of the illuminated section. After a slight hesitation, the hallway ahead of him grew brighter. Another few paces. The glow seemed to run ahead of him, beckoning. The corridor stretched another thirty feet straight ahead, then forked into two, a right and left turn at sharp angles.

"Guess it wouldn't be prudent to split up," Jack said. He moved a bit further down the corridor, counting steps. Maybe the people who'd built this place could tell one hallway from another, but there was no chance he'd be able to. Each wall was the same, as far as he could tell. Of course, the writing was probably different, and maybe Daniel could tell, but to Jack's untrained eye it was as meaningless as chicken scratch. Less, even. Sebek didn't seem like he was going to offer up any advice, though, so Jack could be wrong about Daniel. Or maybe Daniel was clamming up in there, somehow. Wishful thinking.

"Choose a direction," Sebek ordered.

Jack turned back to make a smart remark and was momentarily startled by the sight of Daniel's face, watching him intently. No matter how long they were at this, the sight of not-Daniel was going to be a nasty shock every time. But then his attention was captured by something else. "Hope you weren't planning on leaving anytime soon," he said, and pointed back the way they'd come. The ambient light lingered behind them, slowly fading now, but augmented by a weird, shifting glow. Where the door had been, there was now a seamless patch of wall, black, without writing. The dark surface was vaguely iridescent, oddly slippery to the gaze, like it was there, and it wasn't, like it was solid and somehow fluidly rippling, too.

Aris shouldered past Jack and Sebek and holstered both his

glowstick and weapon, so his hands would be free to touch. He ran his fingers around the outline of the door, then across its surface, and his frown cleared. He nodded, confirming an unspoken assumption. He thumped the barrier with the back of his knuckles, snatching his hand back quickly and shaking it vigorously. "Force field," he reported. "Not rock or metal." He looked down at his hand and rubbed his knuckles. "Tingly."

Jack started back toward him, but Sebek stepped into his path. "Our goal is that way," he said, aiming his chin over Jack's shoulder. "Move."

Jack turned and looked down the corridor toward the juncture. He sighed. "Onward, then."

"Looks like it." Aris made no move to come back to the front, and Jack pursed his lips. He should have known.

Something brushed past him.

He turned, arm outstretched, ready to strike with the flashlight, but there was nothing there. The low-grade nausea that had been dogging him since his first hour down in the mine rose, bile burning the back of his throat. He lost his balance and staggered sideways, crashing into one of those blank pillars. Not enough support to keep him on his feet, though, and he pitched over onto the ground. He beat back panic – so not like him; he and panic weren't that well acquainted – and tried to focus. Something was making him feel this way, something out of his control. He had to *get control.*

Dimly, he could hear Sebek moaning. Too bad he couldn't get over there to shake the damn snake loose – he could snap his neck so easily…Daniel's neck. Jack put his hands over his ears and struggled to catch his breath. He couldn't hurt Daniel. *Not now. Not yet.*

Aris knelt beside him and hauled him up to a sitting position. "Fight it," he growled. "Pull yourself together."

"We have to get out of here," Jack said through gritted teeth. "We can't stay down here."

"We don't have a choice," Aris hissed. Behind him, Sebek thrashed on the ground. Jack stared at him, until Aris shook his shoulders, hard. "You're going to help me, and then I might help you. *Might.* But you have to get up. Get moving. Fight this."

"Fight *what*?" Jack shook his head, but the dizziness came back with a vengeance. "What the hell is it?"

"Guess we'll find out soon enough," Aris said. He pointed down the corridor. "As soon as you choose. Right or left."

"Damn it," Jack said. He pushed Aris's hand off his arm and crouched by the wall, half sitting, half standing. Sebek had rolled over on his belly and was quiet. "Guess you'd better pick him up, too."

Aris gave him a sharp look. "Don't even think about killing him."

Jack opened his mouth to say that was his *friend* trapped in there, that he wasn't going to consider that option now...but he'd be a liar. He had pictured it all, in those moments of rage, down to the sound Daniel's neck would make when it snapped, the crunch of bone beneath the force he'd apply. He shuddered and closed his eyes. "Hurry up," he told Aris. "Let's get to it."

# CHAPTER NINE

The watery sunlight seeped through the latticework across the window and drew clumsy, blurred lines of shadow across Teal'c's face, his bared chest. Sam's hands moved in and out of the light as she swiped the rag gently across the burn above his hip and sat back a little to squeeze the blood into the bowl at her knees. With a grimace, she leaned in close and peered at the wound. It was ugly, a charred arc glistening black. It would be red if the sun weren't so wan. But the staff blast had hit obliquely and the wound wasn't deep, thank goodness. It was painful, but hopefully not life-threatening. Sam suspected that she'd do better to worry about the quality of the water and the rags she was using to bind him up. The cloth was blackened with soot, and an oily film floated on the surface of the bowl, making slow-moving rainbows that scattered when she finally dropped the rag into the bloody water for the last time.

Teal'c's chest rose and fell slowly but regularly, and his eyes darted behind closed lids. As she sat on her heels, watching him, her teeth in her lip, Sam tried to make her brain think forward. Without the tretonin there was no way for him to fight off infection. She closed her eyes briefly and rubbed the nails of her curled fingers against her lips. "Damn," she breathed.

From where he sat huddled on the other side of Teal'c, Aadi narrowed his eyes at her and repeated the curse softly as if trying it out. Sam was too tired to bother explaining.

"Perhaps some food," a soft voice said from beside her, and small, rough hands lifted the bowl, passed it to someone out of sight.

Sam looked at the woman who settled down next to her. She wasn't exactly pretty, Sam decided, or not anymore. She looked hungry, and probably older than her years. The hair pulled back from her face and escaping from a knot at her neck was black shot with grey. The same black soot that drifted down over the whole city had worked into the lines around her eyes and mouth, as though she were a pencil drawing, sketched in haste. Her face was angular, with prominent cheekbones over hollow cheeks, and her upper lip puckered at the corner with a scar that curved up along her nose and out to the corner of her eye. A close call, that one.

The woman raised a hand and laid two fingers on the scar. "My brother," she said, and her eyes were pale like the water in the bowl, dully reflecting the thin light but alert.

Sam's eyes narrowed. "Your brother did that?"

She nodded. "Sebek's Jaffa, they are often hungry." Her hand fell and a grim sort of smile tugged at her lips, made the puckering of the scar more noticeable. "They like pretty things."

Sam looked away. "Right."

She'd heard this story before, on planets scattered so far from each other they weren't even pinpricks of light in the sky. Goa'uld appetite was another galactic constant. She found herself picturing Daniel, wondering if that kind of hunger—

Her gut twisted sharply and she had to physically scour the thought from her brain with a scrubbing fist at her temple. When she opened her eyes, the woman was watching her closely, knowingly, and Sam felt an unreasonable flare of anger at the thought of this stranger thinking about Daniel like that. But the knowing look softened a fraction to something a little like sympathy, making the scar twitch on the woman's cheek, and Sam's anger faded. She was too tired for that kind of anger. There were more practical things to be angry about.

*Focus.*

The room was crowded now. While she had been tending to Teal'c, several others had arrived like gloom coalescing in the corners. Now they were hovering silently against the walls. Like the woman, they were thin angles of hunger, sketchy suggestions of people. The one nearest Sam had his feet wrapped in rags and tied round with twine, but the rest were barefoot, and even in her boots, Sam's own toes were a little numbed by cold. The men shuffled constantly in the shadows, taking turns near the tin-can stove and the warm brick hearth. While she worked, she'd kept track from the corner of her eye and now she placed the room's occupants on the mental map in her head: nine in the narrow, low-ceilinged room, plus the woman, who was still watching her attentively. There were three men between Sam and the doorway. She had one hand on the *zat* beside her, for all the good that would do against these people, except that, really, they didn't look like they'd put up much resistance, even if she'd gone for them hand-to-hand. But Teal'c was heavy, and there was no way she'd be able to heave him out of here unless he were conscious and helping. She scanned the men in the room and wondered which one was the brother with the knife.

"What's your name?" she asked the woman.

"Brenneka." With a nod toward Aadi, who was still crouched at Teal'c's head, hands tucked up inside his shirt and eyes rodent bright, she smiled again. "That one calls me Bren, though I tell him I will wear his skin for shoes."

Aadi's grin was wide and he bounced a little as he nodded his head. "Have to catch me first," he answered in a sort of toneless sing-song that said this was a game they'd played many times before.

"Not so easy these days," Brenneka admitted with faintly amused disappointment. "He's mostly legs and big feet, like his father, my brother."

Sam's eyebrows shot up. "Aris Boch is your brother?" Involuntarily, her hand came up and she pointed a finger at Brenneka's scarred face.

"Yes, but not that one. Sebek killed that brother three days ago, at the vault." Her face was hard, smeared with grit and shadow.

"Oh." A small part of Sam relaxed, and she felt a little less nervous about the men at her back. "I'm sorry."

With a shrug that said that sympathy was useless, Brenneka looked at Teal'c, tilting her head pensively for a moment and then reaching out to trace the edge of his tattoo with a tentative finger. Sam's hand tightened around the *zat* while she wished again for her Beretta.

"Are you sure about him?" Brenneka asked.

"Of course."

She turned back to Sam, a frown notched between her brows.

"The Jaffa are followers, like insects, each one with its job, its place. Drones."

"That's not true of Teal'c."

Brenneka didn't look convinced.

Sam leaned in to lay a hand on Teal'c's forehead, displacing Brenneka's. His skin was hot. "Teal'c has raised armies to fight the Goa'uld and free the Jaffa from enslavement." She decided she'd give a lot for aspirin right then. The last thing he needed was a fever. "You know, maybe you have more in common with them than you think."

A hiss of dissent ran through the room, half-suppressed curses escaping between teeth. Only Brenneka voiced hers aloud and punctuated it by spitting onto the bricks around the little stove. "In common." The scar twitched as she curled her lip derisively. "We're the broken bones. The Jaffa break us."

"And the Goa'uld break them," Sam said.

"Good." Brenneka struggled to her feet, then shoved her way through the small crowd and out into the thin, grey light. The men murmured their agreement and one by one drifted away like dispersing fog. In the corner, the coals in the tin-can stove glowed dully and cast no shadows.

Sam zipped her jacket up to her neck and crawled closer to Teal'c, settling herself against the wall beside his shoulder, the *zat* on her lap. She could always use it as a club, she figured. And it would work on Jaffa, still. On the other side of Tealc, Aadi squatted with his legs and arms pulled inside his long shirt and watched her with pale, dimly curious eyes.

"What did she mean, when she said your dad thought we'd be worth something?" she demanded.

He pulled a hand out from inside his sleeve and chewed his thumb for a moment. "Maybe trade you," he answered finally. "Maybe use you."

"Use us for what?"

He shrugged that shrug again, and Sam had to count in multiples of seven until the urge to *zat* him went away. *Insolence*, she thought wryly, as she leaned forward and pulled Teal'c's jacket closed and zipped it up. He murmured something and her hands hovered unmoving over him while she waited for more, but he settled again into stillness. The wash of sunlight across his face faded slowly and brightened again as clouds shuffled and parted for a moment. Then the light went out for good, and a sudden rain drummed heavily on the tin roof of the shelter. She could hear feet splashing in the mud outside, a few distant shouts, and one closer before a tarp was pulled down across the latticework. It blocked out the rain and left them in a shifting, watery darkness warmed by the glow of the coals and the dim square of daylight that shone through the plastic sheeting that served as a door.

Aadi shuffled around like a dog turning in his bed and hunched deeper into himself, dropping his head onto his folded arms on his knees. Sam let her head fall back against the crumbling brick of the wall and tried to get her bearings. It wasn't easy; the rain seemed to hollow out her head and leave nothing but throbbing behind. Raising a hand to her temple, she winced at the tenderness there and followed it along her cheekbone and around her eye. Probably a hell of a shiner, she figured, and maybe, since they were so lucky, a bit of a concussion. She didn't even bother trying to inventory the bruises she'd earned falling down a flight of stairs tangled with an armored Jaffa.

"Focus, focus," she told herself and forced her eyes open to stare at the ruddy mouth of the stove. They weren't all that far from the bunker they'd escaped, right on the edge of the *ha'tak*'s late-morning shadow. Her eyes strayed to the faint outline of the lattice window. She wondered which way the sun was moving, and pictured that shadow sliding like the blade of a sundial across the valley floor, marking time.

Beside her, Teal'c's hands twitched fitfully and he mumbled something she couldn't quite hear. Patting his shoulder, she said, "shh shh," and continued pacing out the city in her head. This little hovel was, in fact, pretty swank compared to most in the neighborhood, what with two actual brick walls and a door covering and all. It sat at the centre of the shanty town sprawled on the edge of the black river. The *ha'tak* stood between them and the entrance to the mine. She'd glimpsed the glowing geometry of its gold apex between the leaning remains of towers and the slumped and tumbled ruins of what had once been pretty impressive buildings.

But she'd had to keep her eyes on her feet for the most part to keep from tripping on the heaved and uneven surface of the alleys and dropping Teal'c – again. The third time, two of Brenneka's men had finally done more than get her and Teal'c on their feet, the larger of them taking some of Teal'c's weight and helping her guide him down the narrow passageways deeper and deeper into the ramshackle settlement. That last time, they'd fallen onto a broken face, a blue mosaic eye as wide as she was tall staring up past them at the grey sky. Pulling herself to her knees and then to her feet to sling Teal'c's arm over her shoulder again, she'd noticed that none of the six people with them had stepped on that eye, each of them skirting it carefully. Behind her Aadi and Brenneka had whispered in unison as they passed, but she hadn't been able to make out the words.

It had taken forever to cover what couldn't have been more than a kilometer, and Teal'c had gotten heavier and heavier until, by the time Brenneka had pulled back the sheeting and ushered them into the shelter, Sam and her helper had had to drag him, his boot-heels bumping over a mosaic sea, curling waves made of tiny squares of glass embedded in the floor. Now, she absently picked at the grout between the squares and wondered what the Colonel was up to, how long Teal'c would be out, whether or not they should eat the remaining power bar or save it for trade, and finally, whether she and Teal'c were grateful guests or prisoners. Mostly, she tried not to fall asleep, because two stoves floated in the gloom in front of her eyes sometimes and sometimes just one, and her head was pounding so hard that the sound of the rain seemed to rise and fall, now nearer, now farther away, like she was swaying…swaying.

"Eat," Brenneka said.

Sam's head snapped forward as she woke, making the floor rock and twist as if it really were an ocean. She flattened her hands on the mosaic either side of her, and sucked in a few deep breaths while she waited for the world to settle again. Brenneka was holding out a bowl and thrust it forward against Sam's knees.

"Eat something. You look terrible."

Sam couldn't stifle a laugh, and when she tried to duck her head, pain shot up her neck and made her wince. Rain was still rattling on the roof, so she couldn't tell if the sound Brenneka made was an answering laugh or not.

She accepted the bowl, tipped it to look at the thin, whitish slush at the bottom. "What is it?" she asked, trying not to grimace. It didn't smell like anything at all.

"Nutrient paste." Brenneka sat down and leaned back on her hands. "It doesn't fill you up, but it makes the machine burn well enough." She pointed at the window, then leaned back again. "They shovel it out for us every two or three days in the square. And on special days, if we are quick, like Aadi there, and if we can get into small spaces, there's squig."

Sam stopped with her cupped hand halfway to her mouth. "Squig?"

Aadi stirred and held his curved fingers up to his mouth to imitate fangs. "Little hairy things with thin tails and tiny eyes. Live down in the dark places."

"Rats," Sam said. Another galactic constant.

"The eyes are the best," Aadi added with a wistful lilt to his voice. "I always get the eyes if I catch them."

Sam licked the paste off of her fingers and tried not to think about rat-eye delicacies. The paste didn't taste like anything either, which she decided to take as a blessing – although the bowl was empty too soon. She eyed the second one next to Brenneka's hand.

"For the Jaffa," Brenneka said. "If he wakes up."

"When," Sam corrected.

Brenneka's shrug was identical to Aadi's, part indifference, real or feigned, part caginess. "The worm should have healed him by now."

Putting down the empty bowl, Sam laid a hand on Teal'c's forehead. His skin was hot, but the tattoo was cool under her fingers. She wondered if he could always feel the shape, the weight of gold stamped into him.

"What is it?" Brenneka asked, and Sam looked up to see her

pointing at the tattoo. "I've not seen this one."

"It's the mark of Apophis."

"But what is it?"

Sam tilted her head and peered at the gleaming image, more silvery than gold in the rainy light, ran her fingers gently over it, realizing that she'd never asked Teal'c to explain it. It hadn't seemed right to talk about it. Daniel would know, though, and she wondered why she'd never asked him. She would, first thing when he was back. With a tentative finger, she traced the arcs and curves, and she sighed. "It's a serpent at the center of the world," she speculated, her fingers moving along the lower half of the oval, "Earth," the inner cupped line, "sea," and the top half of the oval, "sky." Part of her wished that Teal'c would wake up and be affronted at this intrusion.

"Arrogance," Brenneka observed.

Sam caught herself shrugging. "I guess after a few thousand years they start believing their own advertising."

Brenneka's expression of hatred was eloquent. "A worm that declares itself a god is still a worm." She picked up Sam's bowl and inspected it for scraps, running a finger around the inside, then licking the residue off of it. "We remember the gods. Sebek isn't one of them."

Sam thought of the giant mosaic eye staring blankly at the sky. Was that the god or was it the people looking for one? She stretched out one leg and then the other, wincing at the stiffness in her knees. It sure didn't seem like there was anybody looking back at this place. Walking through the Stargate for seven years had taught Sam what godforsaken looked like. The rain seemed to drum directly on her skull and, as she slumped back against the wall sodden with weariness, it seemed like the whole galaxy was filled with broken people, broken, angry and indifferent gods. Good riddance to most of the latter. But still, the eye stared up at the sky, waiting for something. The edges of the tiles on the floor bit into her palms as she tried to find a comfortable position against the uneven bricks. Teal'c mumbled again, his hands clenching and releasing.

Brenneka was right: the symbiote would have been well on the way to healing him by now. Giving up on the idea of getting comfortable, Sam said, "We – I have to get back into the bunker."

Brenneka laughed, a short, disbelieving bark.

"I'm serious. If I don't get to our gear, Teal'c will die." Remembering Teal'c's warning look when she'd been about to mention his need for tretonin to Aadi, she hesitated. No show of weakness. She glanced down at Teal'c's paling face. Too late for that. "Not just from the wound, either. He needs a special medicine."

Brenneka looked skeptical. "The worm—"

"There is no worm. He lost it."

"He's Jaffa."

Sam could see her struggling to put what seemed like mutually exclusive facts together. Sam shook her head impatiently. "Yes, but he's different. The Goa'uld destroyed the Jaffa's immune systems when they engineered them as hosts, but we've been able to synthesize a drug that releases the Jaffa from their dependency on the symbiote. Without that drug, they die."

Brenneka considered this for a moment. "Seems to me that you've given them a new kind of slavery. Maybe he's better without it."

"He'll die."

"You say he fights for freedom. Well, freedom has its price."

Sam yanked on the thong around Brenneka's neck and pulled the small vial at the end of it out into the dim light. The *roshna* inside was a pale blue glow. "For you, too?"

Brenneka snatched the vial back, stood, and walked out of the hut. If there had been a door, she'd have slammed it.

Although they weren't prisoners in any meaningful sense of the word, no visiting Tok'ra was ever allowed to leave the base without escort, and they were always under the watchful eye of security forces while at the mountain – even Jacob, whose security clearance had been the highest possible before he left the Air Force. But now the military considered him alien, apart from them, inseparable from his symbiote. It was hard for Jacob to remember a time when this hadn't been status quo for him, this combination of trust and mistrust, friendship and suspicion, with which even old friends now greeted him. Even George had his moments of doubt, and Jacob couldn't blame him. If someone had told him ten years ago he'd finish his days living on other planets with a snake sharing his body, he would have had them locked up in a padded cell. Tough to wrap his head around, even now.

*Snake?* Selmak's thoughts slid into his consciousness, like slender golden threads. *You have learned this term from O'Neill. It is a most derogatory way of thinking of your brethren.*

*I know.* Jacob didn't have to apologize. Selmak was already aware of his feelings on the matter. Not like he was able to hide them.

*Malek means well, but he pursues an agenda separate from that which benefits our Tauri friends.* Selmak was watching Malek, seeing him through Jacob's eyes. He prowled around his quarters like a trapped cat. Jacob was familiar with that restless anxious feeling. It never went away when he was underground. He'd grown accustomed to living in the tunnels, but he'd never managed to overcome that feeling of being locked away inside the earth, buried. Trapped. Like a vampire, hiding in the dark.

*Vampires?* Selmak was deeply amused. *Your analogy leaves much to be desired.*

*Not literally. Well...maybe a little bit. But it's only an expression.* Sharing nearly every thought and feeling with Selmak had become easier over the years, but once in a while, Jacob felt a pang of regret for his lost privacy. Selmak always understood and withdrew at those times, but he was always at the back of Jacob's consciousness, a sentient hum underlying all of his other senses.

It was odd, standing inside the mountain that was so familiar to him while carrying on a conversation no one else could hear. The thought made Jacob smile, and it amused Selmak as well. *Crazy old human*, Selmak said fondly.

*Not as old as you.*

Malek glanced up at the open door and frowned as the SF passed by on his routine rounds of the level. "I do not believe we should remain here at the beck and call of the Tauri."

Jacob quested gently to see if Selmak wanted to handle the conversation, but he was content to let Jacob continue. Unlike Malek, who usually dominated his host by mutual agreement, Selmak had no such presumption that his voice and presence were superior. Jacob wasn't troubled when he encountered a dominant symbiote, but he was often grateful Selmak wasn't one of them. "Only a few operatives have reported back, and none of them had any information."

"But you believe they will." Malek tilted his head and gave Jacob a calculating stare.

"I believe it's possible, yes. I went through the list of old enemies George's people drew up. There are a few leads there, but not much we can follow up quickly. It's going to take time."

"I do not intend to remain here until they are found," Malek said. "I can be more useful elsewhere, engaged in the search."

Jacob knew that for what it was – he'd been just as desperate to get out of various tunnels. Malek also wasn't the type to sit on his hands. "George hasn't asked me directly, but if we do get intelligence, I think he's hoping we can do something about it."

"And this after he said explicitly he did not expect such a thing."

"To expect and to hope are two different things." *Not in the case of most Tauri*, Selmak chimed in. Jacob ignored him. "At any rate, Selmak and I are agreed: if it's possible, we'll offer our help."

"Your agreement is irrelevant, Jacob. Your desire to assist is commendable, but I doubt the Tok'ra Council will sanction it."

"Your point being?"

Malek's eyes narrowed. "My point is simply that the position of the Council has not changed, regarding what must be done."

Jacob glanced up at the SF again, then pushed the door of their quarters shut. Malek barely had time to react before Jacob shoved him back toward the wall, one hand on his chest like a ten ton weight. A flicker of fear crossed Malek's expression, swiftly replaced by disdain.

"That's my daughter we're talking about," Jacob said softly, and shoved Malek again. "Do you understand that? I'm not going to let anyone kill her if it's within my power to prevent it." One more small push, and he closed his fist around a handful of Malek's tunic. "Certainly not you."

*Restraint, my friend*, Selmak said, and this time he was harder to ignore. Reluctantly, Jacob released Malek. Selmak eased away, satisfied that Jacob was able to control his temper.

Malek didn't attempt to move away, but he squared his shoulders. "You were a soldier before you came to us, were you not? You have been a soldier with us, as well. You know what it means to protect our secrets."

"Not before other methods have been tried."

"Even if it means the death of your comrades?"

Selmak pressed up, demanded the right to answer. Jacob allowed it, let himself retreat into a corner of his own mind as Selmak took his voice and said, "Even then, Malek."

"Selmak, I mean no offense," Malek began, but Selmak turned his back. Jacob was acutely aware of Malek behind him, the heat of his host body, his proximity to the wall. "I only speak the truth."

"You do offend me. You mean well, but you allow yourself to be blindly led by the Council."

"At least I can still be led."

Selmak returned control to Jacob, and there was a slide of possession; where before Jacob had been the passenger, he was now the driver again, turning, looking out of his own eyes and into Malek's.

There was a rapping on the door, a pause, and then it opened.

"Sir." The SF was standing in the doorway. Both Malek and Jacob turned to him, but the 'sir' was a leftover courtesy to Jacob's former rank. "General Hammond wants to see you now, sir."

*We would be better off if Malek were to be assigned duties which took him away from Earth*, Selmak said. Jacob watched the stiff set of Malek's neck, the unbending line of his shoulders as he walked toward George's summons, and silently agreed.

They found George standing in front of the briefing room window looking down at the inactive 'gate, his hands clasped behind his back. "There's been word from your operative on P44-211," he said, without shifting his gaze. "The Tok'ra have been given intelligence that indicates SG-1 may have been captured."

"Well, we were pretty sure of that before," Jacob said. "The question still is, who's got them?"

"Nothing specific," George said. He turned then and looked Jacob squarely in the eye. "But they mentioned a bounty hunter. Someone who set out to capture SG-1 with a specific purpose in mind. And as it happens, SG-1 has previously encountered someone who fits that description to a T."

"Aris Boch," Malek said. Jacob glanced at Malek, who stiffened even more under his scrutiny. The SGC shared their mission intelligence with the Tok'ra on a sporadic basis as required by their formal treaty, but Jacob was truly surprised Malek had bothered to read it. Very few Tok'ra thought the information worth sifting through. "He was responsible for the rescue of one of our Tok'ra operatives several years ago."

"Rescue?" George said, giving Malek a hard look. "Not quite the way I'd put it. *SG-1* rescued him. Aris Boch planned to hand him over to the Goa'uld at his earliest opportunity."

"Until Teal'c offered himself up in Korra's place," Jacob added. His mind raced. Aris Boch was as unpredictable as he was efficient, and if he had SG-1, it was unlikely he'd be stupid enough to leave a trail to follow.

*Give our people time*, Selmak cautioned. *Do not allow Malek to use this to his advantage.*

As if he had read those thoughts, Malek said, "Then we can do no more. You have the information you require."

"Not exactly," Jacob said. "We still need to know why. A little more poking around will probably give us the answer."

"We have no idea where this bounty hunter has gone," Malek said, turning on him with a flash of anger in his eyes. "Why do you continue to insist we waste our time in this manner?"

Jacob studied him. "Why do you continue to insist we don't?" Malek's eyes narrowed, but he didn't bother to answer. *Score*, Jacob thought, and was rewarded with a rumble of amusement from Selmak. "Listen, we've got nothing to lose by looking a little deeper, right? Maybe, best case, our people can figure out where he's gone, or if he's sold them, and where they've been taken. If that's the case, we can help you mount a rescue."

George wasn't looking at Jacob, although Jacob was certain he'd heard every word. His attention was fixed on Malek, and on the distinctly uncooperative words that were still hanging over them in that room. "I'd appreciate that, Jacob," he said, still staring at Malek. "I'd appreciate that a great deal." Finally, he turned his head to meet Jacob's eyes, with steel-grey resolve. "And I'll take you up on it."

# CHAPTER TEN

"**D**amn, damn, damn," Sam chanted to herself as she paced the small room with her hands tangled in her hair, torn between staying and going. Aadi watched her from his corner, still wrapped up in his shirt. She dropped her hands and thumped her thighs with her fists. Her available options were both lousy: stay, do nothing, and watch Teal'c die; or go find his tretonin and leave him here to be turned over to the first passing Jaffa with an extra ration of glue-food to offer. She made another turn around the room as Aris Boch's voice rumbled in her head: *choiceless.*

"Damnit," she spat and bent to grab the *zat.* As she tucked it into her waistband, an idea struck her – not something she was totally comfortable with, but better than nothing, and it always seemed to work for Daniel. She took the last power bar out of her pocket and waved it at Aadi, forcing her face into a friendly expression. His eyes followed the bar like it was a pocket watch and he was being hypnotized. It was chocolate and nuts, and who wouldn't risk his skin for chocolate and nuts? "If you take care of Teal'c for me, and come for me if anyone tries to get to him, this is yours."

The power bar seemed like slim ground for bargaining, and Aadi could offer little protection for Teal'c, but time was a-wasting, as the Colonel would say. Besides, there was something about the kid that made her think he might be bright enough to see the advantage in helping them, not that she could have explained why she felt that way. He'd barely spoken since they made their escape. It was a gut instinct, and she trusted that feeling. She unwrapped the end of the bar so the sweet smell of chocolate could help her seal the deal. Aadi stared at it, and then at her, until his suspicious squint eased and he nodded. He held out his hand, but Sam put the bar back in her pocket.

"Teal'c's okay when I get back, you get the bar. Deal?"

He hesitated, so she squeezed the pocket a little to make the wrapper crinkle. Finally, he nodded again.

"I'll be fast," she said as she headed for the door, but the reassurance was more for her own benefit than for his.

She was ducking around the sheet of plastic when she found her way blocked by the solid bulk of Esa, the man from the laundry. He put a hand on top of her head and pushed her, not too roughly, back into the hovel. Sam retreated to give herself some room, then curled her fingers around the *zat* but didn't draw it. It was really only a security blanket for her where these people were concerned, but at least it showed that she was willing to fight them if she had to. And it had to hurt, getting clobbered on the head with a *zat*. Esa's pale eyes drifted down toward it and then back up to her face. They weren't cruel eyes, but they were heavy with the kind of exhaustion that didn't go away with sleep. The soot-filled lines on his face made him look sixty, but Sam figured he was probably twenty years younger than that. His head was shaved and showed scabs. He smelled like harsh industrial soap, like the inside of a hospital.

"I don't want trouble," Sam said levelly, letting go of the weapon and holding her empty hands out so he could see them. "I have to help my friend."

Without answering, Esa took a step closer, and Sam automatically fell into a fighting stance, hands closing into fists, before she realized he was only making way for Brenneka to enter.

"Here," she said, coming around Esa and dropping a bundle on the floor at Sam's feet. "My brother gave this to me before he went into the mine."

Sam stole a glance downward. The rough cloth knot had come undone when the bundle hit the tiles and some of the contents had spilled out, foil packets catching the light. With a quick look at Esa's face to make sure he was still watching passively and not making any aggressive moves, she knelt and pulled the cloth away. Inside was a jumble of supplies from their packs: iodine pills for water purification, first aid packets and sterile bandages, Daniel's antihistamines, Tylenol, and Teal'c's tretonin autoinjector.

Sam threw everything but the tretonin back into the cloth and gathered up the ends. "Thank you," she said to Brenneka, putting as much sincerity into it as she could.

Brenneka simply waved her gratitude away and went to stoke the stove. Esa squatted beside her, his shoulder brushing hers, and held his hands out to the glow.

Sam edged around them and back to Teal'c, who hadn't moved at all. She shoved up his jacket sleeve and pressed the autoinjector into his arm. The knot under her ribs relaxed a bit at the sound of the drug hissing into his blood.

Then she looked over at Esa. "Could we have some water?"

With a brusque nod, he heaved himself to his feet using Brenneka for a brace. Her eyes still turned toward the fire, she reached up and squeezed his hand as he leaned on her shoulder, and a brief smile warmed her face as Esa shuffled out the door. Sam went back to pulling open Teal'c's jacket and treating the wound. Her cold, stiff fingers gave her trouble with the wrappings of the bandages and she had to use her teeth. By the time Esa was back with the bowl, Teal'c's wound was hidden behind white gauze and tape. Somehow, that seemed to make all the difference, as if he were healed already. A part of her wondered why he didn't sit up and get on with it. She took the bowl with a murmur of thanks, crushed two aspirin into it and stirred it with her fingers.

To her surprise, Aadi helped her prop Teal'c's head up so she could tip the bowl at his lips. She was pleased to see Teal'c swallow and open his mouth for more.

"Easy," she whispered. "Don't choke." His lids fluttered but didn't open. His hands relaxed at his sides as Aadi eased him down again.

Sam scooted back against the wall, elbows on her knees, and rested her forehead on the heels of her hands. She closed her eyes, drained. The relief seemed to take more out of her than the tension and worry had. Aadi had to call her name a few times before she recognized it and looked blearily over at him.

"Can I still have the food?" he asked, almost shyly.

Wordlessly, Sam pulled the bar out of her pocket and tossed it over Teal'c into Aadi's lap. He tore the wrapper off, bent his head low and measured the bar by laying his fingers across it. Then, with careful attention, he broke it into three equal pieces and scrambled up to give one each to Brenneka and Esa before crawling over Teal'c's legs and back into his corner to eat his share. A small smile played across Brenneka's face as she watched him. When both he and Esa were done, she broke her own piece in two and handed Sam half. Sam ducked her head in thanks. She put the morsel on the edge of Teal'c's bowl, where it slid down into the unappealing paste.

The rain fell and the light turned bluer as the minutes passed, so that the three pairs of eyes watching Sam seemed white-pale and cold.

Eventually, Brenneka pushed herself to her feet and tapped Sam on the top of her head to get her attention. "Come with me," she said, and turned toward the door. Sam looked from Brenneka to Teal'c, but didn't move to get up. "He'll be fine here with Esa," Brenneka reassured her impatiently.

"If the Jaffa know you're Aris's sister, they're going to come here looking for us."

Brenneka's smile showed a broken tooth at the spot where the scar puckered her lip. "They've already been to my house, on the other side of the city."

"Then where are we?"

"The pest house," she answered with that abrupt bark of a laugh. "No one will come here until they've checked every other possible place." She turned again and slipped out the door.

Sam followed. "The pest house? As in disease?" she demanded as she stepped out under the awning and hunched away from the wind.

"As in the dead," Brenneka strode out into the rain and headed off down the narrow alley.

"That can't be good for Teal'c," Sam said. "Or for you."

Brenneka shrugged and disappeared around the corner. After a moment she leaned back around it and glared in Sam's direction. "Are you coming or not?"

Casting a last look back through the plastic at Esa, who was still warming his hands at the stove, Sam pulled the collar of her jacket closed at the neck, then dashed out into the downpour after

Brenneka. She tried to keep her bearings, counting lefts and rights, but she had to move fast to keep Brenneka in sight as she wove her way down the tight alleyways of the shantytown. There were few people in the open. Most of them drew back into doorways and shadows and watched Sam with hollow eyes as she passed. Sam wished she had some local clothing to wear. Any one of these people could tip off a Jaffa patrol that there was a stranger in the quarter, although they seemed too indifferent to be dangerous. No way to know for sure.

Mulling this over and trying to ignore the slither of cold, silty water down her neck, she rounded a corner and ran headlong into Brenneka, who pushed her back into the shelter of a doorway as three Jaffa tromped by. Rain spattered on the crocodile-styled helmet of the leader. Brenneka leaned hard on her, shielding Sam with her back to the passing guards, elbows braced against a corrugated tin wall on either side of Sam's head. Peering over Brenneka's shoulder, Sam could make out the last Jaffa turning his head toward them, but, seemingly as incurious as the people, he looked away. They continued down the passage and out of Sam's angle of vision.

Brenneka's thin body relaxed, and she exhaled a sour curse into Sam's neck before pushing away. They set out again into the rain, following in the Jaffa's steps and then ducking down a side alley. While Brenneka could walk comfortably upright under the makeshift roof that ran the length of the passageway, Sam had to bow her head and turn her shoulders sideways to avoid catching herself on the rafters or the walls.

"There were a lot of people in that house who saw us," Sam said, lagging behind. "How do I know that they won't sell us out to the Jaffa?"

"Because they are members of the Order. They won't betray you. Unless…"

Sam stopped. "Unless what?"

"Unless I tell them to," Brenneka answered, without looking back.

Sam was about to protest more, but they suddenly stepped out into a tiny courtyard. Her hair snaking across her forehead and stuck to her cheek, Brenneka tilted her head back and pointed up at a small square of sky. Sam blinked up into the rain and followed the line of her finger to the tip of a silvery spire that leaned at a precarious angle against the clouds. It was impossible to judge distances in the Byzantine space of the town, but Sam guessed that the tower wasn't far away and was quite tall, at least a couple of hundred feet. She could remember seeing it from the ridge above the city when they'd left Aris's ship, one of the few spires still standing in the ruins. She had her bearings now, could place them within the tumbled geography of the city.

"It's part of one of the great ships that brought us here," Brenneka explained. "It never gets old. It will outlast the Goa'uld, I think."

It certainly didn't look like Goa'uld technology. Before Brenneka could continue on through the gate at the far side of the courtyard, Sam put a hand on her arm. "Wait. You mean the Goa'uld didn't bring you here?"

This time, the smile wasn't bitter, but brightened by pride. "We brought ourselves. With help from the gods."

"The gods?"

"The Nitori."

"I don't think I've heard of them."

Brenneka pulled her arm free and ushered Sam ahead of her through the gate. "When the Goa'uld took the Homeworld, we fled. The legend says that the Nitori left us knowledge and chose one of our people – the Inspired – to entrust with the knowledge. He learned how to make the ships." Glancing back, Sam saw her make a brief gesture with her hands, like she was setting a bird free. She remembered seeing Aadi do the same when they'd crossed the mosaic face. "The ships brought us here. This was a beautiful place, once. And a long time later, the Goa'uld found us again." Her mouth was a grim line broken by the end of the scar. "The Inspired was gone, and there were no more ships." Pushing past Sam, she pointed ahead. "It's here."

Brenneka reached into the pocket of her trousers and pulled out a key on a fob. She slipped it into a tiny gap in the wall. It turned with a click, and a door Sam hadn't even been able to see opened a crack. Brenneka pushed it open and stooped to enter, Sam close behind. They found themselves at the top of a spiral staircase, all but the first few steps lost in darkness. Reaching into a small niche near Sam's head, Brenneka pulled out a baton of about the length of her forearm. She rapped it sharply on the brick, then shook it until it began to emit a cool, blue light.

"This way."

Sam had to walk fast to keep within the small illuminated circle. Made of worn stone, the stairs were uneven triangles set into the wall and winding tightly downward around a central point like the steps inside a lighthouse. Brenneka's bare feet were sure, but Sam's boots felt clumsy and too large and she had to hang onto the rough brick to keep her balance. There was no way of gauging how far they went, except by counting steps. Sam had counted two hundred and four when the stairs ended on a landing in front of another narrow door. Again the key came out, and the door opened silently on oiled hinges.

She couldn't see to tell for sure, but the room they entered seemed cavernous and the cool, slick, green-smelling breath of air that washed over them as they moved deeper into the clammy chamber suggested an underground river nearby. Sam listened carefully but couldn't hear any running water, only her own breathing and the echoing of her boots on the stone floor. Her skin was crawling with uneasiness. She hovered near the door, one hand groping for the wall and guiding her backward until her shoulders were leaning against brick. Brenneka looked over her shoulder, a ghost in her halo of blue light, then continued on to the left. After a few steps, she reached into another tiny alcove in the wall and a soft, yellow glow bloomed from sconces high up near the vaulted ceiling. With a shake, Brenneka extinguished her torch.

Sam looked up at the gilded ceiling, a good three or four stories above their heads, and thought of medieval churches. The walls were a mixture of brick and the black native stone. The floor was another detailed mosaic, faces and waves, stylized stars and solar systems, massive fish and featherless birds in a kaleidoscope of color. At the far end of the room a dais stood in front of a wall that seemed to be made of the same silvery metal as the spire outside, pitted and scored, blackened around the edges. The skin of a ship, Sam figured.

Brenneka regarded her through narrowed eyes. "Why are you here?"

A bit taken aback by the question, Sam blinked a few times while she looked for an answer other than the obvious. "Because your brother kidnapped us."

Brenneka's face fell into sharp lines of impatience. "You travel through the Stargates. Why are you out here?"

"Well, because we're explorers."

"Exploring."

"Yes."

"No."

"No?" Stepping closer, Sam looked at the remains of the ship. It seemed like that whole wall, all three stories of it, was of a piece. She couldn't see any seams under the scarring. "Okay. Not just exploring. We're looking for ways to fight the Goa'uld."

"To save yourselves."

"To save everyone the Goa'uld oppress."

The sharp bark of Brenneka's laugh clattered around in the rafters and was swallowed by the room. "A whole galaxy of worlds."

"Nobody pretends it's easy. That doesn't mean it's not worthwhile." Sam held a hand out toward the other woman, thinking of Teal'c back at the pest house, held safe only by the strength of Brenneka's word. "And we need allies. All the friends we can get."

"We have nothing we can afford to give you. You see the way we live. Even if the Goa'uld were gone tomorrow, in a hundred lifetimes we'd never be what we were." Brenneka gestured toward the remains of the ship behind her. Against the backdrop of the metal skin of the wall, her eyes were colorless.

"We could help you."

"The mine is spent. We work twice as hard and bring out half as much. There's nothing for you there."

It was all Sam could do not to sigh, so she closed her eyes instead. "Maybe we'd help you because you're people. Just because you're people. And we're all the same to the Goa'uld."

When she opened her eyes again, Brenneka was at the dais, leaning her elbows on it with her hands clasped together, watching her. "But you're wrong, aren't you. We're not all the same. We're different from you." She touched the back of her neck, then her throat. "They can't use us like they use you, like puppets."

Hooking her fingers on the edge of the dais, Sam looked up at her. "See, that's it. We can learn from each other. This immunity you have. You must know what that means."

Brenneka flattened her hands down on the dais and carefully smoothed dust from its surface. "When we left the Homeworld, there were eighty thousand of us. We came in three ships, sleeping, and when we arrived, each ship became a city. We weren't fighters. We wanted to make beautiful things. With the knowledge of the Nitori, we were given a chance. We changed ourselves, the story says, as the Inspired taught us before he was absorbed by the Nitori, became one of them." Her smoothing hands slowed to a stop. "By the time the Goa'uld found us again, we were almost a million, and we were different, in the blood, but still the same. We still weren't fighters." When she met Sam's eyes, her gaze was piercing. "Now there are six thousand of us. *Six thousand.*" She leaned lower so that her face loomed over Sam's. "That's what it means. The Goa'uld destroy what they can't have. And when we learned to kneel, and to beg—" She cut herself off and turned to look up at the fragment of the ship. "Who can blame the Nitori for leaving us?"

Sam thought of the mosaic eye, watching the sky, waiting, all in pieces.

"But," Brenneka continued after awhile, "we *never* knelt to worship a worm. And maybe that will redeem us."

"I'm sure it will. That's a beginning."

"Maybe your friend, Dr. Jackson, will help us," Brenneka said as she turned the key in a lock and raised the lid of the dais.

The mention of Daniel sent a sliver of pain through Sam's chest, and she grimaced. "He's…compromised. I wouldn't count on him now."

After lowering the lid and placing a stone tablet flat on it, Brenneka crooked a finger at Sam, inviting her to join her on the raised platform. "Sebek will use what he knows and they will open the door. It doesn't matter if Dr. Jackson helps willingly. It'll still be help, won't it?"

Revulsion ran through Sam at the way Brenneka casually dismissed Daniel's life, but she said nothing. Instead, she leaned over Brenneka's shoulder to run her fingers across the tablet. About the size of a dictionary, it was black like the stone of the mountain and deeply carved with familiar blocky shapes. "This is the same form of writing that's on the door." Pieces fell together in her mind and the Nitori took on a familiar shape: Ancients.

Brenneka's cheek rounded with a smile.

Trying to keep her excitement out of her voice, Sam asked, "Can you read it?"

When she shook her head, water droplets scattered from Brenneka's hair onto the tablet. "No. But I know what it means." She laid her hand reverently on the stone and wiped the water away. "This is the sacred writing of the Nitori. They've left us a message in the mountain. They've left us something there that will save us, as they did before."

"Brenneka, I don't think—"

She turned on Sam, her eyes alight. "Sebek, Dr. Jackson, they will open the door and my brother will find what the Nitori have left us, and he'll destroy Sebek and prove that we're not worthless. We're not cringing vermin."

Sam's mouth was dry. "Destroy Sebek."

"Yes!"

"And what about Daniel?"

"He is a vessel of the gods now. He has his part to play. We can't interfere."

"You know," Sam said, barely controlling her anger, "we would have helped you. We didn't have to be coerced. Daniel didn't have to be—" She almost said 'lost' but she snapped her teeth down on the word. "—put at risk." When Brenneka's hard expression didn't change, Sam sighed and ran her fingers over the raised shapes on the tablet. "Why did you bring me here?"

"To show you that this is all much bigger than you, or your friend, or the worm, Sebek. What you *want* is irrelevant. Your friend has been brought here to serve the ends of the Nitori."

"And you think that the Nitori want him to die?"

"We can't know what the Nitori want. We can only see what they put in our path." Now her face did soften with compassion, but only for a moment, as her hand covered Sam's and then slipped away. "He'll be free. Freedom has its price. I'm sure if you could ask him, he would agree."

# CHAPTER ELEVEN

Daniel's body – if he could even call it his own anymore – was numb. But it wasn't numbness, not really, because he recognized sensation, the way he would know that the punching throb against his eardrums on a crowded dance floor was music even if he couldn't hear it. It was as if the world was too loud, so loud that his body was full to the point of being empty, overloaded to the point of white noise and nonsense, and all he had in his head to name it was 'numb.'

He was too small for all that feeling.

Sebek thrashed inside him, and Daniel saw the floor close to his face, black stone with a blue sheen from some light source he couldn't place. He saw his own hand splayed a few inches from his eyes, the fingers stiffly straining, the pads of each one white, and the nails white, too, except with a rim of red at the quick because of the way the hand was pressing hard against the stone. Sebek was trying to lever himself upright, but Daniel's body was heavy and numb and full of noise, and he fell again – the floor right next to Daniel's eye now, his face pressed against stone. Sebek made a sound with Daniel's throat, a growl of frustration that Daniel felt inside his head and not in the body at all, but it was some kind of coherence to cling to, and so he did. The noise and numbness started to resolve again into thought and feeling, distantly: the cool stone against his cheek, a cold ache inside the globe of his knee, and the jutting bone of his hip where he'd fallen. Flares of color in the whited-out landscape of his being.

He could hear Aris's voice, Jack's, and a moment later, a heavy hand fell on the back of his neck, squeezing and then shifting to his shoulder. A wall loomed in front of him, with shadowed etchings, dancing figures, then skewed away into the blankness of ceiling. He was on his back now. Aris's face came into view, wearing an expression of unconvincing concern, or so it seemed to Daniel. Those pale eyes held a distinct glimmer of satisfaction as he looked down at his Goa'uld master.

"My lord," Aris said, the honorific colored by barely suppressed mockery.

Sebek was not in the mood for amusing ironies, it seemed, and his anger scraped a livid path through the static inside Daniel's head. Daniel's hand, the one without the ribbon device, passed through his field of vision as Sebek raised it. Aris gripped his hand and leaned back against his weight to pull him up; the walls angled around him, and Jack was suddenly there, on his ass with his legs askew and his fists pressed to his temples, broken finger sticking out with incongruous daintiness.

Jack must have known he was being watched, because he dropped his hands and followed Sebek's progress. In the dim ambient light Daniel was close enough that even without his glasses he could see the red rash left by the ribbon device there between Jack's eyebrows, the broken blood vessels a fine webbing on the skin on either side of his nose and around his bloodshot eyes. Jack rested his weight on his broken hand and then, with a hiss of pain, sat up again and cradled it for a second against his chest. Something about the gesture seemed to clarify the numbness in Daniel's body – some memory of pain, maybe – and he could feel his legs again, fully, the weight of the ribbon device on his dangling hand, the fleeting touch of Sebek's attention along his limbs as the bruises on his knee and hip were repaired and erased. Sebek drew his body up straight.

Jack screwed up his face in that expression that usually preceded a smartassed remark and, true to form, said, "Nice impression of a fish on the bottom of a boat. Not very godlike, though."

Daniel could feel the rage in the middle of his chest – Sebek's chest – a tightening that started under the sternum and spread outward along the muscles and into his arms, tendons going taut and fingers curling, clenching into a fist, and if that feeling had a color it would be seething red. His centre of gravity shifted, his weight moving from his left foot to the right as Sebek pulled his left arm back and up. There was a sudden release of energy as the arm and its fist swung down and smashed Jack across the mouth. Daniel felt the give of muscle and the resistance of teeth and bone before Jack spun away with the force of the blow, and the shifting of weight again in the follow-through, anger boiling away and leaving behind the oily residue of satisfaction.

Daniel felt it all, a detailed parsing of his own body, because that was what Sebek could feel. Sebek enjoyed the violent art of the machine.

His mouth stretched into Sebek's smile as Jack, knocked onto his shoulder, rolled to his knees and stood up, using Aris for balance. When Jack turned to face Sebek, the back of his hand was red with blood from his lip.

"This is godlike," Sebek said, low and warning. "We are infused with the power of this place, and we are strong." A tremor of fear rippled through the sharpening space of Sebek's mind. Daniel tried to follow it, but Sebek smoothed it away.

"Strong enough to hit a guy when he's down, anyway," Jack answered, dabbing his lip with his sleeve.

The satisfaction wilted to disdain as Sebek turned away. Daniel watched Jack in his peripheral vision while Sebek turned his attention to Aris. Jack leaned to the side, one hand on Aris's shoulder, and spat blood onto the floor. No teeth with it, at least. Daniel wondered what it would feel like to strangle himself – to strangle his own body. Serve Sebek right.

Sebek's answer to that was immediate; there would be a price for insubordination. Daniel shrank back from what Sebek showed him – promised him – a threat, enacted from the twisted wreckage of Daniel's own memory – Jack falling – and Sebek's vision – a snake's-eye view of a host being taken. Jack's contorted face, now, as *no* worked its way between his clenched teeth. Sebek got that image from Daniel, Daniel's memory of Jack in Hathor's bunker, tied in the cryo-bed while the snake took him. Daniel could *feel* the tusks as they carved their way into flesh, Sebek's experience relived time and again, the slight pressure of resistant skin giving way and then muscle quivering, resisting but unable to keep him out; the sideways slither around bone, the sinewy body winding, slick with excreted enzymes, ducking between tendons, sliding over the points and angles of vertebrae, seeking the way to the brain, already starting to divide, ganglia extending into the spinal column. Daniel heard the echo of distant screaming, the host mind recoiling, and that became a picture, Jack crabwalking backward, scrambling away, away from Sebek, from Daniel, nowhere to go, and there was no place in Daniel's memory where Sebek could have got that image because Jack never crawled in panic like that. Daniel's mind had created this from fear, had made that picture out of the screaming, made Jack crawl, and there was nowhere to go. Sebek would take Jack, and Daniel would be dead, and there would be no way of stopping him, then.

Inside, Daniel went blank.

When he could see again, they were walking, Jack up front, Aris behind. The hallway curved to their left, dark beyond ten or fifteen feet or so. Wherever the light was coming from, it seemed to be rationed, because it faded behind them and crept ahead of them reluctantly, tantalizingly. Their boots clattered on the black stone, and echoes ricocheted along the narrow space so that sometimes it seemed like there was an army in here with them. On either side, the walls were alive with those still figures, caught midway through their dances.

Sebek hummed inside with satisfaction as he carried Daniel long between the murmuring walls, but the purring smoothness was deformed a little, silk folded around the shape of something underneath. It wasn't precisely fear, but the symbols on the wall seemed to vibrate in his head, below the threshold of understanding, and it was a fine-toothed abrasion of his control. He strode on faster than the blooming light, pushing them toward…something.

Daniel watched Sebek as he traced a worn path through a list of grievances, lost opportunities, humiliations, felt the Goa'uld's anger, his self-righteous conviction that he deserved more, always more. It was as though the place were singing in sympathy for his outrage, and each step they took brought Sebek closer to – *revenge* – fulfillment. Sebek, Daniel realized, believed that the silence was speaking to him, and the path that started in his failure wound its way inward, forward, toward promise. Aris was at his back, and Sebek knew that his hold on the bounty hunter was slight. Again, a shiver of fear, but Sebek crushed it. He was a god. A sudden, gro-tesque series of images slid up out of Sebek's memory and assaulted Daniel: a crying child, a dead woman, Aris falling under the rain-ing blows of mailed fists. A god would never fall to a slave. There was no thought of going back without his prize, no matter what risks were to be faced, or how terribly the place ravaged his host. And in any case, Sebek had options. With his gold-capped hand, he reached out and gave Jack a shove.

When Daniel tried to follow the contours of that uneasiness in Sebek, he found himself looking at the back of Jack's neck above his collar, the slight indentation at the base of his skull below the brush of silver-grey hair. He tried not to, but Sebek kept his eyes on it. Eyes on the prize. Sebek's threat was clear. If Daniel didn't want to feel Sebek's predatory gaze on the entry-point in his next host's body, he'd have to retreat. He didn't want to retreat. He was afraid that if he did, he'd lose his way. So he watched the back of Jack's neck while Sebek caressed memories of takings, a snake charmer holding up his darlings in front of an appalled, fascinated audience. That weird, inside-out metaphor should have made Daniel falter, but Sebek walked steadily along, his boots on Jack's shadow.

Sebek shoved Jack again.

This time, Jack was braced for it and, instead of staggering for-ward, halted and turned to face Sebek with an irritating expression of calm affability. He smiled tightly and stepped to the side, sweep-ing his arm wide to show the way. "If you'd like to go first, be my guest," he said, still smiling with his own threat in his eyes.

"You will continue…" Daniel could feel Sebek searching Daniel's own vocabulary. "On point. Aris will watch our six." That hum of satisfaction keyed up a bit when Jack's smile faltered as he heard those familiar words in Daniel's warped and unfamiliar voice. Their language, stolen, to make a point. "And we will move faster." That agitation in Sebek was a thin whine, and it seemed to spin out like a ribbon along the hallway, into darkness. "Move."

Jack pointed ahead of them to where the wall curved away, its lines of symbols dancing away, luring. "I don't think faster is neces-sarily the best strategy," he said, as he put his hands in his pockets, and then, wincing, pulled the one with the broken finger out again. "I mean, didn't you *see* any of the *Indiana Jones* movies?" Tilting his head back and cocking a finger gun at Sebek with his splinted hand, he added, "Wait, I forgot. Of course you didn't. Take my word for it. Caution is what we learn from Dr. Jones."

Impatience prickled along Daniel's skin as the ribbon of agitation went taut, urging Sebek forward. But he took a fraction of a second to rummage through Daniel's memories again and came up with the image of Indiana Jones running from a giant rolling boulder, dodging poisoned arrows. Sebek grunted out something like a laugh. "That is why you are on point, O'Neill," Sebek answered with a smile of his own. "If there are traps, you will know about them first."

Behind them, Aris let out a brief gust of laughter. "Sounds like an excellent plan. Plus, I didn't get any lunch, so I'd love to wrap this up as soon as possible."

Shrugging, Jack turned around and kept walking, at the exact same pace he'd set before. "Whatever," he muttered and then waved an admonishing hand at them over his shoulder. "But you really should see the movie first, is all I'm saying."

Sebek could see it, or at least what Daniel could remember of it, scattered fragments, lost in the clutter of associations: hot asphalt under his sneakers reflecting the summer heat into his face as he walked to the theater; Sarah, reading over his shoulder faster than he was, reaching down and turning the page of his book to reveal a full-page image of the South American jungle, impenetrable green and a startle of tropical bird-red at the top of the canopy; the smell of dust and cobwebs in the ziggurat on P2X-338, a skittering in the darkness, and the sarcophagus heavy and silent, pried open and empty but for gnawed bones; the lingering scent of Russian cigarettes, and the burn of vodka in his throat. Sebek had all this to assimilate, with Daniel's low-grade annoyance at the piratical archeology of Indiana Jones and his own feelings of hypocrisy as the relics of a hundred worlds accumulated in his lab in the mountain and at Area 51, waiting to be cracked open and – *exploited* – explained.

Sebek watched the settling layers of Daniel's experience with the bored attention of someone thumbing through the pages of the phonebook.

"Your friend's mind is undisciplined," Sebek said to the back of Jack's head.

"You should see his office." Daniel could tell from the sudden, barely-perceptible flexing of the tendons in the back of Jack's neck that he regretted saying that.

Daniel regretted it too, because now Sebek was in his office with Daniel's books, his files. Before he could imagine hiding it, the pang of protective homesickness shot through him, sharpening Sebek's idle searching. Daniel tried to focus on miscellany, ritual objects without strategic significance, requisition forms piled messily on the corner of his desk, the volumes of Budge's *Egyptology* still on the bookshelf behind a forgotten mug half-full of stale coffee. But he thought of the way Jack's neck tensed, belated, the words already out when Jack, Daniel knew, had sworn not to give the snake an inch, not a word, and it was like that in Daniel's head now, where trying not to think about things that needed protecting only pointed Sebek toward them. The slope of Jack's shoulders as he paced ahead of them was the same now as it had been the day of the summit at the SGC, when the Goa'uld System Lords sat around the conference table with Thor and debated the best way to – *subjugate* – protect the Earth. On the break, Jack in his dress blues had stood wordlessly in Daniel's office, perfectly ironed on the outside and crumpled with fatigue and frustration on the inside. Daniel knew Jack hated politics. He hated talking. He hated being the one it was all resting on. Jack had said as much when he'd hinted it should have been Daniel spinning the whole world on a thread of words and lies.

Daniel tried to forget the lies. But of course, trying to forget only brought them to the surface where Sebek snatched at them. The Asgard were besieged in their own galaxy. The Protected Planets Treaty was based on a bluff. Sebek laughed out loud.

"Something's funny?" Aris asked. The 'my lord' was conspicuously absent, but fortunately for him, Sebek was feeling generous and let it slide, keeping his eyes on Jack.

"Your friend is a source of much useful information," Sebek taunted.

"Oh, he's full of it, all right," Jack answered without turning around.

It took Sebek a second to scan Daniel's store of idioms and appreciate the double-entendre. "It seems your protectors, the Asgard, are not as powerful as they purport to be." Jack slowed to a halt and turned to face him, his face impassive. Sebek pulled Daniel's lips into a satisfied smile. "I'm sure Lord Yu would pay handsomely for this information."

"I'm sure." Jack sounded so disinterested that Daniel couldn't stop himself from thinking about Yu, crazy Yu, whose host body was beginning to deteriorate. Soon he wouldn't be able to keep his host alive, and he would no longer be a threat to anyone. Sebek seized that idea, turned it around in triumph. Now was the time to strike, and once Sebek had acquired the appropriate weapons, he would dispose of his infirm master. Daniel's despair deepened.

"Yes, your friend is useful. He gives up easily." Sebek waved Jack on, an implied order to get moving.

Ignoring Sebek's command, Jack narrowed his eyes at him. "I doubt that." His expression softened into mock pity and he added, "He can be a real pain in the ass. *I* wouldn't want to be stuck in there with him." The softness hardened again into serious lines and planes of shadow. "But if he's so useful, you might want to treat him nicely." The threat was implicit, and ironic: Jack could kill Sebek, but he'd have to come through Daniel first – literally.

A part of Daniel's mind thought that might be a good idea. But another part, a part he hoped was small enough to go unnoticed, was struck by what Jack said about usefulness.

He considered the ribbon of agitation that ran through Sebek and down along the hallway ahead of them, a keen thrumming of desire that was verging on physical pain, like the irresistible drag of addiction. That was a familiar feeling. He could understand that. The memory of the sarcophagus coalesced, bringing with it the ghost of elation, a wash of wellbeing, of strength and power. And anger and hatred and need. How many times had Daniel gone through the cycle of death and life, injury and repair, and finally hunger and fulfillment while Shyla waited for him to become bound to her by dependency? He'd deliberately not kept track. How many times had Sebek crawled into the gold coffin and waited to cheat time? A hundred? A thousand? Power and elation, anger and need. They coursed through Daniel now, barely attenuated by the years, and he realized, suddenly, that he didn't know if these were Sebek's remembered feelings or his own.

Daniel struggled to keep his focus, and to do it quietly, if that were even possible. But this could be useful. Sebek's need could be just the thing. On all sides of them, broken only by the occasional empty column, the cryptic symbols marched on, luring Sebek down into what Daniel believed to be an elaborate maze. It had a structure, a symmetry; nothing about the patterns they were following was accidental, and it certainly wasn't intended to get people lost. Confuse them, perhaps, or slow them down – that was possible. But whatever was behind the design here, it wanted to be found. Even Daniel could feel it, the seduction of it. The Ancients knew something about this place; they'd been here, left a warning, locked the door. The answer to the place had to be, at least partly, with them. And what the Ancients had was once his, though he couldn't access it consciously.

Once before, he'd gained control of his body, and Sebek had been pushed aside. But why? The external dissonance of this place had helped, but there had to be a way to open the door, to gain some advantage. If only he could find it.

Sebek could sense Daniel hiding his thoughts. He gave Daniel pain, a long, slow burn of sensation across his nerve endings – Sebek seemed immune, but Daniel's agony bloomed through every portion of his consciousness. Then came the vision again, the image of Jack, scrambling away from the horror of being taken as host.

*You won't*, Daniel thought as clearly and as loudly as he could.

A tiny tendril of Sebek's attention turned from the symbols and their progress along the gloomy hall to wonder, not terribly intensely, why Daniel thought so, because clearly, Sebek would do whatever he chose.

*You won't because of this*, Daniel thought again, and this time, he didn't resist when the scent of ripe, pink flowers flooded his mind. It was like throwing himself backward off a cliff, falling through the smell of rot and the exquisite singing of pain and death and dissolution, all the way to the brink of all that was the Ancient in his memory, everything his conscious mind refused to remember. He could feel Sebek following him, the way he'd followed him into his office, along the winding way from Indiana Jones to Sarah to the Asgard, to the edge of the disorienting swirl of Ancient knowledge Daniel could barely feel because it was too vast and his body was so small. *This is why*, he snarled into the noise. *Because you need me.*

Jack didn't bother to stop walking when he tossed his reply over his shoulder. "Believe me, I could muddle through fine without you. In fact, the galaxy took a vote and we'd all like to try getting along without the whole lot of you."

"What?" Daniel said numbly as he faltered to a halt. Aris, not paying as close attention as he should have been, managed to pull up before running into him. His armored chest brushed Daniel's back before he stepped to the side and leaned around to look at him expectantly.

Jack continued along for a few steps until he noticed that no one was following and turned around. "What?"

"What?" Daniel repeated.

Shooting Jack a quizzical look, Aris said, "What?"

"It worked," Daniel said and the relief and the excitement at the sound of his own natural voice pushed the air out of him in a startled, incredulous laugh. "It worked. Jack."

Jack cocked his head and folded his arms. He needed a P90 to rest his hands on though, to complete the familiar 'cut the bull' posture. His suspicion seared through Daniel. Of course. Jack had no reason to believe, no reason to trust. A new kind of despair caught at Daniel's throat. He had information Jack needed, that he had to give him, even if Jack didn't believe. If only he would listen and remember what Daniel said.

Daniel held out his hands, remembering too late that one of them was still in the ribbon device, which was now aimed at Jack's chest. He dropped it hastily and took a step toward him. "I know. I know. Just…just listen to me. I don't know how much time I have, so just listen."

Jack shifted his gaze to some spot on the wall and sighed out a weary, "We danced this dance already."

"I know. You have no reason to believe it's me. But it is, Jack." Daniel's heart was pounding so hard he could barely hear his own voice. He wondered when Sebek would tamp that down again. But he didn't want to think of Sebek. Speak of the devil. He felt Sebek pressing, shoving, battering at him; he ignored it, and the small waves of pain beginning to track through his body. "Remember all those times we've seen the symbiote suppressed by…by technology or…design. When Sha're was pregnant and, and, and when…at Skaara's trial, the Tollan had that disengagement device that allowed Skaara to speak freely. Remember?" Jack's face was expressionless, his eyes still staring at nothing. "You remember. And this, this is like that. Something here is doing it, like we saw before, in the way the Jaffa were affected." Daniel took another step and Jack moved away, keeping his distance. "Okay, fine, then you can listen, just listen to me."

Aris was keeping pace with him, his forehead wrinkled in an eloquent frown that was part confusion and part bemusement.

"Sebek isn't in complete control. I don't know why for sure. But he's obsessed with this place and whatever he thinks is in here. A weapon, something that will make him powerful, that he can use to challenge Yu, maybe. It doesn't matter. He's…broken somehow – of course, they all are, but he's extra broken. There's something wrong with him. He'll threaten you. He'll threaten to take you as a host, Jack, but he won't follow through. Not unless I become too weak to support him."

Now Jack's gaze stabbed through him again.

Daniel smiled and shook his head. "He says he'll take you. He says that to keep me quiet, but he won't do it, because he needs what I know, what the Ancients left in me. The threat's empty, Jack. You can use that." Tapping himself sharply on the temple, Daniel came forward again and this time Jack stayed put. "Everything's there, Jack. We can use it. We can use Sebek to get it for us. Everything that happened to me. The meaning of life st—"

He didn't have a chance to finish his sentence because Jack was moving fast, stepping into his space. Jack grabbed his pleading hand and twisted it behind his back, using his momentum and his weight to propel Daniel forward, away from Aris, face-first into the wall, his other wiry arm pinning Daniel across the back of his neck. Daniel could feel the vibration of Jack's rage as he leaned in and pressed him harder against the stone. Fighting his own reflexes, augmented now with Sebek's power, Daniel forced himself not to resist. Distantly, he noticed that he was leaning against one of those blank columns, and above his head, a watery light glowed from a narrow groove where the ceiling met the wall. One mystery solved.

Jack's breath was hot against the side of Daniel's neck when he spoke, a low, furious whisper. "*You* listen. I'm not the sharpest knife in the drawer, but I'm not as stupid as you seem to think I am. And if you use Daniel's voice to talk to me again, I swear, Aris will not get to me before I get to you."

To make his point, Jack twisted Daniel's arm a little harder, enough to make Daniel's mouth fall open in a silent gasp of pain. External pain was bad. Pain threatened static and loss of focus, and Sebek was close to the surface. Daniel considered throwing Jack off of him. He could do it. Sebek was strong enough.

"Jack, please," he managed, but the words were drowned out by a click and rising whine. Out of the corner of his eye, he could make out Aris's looming shape, and the gleam of light along the muzzle of his blaster. It was resting against the side of Jack's head.

"Yes, Jack, please," Aris repeated with a mocking sneer, then pulled back and shot him.

# CHAPTER TWELVE

It was dusk when they returned to the shelter. Deep twilight had settled over the sooty valley and brought a sharp chill on its heels. When Sam pushed aside the thin curtain and stepped into the shack, she found the room still full of strangers, but she was less wary about making her way through them this time. No one stood in her way, although they muttered amongst themselves as she passed. She wondered if maybe they were trying to make up their minds about her and Teal'c – whether to turn them in, or send them out on their own – but she was too tired to worry about it now. If it was going to happen, she couldn't stop it.

Teal'c was awake, half-sitting against the wall beneath the latticed window. He was peeling back the fresh bandage and poking beneath. With a nod to Aadi, who was crouching by the fire, she knelt at Teal'c's side.

"Teal'c. It's good to see you awake." She covered his hand with her own, squeezing a little, and pressed the bandage back in place. "We don't have much gauze for sterile dressings."

"It does not matter," Teal'c said. Pain creased his forehead. "I needed to see the depth of the wound for myself, but it appears to be healing well."

"The tretonin probably has something to do with that."

"Indeed." Teal'c's gaze shifted to Brenneka, who stood beside Sam, silent as stone, then to Aadi, who had inched marginally closer. "Thank you."

"Thank Esa," Brenneka said, in a clipped tone. "He's the one who risked his life for you. My home was crawling with Jaffa when Esa stole these things from the hiding place there." It was the way she spat the word – *you* – as if Teal'c was the lowest form of life in the room. Sam frowned, but Teal'c's expression was calm, so she let it go. They had saved Teal'c's life, and she wasn't in a position to complain.

Esa wasn't among the strangers still cluttering the small space in

the room, so Sam shook her head at Teal'c. He nodded his understanding. Slowly, he looked around the room, watching each person
for a short time and taking the measure of each man in turn. She'd
done it herself, earlier.

"Teal'c, these people are Aris's kinsfolk," she said. "You've
met Aadi…and this is Brenneka." She didn't bother with trying to
remember the names of the others; even if they had been identi-
fied, she had relegated the information to the back of her brain as
not important now. Teal'c inclined his head toward Brenneka, who
gave a curt nod before turning her back on him.

Sam eased herself down to the ground beside Teal'c and scooted
back for the support of the wall. Every bone in her body was aching,
and hunger and exhaustion were catching up with her. One thing
after another since they'd been captured…her skin felt stretched
too tightly over her bones, as if it might crack and she would spill
out in the margins. She turned her face toward Teal'c, to speak as
privately as possible – not like that much privacy was possible here.
Aadi would hear all they said to each other in these cramped quarters.

"How are you really feeling?" she asked, under her breath.

"It appears to be a superficial wound. I will be able to travel
within a few hours."

"Even without a symbiote?" she said, and then cringed. Of course
she didn't need to remind him. Maybe she was reminding herself.
Teal'c had been able to avail himself of a symbiote's healing powers for so long that she'd never considered what might happen if
that ability was stripped away. She was sure Teal'c had, though they
had never talked about it.

"Even without a symbiote," Teal'c confirmed. Sam sighed,
and her body relaxed another fraction of a degree. Part of her had
expected him to say it would take longer, or that he was in serious
pain. That same part feared they were going to be stuck here, or lose
Daniel, or the Colonel. It was the part of her that was clueless about
how to get out of this mess.

"I don't have a concrete plan," she told him up front, confessing
her failure as a tactician. "So much has happened." Brenneka was

kneeling by the hearth, but her head was angled toward Sam. No doubt she was absorbing everything. "The bottom line is, Aris is going to kill Sebek, and Daniel in the process. He wants whatever is in that vault. These people think it's a weapon the Ancients left for them." She watched this register with Teal'c, watched his eyebrow raise and his expression harden. He pushed himself upright with a grunt, leaning heavily on one arm.

"We must attempt a rescue before Aris Boch makes his move."

"Agreed," Sam said. "But with what?" She tapped the *zat*, secure at her side. "Against dozens, maybe hundreds of Jaffa? We're in no shape to take on even a small portion of his army."

"What do you suggest?"

She looked into Teal'c's eyes, warmed by the confidence and trust there. No way was she going to open her mouth and say *I don't know* and blow all that out of the water. So instead she said, "We need more weapons, and people to handle them." If they'd been alone, she might have told Teal'c she suspected Brenneka and her Order had more up their collective sleeves than cold huts and gruel, but she had no proof.

Teal'c glanced back over at Brenneka, at the stiff lines of her back. "Are these people able and willing to fight?" he asked Sam.

At this, Brenneka turned on her knee to face them. "For you? No. Nor will we give you weapons. If your plan is to use my people for gun fodder, you'll sleep in the street until you are discovered, Jaffa – no matter what you have done for Aadi."

"Brenneka, no one is suggesting that your kinsmen should die for what we need to do," Sam began, but Teal'c threw off the blanket covering his legs and forced himself to sit up, one hand clutching at the crumbling brick to balance himself.

"I *am* suggesting it," he said. Sam touched him on the arm, trying to warn him away from the subject – now wasn't the time – but he ignored her. "Your people live in misery, yet there are but a few hundred Jaffa to control you. Why didn't you rise up?"

"Is it so easy for you to judge, Jaffa? Why didn't *you* not rise up, in all the thousands of years your people have been killing my kind?" Brenneka reached into the pocket of her trousers and pulled out a tiny blue packet. She turned it over between her fingers, then gestured to Aadi; he handed her a cup of water, and she emptied the *roshna* into the cup. The liquid fluoresced to a vivid green-blue for a few seconds before the color faded, leaving only a grainy scum on the top of the water. Sam knew what it looked like. She'd helped the chemists work with it for a few days in the lab, trying to wrench all the secrets from it in the hopes that it was responsible for some immunity to Goa'uld possession, but she'd never been able to find anything of use. Like most other things, they'd handed off the remaining sample to Area 51, where it waited its turn in the scientific queue.

Brenneka drank deeply, emptying the cup in one long swallow. A moment later, she flung the cup into the corner, inches away from Teal'c's head. "You know nothing of my people or our struggles here."

"Perhaps not," Teal'c said. He met Aadi's eyes, where there was curiosity and fear in equal proportion. "But I know what it is to depend on an outside source for strength and life. And I know what it costs to be free."

"And you would have us pay this price. For you."

"For your freedom," Teal'c said fervently.

Brenneka laughed, a scratchy sound, without humor. "It's as I thought, from the beginning," she said, with a hard look at Sam. "You fight to save yourselves. You persuade for your own cause. Not for ours." She jerked her head at Aadi, motioning him out of the room, and Aadi scrambled to obey, with a last curious look at Teal'c. "We will not help you."

"You already have," Sam said wearily. "It's a little late to back away from that on principle, don't you think? We're here, you're hiding us. We have nowhere to go."

Near the doorway of the hut, one of the men standing there spoke quietly. In the dim light, his face was cut with shadows. "Brenneka. Perhaps we should hear the words the strangers are saying, rather than judging them half-said."

"Perhaps, Hamel, you're anxious to throw your life away." Brenneka turned her head to glare at him. "You've been waiting for an excuse, haven't you? This is not what we agreed upon."

"No, but then again, opportunities like this don't present them-selves often." Hamel approached and squatted down next to the hearth; his grey hair glinted silver in the flickering light. "We have two warriors, ready to help us, and Aris is in a position to rid us of Sebek. What more can we ask? How much longer can we wait?"

"Until we are ready," Brenneka said. Her fingers flexed and pulled at the fabric of her trousers.

"That day will never come," Hamel said. He cupped Brenneka's chin with one hand and raised it gently. "We will spend our lives preparing to fight and die without having fought. I don't want to die a slave."

Teal'c said, "Hamel is correct. When the moment comes, you cannot step aside and wait to fight another day."

Sam had a flash of memory: Teal'c's anguished expression, and the profound sadness on his face, at the moment when he'd switched sides to join them.

"Self-serving words," Brenneka muttered, but she no longer sounded so convinced.

"We are not afraid to die for those things in which we believe, if others may live free," Teal'c said. "We do not serve only our-selves."

"But we want to save our friends," Sam said. "And we're going to try to make that happen, with or without your help."

Hamel pointed to Teal'c's bandaged side. "You won't get far without us. Unless you have a clever plan you haven't told us about." He tilted his head to the side. "Do you?"

Sam smiled in spite of herself. "I'm a little short on clever plans today."

"Because you don't know this place, or the mines, as we do." Hamel smiled back at her, but his smile was cold. "I can help you."

"Hamel," Brenneka began, but he shook his head.

"The time for discussion has finished," he said. "You may do as you wish, but I will do what I can to help them."

"You go alone," Brenneka said. "The others will not follow."

"Be that as it may," Hamel said. Like someone had snapped a wire between them, he moved away from Brenneka and settled next to Sam with his back against the wall.

"Thank you," Sam said, quietly.

"Don't thank me yet," he said, watching Brenneka, whose eyes glittered as she turned her back on him. "It is likely we will all die. Certainly you cannot save your friend, the one Sebek took."

Sam and Teal'c exchanged a glance full of meaning. They were going to have to find a moment alone to talk about their options. Even if they got into the mine – even if they found the Colonel and Daniel – Sebek would never go willingly. The chances of getting Daniel back had already dwindled to near zero.

"You have weapons," Hamel said, making it less a question than an invitation to tell him more.

"Just a *zat*," Sam said. "Aris took our Earth weapons, and the ones we picked up in the bunker seem to be missing." Sam raised her chin pointedly at Brenneka, and Hamel nodded, chewing his beard thoughtfully.

"We may be able to do something about that."

"We?" Sam asked, not entirely sure if he was including Brenneka's people in that broad category. She didn't dare hope there would be enough of them to overpower even a small squad of Jaffa. Whatever plan they made would have to be less about brute strength and more about cunning, and she was feeling pretty short in the idea department.

Hamel's gaze shifted back to Brenneka, who was now busying herself around the room, studiously avoiding the area where the three of them sat. "She will consider it, and when she puts aside her anger, she'll see the wisdom of striking now."

"It is not easy to stand up, when one has lost the will to rise," Teal'c said. "Nor is it easy to know if one's efforts will succeed."

"No," Hamel said. "And we'll only have one chance to get it right. Brenneka doesn't want to jump until the pond is full of water."

Sam watched Brenneka and reconsidered everything the woman had told her about the Ancients, hoping to remember something she could use, something to sway Brenneka to their point of view. Too bad Daniel wasn't here to make helpful suggestions. He was a master of re-contextualizing myths into persuasive arguments. But if Daniel could do it, so could she. It was a matter of finding the right buttons to push.

Her eyes drifted closed, and before sleep claimed her, she saw the image of Daniel's smile in the darkness, and the Colonel's face, etched with worry.

At first he thought it was a dream, but no dream was ever that vivid, so gradually Jack decided it had to be real. He could smell dinner cooking in the kitchen – meatloaf, maybe. Something with the tangy odor of burned ketchup, and then there was the scent of salted water steaming the air. Probably noodles, for macaroni and cheese. He smiled and shifted on the couch. Saturday afternoon naps were the best, and then there was always his son, Charlie, who would be waiting for him in the yard so they could play catch. Best part of the weekend, bar none. He wished he had more time, for his family, for Sara, for everything that mattered. A stretch and a yawn, and he'd open his eyes and Charlie would be there.

*Jack.*

He frowned. That voice was familiar, but it didn't belong here. Charlie was calling to him from his room, but his voice was fading, and suddenly the memory went rushing past like ice water over Jack's skin, gentle afternoon sunlight and comfortable sounds twisting fluidly into screams and blood and terror. *Not this*. He shoved it away as hard as he could, and the world fell away underneath him.

*Jack!*

So insistent…words, modulating from one range to another, familiar and yet not quite the same. He knew the sound of that voice – *Carter*, he thought at first, and then *Teal'c*, but he knew immediately that wasn't right, either. *Daniel*.

His eyes snapped open, and he thrashed for a moment, unsure of where he was. Someone was leaning over him, staring at him through silver eyes, glittering circles like funhouse mirrors reflecting his entire life back into his mind. He blinked rapidly, trying to

clear his field of vision, but now he could see the shape of a face
behind those eyes. Light caught and scattered off its skin, which
shimmered with tiny rainbows. Iridescent, like…*scales*, he thought,
and swung up with one closed fist. The vision shattered, fragments
flying apart like a prism, and he gasped out loud.

"Bad dreams?"

Jack sat up and twisted in the direction of Aris's voice. They
were only a few feet apart; a safe distance for Aris, since he was
out of arm's reach. The scant illumination that had helped them find
their way earlier seemed to have disappeared completely, for the
time being. Jack held his hand up to block the light Aris was aiming
at his face. "Put that thing down," he ordered. Aris leaned the flash
against his knee, its glow narrowed to a thin beam. Jack blinked
away spots. "You had fun shooting me, didn't you?"

"I always do." So smug. Jack wanted to rip that satisfied smile
right off his face. A faint tremor went through his body, unused
adrenaline built up with nowhere to go and nothing to fight. He
glanced around him, half expecting to see a physical manifestation
of his dream, but there was nothing there. No point in asking Aris
if he'd seen anything; he was sure now that he'd imagined it. Jack
shook off the sensation of those eyes, shining straight into him, and
the sound of his son's voice. *Not now.*

After a moment, it dawned on Jack: no Sebek. It had taken him
far too long to realize that the snake wasn't standing there baiting
him, and it was still taking too long to get his bearings. Not like
him, to *forget* to threat-assess. *Get a grip.* He glanced around and
saw Daniel face-up but unconscious, sprawled on the ground at the
edge of the area the light could reach. "What happened to him?"

"I shot him, too."

"Isn't that going to piss him off a little?"

Aris shrugged, his armor creaking. "I'll say it was collateral
damage from when I tried to save his life." He waggled his blaster
in Jack's direction. "Overflow, proximity." He grinned a little at
his own cleverness and shrugged again. "I needed some peace and
quiet. You two are like bickering children."

"Nice way to talk about your god," Jack said.

Aris shot him an ominous look. "You know better than to call *that* my god," he scoffed, as he indicated Daniel with the blaster. He sighted along the muzzle, his finger twitching on the trigger. "But if you don't stop interfering, I'll have to kill you, and that would be a shame."

"I'm not the enemy."

"I don't have enemies. I have associates, and I have people who get in my way." Aris fished for his canteen, then for a small packet of *roshna*, which he dumped into the water. "Don't be the latter."

Jack watched him take a long swallow of the blue mixture, and had a flash of craving, so strong that his stomach cramped and his skin went clammy. "You'd do anything for that, wouldn't you?"

Aris said nothing. Instead, he held out the canteen. "Thirsty? Shame I forgot to ask earlier."

Jack grimaced. "No thanks."

"Smart move." Aris took a bite of something he held in his hand.

Jack's stomach rumbled, right on cue. "Don't suppose you have any more of whatever that is?"

"Sure I do." Another bite, and Aris made no move to hand him any. Jack raised his eyebrows. After a moment, Aris sighed impatiently. "Oh, all right." He dug into one of those strange hidden pockets in his armor and pulled out the scant remains of a crushed power bar, half-unwrapped.

Jack caught it in mid-air and tore it out of the plastic. The smell alone made him vaguely nauseated. It had probably come out of Daniel's pack, since Daniel always carried extra food for bribing natives. "Nice of you to bring along some stolen supplies."

"Finders keepers."

"Your motto, clearly." Jack took two large bites, watching Daniel as he chewed. "Why is he still out?"

"I told you already, Sebek is weak. He hasn't been able to sustain a host's strength for more than a day or two, and he hasn't been in the sarcophagus since at least a full day before he took Dr. Jackson as host." Aris picked up the light and shone it on Daniel's motionless body. "Maybe he's having a tough time blending with him."

"Who wouldn't," Jack muttered. He finished off the power bar, licked the wrapper clean and tossed it aside, then felt around on the floor for his flashlight until his fingers bumped up against it in the dust. Turning away from Aris and Daniel, he clicked on the light and aimed it down the passageway in the opposite direction.

"I've already had a little look around," Aris said. "You know how it is." Jack did understand; he'd been thinking of doing the same thing. No reason not to take advantage of the fact that Daniel was out cold. "As far as I can tell, this place goes on forever, all sharp corners and tight turns. Still don't see any way out. At least none that's obvious."

"I'm sure you won't mind if I take a look myself," Jack said and pushed up from the ground without waiting for a response. Despite the fact that he carried his light source in his hand, he had the sensation of rising into space without stars, and for a split second he was back in the X-301, in the co-pilot's seat behind Teal'c, drifting out toward his death. "Damn," he murmured, and closed his eyes. It was like vertigo, but not as strong, and he couldn't control the images. Weird. He took a few cautious steps back in the direction they'd come from…or at least, he thought he did. It was too easy to get turned around, and he had nothing that looked remotely like a landmark. He'd have to start doing something about that before they moved much further in.

Jack moved the beam of light around, left, then right, and saw what Aris had described: walls, angles, corners. Nothing more. No exit.

"I hope to hell Jackson knows something about the inside of this thing," Aris said.

"That's assuming he has any input," Jack said. He turned back to look at Aris, who reached up and tapped the wall.

"Don't forget, Sebek is getting the information from somewhere in Dr. Jackson's brain."

"And that counts as input," Jack said dryly. "Right." He clicked off his light and stowed it in his pants pocket, then sat down again. Daniel still hadn't moved, and it crossed Jack's mind that maybe Sebek was hurt in there, somehow, or that Daniel was—

"He's not dead," Aris said, then added, "Not yet."

For the moment, Jack ignored the implicit threat. "So do you have some kind of plan?" Jack asked. The fact that he *didn't* have one of his own sowed a tiny seed of doubt in the back of his brain. He should be thinking faster than this. He should be paying better attention, not losing it over tricks the snake was playing. It was as though his brain were mired in molasses.

"Other than killing him once we get to where we're going? No." He met Jack's eyes. "There's nothing you can do for your friend. Most men would welcome death rather than be host to one of those things."

Jack was silent. He'd seen Daniel offer himself up as a host, once – on their first mission to Chulak – but that was before they'd really understood what it meant to be subjugated to a Goa'uld. Daniel had been desperate to be with Sha're and half out of his mind at the time. Jack knew better than anyone how far from that moment Daniel had come on the subject; he didn't want to be host to a snake, even on a voluntary basis. The first time the offer had been made, by the Tok'ra, Daniel's quiet but firm refusal had struck a sympathetic chord in Jack. Not even the chance for a deeper understanding of Tok'ra culture had been enough to sway Daniel, and that was something Jack hadn't expected. Daniel had always seemed open to new experiences, but that clearly wasn't one he wanted to check off his list.

After the incident with Jolinar, Carter, too, had made her wishes clear: a quick kill, rather than a living death. Daniel had taken a little longer; maybe six months after Sha're's funeral he'd mentioned it, offhand, as though they were talking about what kind of pie to have for dessert. It had been a bad period for Daniel, so Jack had asked him again, a few months later. Just to be sure.

*That's not living*, Daniel had said, with quiet grief in his voice. *Think of the things they use the host to do, Jack. Don't let a Goa'uld use me to hurt anyone else.*

"There's no chance that was your friend talking, back there," Aris said, as if he thought Jack's silence was a sign that his captive needed convincing. Maybe it was. Jack knew what Daniel wanted.

He knew what had to be done. His hands were shaking.

Daniel-Sebek stirred and moaned softly. Jack watched him until he lapsed back into unconsciousness, then turned his attention to Aris. "Why don't you take your son and get the hell off this planet?" Jack asked. "You're resourceful. You should be able to find a way, right?"

Aris took another swig from his canteen and capped it. "You have a simplistic view of the situation."

"The kid is enslaved, and you're a snake lackey. That about covers it."

"I'm no one's lackey." Aris sat forward, staring at Jack. "I'm a businessman. A hunter. The Goa'uld trade with me because I make it worth their while."

"Who makes it worth your son's while?" Jack said. Aris's eyes narrowed. "Or are you planning to live the good life forever while he rots in a cell somewhere, and make excuses about how you hope to buy his freedom someday?" It made him feel better, gouging a few verbal holes in Aris's armor and twisting the knife down from heart to belly.

Aris set the canteen aside and picked up his blaster. "I don't owe you any explanations," he said. "Drop it now."

Jack made a dismissive sound through his teeth and lay down on the cold ground. If there was a ceiling above them, it was completely concealed by the darkness, and Jack was unnerved by the way the chamber seemed to stretch out forever. A trick of the dark, but an effective one.

"It's been one Goa'uld after another," Aris said slowly. "Sokar, Apophis, Sebek. I thought one of them would do the honorable thing and let me buy my son out of slavery, but my reputation was already too great. They needed me to get things for them, to move in circles where they couldn't function themselves."

"And they held your son prisoner to make it happen."

"They had him in the mines," Aris said. "Every breath was killing him. It was Sebek who put him…in chains." His voice wavered on the last words, then steadied. "Sebek promised me that your capture would more than equal his price, but he had no intention of freeing him. Even so, I had to try."

If ever there was a motivation Jack could get behind, it was that one. With any luck, Teal'c had broken the kid out of jail and they were hiding somewhere in the city. Or maybe they had found a way off the planet. Even better. "Why do the Tok'ra think you lied about your family?"

"I lie when it suits me," Aris said, chuckling. "Half-truths help me do my work. Besides, the Tok'ra intelligence is weak."

"That must be where you buy yours," Jack said, risking a wild stab in the dark. Aris said nothing, and Jack made a mental note to pass that along to Hammond. More confirmation of the leaks among their 'trusted allies'. "Is Sebek in service to Yu?" Jack asked and, for once, he didn't go near the pool of Yu jokes.

"Yes. And Yu already knows you're here." Aris paused, then added, "Not my fault. Sebek contacted him."

"Of course he did," Jack said. No chance they were going to catch a break at any point in this gigantic snafu. "And you still think there's something in here that will help you do…what? Defeat Yu?"

"Hard to say. But I told you, I've got nothing to lose."

"Yes, I heard you." Jack had a flash of Charlie's face in the darkness, and then Aadi's. "But that's not really true."

"Fine. I have more to gain than to lose. How's that?"

"At least it's honest."

A few minutes of quiet passed. Jack tried to rest his body, simple preparation for whatever fresh hell was coming next. When Sebek got up off the ground, things could only get worse. Aris's voice, quiet and rough, broke into his thoughts.

"There's only going to be one chance to rid my world of Sebek, and I'm going to take it."

Jack's memory slid off without his conscious will again, and he was there at Daniel's deathbed, beside Daniel's bleeding body, asking Jacob to let Daniel go. He allowed the memory to play out, then tucked it away where it belonged, in that place where he kept these things, stuffed down as deep as he could manage, so deep it barely existed anymore. He didn't quite trust his own voice, but the words came out without a hitch. "When the time comes, I'll be the one to do it."

Aris nodded once, the acknowledgment of an agreement made. "When the time comes, if you don't, I will."

There was no answer to that, so Jack closed his eyes and made his mind a blank. It wasn't hard; he wasn't processing information well.

"He's coming around," Aris said.

As if in response to Aris's prompt, Daniel stirred. His lips moved, and words whispered out in languages unfamiliar to Jack. Abruptly Daniel sat straight up, then turned his head to stare at Jack first, then Aris.

When he spoke, all pretense of being Daniel was gone, and it was Sebek's imperious anger. "How dare you injure us?"

"You're not hurt," Aris said tiredly, and Jack felt a tiny – barely there – twinge of sympathy for him. "So get up and let's go."

"You do not give us orders," Sebek said and lifted his hand. The ribbon device flashed golden in the dim light. "Or we will remind you of your place."

One corner of Aris's mouth quirked up in a smile. To Jack, he said, "That one works on me. For future reference."

"Good to know," Jack said, ignoring the muted growl from Daniel's throat.

Sebek got to his feet slowly and folded his arms across his chest. "We do not wish to delay further. On your feet."

Jack rose, though his body protested the loss of the nice hard ground to rest on. Aris stood up beside him.

"You first," Aris said.

Jack pulled out the flashlight and clicked it on, then got moving, passing Sebek without looking at him.

"I really have no idea where I'm going, you know," Jack said. He stood at the juncture of two passageways and thought he might as well flip a coin; they were probably going to die in here, lost and starving to death, and that was *such* a pleasant thought.

Sebek's hand landed on his shoulder. "To the right," he ordered. Jack didn't bother to ask why or if he was sure; it didn't matter anyway, at this point.

When they rounded the corner, Jack allowed the flashlight to strike the edge of the wall. A fine chip appeared and dust silted down to the ground.

Not exactly bread crumbs, but it would have to do.

# CHAPTER THIRTEEN

It was singing that drew Sam from sleep. At first it sounded like a nursery rhyme she remembered from school, maybe, something she chanted while jumping rope. *Apples, peaches, pears and plums. Jump right out when your birthday comes. January, February*...But the words were all wrong, even if the rhythm was right. She peered into the darkness, straightening her neck and wincing at the crackle inside. It was night now, rain still pattering on the tarp over the lattice. Beside her, Teal'c was upright in his half-lotus. His eyes were pricked with light from the little stove as they met hers and then slid away. The room was, if anything, more crowded now; she could still feel the shift and press of at least a dozen of Brenneka's kinsmen, a couple standing near the drifting plastic over the entrance, the others kneeling on the mosaic floor. Sometimes wavering and sometimes solid against the dim glow from the fire, their outlines swayed slightly in time with the barely vocalized chant. Closest to the fire, facing them all, Brenneka knelt, bowed over her clasped hands, Aadi close beside her. As if feeling Sam's gaze on him, Aadi lifted his head and returned her stare. She couldn't see what expression his face held. The firelight glowed through his spiky hair and made him seem like a lit match next to Hamel's hunched and crooked form, his own fire long burned out.

"Some army," Sam muttered as she pressed her hands to the floor and hitched herself up straighter against the wall.

"Indeed," Teal'c answered. His voice thrummed just above a whisper. "A boy and an old man."

"And a concussed Major and a wounded Jaffa. Don't forget that."

She could make out the tiny shift of shadows around his mouth that indicated an ironic smile. "No. I have not forgotten."

"And a man on the inside," she added. Unless the Colonel was dead. Calculating assets without proper intel was a pain in the ass. She stopped gingerly probing her black eye with the tips of her fingers. "Wait a minute. A boy?"

Teal'c nodded toward the circle of singers. "Aadi has agreed to assist us."

"Why?"

"He wishes to help his father."

"Isn't he kind of young?" Sam cast Aadi a glance. He was still watching them.

"I began my training at a younger age," Teal'c answered. "As did my son, once he was freed from servitude."

Sam shifted uncomfortably. Aadi bowed low and leaned back to perform that gesture with the rest of them, an opening of his grubby, clasped hands as if he were setting free a bird. "He's a kid."

"This is war. There is no time for innocence."

"That doesn't make it okay."

"No, it does not." Teal'c inclined his head in sad acceptance.

Their prayers ended, the men rose stiffly to their feet. A couple of them slipped out through the plastic and into the rain. A few shuffled for position a little closer to the fire, hands held toward the heat, while the less lucky hunkered down again inside their long shirts and waited their turn. Here and there, Sam caught the cool gleam of *roshna* packets. The two who had left returned with stacked bowls of water – rainwater, Sam guessed, and grimaced to think what was washed out of the roiling air along with it – and the bowls made their circuit around the room. Once those present had emptied their packets into them and swallowed the contents, the room lapsed into a dull stillness, the bodies relaxed without much release of tension or pain. Sam was keenly conscious of her own muscles twisted tourniquet-tight around her bones. She leaned her head left then right, listening to the snap, crackle, pop. If Teal'c was good to go, then they had to go before her tendons snapped her neck in half.

As if hearing her body's protests, Hamel craned his neck to look at her, then rose and weaved his way around the gathered bodies. With a sigh, he dropped to the floor beside her. He leaned his balding head back against the brick and closed his eyes. His lean face was slack with exhaustion and deeply shadowed in the shifting light. Sam couldn't tell how old he was; he moved like an old man, but a life of hard labor could have aged him well beyond his years. She thought of her father and couldn't help wondering if Jacob knew she was missing.

Teal'c didn't bother to hide the appraisal in his eyes as he studied Hamel, the senior member of their army. Sam wanted to think of Hamel as the older man, but it was unlikely any of these people were older than Teal'c. She watched him tilt his head attentively toward Hamel and realized that maybe the years would start to weigh on him like they did on the rest of them, now that he didn't have a symbiote to slow his aging process. Unless his genetic makeup was sufficiently modified for longevity – but that seemed a little too generous on the part of the Goa'uld. She thought of Apophis and his host dying in the SGC, thousands of years catching up with the body in hours. Teal'c looked the same as he always did. What did a century of life feel like? Hamel looked like he'd know.

"To whom do you pray?" Teal'c asked him.

Hamel offered a wry smile while he considered the question. "Don't worry. Not to that worm, Sebek." He made a small, sharp gesture with his fingers as if he were squashing a bug. The men within earshot did the same. "No, we remember the Nitori. Give thanks."

Teal'c regarded him in silence for a moment, then said, "You have little to give thanks for."

This time, the smile became a low chuckle. "We have this world. It's not all ugly, you know." He waved his hand vaguely toward some distant place. Sam wondered if he'd ever seen it himself, and if he ever would. "We have today. Maybe, if things go our way, we even have tomorrow." He eyed Teal'c a little critically. "You were a slave. You should know what a gift that is."

"I have since learned to hope for more."

"Well," Hamel said, pulling his scrawny legs up inside his shirt, "maybe you can teach us that, too."

Sam leaned forward and looped her arms over her knees. "We have to get moving. It's already been too long. How many of your people can you count on?

It took longer for Hamel to calculate his answer than the final sum seemed to warrant. "Me. Aadi. One or two others here and maybe a few more in the mine." When Sam sighed and dropped her head for a moment onto her arms, he added, "And more, if Brenneka can be convinced.

"How many more?"

"Hard to say for sure, but maybe a hundred, if word spreads. *If* Brenneka can be convinced," he repeated, although he didn't look too optimistic.

Sam's frustration came out in her voice, and she had to remind herself to speak softly. "This is what I don't get. She talks about standing up to the Goa'uld, but she won't help us do that. We have a better chance together than apart."

Hamel picked at the tiles with broken nails. "She believes her brother will take care of Sebek, bring back the gift the Nitori left us. She won't act until she knows that she can win. She doesn't want our victory to be tainted by the interference of offworlders." He flicked a bit of grout from his fingers and watched Brenneka gathering the bowls, stopping as she did to speak to each man still hunkered down on the floor. One by one they nodded and made that gesture again, a bird escaping. Aadi followed close behind, taking the bowls from her and carrying them in a wobbling stack he kept upright by bracing it with his chin. When she passed to the far end of the room, Hamel went on. "She and others in the Order believe that the Nitori will come back to us when we are worthy of their attention. This is a test of our will and our faith."

Teal'c met Sam's eyes. She answered his unvoiced question with a shake of her head, and his mouth thinned to a disapproving line.

"Do you believe that?" Sam asked.

In his lap, Hamel's hands made the reverential gesture. "I'm a pragmatist," he answered at last. "I'm not above inviting a friendly god to supper. Especially if he's bringing the food. But I'm not going to sit and starve while I wait." He shrugged. "It's not much of a faith, but it's better than no faith at all." His grin showed a mouthful of blackened teeth. "Some pray and wait for grace. I say, pray while you're running, meet the god on the road."

Sam had to agree, but Hamel didn't look like he was up for much running. "What would convince her?" she asked with a nod toward Brenneka, who was now in conference with Esa by the door.

"A sky full of Nitori, each one bringing a whirlwind and lightning."

The rain intensified and hissed against the tarp and the cobblestones outside. No lightning, though. Sam considered their options, making sure to avoid Teal'c's eyes. She knew what his response would be. With a curt nod to herself, she walked her hands up the wall until she was upright and steady, then stepped over the sprawled men, carefully making her way toward Brenneka. They needed more than an old man and a kid. They could probably sneak into the mine with a small party. But if it came down to a fight, they needed Brenneka's army of believers.

Brenneka nodded at her approach and said, "Esa has returned from the mine. Sebek and your friend and my brother have entered the vault. But the Jaffa were prevented from entering with them." She did Sam the favor of not smiling, but her pale eyes glittered with anticipated triumph. "It won't be long now."

"Until Aris kills Daniel," Sam finished for her. It was impossible for her to keep her voice down now.

"Until he kills Sebek. Your friend is already dead."

"We know that's not true. We know the host survives. If we go now, if you help us, we can stop this. We can stop Sebek, and we can get to whatever's hidden in that mountain. We can do it together."

"And you will take the gift and keep it for yourselves."

"No. *No.*" Sam counted to five, mastering her temper. It was time to *do* something. It could already be too late. There was no way the Colonel would let Aris do that to Daniel. No way. The thought of the Colonel having to kill Daniel himself with nobody there to share the burden of it made her brain white out with static. This time she had to count all the way to ten before she had her frustration tamped down again. Firmly, but calmly, she met Brenneka's eyes with all the sincerity she could muster. "That's not how it works. It's not how *we* work. Please, Brenneka."

The small woman shook her head brusquely and tried to push past her.

"I've seen the Nitori," Sam blurted. "Your gods."

That worked. Brenneka stopped and turned slowly to look at her. In fact, everyone in the room was looking at her. Including Teal'c, who didn't look happy at all.

Brenneka's expression didn't change. She watched Sam suspiciously, her arms wrapped around her body as though she'd suddenly gotten colder. "You said you didn't know the Nitori."

"Well, not as Nitori, no. We call them the Ancients." Sucking in a bracing breath, Sam kept her eyes on Brenneka's. On the other side of the room, Teal'c was on his feet. "And Daniel's one of them."

It took a long time for Brenneka to decide what to do with her face. She settled on indignation. "*We* are the people of the Nitori," she hissed.

Behind her, the room was starting to buzz, the sprawled men sitting up and whispering to each other. That curse made a ripple through the room, but Sam noticed that not all of the men took it up.

"Yes, of course you are," Sam answered, letting her gaze slip significantly to the crowd before meeting Brenneka's again. "But it's a big universe, and the Nitori got around. You aren't the only ones, Brenneka." She pointed behind her in the general direction of the mine. "And if you let Aris kill Daniel, you'll be killing—"

"Major Carter," Teal'c interrupted from the far side of the room, but Sam aimed a warning look at him and hurried on.

"You said that you were taught how to build the ships by someone…the Inspired. And that person was absorbed by the Nitori."

Another flutter of voices in the room, heads bowing briefly over clasped hands.

"It was a gift," Brenneka said, her voice hard, but brittle.

"Well, that same thing happened to Daniel. They call it ascension." Struck by a realization, Sam came forward and started to move the gathered people aside, ushering and urging them toward the edges of the room until there was an open space of floor, only Brenneka still standing there alone amid the swirling colors of the broken tile mosaic. Sam pointed at their feet. It wasn't an image of waves like she'd first thought. "See? I know this." With her toe, she traced the tendrils of white on their background of blue. "This is the Nitori. This is what Daniel looked like when he left us." Her voice catching on the last words, she blinked back sudden tears. God, she was tired. "And you said there was a cache of knowledge that was left and the Inspired took it all in. That's what happened to the Colonel, years ago. He learned all that the Ancients, the Nitori, knew. He learned enough to go to another *galaxy*."

Holding up both hands, Brenneka turned her head away as though from the burning heat of a house fire. Around them, the kinsmen were silent and perfectly still.

Sam pressed on. "There was a device at a special meeting place. It reached out and grabbed the Colonel by the head and there were lights—"

"And the Nitori enfolded him, and the lights filled him and when he spoke the world changed—" It was Hamel, coming forward, nodding.

"—and the people changed and—" another man said, his voice wavering, fearful, faltering before another picked up the almost-song.

"—the universe opened like a flower and—"

"—the people were like seeds blowing in the dark sky—"

"You lie," Brenneka said flatly, with the same common sense conviction she'd use to say that the rain was falling.

"Why do you think Sebek wanted Daniel, specifically Daniel? There are lots of people in this galaxy who could eventually crack that message on the door. It's because of what Daniel wa— What Daniel is, what the Colonel is. What they know." Sam was right next to Brenneka now, using her greater height, looming over the woman. Her back was prickling with the intensity of the attention on her, and her gut was twisting with distaste for what she was about to do. "If you let Daniel and the Colonel die, you'll be killing the closest link you have to your gods. How worthy will you be then?"

When she glanced over Brenneka's head, she found Teal'c on the edge of the crowd, and his face was stone.

Daniel was beginning to understand: isolate the pathways, sneak through the nervous system into the framework of his body as if it were a spider's web of conduits, and find the place where action was needed. This was why, for the past half hour, he'd been twitching his little finger. Not much, just a fraction of an inch. Barely any energy was required to make the connections, and Sebek was preoccupied with the maze and the path they were walking.

So far, Sebek hadn't noticed.

His finger twitched, twitched, and Daniel curled up at the back of his own body, waiting for another chance to drive. Now that he knew he could do it, he only had to wait for the chance to shift forward and exert control.

Everything was trial and error, experiments performed on a wisp of hope that Sebek wouldn't discover his intentions and turn on him. The torture Sebek inflicted on him for failure to comply was like acid in his brain, seeping through his thoughts and shorting him out, until Daniel wasn't a coherent presence anymore. When Sebek punished him, Daniel became a mass of disorganized impulses, misfiring. He knew that sensation, a weightless fear, as if he were falling up, uncontained by gravity.

He was getting the hang of drawing a curtain between his memories and Sebek's insistent probes. As long as Sebek didn't seek specific information, Daniel could keep his thoughts neutral, shrunk down like blips on the radar, appearing and disappearing before Sebek could be distracted into paying attention to them.

Twitch, twitch. The hand his finger was attached to began to tremble, the muscles spasming – not his doing, not his control. He felt the weakness seize his body and shake it, throwing Sebek back and Daniel forward, and he gasped, unprepared for the sensation of boundaries collapsing. All he needed was a few more minutes, and he would find a way to convince Jack. There had to be a way, but he didn't dare think about it too closely, for fear Sebek would steal any workable idea from him and use it to trick Jack. Sebek pressed, twisted inside him, and Daniel retreated ahead of the wave of mind-shattering fire. This time, when he gasped, it wasn't audible.

The barriers between them were beginning to fall and rise without warning, like a wave cresting, then collapsing back down to the dark water, only to repeat again moments later. If only he could figure out how to be on top of the wave. He *had* to get himself in position to seize the chances. Sebek was weakening; Daniel was sure of it now. The Goa'uld's control of Daniel was taking all Daniel's strength, and the aching palsy of his muscles was only a symptom of it. His eyesight was getting worse in increments large enough for Daniel to perceive, like the changing of a lens over his eye. He knew, though he wasn't sure how, that Sebek could not heal his eyes. He needed his glasses, but they'd come too far to go back for them now – another thing Daniel could use to his advantage, provided he wasn't blind by the time he had a chance to strike.

Vividly and without warning, the image of Sha're flashed through his thoughts, a burst of light that brought with it the heat of her body and the fresh-scrubbed soap scent of her skin. This must have been what it was like for her, trying to reach him – to thrash and push against invisible bonds, working all the time, from within, fighting for moments of dominance, every thread of information she gave to him, in the last seconds of her life. He shuddered under the weight of her memory, and Sebek staggered, knocked off balance by Daniel's attempt to bury the thought of his dead wife. Instantly he turned inward to see what Daniel was hiding, crashing through all the futile roadblocks until he had all of the memory: all the things that hadn't been true, all the cues and clues, dissolving into the sight of her pale, dead face inches from his own. Sebek's satisfaction was clear as he discarded the image as unnecessary, and Daniel let himself see Sha're as she had been, so beautiful, before she'd been taken as a host. He could hear her voice, soothing him, before he locked the image away.

Ahead of Sebek in the passageway, Jack was walking slowly. In the dim light, Daniel could make out the fuzzy lines of his torso, but Aris was nowhere to be seen. Daniel couldn't tell where the bounty hunter was, because he didn't have access to all his senses, but he thought Aris must have been behind them all along. Daniel was able to sense things Sebek was shielding from him, a dull, distant perception, like sound dampened by cotton. Frustration seeped through, and a simmering anger, something Daniel interpreted as hatred of Jack, of Daniel, of his own weakness. He shied back away from those thoughts and watched Jack as well as he was able.

At each turn, Jack stopped, then chose a direction. It looked as though he had no idea where he was going, and Daniel had no way to help. Even if Sebek had allowed him that much control, at this juncture Sebek wasn't interested in knowing any more about the walls or the writing or the secrets at the heart of...wherever this was. He only wanted to *arrive*. Jack was moving only because he had to bide his time. Daniel had no idea what had happened to Sam and Teal'c, and he knew it was on Jack's mind as well.

Jack slowed at the corner, as he had at every other corner. He rounded too close to the wall and his flashlight crashed gently into the wall, gashing the edges. The dent obliterated a panel of glyphs, slashing across them like an eraser. Daniel would have snapped at Jack to be careful, since they didn't know what they might need to make their way out again, but he had no voice to do so. Still, the thought ran through his mind.

Too late, he realized that his concern was loud enough to be felt by Sebek, who lifted Daniel's hand. In an instant, the flow of naqua-dah in Daniel's blood burned and ignited, coalescing at the point of power in the palm of Daniel's hand, and he watched helplessly as the energy burst from the hand device, hit Jack squarely in the back and sent him sprawling to the ground, still and quiet. Daniel's outrage was a small, silent thing in the back of Sebek's consciousness, and Sebek squashed Daniel's protest that they needed Jack, that it wouldn't do any good to harm him now. "Get up, human," Sebek said coldly, without bothering to inform Jack what his transgression had been.

Sebek glanced at the damaged wall, and Daniel replayed the scene in his mind's eye: Jack's hand, moving, striking – he'd seen Jack do this, or a version of it, a hundred times, a dozen different ways of leaving a trail for himself to follow, or a trail to lead others to him. He'd shown Daniel how, in his first year on the team, and told him that it was always crucial he leave a trail if he was captured. Daniel had *done it*, more than once.

*Sebek mustn't know*.

Daniel tried to forget the realization, erase it from the places in his mind where Sebek was always watching, but too late; it was impossible to remember every moment that his fleeting thoughts could be so easily captured by Sebek. He stared at Jack, who was pushing up slowly from the ground as if he was tired.

"So," Sebek said, with a trace of harsh glee. "You formed a plan of escape. You could not truly be so stupid as to believe we would not discover it."

Jack's eyes narrowed; Daniel had the impulse to squint, to see more clearly, but he wasn't able to control his body. Jack raised his hands in a mock gesture of supplication. "You caught me," he said, still staring at Sebek with contempt clear in his expression. "Good for you."

"We will not tolerate insolence," Sebek growled, and Jack snorted.

"Oh, there's that word. Insolence." His face scrunched, as if he smelled something foul, and then he said, "If you weren't running around in Daniel's head, you would never have figured it out. You're not too bright, for a snake."

Sebek's impulse was immediate. He raised Daniel's hand, but something stopped him – the image of the former host, ravaged and burned out, seared across Daniel's mind, leaving a scar – *fear* – behind it. As much as it made Daniel cringe to do it, he summoned up the same image Sebek used to torment him: Jack saying *no* as the snake burrowed into his neck, and then Sebek's remembered satisfaction at the sensation of bringing a new, strong host under his control. Sebek lowered his hand.

"If you attempt any other tricks, we will kill you where you stand."

Daniel barely contained his relief before it rippled out across Sebek's attention.

Jack regarded Sebek for a long moment. His gaze shifted to Aris, who was standing where Daniel couldn't see his face, then back to Sebek. "Listen," he said. "Do you have some kind of plan? Or are we going to wander around in here until we starve to death? Because we are getting nowhere."

The Goa'uld tilted his head to look at Jack, and suddenly he was pushing and clawing his way through Daniel's thoughts again, raking out the pieces he'd examined before. Daniel let him have them without a fight. There was no point; he could take all that, and more besides, and Daniel still wouldn't know how to read the walls. After a moment, Sebek said, "We will continue until we reach an end."

"Fabulous plan," Jack said. His eyes were dark, and there were bruised-looking circles beneath. "But what if I won't keep walking?"

"Oh, you will," Aris said. Jack glanced back at him, and something shifted in his expression, so subtle that Daniel almost didn't catch it. His jaw tightened, and he looked back at Sebek, into his eyes. For a moment, Daniel felt as though Jack could see through Sebek, down to where Daniel was locked away. Then Jack turned and stretched, easing tired muscles. He rested a hand on the wall, above the gash.

The wall turned to light beneath his touch.

All the glyphs within three feet of them were ablaze, patterns of cool white and yellow fading back and forth across the dark background of stone. Jack jerked his hand away and stared at it. "Huh," he said, and looked down at his hand, as if it were a foreign appendage.

"Why have you concealed this from us?" Sebek said, furious, but Daniel was watching the play of illumination over the symbols. If he could discern some kind of pattern...

"I haven't concealed anything," Jack was saying. "Well, okay – I was hiding something, but not *this*." Daniel knew it was true. He'd seen Jack touching the walls on and off throughout this entire nightmare, and nothing had activated because of it, until now. But why now? The technology here wasn't Ancient; it was something quite different. Shallow golden light fanned across Jack's face, then across Daniel and Aris. Sebek turned to it, entranced by the possibilities of what it might signify, but he didn't interfere with Daniel's examination of the text.

"Whoa," Jack said. Sebek gave him a cursory glance, in time for Daniel to see Jack raise his hands to his face to press the heels of his hands against his closed eyes.

*White light, and the illusory face of Oma Desala. Grief. Peace. Resignation. Sam, crying; Jack, watching him with haunted eyes. A sense that beyond what he could understand and perceive, there was knowledge waiting for him. A chance to do good.*

Sebek slapped at Daniel's head, keening a sharp cry as the memory ripped through Daniel's consciousness: Daniel's thoughts at the moment of his ascension – moments he hadn't dwelled on, because he couldn't bear to think of them. Sebek thrashed within Daniel's body, and Daniel felt them falling, felt the jolt to his knees as they landed on the hard ground. Violent nausea welled within him, and confusion – Sebek's confusion. Daniel wanted to take control, but he was lost, swimming among the glittering fragments of his life. There was no air, nothing to breathe, or maybe it just felt that way. Daniel's chest felt crushed, and Sebek's shrill wail filled his head until he could hear nothing else.

Slowly, the onslaught of memory eased away. Sebek retched, his misery apparent. Daniel had a moment of vicious satisfaction. So much for Goa'uld healing, in this place. He watched Aris dragging Jack upright, saw them exchange words, but he couldn't make them out. Sebek lifted Daniel's body and got to his feet, turning his attention back to the wall. The bright fire behind the symbols had faded, and now glowed like banked-down coals. Sebek took a step forward, then another, with Daniel's hand outstretched. Daniel could feel the pull of the thing, the compulsion to touch it.

*No*, Daniel thought, as loudly as he could, and Sebek jerked his hand back. Daniel communicated to Sebek that he mustn't touch it, no matter what. No time to worry about helping Sebek do whatever he planned to do, at the end of this. Right now he was only concerned with making sure no one did anything stupid. He wanted to speak to Jack, tell him not to touch the wall again under any circumstances, but Sebek's calculated strategy didn't include warnings for Jack. He moved closer to the wall, not touching it, but tracing the lines of the symbols with his gaze. Daniel could feel it, too. They were close to understanding…something.

Sebek looked at Jack, and then back at the wall, and he used Daniel's mouth to smile. Daniel knew then. Jack was not the guide.

Jack was the guinea pig, the test dummy. Daniel knew that Jack would be used, one way or the other.

When he surged forward, wrestling for a moment's control, Sebek crushed him back, strangling his thoughts into silence.

# CHAPTER FOURTEEN

Hammond was beginning to think that if the mess sergeant could mix up a vat of coffee large enough, he might as well bathe in it and get it over with, since coffee seemed to be coming out of his pores. It was par for the course, but the stress of the search for SG-1 was beginning to tell on him, which was undoubtedly why Janet Fraiser had attached herself to him early that morning. Wherever he went, she seemed to pop up, bright and cheerful, urging him to eat, to sleep, and to rest – completely without subtlety. Hammond knew a lost cause when he saw it, which was how he'd ended up in the commissary, putting back a sandwich and some coleslaw as if he was actually enjoying it.

Janet passed by on her way out the door and eyeballed his coffee. "You really should cut back on that, sir."

"Yes, I should," he said, and pulled his cup a little closer, in case she had any ideas of saving him from himself and tried to kidnap his caffeine. She shook her head at him sadly, a promise of much lecturing to come.

"Mind if I join you?" Hammond looked up to see Jacob, tray in hand.

"Have a seat," Hammond offered. "But watch out for rampaging doctors." Jacob smiled in the direction of Fraiser's retreating figure and set his tray down on the table. Hammond pointed at the greenery all over Jacob's plate. "Not even a cup of coffee to wash that down?"

"Not that I didn't want some, but Selmak revoked my free pass," Jacob said. "At least if I sit with you, I can smell it. That'll have to do." He sat down and leaned closer, as if to take a whiff of Hammond's cup. "I came down to tell you that there's word from some of our outlying operatives. Aris Boch has been sniffing around on a number of the bigger Goa'uld trade worlds, trying to get information about SG-1's recent missions. We're fairly sure he was trying to track them down."

Hammond set down his mug. He'd been expecting the Tok'ra to stop cooperating after his square-down with Malek – not that Jacob would refuse help deliberately, but he wasn't the one with control of the information flow. "Do they know where he may have taken them?"

"Yes and no. Yes, in that they know where SG-1 isn't, but no, in that they haven't narrowed it down to where they are. Yet." Jacob picked at his salad for a moment, pushing it around his plate without taking a bite. "I can give you some educated guesses, though, if you're interested in speculation."

"You know I am."

"If it really is Aris Boch who has them, I'd say he probably took them to his homeworld, but we haven't been able to get confirmation. We don't have any operatives on that world – the Goa'uld running things there, Sebek, isn't much of a power broker, so we don't have time for him."

"Any Jaffa operating on the inside?"

"We're having some trouble getting concrete information out of the fifth column as well. They appear to be having some of the same issues we are, with security and trust. In their case, it's trust of the Tok'ra." Jacob took one bite of his salad, then said, "If you have any contacts among the Jaffa, you might want to try them."

"We already did." When Jacob gave him a wry smile, the one that said Jacob had expected as much, Hammond smiled back. "You didn't think I'd sit on my hands and put my faith in Malek, did you?"

"I should hope not."

Hammond shook his head. "They had nothing. Even less than your people did. Most of them are buried so deep within the ranks of the Goa'uld they serve that they don't see or hear much of any use."

"Well, it was worth a try." Jacob glanced wistfully at Hammond's cup, then sighed and said, "Sebek works for Yu, and though Yu's never been especially interested in SG-1, that could change, given the current climate among the System Lords. They're paranoid, and it's hard to predict what they'll do."

"SG-1 would make a good bargaining chip," Hammond said. "Even if Yu doesn't care about them personally, he might have something in mind. A trade."

"He's certainly not above it, but it doesn't seem like his style. And Boch has been keeping a low profile lately; it's only because of the questions that we caught his trace. People remember questions about the Tauri."

"Lucky for us," Hammond said. Luck was, in fact, the only thing sustaining his hope that they might find SG-1 alive somewhere.

"You should know that according to our operative on Yu's mothership, he's on his way to Sebek's homeworld, Atropos, at full steam." Jacob set his fork down and pushed his tray away. "So whatever we're going to do, we'd better do it fast."

Hammond sat back in his chair; he'd already been ticking off options. But it couldn't hurt to have a sounding board, and Jacob knew their resources well enough to be of help. "Can we 'gate to Atropos?"

"Maybe. There's a 'gate there, but last time I had accurate intelligence, it was in Sebek's palace and heavily guarded."

"Too much risk to send a MALP or a UAV, then."

"It'll only tip them off that we're nosing around."

Hammond nodded. Without a MALP, he couldn't risk sending any personnel. Four people was an acceptable threshold of loss to the program, no matter who those people were, but he wasn't about to risk additional lives unless he knew there was a chance of success. Frustrated, he scrubbed a hand over his face. "We're running a little short on solutions, Jacob." Hammond tossed back more of his coffee, then said, "Give me something, here. Anything I can work with."

Jacob sighed. "Listen, George. I'm going to lay it on the line. I can get a ship and go after them, but I don't know anything about that planet or where Boch might be holding them. When you consider I've also got Malek nipping at my heels like a pit bull, things get a little tricky."

Hammond looked at him steadily. They'd been friends far too long to play games. If Jacob was going to offer help, he'd do it without beating around the bush, but he seemed reluctant. At that moment, Jacob lowered his head and closed his eyes, and when he looked up, Hammond knew without hearing him speak that Selmak was in control. No matter how many times he saw it happen, it still raised the hair on his arms.

"General Hammond. You are an honorable man with much political experience, and I do not think I need to describe for you the danger of defying the Tok'ra Council. What Jacob is considering is dangerous for us, and for you. Malek will insist that he be allowed to come along, and so we must convince him to assist in a recovery rather than an assassination."

"What do you suggest, then?" Hammond asked.

"We have no choice but to proceed. If we do not act, SG-1 will be lost. However, I must caution you that Malek's agenda seems clear and certain, and if we fail to dissuade him from the course he has been set upon, he will carry out his plan."

"I'm not going to give my sanction for it," Hammond said, eyes narrowed.

"Practicality, General. This is the risk you will take if we proceed. Is this risk acceptable to you?"

"If you don't go, they die. So, yes." Hammond felt as though he'd been shoved over a barrel. Not Selmak's fault, or Jacob's either. Not even Malek was to blame. Hammond had participated in his share of dubious acts to ensure an operation's security, and he understood even if he didn't like it one damn bit.

Selmak bowed his head, and as soon as he raised it again Jacob said, "Okay, then. We go. I'll talk to Malek."

"Now's your chance," Hammond said. He nodded at the doorway, where Malek stood, looking uncomfortable as he surveyed the crowded room.

"Selmak has had a lot of practice dealing with stubborn Tok'ra," Jacob said under his breath, as Malek approached their table and inclined his head in greeting. "It'll be all right."

"General Hammond," Malek said, with barely a glance at Jacob, "I wish to apologize for any offense I have given. I did not mean to be disagreeable."

"I understand," Hammond said, and though he meant it, the words came out a little harsher than intended. He gestured to the third chair at the table, without making an overt invitation. Malek looked as though he'd much rather leave, but he pulled out the chair and sat down on the edge of it.

"The Tok'ra's numbers continue to dwindle, General. It falls to those of us to remain to preserve our brethren in any way necessary, so that we may continue the resistance that benefits your people, and mine. It sometimes causes me to be…" Malek paused, shifted his glance to Jacob, then back to Hammond. "Somewhat hasty in my judgment."

"We all have those moments, from time to time." Hammond watched Malek's stiff nod and wondered if Malek had been directed to play nice by the Council, or if he had experienced some sort of perspective shift. It could be either, but it didn't matter; he had settled the issue as much as possible with Jacob and Selmak, and soon it would be up to them.

"I've offered George our help," Jacob said, his direct gaze fixed on Malek. "We should leave as soon as possible; we'll need to gate to P32-119 and pick up some transportation."

"I will not say it is a fool's errand, but you understand I believe we have little chance of assisting your people," Malek said quietly.

"I do," Hammond said, and left it at that.

Malek stood up, waiting for a moment for Jacob to follow. "I will meet you in the embarkation room," Malek said, and took Jacob's half-smile as an answer.

When Malek was gone, Jacob reached over and sneaked a sip Hammond's lukewarm coffee. "This is going to be a long trip," he said, by way of apology. Hammond couldn't tell if it was directed at him or at Selmak.

Sam stared down at the driving rain on the cobblestones and hunched her shoulders against the wind that whipped down the alleyway, blowing greasy water sideways into the meager shelter of the overhanging tarp. Above the wall on the other side of the alley, the clouds glowed red with the *ha'tak*'s reflected light, the towering remains of the Ancient ship slicing up into it like a faintly gleaming talon. Over the sound of the storm, she could hear the growing whine of a death glider doing its sweep over the city and instinctively she drew back further into the shadows, coming up against Teal'c's solid presence.

"I didn't lie," she said at last.

"Only by omission."

"My call."

She had already let him off the hook – she was taking the rap for this one – but he wouldn't let it go. She'd known he wouldn't.

"You would use their faith against them. Let them trade one false god for another."

She tilted her head back to stare up at the Ancient tower. What part of the ship was that? Communications? Command deck? Something she couldn't imagine, probably. "Maybe," she sighed, and closed her eyes. In her head she could hear the Colonel's voice. *You say false god. I say potahto.* "I don't know. The Ancients can seem pretty godlike."

"They appear to have abandoned these people. And in any case the writing on the door in the mine is not an invitation. It may be irresponsible to allow them to persist in their misunderstanding."

She let the white noise of falling rain soothe the throbbing behind her eyes. What people hasn't felt abandoned by its God? She squared her shoulders. This wasn't the time for metaphysics, even though a part of her brain reminded her that this wasn't a metaphysical argument at all. It was plain old human politics. Manipulation. Maneuvering. Tactics. She turned to Teal'c. "So, what? I'm supposed to let them kill Daniel and probably the Colonel, too, in the process?"

In the dim light from the Goa'uld ship, she could see his features soften for a moment and then resume that stony determination she knew well. "It is likely that Daniel Jackson will be killed in any case. Aris Boch—"

"*It's not his place.*" She surprised even herself with the vehemence in her voice. When he made no reply, she jerked her chin toward the door. "Go get Hamel and whoever else will come. *Not*

Aadi. It's time to move."

Teal'c hesitated, the argument unfinished, but did her the favor of obeying without comment.

"My call," she repeated to the rain.

Once he was gone and the plastic had settled again behind him, she allowed herself thirty carefully measured seconds to listen to the rain with her eyes closed, to let it sheet across her mind. But even thirty seconds seemed too long now. Too much waiting. When she opened her eyes, the Ancient tower pointed up at the clouds and, somewhere behind them, the stars. It was time to get off this damn planet.

She ducked through the door, her nose wrinkling at the acrid, sooty bite of smoke and the heavy-sweet smell of unwashed bodies. No one turned to look at her, though. They were all watching Brenneka, still standing where she had been in the middle of the room, planted at the center of the swirling mosaic body of the Nitori. At her feet, Aadi lay sprawled in the curling embrace of the glass Ancient, his hand cupping his cheek, his eyes blazing.

"They *lie*," Brenneka hissed at him, the force of her anger making her bend toward him, lashing out like a snake.

Aadi recoiled but didn't scramble away from her. "It doesn't matter!" he shouted back, his voice was thick with unshed tears. "He's *my* father and I'll—"

"They'll kill him to save their friend!"

Sam shouldered her way through the people by the door. "That's not true." This time, she didn't bother to hide her exasperation and her anger, but she saved at least some of it for herself. She nodded at Teal'c, who started to make his way toward her, keeping to the walls. No one, it seemed, wanted to get too close to Brenneka.

"Bren—" Hamel interjected from somewhere on the far side of the room.

Brenneka speared the old man with a furious gaze.

"What if they aren't lying?" Hamel came forward, then bent to heave Aadi to his feet by the collar of his shirt. "If the offworlders are the Inspired—"

"*We* are the chosen of the Nitori," Brenneka insisted. Sam

flinched inwardly a little to see the disappointment and the denial struggling in her. "They will take what is ours. And if you help them steal our gift, the Nitori will—"

"What?" Hamel waved a bony hand at the scarecrows gathered in the room, the broken city outside. "Punish us? Leave us?" His laugh was ironic and bitter. "What if the Nitori have already done something, Brenneka? What if these offworlders are the gift?" A murmur of agitation rippled through the gathered men. After smoothing Aadi's shirt and patting him gently on the side of the face, he raised his eyes to Sam's, then turned to meet Brenneka's sparking resistance. "Maybe it really doesn't matter whose story is right. We can help Aris. And if they can get their man back, isn't that a worthy thing? He doesn't have to die, their Colonel, and weigh us down with his death. The other—" He shrugged. "If he is what she says he is, he'll do for himself. And if he is what he says he is, maybe he'll do for us, too."

Sam ignored Teal'c's low, dissenting grunt as he came to stand behind her.

Brenneka's fists opened and closed at her sides, once, twice, before she looked down at the tendrils of light captured in glass at her feet. "Do what you want," she said finally. "I believe in my brother. Sebek will die." Shooting Sam a venomous look, she made that small, snapping gesture again. Most of the gathered men made it with her, but a few looked anywhere but at her, their hands hanging still by their sides or tucked up inside their sleeves. Sam was more than a little surprised to see that Esa was one of the latter. Apparently, Brenneka was surprised, too, because her face fell as Esa looked at his feet.

"We have to go. Now," Sam announced. "We'll take anyone who wants to help." When Aadi stepped forward, she aimed a finger at his chest. "Except you." Predictably, Aadi opened his mouth to protest, but she cut him off. "You're a kid, and a liability. No time to baby-sit." Gathering Teal'c and Hamel up with a sweep of her gaze around the room, she ordered, "Let's move out," and left before Aadi could say any more.

In the alleyway, Sam hunched inside her jacket and counted the men as they filed out after her. In addition to Teal'c and Hamel, there were four others, two about Hamel's age and two who were much younger. In the swinging circle of Hamel's lantern, she could see that one of the younger ones had only one eye. Terrific. This was going to be a disaster.

Hamel must have seen it in her face because he raised the lamp higher and inspected the little group. "They know the city and the mine. They know the Jaffa. There's more to war than fighting."

True, except that there was fighting, too. Still, they needed someone to watch their backs, and these guys could shout a warning as well as anyone. And it didn't take a lot of strength to fire a *zat*. Maybe, if things went well and they could do this by stealth, even that wouldn't be needed.

"Thank you for agreeing to help us," Sam said to the men. "We'll all get what we need from this."

His mouth turning up in a wicked grin, the one-eyed man, Behn, clapped his hands together like he was ready to get down to work. "Dead Jaffa!" he all but shouted, ducking a little when Hamel swatted him across the back of the head, but not losing the smile. The others nodded their agreement. Teal'c arched an eyebrow at them and the nodding lost some of its enthusiasm.

Okay, armies could run on vengeance and bloodlust if not on principle, Sam conceded with a barely suppressed sigh. They didn't run *well*, but then again, nothing went well here. "Right," she said. "Maybe. But the trick here is to not attract attention. You have to follow orders, lay low. Can you do that?" Another round of nods that was less convincing than Sam had hoped. *One problem at a time, Major*, the Colonel reminded her in her head. *Torch the bridges when you get to them.* Turning to Hamel, she asked, "Where are our weapons, Teal'c's staff, the other *zat* we had when we escaped?"

In answer, Hamel pointed down the alleyway and took off at an ungainly trot, the rest shuffling after him, bare feet slapping in puddles. Sam cast a last look back at the house. Esa was in the doorway, his hand raised, maybe good riddance, maybe goodbye.

They hadn't gone far when Sam brushed her hand against Teal'c's back and waved him into the shadow of a doorway. She waited a beat while the extra set of footsteps came closer and then shot out her arm and caught the passing shadow by the back of the shirt.

"You don't listen, do you?" she whispered roughly.

Aadi twisted out of her grip. He backed himself up against the far wall of the alley and planted his feet like he was expecting her to start dragging him back to the house. Up ahead, Hamel and the others were waiting in the diluted light of the lantern.

"You—" Aadi began.

Sam held up a hand and searched her memory for an angry mother voice. Coming up empty, she settled for 'annoyed military commander.' That, she had plenty of examples to draw on. "Go home, Aadi."

He thrust his chin out and didn't move. After a second, though, he started to fold a little and wiped his nose on his sleeve. Water ran down his face and off the end of his chin. His skin was pearly blue-white with cold where it showed above the ragged collar of his shirt. He wrapped his arms around himself and looked up at her, his mouth pinched with the effort of not looking as scared as he felt. "You want to kill my father?" he asked, through barely moving lips.

Sam blinked up into the rain. "No," she answered wearily, as she allowed her head to fall back against the corrugated steel of the wall behind her. "I don't want to kill your father, Aadi."

"If he will listen to reason," Teal'c said, "perhaps no one will have to die."

Sam lowered her eyes to meet Aadi's. He watched her and Teal'c for a long moment, but she couldn't tell what was going on inside his head, and frankly, at this point she didn't have time to puzzle it out. "Go home," she repeated and pushed away from the wall, waving at Hamel to lead the way. She didn't turn around when Teal'c's following footsteps were doubled by Aadi's. "Go *home*, Aadi." The footsteps continued. Finally, she stopped and faced him.

"I know the mine. And my father will listen to me. I'm not a—" He broke off to search for the word. "A liability. At least I have two eyes," he finished, jabbing his finger at Behn, who offered no contradiction. When Sam looked skeptically at him, he pointed over his shoulder, adding, "I could go now to the mine, meet you there."

"Fine," Sam sighed, but she pinned Hamel with a stare. "He's your responsibility." Then, to Teal'c, "No weapon." Teal'c nodded and she was glad that Teal'c, at least, followed her orders, even if she got worn down by a thirteen-year-old. "Let's go get the Colonel, okay?" she mumbled as they got underway again. Let *him* deal with the kids.

# CHAPTER FIFTEEN

"**Y**ou know what?" Jack told no one in particular. "I really, really hate this place." He sat in the middle of the passageway and pressed the heel of his good hand to his brow, trying to blunt the point of the ice pick behind his eye that was boring through his skull from the inside. He didn't close his eyes, though, partly because he wanted to keep Aris and Sebek in sight, but mostly because there were tendrils of…something – visuals, maybe, only more than that – still trailing and twisting through his brain like the tentacles of some giant passing jellyfish, each with a sting on the end.

Whatever had happened to him, Sebek had recovered fast, way faster than Jack had, and was crouching in front of him, hands hanging loosely over his knees. His eyes were narrowed and his mouth was curled up in a thin smile.

"What?" Jack demanded testily. That smile was irritating and the clearness in Sebek's eyes, compared to the bleariness Jack felt, was insulting. Of course, Sebek hadn't actually touched the wall and he hadn't felt his brainpan splitting to let…stuff…freaky stuff…in, and he hadn't been ribboned six ways from Sunday, either.

"What did you see?" Sebek asked him. He raised his eyebrows like Daniel used to when asking that kind of question.

"I didn't see anything," he lied. *Screw you, Sebek*, he thought. He could still feel the prickle of intense heat, like a blast furnace against his face, and when he blinked, the after-image of a bare, stony plateau and two rising suns glowed behind his lids. One sun was swollen and red, the other tiny and blue. He tried to remember the designation of that planet, but nothing came to mind. He was beginning to think he'd never been there before.

But he *felt* like he'd been there. He could *feel* the thinness of the air as it rasped through his lungs, gritty with dust. The cracked sandstone was too hot to touch, and his palms itched, the pads of his fingertips burning. His hands. Why had he been on his *hands*?

Dropping the one from his forehead to look at it, he was momentarily surprised to see four naked fingers and a thumb instead of... what? Webs. Three scaly, webbed toes. And feathers.

"What the hell?" he breathed and resisted the urge to screw his fists into his eye sockets.

Sebek's smile was wider now and he nodded slowly. "You did see something."

"Maybe. But I see lots of stuff. It's a side effect of being half-starved and sleep-deprived and, oh, maybe, being *shot in the back* every five minutes."

Jack could still feel the percussion of the energy bolt from Sebek's ribbon device, like an enormous, knuckled fist slamming between his shoulder blades. He focused on that. It was better than the lingering feeling that he was a feathered quadruped, and it made him angrier and more alert, instead of a little on the loopy side.

"We would not have to punish you if you were compliant. Whatever you suffer is your own doing. For instance, in this case." He aimed the ribbon device at Jack's forehead. "You can tell us what you saw, or we can cause you great pain. And, we should tell you that your friend finds your pain very distressing." Sebek tapped his own temple with his empty hand. The crystal in the other glowed livid, causing an anticipating flare in Jack's head.

Instead of answering, Jack lunged forward, which wasn't easy from his position sprawled on the floor, but he managed to get enough momentum behind it to throw Sebek onto his back. Jack scrambled on top of him and grabbed the arm with the ribbon device, barely feeling it when he brought the hand – and his own broken one – down hard onto the stone. He wasn't thinking of much except breaking that damn crystal, but Sebek was strong, stronger than Daniel had ever been in sparring, and Jack couldn't twist his wrist enough to get the hand turned over so that the next blow would smash the crystal against the floor.

But he didn't have the time, either, because Aris was on him, an arm like a tree trunk across Jack's windpipe pulling him up onto his knees and away from Sebek, squeezing off the breath Jack needed to shout the curse that was lodged in his throat.

As his vision was narrowing and going grey at the edges and Sebek was rising and leaning into the shrinking centre of clarity, Jack blinked. It wasn't Sebek's eyes on him anymore, but mirrors half the size of his palm, eye-shaped in a delicate face of iridescent glass, his reflection floating, distorted by the curvature, at the center of each mirror. Beneath the small, underdeveloped nose, the mouth opened to show a tongue shockingly pink against the bloodless white of the lips, and a thin, high voice seemed to tumble like water over him, soothing, soothing, the only thing left to hang on to as the world started to go black. It flowed through his grasping fingers.

*Tell him,* the hallucination said to him, gently. *He will hurt you if you don't tell him. It is a small thing, but the reward is great.*

Jack pressed his lips together against the words that leaped up into his mouth.

*Give this little bit, and I will give you everything.*

The voice was so sweet, and under the cajoling words were others. *Give up, give up, give up.*

Jack meant to say, "No," but what came out was, "A desert." The words were crushed by the weight of Aris's arm on his throat.

"What did you say?" Sebek asked, and there was a shadow of motion that Jack figured was Sebek waving Aris off.

The pressure on his throat lessened a little, enough for him to talk. Inside his head, the sweet voice crooned *give up, give up, give up* and Jack thought, *Screw you*, but his mouth was in full rebellion and was saying, "It was a desert. I saw my feet. My hands. Or maybe feet. Whatever. There were feathers."

Behind him, Aris let out a snort of laughter.

"Hey," Jack said, "you asked. Don't blame me if it sounds stupid."

Inside his head, the voice was gone, and he felt inconsolably lonely, which was surely a sign of the incipient crazies.

Sebek was standing now, looking down at him with an expression of mild irritation as he rubbed his wrist and settled the ribbon device back into a comfortable position. "You will not touch us again," he ordered.

Without waiting for Jack's pithy and cutting retort, Sebek turned to the wall and ran the gold-capped hand across its surface. Nothing happened. But when he raised his empty hand, the wall came to life under his almost touch. With the other hand, Sebek flicked his fingers at Aris, and Jack found himself suddenly on his feet, Aris's fist bunched up in the shoulder of Jack's jacket to hold him upright until Jack got his boots flat on the floor.

"Why do you think you saw this place, the desert, the feathers?" Sebek asked him, slowly moving his hand across the tiles of glyphs and watching the color flare and follow the motion of his hand.

Jack shrugged.

Sebek paused over a tile at Jack's shoulder level. "It was this one, I think."

Jack shrugged again. The floor was sort of corkscrewing up-down, left-right, and he was sure that if he could look in the mirror, he'd see the ice pick in his skull stabbing out through his left eye. He didn't want to think about mirrors. He wanted to lie down and sleep until doomsday. But, seeing how things were going, that might not be such a long nap.

While he was having these cheering thoughts, Sebek snagged him by the cuff of his sleeve and lifted his arm. Before he could react, the Goa'uld closed his fingers around Jack's hand, squeezing him with bone-crushing strength, and pressed Jack's fingertips against the wall, sliding his fingers sideways over the rough symbols.

This time it wasn't desert. It was water. He surged upward through shafts of light, breached the surface with a shriek of escaping air, a shudder in his guts, and a wheeze as a new breath filled him. The sky overhead was one swirling nebula, purple winding around a green center. His jaws gaped open as his spine arched, impossibly supple, and he slid backward again into blackness. But before he did, he caught sight of something else, poised like him between sea and sky, a massive bullet-shaped head, a maw full of teeth, a single glassy eye, the sinuous flip of a tail, and he thought, clearly, although in no language he'd ever heard: *love*.

Jack lurched backward as Sebek released him. He put his hands over his eyes, surprised to find them open. When he hit the opposite wall of the passageway with his shoulder, he could see the flare of light between his fingers – glyphs like animals dancing in stone, lit up from the inside – and then the ocean was gone and he was floating against the stars, weightless, and below him was a slowly turning space station, eight rings on a central spindle. Beyond it was a planet wrapped in bands of red and yellow. As he watched, a gun turret at the stationary center of the array swiveled toward him, glowing, firing silently.

Then he was on his knees beside Sebek, his forehead on Aris's boot. The bit of food he'd eaten was making a comeback. He didn't bother to turn his head. With a grunt of disgust, Aris kicked him away, then took a step forward to wipe his toe on Jack's pant leg.

"Nice," Aris said, grimacing.

"Blame your boss," Jack answered, slowly dragging himself to his feet. He almost reached out to steady himself, but caught himself in time and instead pressed three fingers against his throbbing eye. He waited until Sebek, who also seemed to have fallen to one knee, raised his head, and then Jack said, "That was *unpleasant*."

"Sorry, Jack," Sebek said, in Daniel's voice, lifting his hand to ward off an expected blow. "I know, you said you didn't want to hear my voice again. But it's not like I can help it."

A familiar, humorless grin flitted across his face. Daniel had used that grin a lot before he'd ascended, in those last months when he'd been weighed down by doubt. It was the smile he'd used when he'd sat across from Jack in the infirmary and described the effects of terminal radiation poisoning. Ironic, resigned, impotent. Jack had seen that smile every time he closed his eyes for months after. Right now, he wanted nothing more than to kill Sebek for using it.

It must've shown on his face, because Sebek stood up, too, and backed away a little. Above his head, the light in the grooves along the ceiling came to life and followed him, the darkness retreating behind him.

Sebek closed his eyes for a moment and sighed heavily. "It's me," he said. "It's me and I don't know how to make you believe me, Jack. I just…" His arms rose and fell again to his sides, defeated. "Can't you see it?" His face was pleading.

Jack narrowed his eyes, cocked his jaw. *Do not engage*, he told himself. Then he said, in spite of his own good advice, "What I see is a snake with a sadistic streak this wide." He held his arms out to illustrate.

Again with the smile. "Well, I'm not going to argue with that." Sebek squeezed his eyes shut and bowed his head – the way Daniel did when he was trying to bully through a problem, or when thick people weren't listening to reason – and when he looked up again, he seemed to have made a decision. "Okay," he said. Jack waited for more, but that was it.

Sebek held up his hand, palm outward, the crystal in the centre of the ribbon device cold and black. Jack braced himself for another shot. Aris took a step away. But instead of shooting him, Sebek lowered the weapon and started pulling the caps off of his fingers.

Jack almost said, "Daniel?" in the way that invariably made Daniel reply, in the same overly-patient, bemused tone, "Jack?" He ground his teeth together for a second and then asked, in as flat a voice as he could muster, "What are you doing?"

"I'm giving you the ribbon device."

"Well, that's...stupid."

The snake angled his head in a half-shrug of acknowledgment and looked at Jack from under his raised eyebrows, like he would if he were Daniel and was glancing up at him over the rims of his glasses. That smile again. "That's the point."

Jack's own eyebrows shot up. "Stupid is the point?"

Sebek huffed out a laugh as he wriggled out of the coil brace wound around his forearm. "No," he answered patiently, like Jack was one of the slower, if good-natured, kids in the class. "The part where I trust you is the point." He tossed the device to Jack, who caught it against his chest. "Even if you don't trust me."

The device was warm, and Jack suppressed a shudder as he hooked two fingers through the coil and let it hang at his side away from his body. He had to give the snake credit. This was a whole new level of sinister. A wave of nausea churned through him and the ice pick twisted and twisted in his eye. The man in front of him – Sebek – was watching him, nothing in his expression except a trace of hope, there, in the slight dimple at the corner of his mouth where that resigned smile was trying to get out again.

After a few silent seconds, the man raised his now naked fingers and pinched the bridge of his nose, swaying a little. "I'm sorry, Jack," he said, rubbing his eyes with a finger and thumb before dropping his arm like it was too heavy to carry anymore, his whole frame slumping. "This situation…I know this sucks. But you have to decide what you're going to do. I have some control here. I really do. But Sebek is close, and he's not happy. If he gets control again he's going to punish both of us for this, so I'd like this time to count for something." He spread his arms, open, exposed. "Trust me, or kill me." When Jack didn't move, he aimed his gaze at Aris. "Okay, you do it then. It's why you're here, isn't it?"

Aris shifted his weight, but his face betrayed nothing. "I'm here to serve my god," he said. Jack had to give him points for managing that without rolling his eyes.

Sebek gave him a painfully Danielesque 'oh, please' expression. "Sebek knows, Aris. He knows about your little arms-smuggling venture. He knows about your sister and her blasphemous cult, as he thinks of it."

Aris's jaw muscle twitched, but that was it.

Clearly frustrated, the snake went on, faster now, steamrollering the opposition, his eyes blazing, lips thinned, teeth showing – Daniel on a tear. "The only reason he's brought you in here is because the Jaffa get sick and he needs you to ride roughshod over Jack. He knows you'll do as you're told because he knows you love your son. But as soon as he finds what he's looking for, he's going to kill both of you, and then he'll find your sister and all her followers and he'll wipe them out, and he'll do it as brutally and publicly as possible as an example to the others, and all that is going to happen unless you either listen to what I have to say or you shoot me. Put me out of my misery before Sebek comes back. Do us all a favor."

Aris snapped the blaster up, stiff-armed. The power-pack whined as he keyed the safety off.

Jack stepped in front of it.

The ice pick was grinding against his skull like a drill, and in his grip, the ribbon device was heavy and warm and coiled like a snake, and in the pool of light around the three men, seconds stretched out and out until he could feel every heartbeat building, striking, ebbing. Aris didn't pull the trigger. Behind Jack, that thing, whoever it was, stood still and quiet and was radiating despair and anger and impatience.

Jack laid his hand with its crooked, broken finger on the top of the muzzle and pressed down against Aris's resistance. "Whoa," he said in his talking-to-mad-dogs voice. "Let's take a minute here." Half of his brain was shouting at him to step out of the way and get it over with. The other half was thinking about that smile, the resignation, Daniel's voice saying, *Can't you see it*?

It was true: there were times when the snake's control wasn't absolute. Jack had seen it himself, on Tollana, when Klorel and Skaara were in court fighting for ownership of Skaara's body. And before that, when he'd *zatted* Klorel on Apophis's ship, and Skaara had surfaced to apologize – *apologize* – for not being strong enough. He could even feel a skirling memory of his own, somewhere way back behind the noise and the forgetting, Kanan compelled to return for Ba'al's lo'tar, to walk into a fortress because *Jack* would never leave someone behind. But no, he didn't really remember that. He'd been told that, after. But still, it kind of made sense.

Jack would never leave someone behind.

And Daniel was in there, somewhere, and that despair Jack could feel against his back like a hot breath, that was Daniel, maybe.

Or maybe not.

But if Daniel could get control, even for a moment, there was hope.

*Crap*.

Aris's gun hovered over the middle of Jack's chest, humming with violence. Instead of forcing it, Jack dropped his hand and stared at Aris until he met Jack's eyes.

"It's my friend in there. My call," Jack said in a low, steady voice.

"You believe this?" Aris waggled the gun a little to point at

Sebek through Jack's chest.

Jack said nothing for a long moment. Aris's gun moved minutely an inch from Jack's chest, jittering with Aris's heartbeat. "You need him. If you didn't you wouldn't have pulled me off him *twice*."

Aris paused for a long moment and then laughed, one sharp, incredulous bark. Then he keyed the safety and lowered his gun. "Okay, Colonel. But this is not a promise. Your friend – *if* that's him – gets us where I want to go, he buys himself some time." He pressed a key and the blaster powered down. "You didn't strike me as the type to be taken in by Goa'uld tricks."

The feeling of tension sizzling away was so palpable that Jack could almost see it go, electricity arcing and fading. He let out the breath he didn't know he'd been holding.

Behind him someone – Daniel, Sebek – let out a breath, too.

"Nothing's changed," Aris said to Jack, his gaze straying over Jack's shoulder. "You knew he was in there before."

"I know."

"He's playing you for sympathy. He doesn't want to die."

"I *know*."

"One thing *has* changed," Sebek, or Daniel, answered. Jack had to figure out what to call the guy. He considered something neutral, like Lenny. But the guy didn't sound like a Lenny. He sounded like Daniel. Sebek-Daniel went on. "It's harder to kill me now. It was easier to imagine it before when he couldn't hear me."

Jack didn't turn around. He hated snakes. He hated this one most of all, and that was saying something, the whole Kanan thing considered.

"I'm sorry, Jack. I'm sorry you're in this position. I'm sorry I couldn't stop it from happening." There was a pause. Jack could imagine Daniel's eyes darting back and forth as he gathered up the words, and the way he used the time to rein in the panic, pulling back into that deceptively, maddeningly calm voice. But, no, that was Daniel. This was...

Jack closed his eyes.

Daniel, or Sebek, kept right on talking. "I was disoriented and I fell. When I opened my eyes I could see him – it – Sebek – coming, crawling out of the old host, out of his *head* and I couldn't—"

Jack turned then, in time to see Sebek-Daniel rub the back of his hand across his mouth like he was trying to wipe away the taste of something nasty.

"At least I won't have a scar," Sebek-Daniel said, with that ironic smile again.

"Small mercies," Jack replied before he could smother the sympathy behind it, so he dropped the ribbon device on the floor and ground the crystal under his heel instead. "All right, Daniel." He made sure the skeptical quotation marks there were audible in his voice. "Then let's get out of here." A new wave of nausea almost knocked him off his feet again, but he squinted his eyes against it and hooked a thumb over his shoulder the way they'd come. "Daylight's that way."

Daniel didn't move, but he frowned that schoolmarm frown at him again. "Uh, no."

"I'm sorry?"

"We have to go that way." Daniel pointed behind himself where the wall curved into darkness.

"Why?"

Daniel didn't say, 'duh,' but the look on his face was the next best thing. If this guy wasn't the genuine article, he was at least as annoying. "It's what we came for."

"No," Jack corrected in a tone whose patience conveyed how not patient he was. "*Sebek* came for it – and you don't even know what 'it' is. We're just along to do the heavy lifting." He included Aris in the circle of indentured help.

"I think—"

Jack sliced the air with the blade of his hand. "Did you or did you not just say that Sebek was going to come back, and he was going to kill everybody in a spectacular and bloody way?"

"That's what *he'd* do, yes, but—"

"Then the prudent thing to do is to get Sebek out of here before he does that, don't you think? And since he's currently piggy-backing *on your brain*, you should come with." Shifting his weight, he started to loop his hands over his P90, remembered belatedly that it wasn't there, and had to settle for folding his arms. "*If* it's really you, that is."

"Jack—"

"You want me to trust you? Come back to the SGC and give yourself up. Then I'll trust you. Maybe." And that was a hell of an ultimatum. Jack tried not to think about what life would be like for Daniel on Earth – maybe locked up in some basement level of Area 51 – if they couldn't find a helpful Tok'ra to winnow Sebek out of there. But he could only deal with one gut-wrenching ethical dilemma at a time.

Daniel looked past Jack toward the entrance and then back the other way, his face screwed up like he was in physical pain. And maybe he was. Just thinking about winding their way back through all those dark corridors was enough to make Jack feel like there was a sack of bricks on his back. But he thought of his kitchen and his refrigerator and that last beer all frosty inside it and about how all of that was waiting for him way, way, way, *way* the hell back there, and it was enough to make it seem worth it. The fact that he wasn't actually running toward that beer was a problem. He wanted to go. He was standing there, not going. And not because Daniel was dragging his feet, either. That image of his own face reflecting in mirrored eyes flickered across his mind, and he squeezed his forehead with his fingers and thumb.

"It'll still be here after we get the snake out of your head."

"You know better than anyone there's no guarantee of that," Daniel said, looking at him steadily. "Sebek might kill me first, to spite you. It's this place, Jack. Something here is helping me get control. I wouldn't have it for long once we left here. You can't allow that to happen."

For a long, sickening moment, Jack heard the echo of what Daniel hadn't said, what he'd implied. It was what he'd been thinking all along, and Daniel knew it.

"There's more to it than that," Daniel said, and reached out his hand. This time, he touched the wall himself, his fingertips tracing one of the glyphs as Jack had seen him do a thousand times, waiting for some old language to tell him how to read it. The symbols beneath his fingertips shone softly. His head snapped back and he gasped, and he jerked away from the wall and staggered sideways. When he opened his eyes, he blinked at Jack as though he couldn't really see him, until finally, his gaze focused. "It isn't just you," Daniel said. "That's what Sebek really wanted to know. Who can have access to this place."

"So you're telling me anyone can do that?" Jack said, as the alarming possibilities unfolded for him.

"Yes." Daniel took a few deep breaths. "We've won the race to get to it. Even if Yu is on his way, we're here now." He looked down the dark curve of the passageway.

Jack was opening his mouth to say something – he wasn't sure what – when Aris neatly put an end to the argument by nestling the muzzle of his blaster into the notch at the base of Jack's skull. The hum of the power pack made all the little hairs on the back of Jack's neck stand up.

"Yu has no right to this," Aris said. "Neither does Sebek."

So much for his feigned deference to the god. It seemed that Aris, at least, was either pretty sure he was talking to the real Daniel, or that he didn't care one way or the other. In Jack's educated opinion, this was a bad sign.

Aris wiggled the blaster a little and some compartmentalized portion of Jack's brain wondered if it was a coincidence that the muzzle was so perfectly shaped to fit in just that spot. He slowly unfolded his arms and let them hang, hands open. He did the math, though, and still came up on the short end. He met Daniel's eyes and could see him assessing the situation with that studied, neutral curiosity he brought out when confronted with deadly things. But behind that there was the faintest gleam of panic. Both of them together could take Aris, especially if Daniel had any of that souped-up snake-power that made Goa'uld so arrogant and hard to kill.

But Daniel didn't move. Instead, he turned and looked into the shadows again for a long moment before turning back, not to Jack, but to Aris.

Damn. Damn. Damn.

Aris shifted his weight a little behind Jack. "Whatever is in here is meant for us. *My people*, not yours. You're going to help me get it."

Slowly, Daniel raised a hand, a palm-out, soothing gesture. "Okay," he said carefully. "Okay. We both want to understand this place. But you don't need Jack. You can let him go. He can find Sam and Teal'c and get out of here before Yu comes. And you and I can keep going. I'll help you."

"Not an option," Jack said. "Putting aside for the moment the fact that we can't get out, you are not staying here to get picked up by a System Lord." He stabbed a finger at Daniel's forehead where all the classified information was kept.

The whine vibrating through Jack's bones wound up a notch as Aris keyed the safety off. "Nobody's going anywhere."

Now Daniel's patient, placating expression creased into a frown of irritation. "You need me. You don't need him."

"Sure I do," Aris answered, and to demonstrate, he laid his free hand flat against the glyphs on the wall. Nothing happened. No glowing. No fancy colors.

"It doesn't work for you," Daniel said, unnecessarily.

"Apparently not."

"Why?"

Jack felt the gun shift as Aris shrugged. "Same reason we're resistant to Goa'uld technology, I suppose. We were altered by the beings who sent us here."

"The Ancients."

Another shrug. "Your word. My sister calls them the Nitori."

Daniel blinked, accessing his inner database. "Those who glow." A smile warmed his face for a second.

Jack piped up. "Yeah, well, if the Ancients locked the place up and broke you so you can't get the surround-sound-smell-o-vision, then maybe this place *isn't* for you, then, hmmm?" He took a step away from the gun. Aris didn't follow.

When Jack turned around, Aris trained the blaster on his chest.

"Well, I'm no believer in fate or miracles," Aris said, "but someone made *you*, and you are conveniently trapped in here to turn stuff on for me. Which of us feels awful down here, and which of us feels fit and happy and capable of shooting holes in people, hmmm?"

"He's right," Daniel said in that vague tone that meant most of his brain was elsewhere. "The Ancients must have found a way to make his people impervious to the negative effects of this place, whatever it is that's making Sebek crazy. And they made them impervious to blending, so that the Goa'uld couldn't use them to get in here." Daniel cast him a sidelong glance that made Jack's heart sink. He braced himself. "And, truth is, you're the only one who can touch the walls safely, more or less. And that means you're key to figuring this place out."

Jack opened his mouth to protest – Daniel could get the lights jumping as well as he could – but Daniel cut him off.

"I can't do it. I can barely keep a grip as it is. I touch the wall enough to get any real information, and Sebek comes back." He wrinkled his brow in the sympathy-for-the-screwed kind of way. "I'm sorry, Jack."

Jack wished that Daniel would quit apologizing and start helping him get the damn blaster away from Aris. But as soon as he started to formulate a plan in that direction, the vertigo hit him again like a riptide pulling the sand out from under his boots and that image of the mirrored eyes and scales like flakes of glass stuttered and flashed in his head. He started to slump, but was caught under the arm and levered carefully to the floor.

When he lifted his head from between his raised knees, Daniel was crouching beside him, peering at him nearsightedly.

"Why didn't Sebek fix your eyes?" Jack asked.

Daniel grinned a little at the *non sequitur*. "He's too busy trying to keep my head from exploding." He looked over his shoulder at Aris before going on. "Look, Aris isn't going to let you go. And you're too messed up to fight him."

"I could if I had some help," Jack answered testily.

With a wince, Daniel looked down at his hands. "I think I have an idea about this place." He met Jack's eyes. "When you touched the wall, what did you see?" Jack rolled his eyes and said nothing. "Jack," Daniel prodded, literally, two fingers jabbing him in the arm.

"I saw a sea monster and his girlfriend." To Aris's snort of laughter, he added, "You *asked*."

"You saw it, or you felt it?"

Jack shrugged, not wanting to dwell on it, the sinuous bending of his spine, the heavy power of his jaws cracking open impossibly wide and the sea rushing in. "Felt it."

"What else?"

"A planet. A space station or a ship." He decided to leave off the part about the big-ass weapons platform.

"Huh," Daniel said and his eyes went distant. Jack was afraid that when Daniel focused on him again, it would be Sebek looking out. He was more afraid, though, that he wouldn't be able to tell. Sometimes hope was deadly.

"What?" Aris demanded when the silence stretched out and Daniel kept rummaging around inside the maze in his own head.

When he came back to them, he seemed to be Daniel, still. Pushing himself to his feet, he nodded, confirming something to himself. "It's not a weapon," he said. "At least I don't think so."

"Then what?" Aris didn't sound at all happy about this analysis.

Daniel walked over to the wall and ran his hand quickly over the glyphs, an inch above the surface, watching the colored light course its way from panel to panel. He pulled away quickly. "It's a library."

"A library," Jack repeated flatly. "You have got to be kidding me."

"No, I'm not." When Daniel turned back to him, his face was alight with the excitement of discovery. He pointed at the wall. "These panels. They must be recordings. Experiences." He spread his arms wide to take in the maze as a whole. "Millions of them. Some kind of somatic archive. Sense memories." His hands fell as he gazed with a kind of fevered reverence over Jack's head and at the wall on the other side of the passage. "It's…amazing."

Jack squinted skeptically up at him. "Why would the Ancients lock up a *library*?"

Daniel looked incredulous. "Are you kidding?"

"No. You'll know when I'm kidding."

"It's knowledge, Jack. Knowledge—"

"—is power. Yeah, I get it. But please tell me there's more to this than sea-monster porn."

Daniel blinked. "Well, maybe it's not all that kind of everyday stuff. Maybe there's other things here. You said you saw a ship." He licked his lips, letting his eyes roam the walls. "I mean, think about how far we've come into this place, and every single surface is covered with these glyphs. Who knows what there might be in here?" He turned to Aris. "Maybe even something to help your people. Maybe something that can help us all."

"Maybe that's not good enough," Aris growled, taking a step toward him. "Yu is on his way here *now*. We don't have time to touch each panel until we find something useful."

Jack said a silent alleluia.

Daniel looked nonplussed for a second. Jack was getting a crick in his neck.

"Well, there must be a system here," Daniel said with a wave toward the walls. "Categorization of some kind." He pointed to panels in turn as he spoke. "Desert. Sea monster. Ship. Libraries always have a system. This is a maze, not a labyrinth. Order, not randomness. We just have to figure out the system and then—"

"Or we can ask the librarian."

Jack followed the line of Aris's aim toward the curve of the hallway, and damned if his hallucination wasn't standing there watching them. For a second she seemed to be partially invisible, but he realized that it was a trick of her shining scales that reflected the walls around her in shifting ripples. The scales on her upper body were more iridescent than simply reflective, though, and her breasts, shoulders and arms were faintly blue and covered with rainbows like oil on the surface of the water. Her bald head was angled curiously, and the mirrored eyes, even without irises or pupils, didn't seem at all blind as she shifted her attention from Aris to Jack to Daniel. When she smiled, fine, pointed teeth showed between her full, white lips.

A quick glance at Daniel confirmed that Jack wasn't the only one seeing her, but just in case, Jack said, "Are you seeing what

I'm seeing?"

"You mean a woman with mirrors for eyes and glass scales like a mermaid?" Daniel asked, still turned toward the apparition in the passageway.

"Yeah."

"Nope."

"Very funny, Daniel." Jack rubbed his eye with his fist and used Daniel's pant leg to drag himself to his feet. "This must be what going crazy feels like."

Daniel nodded absently, saying, "Yeah, something like this," as he started off down the hall toward her.

Jack hooked him by the collar of his shirt. "Where do you think you're going?"

"To follow the glass lady?" Daniel pried Jack's fingers away. "Who is leaving, by the way."

And she was. Jack could see the shimmer of her skin as she turned and followed the curve of the wall into the shadows. The light fluttered inside the walls, coursing after her, chasing darkness. Jack couldn't be sure, but there was a faint sharpening inside his head, like his alertness was being honed from dullness, and something that seemed like singing, a high, clear, wordless song. The sound was like a ribbon woven between his ribs, tugging at him.

Aris gave Jack a shove. "You heard the man. Follow the nice glass lady."

# CHAPTER SIXTEEN

Sam trailed her fingers along the smooth surface of the alley wall and wondered what Daniel would make of it. Some kind of glazed clay, she thought, but how had they made it in such long, unbroken segments? Under her boots, the ubiquitous mosaic stuttered around potholes and disappeared like interrupted sentences under new walls and the fallen pieces of old ones. There was probably a story there in the pictures, and another, sadder one in the way it had been broken and remade by the makeshift city. Daniel would know how to read both. She'd seen him reconstruct a whole village from the faint lines of buried foundations and the distribution of charred animal bones and broken pots, and his hands had moved through the air as he described the way families had gathered around this tumble of flat stones that was a hearth, had carried water from that spring, had knelt here to scrape the fur from some fantastic animal with a bone tool familiar on two dozen planets and across millennia. With its past and present layered together like graffiti on a Da Vinci, this city would be a treasure for him, echoing with voices.

To her, the city was silent, full of crouching shadows and blank spaces that she couldn't help but mentally fill with waiting Jaffa. But Hamel moved swiftly and confidently from alley to alley, pausing occasionally to peer around a corner before darting out and waving at them to follow. His lantern bounced and swayed, and the city leaped into existence and faded to inference as they passed. It didn't take long, though, for Sam understand where they were headed, once she'd figured out that they were coming at it from a different angle, Hamel's own shortcut. The Ancient tower was like a compass with the whole city laid out around it in her mind.

Even with the darkness and the cold rain, though, this trip seemed to take less time than the first one, and they were crowding into the low-roofed alleyway and crossing the familiar little courtyard in only a few minutes. Adrenaline was going to be messing with her time sense from here on in, stretching and contracting duration. Sam started checking her watch, the first stage in detaching events from her subjective responses. Falling into the familiar routine, she already felt her mind coming into tighter, clearer focus.

At the hidden door, she pushed past Behn and Teal'c and leaned down with Hamel to inspect the lock.

"I don't suppose you have the key," Sam said, remembering that Brenneka kept it in her pocket.

Hamel looked uncomfortable but resigned. "No. We'll have to break it."

Behind them rose a murmur, and she glanced back to see the little team finishing their reverential gesture, their faces clouded with concern. No one looked likely to volunteer to do the desecrating, so she nodded and waved Hamel out of the way.

Sam handed the *zat* to Teal'c and was winding up to deliver a kick to the latch when Hamel's hand on her arm stopped her. Teal'c was already aiming the *zat* out of the circle of light at a bulky shadow in the middle of alley.

"It's me." The gruff rumble of a voice seemed more irritated than scared.

"Esa," Hamel breathed next to Sam's ear, and she could feel some of his tension release as he stepped around her. "What are you doing here?" he whispered.

Esa leaned around Teal'c with a wary glance at the *zat* and nodded at Sam. Like the rest of them, he was soaked, and his clinging shirt showed an impressive bulk of muscle on his squat figure. He wiped water out of his eyes with a thick-fingered hand and continued up over his knobby bald head in a gesture that reminded Sam of Hammond.

"You'll need this," he told Hamel. In his other hand was the gleam of a small key.

Several scenarios in rapid succession ran through Sam's head to explain how Esa might have gotten Brenneka's key, and some of them weren't pretty. "How?" she asked.

He kept his eyes on Hamel as he answered. "It's not right to break into our own house. Even Brenneka understands that."

"She gave you the key." Sam pondered the implications of even this minimal change of heart.

Esa jerked his chin at the door and gave no other answer. Then, without a word, he took the lantern from Hamel, turned, and was gone. Sam tried not to begrudge the loss of all that useful muscle, but a survey of the huddled shadows of the remaining troops made that a little hard.

"Okay, let's go," she said, watching Esa's lumbering shape until it was swallowed by darkness and rain.

A moment later the rest of them were winding down the staircase, her boots and Teal'c's ringing on the stone steps, everyone else cat-quiet and ghostly in the cold blue of the flash Brenneka had used on their first trip down here. The steps were slick from the water dripping off all of them, and she was certain that the chattering of her teeth was audible over the racket of their climbing. Ahead of her, Aadi's shivering shoulders were up as high as his ears, goose-bumps like plucked chicken-skin on his bare neck. Behind her, Teal'c was a moving wall of cold. She wondered again about fever and then put that aside for now. He'd know what he needed, and his inside pockets were bulging with all the meds from the stolen packs, along with his tretonin injector. Soon, hopefully, he'd be back at the mountain, with Janet hovering over him and pointing out, with the resignation peculiar to armed forces doctors, that it was pretty stupid to go running around in the rain with a crispy hole in his side.

Once in the cavern, Hamel brought up the lights in the sconces and crossed the wide floor, detouring around the dais and finally kneeling at the foot of the scored wall of Ancient metal. His hands smoothing over the surface, up, out as far as he could reach, up again, he muttered something she couldn't make out – that jump-rope cadence again – and a panel about five feet across popped outward and slid aside with the hissing resistance of hydraulics.

When Hamel twisted to look at her over his shoulder, his face was wrinkled up with a wide smile. "Your weapons," he said, "and a few other things."

That was a nice understatement. The 'few other things' turned out to be a small arsenal. Sam crouched to peer inside, her hand steadying her on the upper edge of the door. She could make out a narrow crawlspace extending beyond the reach of the light stick. In neat rows along both walls were *zats* and staff weapons, the former hanging from a rail, the latter leaning at a steep angle between pegs. A quick count of what she could see came up with at least twenty staffs and twice as many *zats*. In a tidy row in the middle of the floor sat four spherical Goa'uld stun grenades and, beside them, an equal number of incendiary ones. Little Bangs and Big Bangs. Excellent.

Raising her eyebrows in surprise, she gave Hamel her best hundred-watt smile. "Not bad," she admitted, deciding she'd better revise her first impression of these people and their whipped-dog passivity. "How did you manage this?" It was unlikely that missing weapons would be overlooked by Jaffa. She'd seen whole villages razed for less significant offenses.

Hamel was gazing into the crawlspace with an expression usually reserved for religious relics. "The mine collapses, Jaffa die. Small people can wriggle into small spaces, bring back things thought lost." He looked at Aadi, who grinned proudly. Apparently, he was good at snagging more than rats for dinner. "The rest, mostly from Aris, smuggled on his ship from his outworld trips. Some, though, have been here for many years." With a grunt, he moved into the storage space on his knees – a ragged petitioner, Sam thought – and started to hand out the weapons. "Some sit and pray—"

"And some meet the god on the road," Teal'c finished for him, earning a rough, phlegmy laugh in return.

In the end, they decided that only Teal'c would carry a staff, since he was the only one able to use it effectively, both for firing and close-quarters fighting. The rest took *zats* – even Aadi, after Teal'c had made a case for him and Sam caved against her better judgment. In addition to her *zat*, Sam stuffed a stun grenade in one pocket of her jacket and an incendiary one in the other, adding two to Teal'c's as well. It was an ungainly arrangement, the grenades inhibiting forward movement of their arms, but the benefits would probably outweigh the disadvantages.

They spared a few minutes to do the fastest small arms training ever, with only one small setback when one of the troops, Eche, the youngest after Aadi, accidentally *zatted* himself. Predictably, it didn't have any effect, except that the look of surprise and then embarrassment on his thin face was a real keeper. Once Behn and the other two, Rebnet and Frey, had stopped falling over themselves laughing, they'd taken turns *zatting* each other. When they lost track of who'd shot whom, Sam learned a useful lesson: two *zats* would kill a normal person, while the average Atroposian was impervious if the *zats* were spaced more than a couple seconds apart. However, two *zats* delivered in rapid succession *would* actually drop an Atroposian like a bag of rocks, leaving the target semi-conscious for about half a minute. While they waited for the gang to lean Frey up against the wall to administer increasingly forceful smacks to the side of his face until he came to with a snarl and swatting hands, she and Teal'c decided that this explained why the Jaffa bothered to carry *zats* at all, given these people's resistance to Goa'uld tech- nology. They tabled speculation about what three shots would do, although continued snickering from the four stooges made her pretty tempted to experiment.

Aadi, at least, wasn't too impressed and sulked against the dais, opening and closing his *zat* with mechanical regularity until Teal'c walked over and laid a heavy hand on the top of his head.

The troops armed, Hamel slid the door back over the hidey-hole and set off, not, as Sam had expected, in the direction of the stairs, but to the right of the Ancient wall. They descended deeper into the cavern, to where the light thinned from more distantly sepa- rated sconces and the elaborate mosaic on the floor gave way first to intermittent patches and then to plain, black stone. At this point, the vaulted ceiling angled sharply downward so that the cavern became a sloping tunnel with a broad entrance like a half-opened mouth. It seemed to sigh out the distant whisper of rushing water on a heavy, cold breath. In here, there were no sconces at all. Hamel shook his light stick again, but the blue glow did nothing except to make the darkness within seem more impenetrable.

Gathered close around Hamel as though the light were an island and the darkness a dangerous sea, the gang shuffled silently, their eyes wide, fingers clenched white-knuckled around the grips of the *zats*. Teal'c raised an eyebrow at Sam. Shrugging, she stepped out of the circle into blackness, then reached back to take the light from Hamel. She didn't actually say *abandon all hope* out loud as, with varying degrees of reluctance, her tiny army trailed along behind her, downward into the belly of the beast.

Sleep hovered around Aris, inviting him into its seductive embrace. He pushed it away. He'd gone longer stretches without sleep before. Besides, he had to stay alert enough keep up with O'Neill. Deep lines of fatigue were etched across O'Neill's face, but that kind of exhaustion could be overcome by a soldier. Aris would have staked his few possessions on the certainty that O'Neill could endure days without sleep on strength of will alone. He knew the type. Times like this, Aris had reason to appreciate the *roshna*; double doses kept him on his feet, but he was running low, and he'd have to cut back soon. He made fists, then relaxed them as his hands jittered and trembled, uncontrolled.

Sebek led their little procession now, a departure from how it had been since they entered the maze. They were following a hallucination, or maybe they weren't. The shimmering woman appeared and disappeared at intervals, leaving them to find their own way, and all three of them were frustrated. Every so often Sebek stopped and pointed, speaking softly to O'Neill, whose posture was still as wary as ever as he listened and responded. Aris watched Sebek's intent stare, the way his body moved, and tried to figure out how O'Neill could think that this was Daniel Jackson. The Goa'uld were good mimics – they got away with pretending all the time. He regretted losing control before, giving O'Neill a reason to align himself – even tentatively – with this other man, whoever he might be. It wasn't impossible, not by any means, that O'Neill had picked up on something, some irrefutable sign, that this really was his friend. Aris had seen too many host bodies give out near this place, too many jumps from host to host, to think the Goa'uld had complete control. Even so, he was having trouble telling the difference between the interests of the two entities. That wasn't something he would share with O'Neill. His plan and O'Neill's plan didn't need to match up. They'd work it out whenever they found their way to a stopping point. Then Aris would make up his own mind about Dr. Jackson, and whether or not he would have to go through Jackson to get to Sebek. The idea didn't appeal to him, but he'd do it.

What bothered him most was that he'd been sure O'Neill was on the same page, until he'd stepped in front of Aris's intent. He didn't like the idea of killing O'Neill, but he'd do that, too, if he had to. He hoped it wouldn't come to that.

"Jack." No deep reverberation; the symbiote was pretending to be the host again. Or maybe not. For the moment, Aris chose to think of that voice as belonging to Daniel Jackson. He might be proven wrong later, but it didn't matter much at this point. Jackson was swaying, his lips parted, head tilted back as if he was listening to something Aris couldn't hear. "Do you sense anything?"

O'Neill stopped and raised his hands to his head as if to block out sound and light, a gesture Aris was becoming familiar with. "Maybe."

"You do," Jackson said, sounding a little too excited for Aris's taste. He moved to touch O'Neill on the shoulder, but O'Neill shied away like a skittish animal, and Jackson dropped his hand. "Is it what you saw before?"

"No. I don't know." O'Neill hesitated, then shook his head violently. "No."

"Something else?"

"Why does it matter?" There was an angry, suspicious edge to O'Neill's voice as he pushed back against Jackson's curiosity, and Aris watched Jackson carefully for signs of the Goa'uld emerging, but he saw nothing but a sympathetic look on Jackson's face. "You want a running commentary?" O'Neill snapped. "Everything that flies through my head?"

"No. But some of it might be important. Especially since you haven't been touching the walls." Jackson stared at O'Neill, until O'Neill nodded curtly. Aris's eyes narrowed. Maybe it really was Jackson; in the way of friends who'd become accustomed to speaking without words, O'Neill seemed to be catching on to something

Aris was missing. It was an interesting trick, but he'd never worked with anyone long enough to develop it.

O'Neill turned away toward the wall and leaned forward as if to rest his forehead against the cool stone, but jerked away at the last second. "I'm not going to activate anything by touching this, am I?"

"No symbols," Jackson said. "No danger. Not that I can tell, anyway."

"That's reassuring," O'Neill said, irony thick in his tone. His head dropped forward and he leaned there, at an angle to the wall, a solid, tilted line of tension. "Some of it's inside my head, and some of it's not," he said, his voice muffled. "Stuff I've seen, stuff I've…done. Memories popping out of nowhere. You don't need me to tell you about those."

"Are you sure?" Jackson's voice was soft.

O'Neill's shoulders tensed. "Yeah."

"Then what else?"

"Stars. Patterns of stars, I guess…I'm not sure. Like star fields. Maps, maybe."

"Of this galaxy?" Aris asked. Jackson's intent gaze shifted to him. "Hey, just asking. There has to be some point to this place, remember?"

Jackson nodded. "Can you tell, Jack?"

Aris had his own doubts about whether the human could even tell one star from another, but a moment later O'Neill said, "There aren't any constellations I recognize."

"Huh." Jackson bit at his lip and his gaze grew unfocused.

"You planning to share or do I get to be the only one on the hot seat?" O'Neill demanded gruffly.

As if deciding whether or not to answer, Jackson glared at Aris and then said slowly, "My memories of Sha're, at first, but other things, too. Almost anything triggers them, and I can't stop Sebek from running off after them. He collects them like…" Jackson's voice trailed off, then resumed, stronger. "Some of the images are so vivid, it's as though I'm watching a movie, or reliving it." Jackson lifted his arms and crossed them over his chest. "Sometimes, I can tell I'm reliving the sensation of being ascended."

O'Neill turned his head toward Jackson. Aris couldn't see his face, but whatever Jackson saw there was worthy of a brief half-smile. "Well, that sounds fun," O'Neill said. "Remember anything useful?"

"Not really. Just a feeling of being weightless. Or…no. Bodiless. Not solid. And drifting, expanding."

"Weird," was all the analysis O'Neill offered, and Jackson nodded. They fell quiet.

In the lull, for the first time since he'd descended down into this hellhole, Aris permitted himself to think of Aadi, unfolding the memories of his son like a piece of fragile paper. His son was no longer a child; he was old enough to control his own destiny. It would be good to give him that chance. He could see traces of his own nature in Aadi – his cunning, most of all. It seemed Aadi had grown ten years in a single night, but there had been many nights, first in Sokar's mines, and then in the service of Apophis, and finally in chains forged by Sebek's Jaffa. When Aris had last seen him, huddled in his cell, he had grown muscles where only skin and bones had been before, and his eyes had held a dull acceptance of how things had to be. That look pained Aris more than any wound or oppression ever could. Away from here, maybe, growing up wasn't the same as giving in. His son's face loomed in the shadows of his memory, and he couldn't tuck it neatly away.

The tips of his fingers shook as a sound trickled through the darkness. He raised his head and listened. It was a child, sobbing. Impossible. He clasped his fingers together to stop the palsied shaking, then glanced at O'Neill and Jackson. They were both silent, their eyes closed, asleep on their feet. Aris groped for the *roshna* secreted in the pockets of his armor, but moved his hand away. The soft sound bubbled up again, one loud wail, subsiding to quiet crying. His son had cried that way when the Goa'uld had taken him from his mother's arms. Aris could see him now, kicking his short legs, his mouth open in a scream of agony that had given way into snuffling sobs. He gritted his teeth and tried to block the memory, but, although it seemed to ebb, it came back stronger, like it had paused to gained strength: Aadi, thrashing with hunger as Aris cleaned his armor and prepared to sell his soul to feed his son. A low shiver crept up his spine.

Jackson and O'Neill were speaking again. With difficulty, Aris focused on the conversation.

"Daniel," O'Neill said. "There's something else. That woman. I've been seeing her longer than you have."

"Is she—" Jackson began, but then his expression distorted, twisted, and he gasped, flailing for the wall. O'Neill straightened and backed up a step, but made no move to help him. Smart man; Aris had always known O'Neill's instincts for self-preservation would come in handy here. They watched in silence as Jackson battled for control of his own body, the struggle playing out in a grotesque pantomime of jerking limbs and facial expressions. Aris's fingers tightened on his weapon. If this was the time, he'd have to do it without telegraphing his intention to O'Neill, or there'd be a repeat of the touching intervention they'd had earlier.

Jackson slammed back against the one of the blank pillars, groping for a handhold, as palpable frustration radiated from O'Neill. Jackson made a strangled sound, and rasped, "Jack, quickly. Tell me."

"Well, what if she's really just a hallucination?"

"Brought on by this place," Jackson said softly. "It's a trick, to draw us in deeper." He slid down the wall, one hand clasping at the other as if they were not connected, and Aris remembered Sebek seating the hand device between his fingers in that way. Jackson closed his eyes.

"He's losing control," Aris said to O'Neill, who nodded once at the obvious but said nothing. All his attention was focused on Jackson. Aris looked at O'Neill for a long, long moment, as a decision formed in the back of his mind. There was no trust between them, but they might be able to help each other.

After a moment, he drew his knife and held it out to O'Neill, offered in his open palm. A muscle in O'Neill's jaw twitched as he looked at it first and then into Aris's face. His expression was stony, but his eyes were wild. "I won't need it," he said, and made no move to take it. Aris didn't need an interpreter. He'd seen what career soldiers could do with their bare hands.

With one swift motion, he sheathed the knife. "When you do," he said casually, the offer implied.

Jackson's eyes flew open and shifted over to them. His body relaxed and he slumped, exhausted, as if he'd been fighting for hours. Aris supposed he had, in a way. "Still here," Jackson said. "For now."

"Good," Aris said. "Enough stories about your touching memories. What does it all mean?"

"I have no idea," Jackson said. He wiped sweat from his face with the bottom of his t-shirt. "There's almost no barrier between us anymore."

"What? Between…?" O'Neill frowned, his finger waving between himself and Jackson and Aris, and then pointing down the hallway at the distant glimmer of fading light. "The woman?"

"Sebek and me. I have better access to his memories, now, when he's trying to get control. Before, I was working at getting at them, but now I can't stop seeing them." Jackson shook his head, then thumped it sharply against the wall. When he looked up at O'Neill, he smiled an odd, humorless smile and said, "I really don't want to see them."

"Join the club," O'Neill said.

"Right," Jackson answered. He pulled his knees up and propped his arms on them. "Sometimes I feel like saying something, and I'm not sure if I'm really the one who's talking. I don't know if it's really me."

Aris winced and spared a moment of gratitude that he'd never know what it was like. Much better to be dead.

"I can't wait to blow up whatever is in the middle of this thing," O'Neill said softly, but with such underlying savagery that Jackson tilted his head to look at him.

"Jack?"

O'Neill squeezed his eyes shut and shook his head violently. Aris's first instinct was to pull him away from the wall, but he realized at that moment that O'Neill wasn't touching anything. "Could someone please explain to me why I've got someone else's memories running around in my head?" O'Neill sounded perfectly rational, but something in his posture…Jackson lurched to his feet.

"Jack, what are you seeing?"

"Dead children," O'Neill said, his jaw set so hard Aris thought it might crack. "Dead planets. Big ugly motherships, Jaffa everywhere. Mines. Some big tower in the middle of a city, and…this mountain, but without the mine." He squeezed his eyes shut, as if he could stop seeing that way. "This planet, I think. Not like it is now, though."

Jackson hissed in a breath. "Uh-oh."

"I'm losing patience," Aris said. In fact, his patience had been lost hours ago, and now his skin was crawling as he watched O'Neill's body go rigid with the effort of driving away whatever was invading his head.

"Those might be Sebek's memories," Jackson said, staring at O'Neill. "Goa'uld genetic memories, maybe; I can't tell. But he showed that to me."

O'Neill swayed. Aris gripped his arm and shoved him roughly against the support of the wall.

"Nice," O'Neill said bitterly. "Like I didn't have enough crap of my own in here." He cast a narrow-eyed glance at Aris, but looked away when he said, "Crying. There's a baby, crying." Again, he screwed shut his eyes and covered his ear with one hand. "Damnit," he muttered tonelessly.

Jackson turned Aris, waiting for confirmation, but Aris kept his face bland, even though all of his skin was prickling.

Jackson nodded, letting it go, and stepped closer to O'Neill, protectively. There was irony there, but Aris wasn't in the mood to appreciate it properly. An insistent ache had been building at the base of his skull for hours; the *roshna* was eating him alive. No way to know how long it would take to reach the center, if there even was a center, and no way to get out. And now this pleasant development.

Things weren't looking up.

"We need to get moving," Aris said, and shook O'Neill by the arm. "Now."

"What's your hurry?" O'Neill pushed Aris's hand off.

"No, Jack, he's right." Jackson began wandering away from them, back down the corridor, but O'Neill caught him by the shoulder and stopped him. Aris glanced down into the darkness and saw nothing, but…the feeling of their guide was with him, as if he could hear her speaking and see her hand beckoning to them. *This way. Hurry.*

"Maybe we shouldn't be so hot to follow her," O'Neill said, staring in the same direction, but clearly he could see what Aris was missing. If he looked askance, though, she flickered at the edges of his vision.

"You have a better option for us?" Aris asked.

"You've got me there," O'Neill said. He released Jackson's shoulder, and Jackson began moving immediately, as if someone had tugged him on a string. Then he stopped abruptly. O'Neill stepped warily toward him. "Daniel?"

The hair on the back of Aris's neck rose as though someone was behind him. He turned, but it was the same darkness as before, nothing of substance hiding there.

Beside him, O'Neill muttered, "What the hell?" and jumped away from him, swinging at thin air. Aris sidestepped and pressed against the opposite wall, his weapon raised.

"Okay, now she's just screwing with us," O'Neill said angrily.

Aris could hear her now, not a voice in his head, but in the echoing maze. *You must hurry!* He glanced over at O'Neill, who nodded at him, and then at Jackson, who was standing perfectly still, staring down the corridor. "Jackson? You hear that?"

"We have heard the voice of our ascendancy," Sebek said, in his strange distorted growl, "and we will use this place to claim our rightful power, and to unseat our Lord Yu from this world, and all the others his hand has touched."

O'Neill winced. Jackson fell forward on his knees. Neither O'Neill nor Aris made a move to pick him up. Too risky to get too close, if Sebek was driving.

"Damn," Jackson said, in the weariest tone Aris had ever heard.

"It's…hard to push him back."

"You sure that was Sebek?" O'Neill asked, and now he did move to help Jackson up. "I've always thought you had a jones to take over the universe."

"That's beside the point," Jackson said, offering a weak smile, which O'Neill returned.

"Let's move," Aris said again. "Get this over with." He stepped up beside Jackson, and the three of them resumed their trek into the dark.

# CHAPTER SEVENTEEN

After her feet skidded out from under her for the fourth time on the slick stone of the tunnel floor, Sam didn't bother cursing under her breath. She cursed over her breath, or whatever the opposite was. The not-very-ladylike word got caught under the low ceiling and the echoes bounced back and forth like there was someone further down the tunnel in the dark who had also skinned the heels of her hands again and whose backside was also soaked. Sam was happy for the commiseration, even though the echoes reminded her that they were trying to be stealthy, and that bitching out loud wasn't exactly textbook.

Still, it felt good. So she did it again. When she got home, she was going to lock herself in the bathroom and curse for five minutes straight. It wasn't much as far as rewards went, but at the moment it seemed pretty damn appealing.

She let Teal'c pull her to her feet, wiped her hands on her thighs, and found Hamel in the gloomy light of the flash stick.

"How much farther?"

If they had to grope their way across the entire city, they'd be at it a long time. Condensation dripped from the ceiling and down the back of her jacket. In the distance, the sound of rushing water pulled at her concentration.

Hamel pushed between Behn and Frey to take the light stick from her. "Not far. Just a little way now."

She waited until the little band of soldiers got moving again and followed the sound of their bare feet slapping on the wet stone. Teal'c fell into step beside her and put out a steadying hand as one foot skidded out from under her again. Her rueful laugh tumbled around in the echoes.

Hamel was true to his word, though. It wasn't much farther. In fact, the next time she lost her footing, she slid into Eche and the two of them ended up knee deep in the river. Or, at least, it was knee deep once they struggled to their feet again, and Sam caught Eche when the current knocked him over before he got fully upright. His momentum almost took them both down again. By this time, Sam's head was ringing with all the cursing she was going to do when she got home.

The frigid water smelled lifeless and oily. She indulged in a brief fantasy about her bathrobe.

"Please tell me we aren't wading the rest of the way," she said to Hamel, who coughed out a chuckle and waved Behn and Rebnet off into the shadows.

They took the light stick with them, and the rest of them stood shivering on the river bank. Sam kept a hand twisted in the arm of Teal'c's jacket and someone, she didn't know who but suspected Eche, had his hand twisted in the waistband of hers. After she'd started to wonder if Behn and Rebnet had abandoned them down here in the dark, she heard them coming back their way, accompanied by the hollow thudding of water against something large and empty.

It turned out to be a flat-bottomed boat with low sides and tall spars at bow and stern, each one with a clasp hanging loose and swinging against the wood.

"In," Hamel ordered and held the boat steady while everyone but him and Frey clambered in and sat down between the moldy ribs.

Their feet slipping every second step or so, he and Frey leaned hard against the current until they managed to get the boat moving slowly upstream. Finally they came to the edge of the landing where the sloping tunnel met the river, and the wall of stone cut off further progress along the bank. Here, Frey scrambled into the boat and helped Hamel attach the clasps to a double rope looped through a pulley waist-high on yet another tunnel wall. Once the boat was attached, Hamel jumped in, and the two men began to draw the boat along against the current by pulling the rope hand-over-hand. The boat moved slowly but steadily upstream, through a tunnel barely wide enough to accommodate it. The tallest of them all, Teal'c had to hunch low to keep from banging his head on the ceiling. After a few moments of listening to Hamel and Frey breathing and grunting, Sam and Teal'c crawled over and knelt next to the rope – the others moving port to balance the boat – and leaned their own weight into the effort. If it hadn't been for the slight variation in shadows on the stone that skimmed along beside her head, Sam would have doubted that they were moving at all.

But they were. Progress. She had to admit that, in spite of the blisters blooming on her palms, and the aching of her bruised back, it felt good to *do* something, finally, and it made a lot of sense to go *under* the *ha'tak* instead of around it. No Jaffa patrols to dodge, no craven city-dwellers to turn them in. As she settled into the rhythm and adjusted her breathing, stretched her arms and flexed her muscles, she let herself fall away from doubt for a few minutes, allowed herself to forget to think ahead, to look only as far as the darkness at the bow of the boat and to think only of keeping the tension up on the rope as she reached for another yard of progress.

It was only a temporary indulgence, but when Aadi touched her shoulder and took her place, her mind was a little clearer. She found a space between Eche and Behn on the bottom of the boat, and set herself to the task of deploying her resources in her head, Teal'c on point, herself on their six with the knife and the *zat*. They'd use the stun grenades only as a last resort. Those would likely be key to any exit strategy that would involve a dash for the 'gate.

But the period of clarity wouldn't last, she knew. She could already feel it, that agitation at the base of her skull and a prickle along her arms like ants scurrying inside her bones, and the well-made plans started to fall apart in her head, too reckless, too risky. She had to force her mouth open a little and put her tongue between her teeth to keep them from grinding. And the nausea was back, too, made worse by the lurch-and-stop of the boat as it labored against the current.

Beside her, Teal'c shifted uncomfortably. "We must be nearing the mine," he observed.

"Yeah. I feel it, too." Craning her neck to look back at Hamel in the stern, she asked, "You people don't feel anything when you get close to the vault?"

Hamel shook his head, and Sam could see the others do the same. "This is why Sebek sent us into that section of the mine, to try to dig around the door. This is how Brenneka's brother – not Aris, the other one – learned of the sacred writing there. But Sebek was impatient, and he finally came himself, and when Ky wouldn't tell him what the writing said, he killed him."

"Ky could read the writing of the Nitori?" Sam asked.

"No, of course not. No one can."

"Sebek would not accept excuses," Teal'c said.

"No."

"He killed him with the light in his hand." Aadi's words were muffled as he leaned forward to reach for the rope. "He wouldn't let me and Bren take Ky home or bury him. He's still there, in the mine, right where he died. People have to step over him to get to work. They're afraid to touch him because of Sebek."

The hatred in his voice was palpable. A whisper scurried along the tunnel and back again as the crew cursed in unison and snapped the Goa'uld's neck between their fingers. Even Frey and Aadi paused in their work to do it, leaving Teal'c to keep the boat from backsliding in the current.

Hamel nudged Sam's thigh with his toe. "Will you be able to fight, like this, when you're sick from the place?"

She didn't hesitate. "Yes, we will." She resisted the urge to scrub at her hair, dislodge the imaginary ants on her skin. "Just follow my orders and we'll be okay."

Hamel looked a little skeptical, but he nodded. "Maybe your friend will help us. If he is what you say he is."

"Maybe."

She turned back and stared at the dark walls passing inches away. It felt as though she were the boat, and the rope dragging her forward was invisible, twisted in her ribs. If she closed her eyes she could see it, tight and urgent, yanking her unevenly toward the vault. It wasn't just the need to get to Daniel and the Colonel, either, but something undefined and insistent, like a craving, like thirst. In her mind's eye, Daniel and the Colonel were pushed to the periphery of her vision and the rope carried on beyond them into darkness. Something was waiting.

But when she tried to focus on it, there was a stirring at the back of her neck, in her throat, her brain, that familiar, alien coiling claiming her. She could feel it cutting the ties between herself and her body. Jolinar had taken her roughly, and the threads had been sliced clean through.

"No," she murmured under her breath.

Not sliced clean through. Sam had remained herself. She'd gotten to be herself again. It had been only temporary, and Jolinar had forced her only because she'd been desperate. That's what made all the difference.

Only it didn't, not where the *feeling* was concerned. She covered her mouth with her hand. *Forget this. It's a distraction. Focus.* In the distance, she could make out the shape of something, someone, waiting for them. She wanted to see the face. But what she kept coming up with was Jolinar looking at her in the mirror, using Sam's eyes.

"Nearly there," Hamel announced in a whisper.

Teal'c was watching her, one hand gripping the rope, the other ghosting over the bandage under his coat.

"Okay?" she asked.

He nodded.

"Here." Hamel shook the light stick, and it guttered and went out.

Instead of total darkness, though, there was a tentative yellow light ahead, enough to show them that the wall on their right was broken by an intersecting tunnel. A few more pulls on the rope brought them to the edge of a sloped landing, where the narrow passage opened up into a small lagoon. After nosing the boat forward until there was enough of the prow exposed to allow them to crawl out, Frey held it steady while Hamel anchored it to a loop of wire in the wall. Water lapped against the hollow sides until the men let go and the boat turned into the current and stilled in the pull.

Crouching next to Teal'c at the mouth of the tunnel, Sam peered up into the shifting light. Torches, still a good twenty, thirty feet away in another cross-passage. No sound except the thudding of the crushers, more a shudder in the chest than a noise. She wondered how close they were to the active sections of the mine. Had to be pretty close if someone bothered to leave the lights on.

When Hamel crawled up beside her, she leaned close to his ear. He smelled like the river – empty, cold. "How far and how many?"

He nodded toward the light. "This place is well-hidden. Jaffa don't come this way." He paused to chew the edge of his stubbly beard. "Usually."

"Then who left the torches?" Teal'c asked without moving his eyes from the tunnel.

"The Order. Word must have spread."

Sam wondered if that was good news or bad. "Any chance there's more up there willing to fight?"

"Not much. But they won't interfere." Again, that pause. "I don't think."

"Just as well," Sam conceded, her voice pitched low as she rose and motioned Teal'c ahead of her. Fewer people to worry about.

Hurrying to keep up with Teal'c, Aadi kept his zat closed and clutched close to his chest. Rebnet followed his lead.

Behn startled her by clapping her on the shoulder as he passed by. "Now we kill Jaffa," he said with a satisfied grin made more than a little ghoulish by the shifting light.

"Not until I say so," she reminded him.

With identical grunts of assent, Frey and Hamel followed, but Eche hung back, hesitating. His usually pale eyes were wide and dark. His tongue passed nervously over his cracked lip.

"Someone should stay with the boat," Sam said.

The relief made him seem a little boneless as he nodded.

Sam squeezed his skinny arm and smiled. "Get back inside it and keep low. Play out the rope until you're in the dark. We won't be too long, I hope."

He nodded again, smiled wanly, part gratitude, part apology. At the top of the slope where the rest were waiting for her at the mouth of the intersecting tunnel, she turned back, but Eche was gone, and so was the boat. She didn't pause for long. The rope anchored in her ribs yanked her forward.

"Let's go," she ordered, and they were moving.

The torches were jammed at irregular intervals into crevices along the new tunnel, leaving long swaths of darkness between them. Hamel urged the group forward at a pace that Sam would have thought imprudent if she hadn't actually felt like *running* toward the vault. She set a part of her mind to work on that problem, the how and why of it. The rest of her attention remained focused on any dark patch large enough to hide a Jaffa.

But there were no Jaffa. At least not in this tunnel. The next one, though, was a problem.

There were three at the intersection, one in a crocodile helmet. From where she crouched in the shelter of the corner, she could hear their voices – one mechanical and echoing – but not what they were saying. She arched an eyebrow at Teal'c, who, standing over her, edged his face an inch around the corner so he could see.

"A disturbance in the city," he breathed, his lips hardly moving as he leaned back and bowed low next to her ear. "They do not know of what nature."

"Okay, maybe good." Then, she twisted on her heel to pull Hamel closer. "How close to the vault are we?"

"Very near. Up there," he hooked a bony finger past the guards, "and down a short passage."

"More Jaffa, probably, then."

He nodded.

Behn hissed between his teeth, and Frey cuffed him in the ear. Rebnet shushed them both and Frey cuffed him, too. Behind them, Aadi stood silently, his eyes glittering, watching Sam closely.

She turned back and studied the guards. The one with the helmet was the priority; they needed to blind the other Jaffa, stop them from sending backup. She was giving the 'go' signal to Teal'c when the sound of boots – lots of boots – in the tunnel made him pull back and flatten himself against the wall. She held out an arm to stop the others as if she were a mother in the driver's seat protecting her kids from a sudden stop.

Six more Jaffa came around the corner.

Sam cursed in her head. Frey cursed out loud, and this time it was Behn doing the cuffing. A guard at the edge of the now-sizable crowd turned his head toward the sound, and Sam knocked her temple against Teal'c's knee when she ducked back around the corner. They waited. She pulled the knife from her belt and rose to the balls of her feet, flipped the blade in her palm so it was aimed down in her fist. She would have to go for the throat, above the cowl, or the seam where the chainmail shirt came together with buckles under the arm. Footsteps came closer as the augmented voice of the helmeted Jaffa rose and rattled around in the narrow space, echoes on echoes, giving orders that all seemed to be depressingly about standing between Sam and the vault. Teal'c was perfectly still. Hamel's fingers stretched out, curled around the *zat*, stretched again. Even in the dim light she could see that his knuckles were white when they finally closed in a tight fist around the weapon. Frey's breathing whistled softly in his chest. The others didn't seem to be breathing at all.

Boots scraped on the stone a couple of feet away. In her mind's eye she could see the intersection clearly, all of the Jaffa facing the one with the helmet, away from their hiding spot. If this one came around the corner, maybe they could take him down quietly, gain a little time. Going back wasn't an option. Even the hint of that thought made the rope knotted under her ribs jerk insistently. She caught her group with a meaningful glance and laid her finger over her lips. A Jaffa-shaped shadow slithered up the opposite wall. She held her breath.

The explosion was muffled by the stone of the mountain, putting it somewhere up near the surface, but it had enough force to make the guard stumble. His bracing hand gripped the corner right beside Teal'c's face. Aadi dropped to his knees, shoulders hunched against a stream of dust and small stones that rained from the ceiling, and Frey hunched over him, deflecting the debris with his back. Sam covered her mouth and nose against the dust while the ground rose up, once, and settled heavily as the shock-wave passed. Some part of her hoped that this wasn't a fluke, but she had no reason to believe it. Still, it was a nice coincidence. The timing was impeccable.

In the silence that followed, it took her a second to realize that the pounding of the crushers was gone. Someone had blown the plant, she guessed, and the naquadah in the ore had added a hell of a kick to the bomb. If she was right, they'd be damn lucky if half the mountain didn't come down on their heads, or worse. But, if there was any luck left in the universe after they'd used up all that credit, the explosion would make a really nifty diversion.

To prove that the universe wasn't quite as perverse and annoying as she'd begun to suspect, the shouting started, followed by a booted exodus of Jaffa in the direction of the mine entrance. She raised her eyebrows at Teal'c, and he leaned a quarter inch around the corner, raising one finger at her. Sam did a silent cheer.

She raised three fingers and lowered them one at a time, counting down. On three, she stepped across the narrow side tunnel to the opposite wall, getting a good view of the intersection as Teal'c lunged around the corner, fell to one knee with the staff level and crackling. But the lone Jaffa was looking the other way and only turned at the sound of Sam's *zat* whining open. By then it was too late for him, and he collapsed with the clank of armor on stone. Sam keyed the *zat* a third time and his body disappeared. Through the soles of her boots, she could feel the tingle of the dissipating charge.

Just as she was waving the rest of the crew forward the wall beside her head exploded under the impact of a staff blast, sending slivers of molten stone into her hair and the skin at the back of her neck. With a shout, she dropped to the floor, discarding her *zat* and the knife to bat the shrapnel away with her hands. Thankfully, her jacket took the worst of it, but she could feel the peppering of tiny burns, hissed as her fingers closed on one larger piece of heated stone and flicked it away. Then Teal'c was stepping in front of her, shoving her back into the wall hard enough for her shoulder to crunch and her teeth to snap down on her tongue. Crouched behind him, she couldn't see what was happening, but she could hear *zat* fire and Behn's voice, a wild, crowing laugh.

It took her only a second to get her groping hand on the lost *zat*, then she was leaning past Teal'c's knees, firing toward a corner further along the passage where three Jaffa were darting in and out of cover. A second staff blast threw up dirt and stone a few feet away, raising a strangled yelp from that direction. Someone fell – Frey, she thought – and a third blast hit its mark, making the body jerk and dance a little in her peripheral vision before it went still.

A quick look over her shoulder showed her Hamel firing from the cover of the tunnel they'd followed up from the river, and Behn, miraculously unhurt, standing in the middle of the intersection firing as fast as the *zat* could load a charge, his mouth open wide in an unvoiced battle cry. Aadi was nowhere to be seen.

"We've got to retreat!" she shouted at Teal'c, pushed off the wall and got herself to her feet. As soon as she'd said it, the floor seemed to rock forward and back, leaving her unable to tell if it was her own dizziness or the shock wave of another explosion. Inside her head a voice snarled, *No retreat*.

She squeezed off another shot, and this time one of the Jaffa went down, sparkling with the discharge. Behn cheered and shot the man twice more before a near miss knocked him on his ass, his *zat* spinning away. The look of affronted surprise on his face was almost comical.

"Go!" Sam ordered.

He blinked owlishly while another blast filled the air between them with debris. When the dust cleared, he was on his back, one empty hand flung out toward Frey's motionless body.

With one step, Teal'c was beside him. He bent and in a single, fluid motion, heaved Behn up by the arm and dragged him across the intersection into the narrow tunnel. A second later he returned, covering Sam so she could make a dash for relative safety. She threw herself against the wall and tried to catch her breath. Beside her, Aadi crouched with his *zat* open and his eyes closed.

"Where's Rebnet?" she panted.

Without opening his eyes, Aadi pointed with the *zat* back the way they'd come.

"Great," Sam muttered.

At her feet, Hamel was leaning over Behn, his ear to Behn's mouth, listening for breath. The dust drifted in the air as Hamel bowed his head to Behn's chest with a silent sob.

Sam laid a cool, sweaty hand against her stinging neck and turned away. "This is not going as well as I'd hoped."

"It never does," Teal'c answered.

"We can't go back." The admission made her feel better, as though any other option was literally too painful to consider. "We have to break through here."

"True."

"A stun grenade's probably not such a good idea."

Teal'c shook his head. "This is a contained space. We would be affected."

"Yeah," Sam muttered. Their banged-up state all but guaranteed that they wouldn't recover as fast as the Jaffa. She chewed her lip and bounced her head gently against the wall, trying to shake something out of the tree. "We have to get them to come to us."

"They will not."

"We could surrender," she said, with a small smile at Teal'c.

Hamel's head jerked up, and he glared at her over his shoulder. "You *will not*."

"Kidding," Sam said, and the smile died on her lips.

"They will know if we do not all step out together," Teal'c objected.

"They haven't seen Aadi." Sam couldn't believe that she was even suggesting it. But it was either this or going in damn-the-torpedoes, which meant that someone else was going to die for sure. She turned to appraise the kid. His eyes were wide, but his mouth was a grim, determined line. He looked, well, about as old as he was – in other words way too young for this stuff. "Can you do it?"

He nodded.

"Okay."

"You must not panic," Teal'c told him. "Wait for your chance. Wait until they are both in view. You need only fell one of them. It will be enough for us to take advantage."

Aadi nodded again, swallowed hard. "Just one. Yes. I can do that."

As Sam swiveled on her knees to poke her head around the corner, she said to Teal'c, "Tell me this is a bad idea."

"It is adequate to the circumstances and our resources."

"Thanks for the pep talk."

A faint smile was Teal'c's only answer.

She held out the hand with the *zat* in it, made a show of deactivating it and tossing it away. "Hey, guys," she called. "You got us. We're coming out." On the floor between her and the Jaffa, Frey was staring at her sightlessly, the hole in his chest still smoking.

With a deep breath, she stood and stepped out into view. Slowly, she held up her empty hands. When no one shot her, she looked over her shoulder and nodded. Teal'c and Hamel both came forward to flank her, their *zats* closed and held over their heads.

"Drop them," one of the Jaffa ordered without showing anything but the end of his staff.

Teal'c and Hamel complied.

The Jaffa strode out into the centre of the intersection and brought his staff to bear. "Slaves and traitors," he mocked, as he raised the staff to fire.

He never got the chance. A low shot from Aadi's direction caught him in the legs, not fatal but enough. He crumpled as Sam and Teal'c lunged left and Hamel right, Teal'c coming up with his *zat*. Before he could advance on the remaining, hidden Jaffa, a staff blast whined and the Jaffa stumbled out from around the corner, clutching his chest. The expression he wore was eerily similar to Behn's as he slumped to his knees and pitched forward on his face.

"What the hell?" Sam said, rising and activating her *zat*.

Brenneka swung around the corner and aimed her staff at the other fallen Jaffa. Two shots made sure he would never get up again.

When she looked at Sam, her grin was wicked with triumph. "And now we will go get your friend, this Nitori. Before I change my mind."

The planet Jacob knew as Heramos was a tiny hunk of barren rock Sam had once said was designated P44-007. This had led to a few truly awful James Bond jokes on Jack's part, and some juvenile mocking by both Sam and Daniel, and then Teal'c had proven he knew more about James Bond than any of them by quoting lines from the recent movies. For Jacob, the memory was fresh in his mind while he tapped in the access code and decloaked the hidden *tel'tak* the Tok'ra had left behind on that world, one of many conveniently scattered around the galaxy.

Malek had been strangely quiet since they had stepped through the Stargate and left Hammond staring after them in the 'gate room. Even more interesting to Jacob, he hadn't attempted to contact the High Council and tell them what the mission status was, or where they were headed. Jacob wasn't sure whether he should be suspicious of the silence or grateful that Malek seemed content to let things follow their own course.

*Be suspicious*, Selmak said, confirming Jacob's instinct. They weren't required to report back – Tok'ra in the field often operated for months, even years, without apprising the Council of their whereabouts or activities – but Malek had been overanxious to do so all along. Now, he was carefully running a status check on the ship's controls, and aside from a small frown creasing his forehead, there was no sign of that earlier firm resolve.

"The vessel is in good condition," Malek said, settling into the pilot's seat without asking Jacob if he would prefer to fly. "We have sufficient fuel for a journey twice the length of what we have planned."

Jacob sat down in the other chair – what he thought of as the co-pilot's seat, although Selmak was always amused by that reference, since no ship could have two pilots – and swiveled to look at Malek, who seemed absorbed by his task. "Malek," Jacob said. "Stop that for a minute."

Malek immediately pulled his hands away from the panel and folded them in his lap, but he did not look at Jacob. Another thing that could be taken two ways: either he was ashamed of his single-minded pursuit of his mission, or he was planning some deceit. Jacob had no idea which, but he liked to think he was a reasonably good judge of character.

*Reasonably good, but not the best*, Selmak informed him, and nudged to take over. Jacob allowed it, and felt himself sliding to the rear of his body, shifting into the passenger role. When Selmak spoke, even Jacob responded to the ring of authority in his tone. "Let us discuss this unformed plan," Selmak said. "And let us discuss what will be required of us when we reach Boch's homeworld."

"I had assumed we would attempt to contact SG-1 and, failing that, initiate a search for them on the planet's surface, using our instruments," Malek said. He glanced up at Selmak. "No different than we have done in countless other situations."

"No different," Selmak agreed. Jacob could tell he was weighing many things about Malek's demeanor, looking for signs he could trust him, but Selmak didn't seem to be finding what he was looking for. While he acknowledged Jacob's impatience, he cautioned against precipitous judgment. Instead, he said, "But I notice you do not say we will attempt a rescue, only that we will attempt contact and search. I must have confidence that we are of similar mind on this, Malek."

"Selmak, I have apologized for my behavior." Malek sat back in the chair and, after a moment, said, "I have not always been wise where the survival of our people is concerned. I do not claim I have been. And I do not claim the Tok'ra are always wise, but they are adept at survival. Perhaps I have absorbed only the latter and less of the former."

"Perhaps." Selmak met Malek's direct, open gaze, and nodded slowly. Jacob could feel the decision forming. "We cannot make a direct landing unless we can find a way to blend among the people. Our efforts may be in vain."

"If SG-1 is dead already, then that is so. If they live still, then there is a purpose to going. It is possible they are no longer held there. There are many variables." Malek paused, then said more softly, "I know Jacob thinks of his daughter. I too would be focused on saving someone I love."

"He thinks not only of her, but of his friends," Selmak said, brushing aside Jacob's defensive bristling, which Selmak felt was irrelevant. "Our friends."

"Of course." Malek inclined his head to acknowledge his error and turned back to the console. Selmak stood and made his way to the supply crates loaded in the cargo hold. In the first crate, six *zats* lay nestled in padding. Jacob didn't try to conceal his satisfaction when Selmak used one of them to stun Malek into unconsciousness before giving control of Jacob's body back to him.

"You were right," Jacob said aloud, as he dragged Malek from the ship and gently laid him on the dusty ground.

*There is purpose to the mission, whether SG-1 is alive or dead,* Selmak answered. *Malek's failure to understand this shows us where his true sympathies may be found, even if he is not consciously aware of it.*

"Better safe than sorry," Jacob murmured. Under his steady hands, the *tel'tak* rose through the atmosphere, bound for Atropos.

# CHAPTER EIGHTEEN

Aris didn't expect the wave of relief that rolled over him and knocked him back a step. He put out a hand to catch O'Neill by the shoulder of his jacket as O'Neill's legs buckled a little. In front of them, Jackson stopped walking and his head fell back, mouth gaping, eyes closed, before he fell, going straight down onto his knees with a crunch that made Aris wince, even though Jackson himself didn't seem to feel it. But Jackson's hands came out to break his fall as he tumbled forward, head hanging, breath panting a little.

"God," he mumbled. "That's—"

"I don't think God has much to do with it," O'Neill said in a whisper that was a sort of freakish combination of reverence and barely-contained anger. He shook off Aris's hand and went to stand next to Jackson. O'Neill's hands twitched as he looked down at him.

Aris's own hand hovered again over the last packet of *roshna* concealed beneath his armor. He wanted it more than he'd ever wanted anything. No. That wasn't true. More than *roshna*, he wanted to make that last turn in the hallway, because that was what the relief was about. The whole place seemed to be shuddering with it. Light was dancing in the walls around them, practically strobing, and somehow, even though it hurt his eyes to look at it, it felt like joy. It was as if he were five steps away from the best thing he could imagine, or something even better than the best thing he could imagine, which was maybe why he couldn't picture at all what it might be. All he knew was that he wanted it, the way he wanted *roshna*, like a physical yearning in his blood and his bones. It was the kind of wanting that could make a grown man fall to his knees.

"Move it," he said. He pushed past O'Neill, stepped over Jackson's legs, and turned the corner.

The sudden expansion of the endless claustrophobic hallways

of the maze into this open space made him stumble, as though he'd looked down and found himself on the edge of a cliff. His arms even snapped out at his sides as though he were falling. And the whole room was bright with swirling light in every color imaginable, coursing away from him along the walls and rising up like flood water to crest and surge along a ceiling high above his head. He raised a hand to shield his eyes as he looked up. There was no way to judge distance. As his gaze swept down and around, he could gauge only that the room was roughly circular, but even that was a guess, prompted by the feeling that he was hanging in the center of a soap bubble, free-floating in shimmering iridescence. He stamped the floor once with his boot to make sure it was still there.

"Whoa," O'Neill said from behind him.

"Yeah," Jackson answered.

These guys were the masters of understatement, Aris thought. He had no idea what he could do with the contents of this room, but that didn't matter much. It was his. He could feel it sizzling inside him, making his brain sparkle. Better than *roshna*. Better than…anything.

Jackson started to move, and Aris shot out an arm to catch him across the neck, stopping him before he could get ahead. "This is mine, remember?" Aris said.

"I thought it was for your *people*," O'Neill said acidly from behind him.

"I am my people."

"You don't even know what you have here," O'Neill went on. "You don't know anything about it. You can't even use it."

"It doesn't want either of you."

His voice low and distant, Jackson was still straining against Aris's arm. For a second, Aris was surprised that he could hear him at all, because the light seemed *loud*, as though it should be drowning out every sound but its own celebration. But Jackson's soft voice carried clearly, making the silence of the room apparent, and Aris got that free-falling feeling again. Instead of stamping his boot, he shoved back against Jackson, who barely budged.

"It doesn't want you," Jackson whispered again, and his eyes were wide with realization. "It wants us." The last words weren't soft anymore. And the eyes weren't blue anymore. Gold flashed there and the mouth twisted into an arrogant sneer.

Aris pushed himself away from Sebek and raised his gun. O'Neill took a step back, too, and he looked pained, betrayed, resigned. Sebek's gaze slid from Aris to O'Neill, narrowed, assessing. His hands closed into tight fists, the tendons in his arms standing out, muscles flexing with withheld violence.

Around them, the light lunged and pulsed, flared white-hot and then went out completely.

The memory of light swirled across Aris's retinas, hot blue and slow-burning red. He blinked it away, and then the only thing visible in the place was the tiny flicker of the power-indicator in the grip of his blaster.

After a long pause, O'Neill offered a hissed assessment: "*Crap.*"

"Yeah," Jackson replied, in Jackson's voice.

"Dark," O'Neill added.

"Yes, seems that way, doesn't it?" Jackson said. Pause. "Does anybody still have a flashlight?"

Aris snapped open a pocket on his thigh and pulled out his light, aiming it in the direction of Jackson's voice before turning it on.

What he saw wasn't Jackson or even Sebek's ugly smile, but his own face, twice, distorted grotesquely. He jumped back and snapped the blaster out to the length of his arm, barely keeping his finger off the trigger. As his eyes adjusted, he saw that the ghosts were reflections in a pair of mirrored eyes. The tiny scales around them shifted a little as the mouth below opened into a sharp-toothed smile, and the movement sent rainbowed sparks of light dancing across Aris's extended arm. He backed up another step and tilted the light so that more of the woman came into view – or didn't, really, as it turned out. For a second he thought she was wearing armor like his. When he moved, the black shapes on her shoulders and chest moved as well, and he realized that this, too, was a reflection. She seemed to fade from existence below the waist, but when the light played across her invisible legs, more sparks flickered across the floor and over Jackson's boots.

Jackson was still there, behind her, O'Neill beyond him, braced for a fight in contrast to his earlier glib tone, with his head tilted so that he could see around Jackson. Aris noticed that the woman didn't cast a shadow, and he wondered what O'Neill was seeing. Probably Aris aiming at nothing, or maybe an outline, like the sun lighting the curve of a planet. O'Neill saw *something* though, because he grunted and tilted his head the other way before saying, "Huh."

His expression rapt, Jackson took a step forward. Aris shifted his aim.

"Back off," Aris ordered.

Jackson blinked rapidly a couple of times, raised a hand to wave Aris out of his field of attention, and took another step. One stride brought Aris close enough to angle his arm over the woman's shoulder and plant the blaster in the middle of Jackson's chest.

"I said back off," Aris repeated evenly. Beneath his arm, the woman stood motionless. Her mirrored eyes were a couple of inches from his chin, looking up at him. He let his gaze slip down to meet them, but his own distorted face glared back and he looked quickly away. Where her body came close to his – not quite touching him – he could feel a chill, a dry cold parching his skin under his armor. He could picture frost feathering upward across his chest and stifled a shiver.

The woman opened her mouth again, ran her pink tongue across her lips. She looked over her shoulder at Jackson. When she turned back to Aris, she said, "Shhhh."

Aris *felt* it pass over his skin like water seething up a beach. Jackson's eyelids fluttered and closed. He felt it too. O'Neill's raised fist loosened and fell to his side.

"At last," the woman said. Her voice was rich and low, but thin, like an echo of something else, something far away. The frost seemed to crackle, crystals growing, spearing through Aris's brain. He had to clench his fingers tighter around the light to keep from dropping it and rubbing at his temple instead. "Have you come for what I offer?"

Jackson's answer was barely a breath of sound. "Yes."

"Daniel," O'Neill warned.

Jackson's head snapped around to look at him. "*Yes*," Sebek said.

The woman smiled again. She stepped away from Aris and ducked under his arm to walk a slow circle around the three men. Where the light hit her, she seemed to flare into existence, sending more slivers of color across the floor, over their skin and clothing as she passed them. Aris tried to make out first Sebek's and then O'Neill's face in her eyes, but failed. It didn't matter. He knew what he'd see: Sebek's expression triumphant, O'Neill's wary.

Her circuit completed, she stopped in front of Sebek and rose up on her toes to look closely at his face. He bowed his head toward her, his mouth opening as if waiting for her kiss. The jealousy that knifed through Aris's chest made him growl, but the woman held a hand out to him, palm outward and, although Aris had been starting to move, he stopped, his changing momentum carrying him back onto his heels.

"I have waited for someone to come. Someone with the intelligence to take what I have to give," she murmured, her lips almost touching Sebek's. "You are beautiful."

"I wouldn't get too close to him, if I were you," O'Neill said from the gloom beyond the circle of light. "He's not as beautiful on the inside."

Her hand almost touching Sebek's hair, she hesitated, shifted her attention to O'Neill. "Are you?"

He hesitated too. Finally, he answered, "No. Not really."

Her smile seemed oddly satisfied when she met Sebek's unflinching stare, her hand still hovering above the side of his face. "I can give you everything," she said, drawing her middle finger – still not touching – down across his cheek, along his jaw, up and over his bottom lip. Sebek's eyes slid shut again, and he shuddered visibly.

"Like what?" O'Neill asked.

This time, when she shifted her gaze, it was a sharp movement of irritation. "Everything," she repeated, her voice colder, like a shard of glass. She waved her hand at the space around them, and the light in the walls started to flow again, subtle, muted. "All that is in this place. Everything I protect." Her lips pulled back a little, showing more teeth before she modulated the expression into a smile. "Powerful things." She caressed Sebek's lip, her finger a hair's breadth away, and he shuddered again. "Violent things. Beautiful things."

"Yes," Sebek said, the hollow rumble of his voice softened so that he almost sounded like Jackson.

Aris's vision dimmed and, instead of the room and the woman and Sebek swaying and stupefied in front of her, he saw a star field, a planet banded in red and yellow, a space station silhouetted in front of it. Arcing around from the night side of the planet were a dozen arrow-head ships. The space in front of them flickered with weapons fire as they bore down on the station. There was a pulse of light from the station, and in an instant the smaller ships were gone, not even debris left to show they'd ever been there.

Aris staggered and recovered, blinking hard. When his vision cleared, he found O'Neill hunched over with his fist in his eye, Sebek where he had been, eyes still closed, but a smile broadening on his face.

"Free me and I will show you more. All of it," the woman breathed against Sebek's lips. "The time is short. We must go now, before all this is lost."

"You won't be giving him anything," O'Neill said, his voice strained as he straightened to face her squarely. "He's not the kind of person you want to be doing business with. Now, me, on the other hand—"

This time, Aris didn't contain his growl. With a quick shift of his weight, he leaned around Sebek and the woman and aimed a shot at O'Neill's head. O'Neill caught the movement and ducked when Aris fired, the shot going over the target and into the wall. Sparks showered out and the screech that came with them sliced through Aris's head so painfully that he dropped the flashlight to cover one of his ears. He was still reeling from it when Sebek caught him by the throat, slipped a foot behind his ankle, and threw him to the floor.

"Don't." It was Jackson, now, who leaned all his weight into keeping Aris still under him. He was as powerful as Aris knew he would be, his strength augmented by Sebek's, and his grip on Aris's wrist was viselike, squeezing until Aris's fingers opened and the blaster clattered free. He brought his face close to Aris's. "You aren't helping."

Around them, the light surged like heaving breath, white-hot, shadow-cold, and the screaming voice rose, thinned, stretched taut to a keening that faded from hearing until it ended in a heart-wrenching sob. A child crying, inconsolable.

Aris turned his head, looked past his empty hand at the woman, whose head was bowed. She was shivering.

"You must not destroy each other," she said, her voice muffled. "You have much to give. So much to take."

Beyond her, O'Neill stood in the wild light, framed by the ugly black scar on the wall. His face was twisted, winced up on one side against the noise. Aris wondered what her tears would look like. If they could slice open skin.

After a moment, her shivering eased, and with the change, the lights changed as well. The room was bathed in a pale, shifting blue glow, like sunlight seen from underwater, and time seemed to slow down. Aris felt Jackson loosen his grip, and he took the opportunity to shove him away and roll to his feet. Jackson remained where he was, lying on his back on the floor, arms splayed, gazing upward. When Aris snagged his blaster again and aimed it down at him, Jackson only snorted out a small laugh and kept staring at the ceiling. In spite of himself, Aris smiled and let the blaster fall against his thigh. He had no fight in him. The light was lilting. He was drifting. Distantly, he knew that this wasn't right. Nothing here was right, but the thought was far, far off, and the woman was right there, looking up at him, and even without real eyes, she looked beautiful, better than *roshna*. His blood felt hot even though the room was cool and he was floating.

O'Neill was still on one knee, cradling his injured hand. His eyes were squeezed shut. He was perfectly motionless, a tight knot of resistance. As Aris sank into the calming light, he felt pity for O'Neill. *Give in*, he thought, and the thought had a high, thin voice.

O'Neill didn't look like he was giving in. Poor bastard.

"Soon this place will die, and all here will be lost," the woman said, with a sad smile. "But I have it all, here. Millions of memories. The lives of thousands. Wonders." She laid a hand on the side of her head. Aris noticed that each finger ended in a silver talon. "I can give you what you seek. If you take me out of here. If you take me out." She was looking at O'Neill, but her gaze slid away, slipped across Aris, and settled on Jackson, whose eyes were closed.

"I was right," he said. "I knew it."

"Take me out and I can show you."

The words seemed to echo inside Aris's head, coming and going like waves on sand. His eyes drifted shut. He swayed on the ebb and flow, and nodded numbly. He held out his hand toward her – he could see her without his eyes—

Someone knocked his hand away.

"Just a minute," O'Neill said. He was right in front of Aris. When Aris opened his eyes to glare at him, O'Neill glared right back. He held up a warning index finger, and then added the one from the other hand for extra emphasis. "Hold on."

Jackson climbed to his feet. Over O'Neill's shoulder, Aris saw the woman turning toward him, arms open, waiting for someone to embrace her. She looked at Aris for a moment and then dismissed him as she focused on Jackson alone. The smile that tugged at her lips was seductive, mischievous.

"So much to offer me," she purred, but the smile faltered, became instead a down-turned frown of compassion. "And yet, so much you cannot comprehend."

Jackson bowed his head. His shoulders slumped into a curve of sadness. The woman cast Aris a long glance and then angled her head so that she could look into Jackson's face. "I can help you. I can help you see." She leaned even closer and whispered right next to his ear, "Give this to me."

At that, O'Neill spun around, keeping a restraining hand in the middle of Aris's chest, and said, too loudly for the gentle light, "Oh, I don't *think* so."

The woman raised her head slowly, aimed her mirrored gaze at him. She bared her teeth again with a hiss.

"He's classified. Everything in there is top secret. And you can bet on never getting clearance."

"Jack—" With his eyes squeezed shut, Jackson looked anguished. "If I could just see…if I could see that time when I was ascended – please—"

"You aren't *giving* anything to anybody. Especially that. And that's an order, by the way."

Somewhere, distantly, Aris could hear a child crying, a thin, weak wail. "I'm so hungry," the woman said, the sound of her voice verging on a whine. "I've been alone so long. I need."

"You need," O'Neill repeated. "*You* need. I thought it was about helping *him*."

"Be quiet, Jack," Jackson interrupted him wearily. His hand came up in a pushing-away motion and fell again. Jackson's eyes opened, heavy-lidded, and he looked down at her. Aris burned inside, but didn't move. Not yet. The far away sound of crying was doubled now by something else, an agitation like a bug caught in a bottle, a buzzing of uncertainty. O'Neill looked at him, and Aris could see it there, in his face. Something not right. Something…

"Tell me your name," Jackson said in a voice Aris imagined people used with lovers. He leaned into her, like he was falling. Closer, and closer still. The woman was within inches of Jackson's face, staring into his eyes as if she could see his soul.

She straightened, smiling. "Lorelei," she said, and beneath the word, a vibrating hum.

Jackson's head snapped up, the spell broken, alarm widening his eyes. "What?"

"You know, you could have come with us from the start," Sam whispered to Brenneka, as they crept toward the vault. They hugged the wall, clinging close to its security, with the others ahead.

Brenneka turned her head. The patterned scarf holding back her hair slipped down, and she tugged it back again. "I'm not sure I should be here now." She wrung the shaft of the staff weapon between sweaty hands. "But maybe the Nitori will make use of you, too." Her lips twisted in a wry smile that made the scar on her cheek twitch. "You are certainly a trial."

"But you let your people help us," Sam said. It was the only explanation. Without her permission, they could never have come away with weapons from the secret cache.

Brenneka inclined her head in acknowledgement. "And if they will meet the god on the road, well, someone has to—"

"Watch their backs," Sam concluded.

"Watch their backs," Brenneka repeated, as if testing out the phrase. Another brief grin appeared and fell away. "A few weapons are no great loss. Those can be replaced. People cannot."

"No," Sam said, thinking of Behn and Frey, and their sightless, open eyes. A burning sensation cut at her as nausea welled again. She pointed ahead, to where Teal'c was crouched. "We're close now."

"Yes," Brenneka said. She laid a hand on Sam's arm, her strong fingers digging through Sam's sleeve, into her skin. "Do not disappoint me," she said, and Sam knew it was not an order, but a plea. She nodded.

"We'll do our best."

Ahead, Teal'c held up a closed fist, a signal to stop and get low to the ground. Sam pulled Brenneka down, then gestured to the others. Ahead in the gloom of the tunnel, Jaffa armor gleamed dully against the shadows. Sam pointed at their shapes, then whispered, "There are only two. We'll take them." Brenneka gave her a sharp look, but nodded her agreement.

Sam crept up to Teal'c's side, staying low. He made a series of gestures to confirm what must be done, though he needn't have bothered. They'd been teammates so long that their strategy agreed: Sam would take the shorter Jaffa, on the left, and Teal'c the taller, heavier man on the right. *Zat* fire was not quiet and would draw attention, so the attack would have to be silent.

On a count of three, Sam's fingers flashing the intervals just as before, they rose and took their victims. Sam held the knife tight and drove it home high, into the carotid artery while her other hand covered a grunt of surprised pain. Out, and then a cut straight across the throat; it was quick, efficient, and bloody, and she shoved the Jaffa away from her before the spray could become a shower, soaking her clothes. The second time within hours she'd killed in hand-to-hand, something she would try hard to forget. She gestured to Brenneka and the others to come forward into the vault chamber. Their stares, admiring and wary, made her stand taller.

"We shall not have much time," Teal'c said, watching the corridor behind her. "We must move into the vault."

Sam nodded, her entire focus on the open doorway. Teal'c stepped forward, but she caught his arm. "Wait," she said. The bloody knife was still in her hand. She tossed it toward the opening; it bounced off an invisible barrier and thudded to the ground. "There's a force field." All her attention shifted to the once-dead mechanism to the right of the door, which now pulsed a muted yellow glow from its recessed panel. She turned to look at her miniature army. They were spread across the chamber, bedraggled, their hopeful eyes trained on her movements. "Teal'c," she said, lifting her chin in their direction.

A moment later, Teal'c was arranging them into a makeshift battle formation, teaching them by placement alone how to take cover, how to choose a vantage point, and Sam felt the ghost of a smile cross her face as they watched him carefully, learning from him. At least this was something he could offer, something they would not refuse to take.

The device seemed as incomprehensible as ever – of Ancient design, but like nothing she'd encountered before. Still, the principles should be the same, and she knew those. She pressed closer to the wall, drawn toward it; the anxiety was smothering her, pulling her in. She had to get in there. It was more than a desire to get to the Colonel and Daniel, much more. With one hand, she reached into the recessed device and began feeling around for a mechanism or panel.

"Major Carter," Teal'c whispered. "Perhaps it is not within the panel itself, but somewhere else within this chamber."

She turned to look at him, and a brief spark of anger welled, then died. Of course he was probably right, but why hadn't it occurred to her before, while they'd been sitting trapped in there, with all the time in the world to figure it out? A few choice bits of profanity floated through her thoughts, but she didn't say them out loud. Instead she took out her flashlight and began examining the walls, looking for seams and cracks. Not ten feet from the vault door, she found the panel, covered over with rock and sand. Teal'c wedged his strong fingers beneath the edge and helped her pry it loose, and she stared in dismay at the workings within.

"Is it not a simple crystal control panel?" Teal'c asked, looking at it.

She shook her head, already dissecting the innards with her eyes. "No. But I think…" She began shifting the controls around, without conscious will. Her hands had taken over, assembling new pathways for the crystals, as if she had the plans in her own mind. "I think this will work."

Teal'c was staring at her, but she ignored him and forced herself to work faster. Nothing was more important than getting in there.

"You feel it too," Teal'c said, as if his meaning were clear. Sam understood him. The desire to move, to hurry, was eating her alive.

"Yes," she breathed, her hands a blur.

"Why would the Ancients have constructed a force field if this place were meant to be found and used?" Teal'c asked, under his breath. He was too close to her now, his shoulder bumping against hers, and she jogged him with her own arm, shoving him away. "We should not succumb to these desires."

"No," Sam agreed. Her hands moved faster and faster.

"Perhaps the discomfort the symbiotes feel – that we all feel – is a warning," Teal'c said. He was jostling her, crowding her space. Irritation flared in Sam. Teal'c was graceful. If he was pushing her, it was deliberate, but she wasn't going to be intimidated.

"If the thing wants us to go away, then why is it pulling us closer?" she demanded, slamming another crystal home. Teal'c caught her hand and yanked the next crystal away from her. She glared at him. "Why would this thing try to chase us away and then pull us in? It doesn't make sense, Teal'c. Think about it!"

"The Ancients were wise about such things," he said, his expression troubled.

"Teal'c," Sam answered, and it was all she could do not to shout it, "if they didn't want people to get in here, they should have destroyed it. Now give me the goddamned crystal!"

"Perhaps they could not," Teal'c said. "Perhaps there was an overriding reason." He stood and backed away from her, and Sam surged to her feet, her hand outstretched.

"The Colonel is in there, Teal'c! Give it to me now."

"Daniel Jackson also," Teal'c reminded her.

Sam looked into his eyes. Nausea filled her belly with cold pain while a growing certainty overtook her. "You want this technology for yourself," she accused, stepping away from him. "That's why you don't want me to bring down the shield. You'd do anything you had to, to defeat the Goa'uld, wouldn't you? Even sell out your friends."

"You speak nonsense, woman," Teal'c said, his voice lowered to a feral growl, his muscles tensed.

Sam felt the truth of her words like the blood in her veins, and she hissed, "I'm not one of your Jaffa women. You don't order me around. Just the opposite."

Teal'c's fingers tightened around the crystal he held. "You would prefer a weak opponent, one of your human males, would you not? Someone you can more easily overpower." He leaned closer; his voice dropped low, and he said, "You will not overpower me. Nor will I allow you to prevent me from taking what I wish. I am fully recovered now."

For a long moment they stared at each other. Sam felt her rage building, seeping out from her pores and covering her. She lunged forward, reaching for the crystal. Teal'c let it fall. She stopped, horrified, expecting to hear the sound of shards exploding as it shattered, but it landed intact, spinning on its edge before rattling down flat on the stone. At that instant she was in motion again, strikes flying toward Teal'c's face, at the wound on his side, all her energy focused on removing the threat.

She never felt the blow he landed on her cheek, but the ground was beneath her, and darkness slammed down over her.

*Sixteen, and sitting at the kitchen table, shouting at her father. Her career defined over her tearful objections as her life was laid out for her, piece by piece in brochures and careful planning, as her course was charted steadily: the Academy and pilot training; a stellar progression of assignments, and then she'd head for space. In that hour she'd seen how much her father wanted her to succeed, how proud he was of her intellect. How much it meant to him that she become everything he had never been able to be.*

Voices. Someone was speaking. Through the fog of intense memory, and the pain of her throbbing jaw, she heard a boy's angry voice – Aadi's voice. "Don't hurt her! Don't!" She tried to rise, got an elbow under her back, but couldn't seem to get moving.

Another voice – Brenneka, his time. "So, Jaffa. You prove yourself to be everything we have suspected you are, and worse. You show us you are without respect for others, and care nothing for us, or even for your friends. Tell us now why we should follow you."

"Brenneka," Sam croaked. The fog was lifting from her mind, chased by pain, and Teal'c knelt beside her. His hand beneath her back steadied her. "It's not his fault. It's this damn place."

"Major Carter," Teal'c said urgently. His stricken expression made her want to laugh, and cry. Without knowing which impulse to follow, she let him help her up, then smiled at him, though the simple act of drawing her lips up made her entire face ache. "Major Carter, I did not—"

"I know, Teal'c."

He stopped speaking, but his jaw was clamped tight, and a muscle twitched there, betraying his tension.

"I am grateful my people are unaffected," Brenneka said softly, touching the growing welt on Sam's face. "We have much to be grateful for, it seems."

"Major," Aadi said, yanking at her shoulder. "Jaffa are coming."

Sam glanced at Teal'c, alarmed. Her ears were ringing from the blow, and she could barely hear.

"Aadi is correct," he said.

He held out his prize crystal to her, and she took it from his hand, with a last look to be sure he was himself again. Not that she trusted her judgment so much right then. A lingering flare of mistrust welled within her, but she pushed it away, tried to keep herself in her head, to focus on the game plan, and ignore the erroneous data her body was supplying. But the pulling, yanking urge was back, compelling her to hurry, and the game plan folded into it seamlessly. She had to get in there, now. Even the Ancients wouldn't have a say.

"I don't know if I can do it," she said aloud, though Teal'c already knew.

"We will cover you for as long as it takes," Teal'c answered.

It was not an answer, because they might not have as long as it would take. But Sam would take what she could get. She crouched by the panel, closed her eyes, and let her hands be led again. No time to waste on false ideas of her own brilliance. This was beyond her now. They had nothing left to lose.

# CHAPTER NINETEEN

Daniel heard the name – Lorelei – but it brought him up short, staggered him a little, because he heard it twice: once from her lips and, a fraction before that, in his head. The echo was dissonant, grating. The light seemed to make everything float, fathomless, and he'd been pulled by it, the ease of it, the gentleness of it. *Give this to me*, she said without speaking, and he'd wanted to give it all to her, the bits he couldn't remember, everything he knew, everything he'd been trying so hard to protect from Sebek. Not to share it, but to hand it over, give it up. *Give up, give up, give up.* He imagined the relief of it, to give it away, and the yearning for that was almost enough to make him cry. Sebek was there too, turned inside-out, opening wide, giving it all up because she'd said she'd return in kind. They were there together, Daniel and Sebek. Both of them, willing. Nothing but willing. He could feel her mouth already, gently drinking, and her crooning was in his throat – *give up, give up, give up* – like the truth, like wine, like the perfect fix for the perfect addiction. So good.

But then there was the dissonance, the hitch: Lorelei.

It was like a sudden connection, a radio finally tuned to the proper channel, and all at once the disconnected parts of his brain were speaking to each other. Lorelei. He'd been thinking of her for a long time, he realized, through all the winding corridors, that irresistible cord twisted in his chest and pulling him forward, onward. Thinking of siren songs, of mermaids and sailors pulled to their deaths by compulsion, irresistible impulse.

*Lorelei.* It wasn't her name at all, just a thought he'd had, a comparison his mind had made. She had taken this from him, directly from his mind, and he hadn't even known.

The maze was a treasure, more information here than he could imagine in one place. He couldn't open his eyes wide enough to take it in, couldn't even make a space big enough in his head to accommodate the idea of it: the memories, the *feelings* of who knew how many species, how far flung, how advanced. Wonders, she'd said. Yes. It was wonderful. Sebek practically slavered at the thought of what he could grasp here, what he could use. His thoughts were purpled with the rhetoric of aggrandizement, nothing but golden thrones, vast Jaffa armies kneeling, the populations of whole planets bowing and laying their riches at his feet, System Lords abased and begging.

But then, there was this cord, twisted, taut, and it was different from lust for knowledge or power. It wasn't lust *for* anything so simple. It was yearning, pure like a single voice singing a perfect note, a sound that made everything in him vibrate in sympathy. He *wanted* so hard that he could feel it like a fist under his ribs, like anguish, and his hands opened and closed around nothing, and all he could do was go forward, forward, and Sebek's plans for dominating the galaxy and his own longing to *know* were pale reflections of that wanting, like a myna bird reciting Shakespeare, like humans singing the songs of angels.

And he looked down, saw himself in her eyes, distorted, smaller and broken and alone, and he wanted nothing but to fall, to give. Anything to take him closer. Her touch burned his skin with cold.

*Lorelei*. His brain had been trying to tell him for hours, days maybe. Lorelei sat on the rocks on the Rhine, and she sang a song of longing, and the sailors drowned in it.

"Lorelei," she said, plucking the name from his mind.

He was drowning.

But now he knew it.

"What?" he said, drawing away from her.

Immediately, the character of the light in the chamber changed, dimming to ruddy, pulsing threads spidering across the walls, writhing with sinuous motion. He could feel it on his skin.

The compassion in her face was gone, but she tried to keep it in her voice. "Shhhh," she said, leaning closer, following him as he backpedaled away from her. "It's such a small thing." Her fingers fluttered in his peripheral vision, one hand at each temple. So cold. "It's such a small thing, this bit I took. And I will give you everything. You want to see. I will help you." When he sidestepped her, circled around Aris to stand by Jack, she hunched her shoulders and turned in place, following him like a bird or a reptile, something predatory. The light traced itself across her body, was fractured against her scales, multiplied, and flung outward again, and Daniel could feel each flake like it was shrapnel, a thousand ghostly cuts.

"I'm *hungry*," she said coldly, her voice deepening. "And it is such a small thing."

Jack stepped between them. Momentary jealousy and anger stabbed through Daniel as Jack blocked her from view. He knew Jack was yearning for her just as Daniel was, but his hands were closed into tight fists, even the broken one with its bandaged finger angled outward, and his neck was stiff, unbending.

"If it's such a small thing, then you could've done without it," Jack said to Lorelei. "How 'bout you tell us why the Ancients locked you up in here."

"They were unjust and afraid."

Daniel nodded. "Because…why? Why do you do this, bring us here?"

"I am what I am."

"And what's that?" Jack demanded, holding out his arm to keep Daniel from getting closer to her.

"A repository of knowledge," Daniel said as the realization took shape in his head. He had to grope for it, though, and he felt like he was abandoning his best friend. She looked stricken, betrayed, and he almost gave up, but Jack's elbow pressed into his stomach and Daniel frowned, dragging his convictions into the light. "She gathers. She records. She *takes*." He thought of all the glowing panels in the maze, thousands of them, memories gathered, recorded. "What happened to them? The beings you gathered from?"

Before she could answer, Aris came up on the other side of her. "I'll give," he said. "Show me the weapons, like those others, the ones on that satellite, how to find them. I'll give you anything you want."

She kept looking at Daniel and Jack. Although her face didn't change and her head didn't move, Daniel could feel her focus shifting from one to the other of them, because each time her attention drew away from him, the ache flared up in his chest, and the loneliness leeched into him like ice water seeping under his skin. She might be taking anything, and he couldn't see it and couldn't stop her.

"You have nothing I need," she told Aris.

Even in the erratic light, Daniel could see Aris shaking with sudden rage. "I brought them here. Me. I brought them and I deserve something." He jabbed the air above his head viciously with one finger. "Do you know what's going on up there? I'm not leaving without something."

"Then bring them a little further," she demanded. She raised her hand and pointed at Daniel and Jack. "Them. There is so much there." She twitched her head to the side, again, like a bird, and Daniel was transfixed by the reflection of Jack's set features in her eyes. "In them are the memories of generations. In them is the knowledge of vast beings, these Ancients, these others, the serpents. These things are worthy gifts."

"Yeah, not going to happen," Jack said.

He leaned backward against Daniel, shoving him toward the door, and Daniel knew he was thinking mostly about keeping Daniel's knowledge away from her. Even so, the cold of loneliness and jealousy in his skin warmed under that protective gesture. But Sebek strained against it. Keen pain slivered its way through Daniel. He opened his mouth to say something to Jack, an apology maybe – as if there were anything that could cover this, the sick irony of Jack being forced to protect what he hated – but Sebek exerted enough control to grind Daniel's teeth together, and to add a sharp jab and twist to the sliver for good measure.

"Bring me out of this place. Bring me out. Bring me out there." Lorelei advanced on them, but Jack held his ground.

"I said no."

"I can compel you," she said, her feral smile a promise.

The light was pounding now, like the worst migraine Daniel had ever had, and the red threads writhed along the walls, and the floor seemed to lurch and sway and the color was as loud as her voice, became her voice, the same words winding and jerking, splitting, doubling back on themselves, alive. They hissed and wailed in Daniel's head, around and around, echoes chasing echoes until he had to put his hands over his ears, and still he heard it, insistent, inescapable. Inside his mind, he ran.

"*Yes*," Sebek said. "Yes." And Daniel could only watch as his own hand closed around Jack's wrist, yanked hard and twisted his arm behind his back. He felt Sebek's quick, hot flash of triumph as Jack crashed to his knees, and Lorelei laid her hand on Jack's head.

Daniel couldn't cover his ears when Jack screamed.

The ground heaved under her feet, and Sam dropped a crystal. Another explosion topside. She hunched her shoulders against the sand and small stones that pattered down around her, took the crystal from Teal'c without looking at him, and slotted it into place.

"Hurry, hurry, hurry," she repeated in a whisper, breathing dust. It was more than she could stand, the need to go faster, the need to get in there, the need…pure need. It yawned open inside her, bottomless, cold, so *physical* that one hand folded into a fist at her breast as if she could grab that need, hold onto it, and keep it from expanding, from swallowing her. Her whisper turned to a wordless panting. She knew that there was something…something on the other side of the force field that she needed to find, someone, but that concern was barely a pinprick of light in the vastness of wanting. Sam forced her hand back into motion and used it to realign the crystals inside the Ancient panel. Someone was crying, a pitiful wail of need and longing. It could have been her. She couldn't tell.

Sam barely registered the sound of staff fire behind her, but she knew when Teal'c left her side and stood at her back – his shadow fell across the panel and she had to lean in closer so she could see. She vaguely heard him shouting orders. The wall a few feet to her right exploded in a cloud of vaporized stone. Sam shielded the panel with her body while heat and shrapnel peppered her back. Another shot, to the left, this one connecting with the force field. The flare of light blinded her.

She kept working by touch alone.

A second shot to the field and now seething static crawled across her skin. A third. The crystals under her fingers were hot. When her vision recovered, she could see them as floating blocks of color. Blue, green, white, red. The crystals flickered, went out, flashed on again, all white.

Behind her, someone's shout was sliced off abruptly. Another began, furious, raw-voiced, and it joined with the crying in her head, louder and louder, until it threatened to crack her apart and she had to open her mouth to let it out.

The ground shook again. She staggered, put out a hand to steady herself, and connected with the shield. Sam let out a screech as her arm passed through. Searing pain, as though she'd been flayed.

Sam sat on the shuddering floor and looked at the arm. It was blue to the elbow where a sparkling line circled her flesh. For a second, before the shield steadied, she had seen each of her bones glowing white through her skin. When she'd tried to pull herself out, she'd almost passed out from the pain. With a deep breath, she got her feet under her and stood, dragging her arm up with her. It was like sliding through blades of glass, but there was no blood.

Gouts of dirt erupted from the ground as another blast hit near the base of the shield. The rocks and sand shot through the flickering barrier like fireworks, tumbling across the stone floor on the other side, and each grain sent out a ripple of light like a knife stabbing through her. One direct hit from a staff against the shield and…well, she didn't even want to imagine it.

Teal'c was down on one knee, steadily firing his staff up the ramp toward the access tunnel. There was no cover for him, but he was unharmed so far. Aadi and Brenneka were on either side of the ramp, flattened against the wall. Brenneka darted out and got off a wild shot, then threw herself back to escape an answering blast from the top of the ramp. Hamel was lying face-down in the middle of the floor.

The whole vault chamber was full of choking dust so that every staff blast and *zat* discharge seemed to expand outward in a halo of soft-edged light. In the haze, it appeared to Sam as though everything were moving in slow motion, dreamily. She watched a bolt of heated plasma slice through the air from the ramp to the wall right beside the shield panel, and the sparks rained out like music, danced on the floor around Teal'c's kneeling form, and died. The shield pulsed. Along its surface she could see the deadly wave of distortion coming toward her.

She lunged to the side, forced herself through the resistant shield with a shout that was part battle cry, part scream of pain. She was being torn apart in layers – skin, muscle, bone – and when she hit the ground on her shoulder and skidded through the gritty debris on the other side, she was numb, stripped of nerves.

It took too many precious seconds to find her limbs again and to get them to cooperate with each other so that she could crawl back toward the barrier. Through the shimmering light, she could see Hamel stirring, drawing his knees up under him, groping for his *zat*. The side of his face was blackened. Aadi was still crouched low in the corner where the ramp met the wall, and he was pointing at her.

Teal'c and Brenneka turned as one.

Sam saw Brenneka's mouth open – "Go!" – before Brenneka spun away, rising from her shelter, staff coming up, laying down cover fire.

Following her example, Aadi sneaked the *zat* up above the edge of the ramp and fired blindly. Hamel half-crawled across the foot of the ramp and rolled off of it into shelter beside Aadi.

Teal'c hesitated for a moment, but it felt like hours to Sam, who watched from the other side of the barrier, still caught in the adrenaline-rush and the memory of pain that distended time and twisted space. But it was more than that, too. It was taking too long to move forward. She had to move forward. Even the fire in her skin couldn't warm the icy desire in her chest. *Hurry, hurry, hurry.*

Once he was moving, Teal'c wasted no time. He flung himself at the barrier, passing through in a corona of intense blue light. Sam held up her hand against it, the bones of her fingers ghostly in blue skin. He tumbled past her and landed in a panting heap, but he was down only for a second before he heaved himself onto his knees and raised his head to look back at the vault chamber.

It was quiet on their side of the barrier, no sound at all except the rasp of their breathing and, from somewhere far away, a child crying. On the other side of the shield the battle raged on silently. Staff blasts gouged holes in the stone floor. *Zat* fire crackled through dust-filled air. Another shot hit the shield. Sam saw it coming and flattened herself, arms around her head. Teal'c did the same, throwing his body over hers. The passing light scoured them. Teal'c didn't shout out loud, but she could feel it shuddering through him.

When they raised their heads, the shield was flickering. It rippled once, and again, then disappeared for a second before flaring back to life. A distant part of Sam's brain hoped that, by the time they'd made their way back with the Colonel and Daniel, the shield would have fallen completely. But that was a distant part of her brain. Most of her didn't want to consider the idea of leaving. Only going forward. Only that.

She was turning away from the barrier when she caught sight of Hamel, lurching up from cover, one foot on the ramp. His *zat* was gone. A Jaffa was standing over him, eyes gleaming red above the cruelly smiling crocodile's snout of his helmet. The staff weapon was angled down at Hamel's head. It crackled, ready to fire. But before it could, Brenneka leaped out from the other side of the ramp, swung her staff in a low arc and connected with the Jaffa's legs. Someone with Teal'c's bulk and power might have been able to sweep the Jaffa onto his back, but Brenneka wasn't Teal'c. The staff snapped out of her hands and spun away with enough momentum to bring it to the edge of the shield. The Jaffa planted the heel of his staff on the ground, twisted with more grace than should be possible in his heavy armor, and caught Brenneka by the throat. She kicked at him as he lifted her off her feet. Behind him, Aadi was straightening, arms stiff, *zat* aimed. The Jaffa jerked Brenneka sharply, twisting his wrist, and her head lolled back, eyes open, as her body went as limp as rags.

Aadi was screaming something as he fired.

"No." Sam took a step toward the barrier but was brought up short by Teal'c's strong grip on her arm. "Aadi!" she shouted and waved him toward the vault. He didn't turn to her or stop firing.

When she stepped forward and touched the field, she let out a yelp as pain sizzled up her arm into her neck. For now, there was no going back through the shield.

"They cannot hear," Teal'c said. The ground heaved again, and rubble crashed silently beyond the tunnel mouth, belching a new cloud of black dust. "The tunnels are unstable. We must go on if we are to find the Colonel and Daniel Jackson."

Hamel picked up the fallen Jaffa's staff and fired over and over up the ramp, Aadi at his side. The dim shape of a Jaffa stumbled away from the rock fall and was caught by Aadi's *zat*.

"We must go," Teal'c repeated with a tug on her arm.

Sam pulled the sleeve of her jacket down over her hand and swiped tears and sweat from her stinging eyes. She nodded and turned to face the hallway behind them.

The erratic light of the failing shield lit their way to the first fork in the path. Sam stood at the crossroads where the two new hallways diverged and peered first down one, then down the other. They looked identical. Narrow, low-ceilinged. The walls were covered with the same glyphs as the vault door, except these seemed to be writhing. It took her a moment to realize that this was an effect of the ugly red light in the walls, which pulsed and flickered like a stuttering heart. After just a few seconds, looking at it made her dizzy, so she looked at Teal'c instead.

Teal'c crouched, fingering the jagged line scratched into the wall. He looked down the passage to the left. "This way."

As soon as he said it, Sam knew he was right, as surely as if a voice had told her she wasn't going to die after all. The relief was so intense that tears prickled in her eyes. All she had to do was follow that feeling, now. She set off down the hallway at a run.

If someone had told Jack way back when that a time would come when he'd prefer being ribboned to death to the alternatives, he'd have raised an eyebrow, but he wouldn't have discounted it. In some part of his mind, he'd always known that the universe had something way worse in store for him than that. For a while he thought he'd felt it when the human-form Replicator, First, had stuck his fingers in his head and picked the locks on all boxes where Jack kept the really painful stuff. If he'd been capable of anything coherent enough to pass for thinking, Jack would have remembered the Replicator's probing as a gentle thing, say, a nine on the agony scale. What he felt as that creature with the mirrored eyes touched him – there wasn't even a scale for this. First had been incisive, slicing and winnowing his way to the core of things, elegant. Even Ba'al had been a gentleman by comparison. This was Jack the Ripper, if Jack the Ripper had been a wolf. With rabies.

Jack knew he was screaming – it was a fierce column of fire somewhere at the edge of his awareness – and that was a good thing. Screaming meant he wasn't really gone, that he hadn't been shredded, or atomized. He still had something that could feel pain. So he willed himself to keep screaming.

Daniel wouldn't like it, though.

Daniel's grip had twisted his arm, brought him to his knees, held him there like a sheep on an altar, offered up to her. Sacrifice. Appetizer. Bargaining chip. Daniel wouldn't like that part, either. A slow-moving slither of darkness wound through the jagged, livid landscape of Jack's mind: regret. Jack should have killed him sooner, before he had to watch his own hands give Jack up to… whatever the bitch was doing to him.

She was eviscerating him. Vivisecting him. If it had been a physical thing, he'd be looking at his own limbs stripped of flesh, his heart there, hanging from bloody shreds in the cage of his bones. She clawed through the meat and matter of him, leaving behind tatters of thought, guts, gored memories, dreams torn open and undone as she dragged herself through his mind. God, she was…huge. She went on forever and ever, scales scraping across his surface thoughts with a hiss of protest, scouring. And for all the reptilian suppleness of her, she was spidery, a million probing, inquisitive limbs everywhere, scuttling into crevices, prying open every closed door, tearing out the contents and dissecting them with dexterous fingers, moving on, moving on, moving on, looking for something.

What?

Distantly, he felt Daniel's fingers like handcuffs around his wrists. Sebek was laughing. *I'm sorry, Daniel*, Jack thought, but the apology barely had a chance to form before it was threshed and discarded, and Jack was left with only the slowly widening pool of loss, wordless, congealing. It had a sound, a long, low note fading under the frenetic staccato of her searching.

For what?

Jack would give it to her, tie it up in a bow and write *best wishes* on the card if it only meant that he could fall down and Daniel's hands wouldn't have to hold him anymore. No. He wouldn't. He would never, never, never. But the spidery thing skittered through him, let him hear Sebek laughing, and told him in its sibilant, insistent voice that he would. He'd give it up if it meant that Daniel didn't have to be an accessory to this anymore.

All at once, there was a pause, a gasp of triumph he felt as an electric shock along his spine, jerking his head back against Daniel's thigh. She crooned with the joy of discovery, and it was blue-black cold fading to pus-green around the puckering of an old wound.

Kanan.

It was Kanan she was after, but there was nothing left of the Tok'ra but a scum around the edges of Jack's memory of Ba'al, an oily residue of Kanan's motivation, his actions that had led only to his host's capture and torture. Mostly there was a blank space scored and pitted by Ba'al's repeated attempts to find out what Jack knew, to harrow Kanan from Jack's memory. For Jack, Kanan was only a thing he'd grasped at and never really found. He was a nightmare, insubstantial and still clinging to the waking world as a shudder of unease, lingering resentment. What she could find was only that Kanan wasn't evil, that he really did believe in symbiosis, but still, he was superior and thoughtless and ultimately Jack was his machine. And she found that Kanan carried in his blue blood everything any snake in his line ever knew. The thrill of elation that passed through the invader in Jack's mind was followed by a sudden frustration that exploded outward as dark, seething anger.

And then she was gone.

Jack slumped forward over his knees, barely caught himself with numb hands before his forehead cracked against the floor. He lowered himself down and gingerly rested his cheek on the cold stone.

"Where is it?" Lorelei hissed, her voice like a serrated blade across Jack's brain.

He felt Daniel's body moving away from him. Near his head were a pair of heavy black boots. Aris.

"There is nothing here," Lorelei said, the edges of her voice jagged. Jack felt a swath of cold slash across the rubble in his head. "There is promise but no…no…no—" Her voice staggered around in the debris, aimless.

"It is here, in us." Sebek's voice.

Jack pulled his hands in under his shoulders and started to heave himself up.

Sebek was still talking. Daniel stepped around Jack. "And so much more. We can take so much more from this vessel. He carries the knowledge of the Ancients. Those who imprisoned you. Those you hate."

Her hiss sizzled across Jack's vision. As he straightened, sitting on his feet now, the room heaved. That may have been in his head, but one look at Daniel, whose feet settled into a broader stance, said that he felt it too.

"We can take it," Sebek said, his voice oil-smooth, insinuating. "You can tear it from him and we can share this, this and all that I know, all that you know. We can rule. We will be great."

Jack managed to raise his head, lift it past the tipping point so that it lolled back on his boneless neck. Daniel's face was ecstatic, his eyes bright in the lurid light. His skin was reddened, his face glistening with sweat. His hands were held out to her. Sebek was offering Daniel to her.

"Nnngh—" Jack said before his momentum started to carry him backward. Aris caught him with his knee and shoved him upright again.

Lorelei's head gave that same oddly birdlike twitch as she assessed Sebek. "I know the host will be a machine to you. I will not be a machine to you." Her chin came up and then fell again as she aimed those lifeless eyes at him. "I am what I am. No less."

"More," Sebek promised, and his smile was wide and ugly.

Jack struggled to get up, but his muscles were jelly and Aris held him in place. He pushed Aris back, knocking him away, but he barely had the strength to get to his feet. Walking would take more muscle than he had to spare; the heavy gravity anchored him to his place. There was no way he could move. Sebek was moving, though, stepping toward that grotesque thing, and she extended her arms to him in a parody of embrace. Her form flickered, disappeared, then reappeared on the other side of the room, her back to the far wall which pulsed with deep blue light. Her arms were spread wide. The winding tendrils of light in the walls converged on her there, pierced her, ran through her. They pulsed like a heartbeat. She was color and light.

"Do not deny me," she crooned. The sound of her voice was a flare of pleasure, stripping will away. Jack focused on hating her, on the threat she represented, and the desire to join her receded. Sebek took one more step, then another, and stopped, his foot inches from the floor, frozen in mid-stride.

"Stop," Jack shouted. "Yes, Daniel, fight her, damn you! Fight this!" His words were felled and flattened by the force of her attraction, which battered him back even as she tugged Sebek to her with invisible strings. The deep red flush on Daniel's skin turned impossibly deeper. He was panting now, a sign of the struggle Jack hoped to God was going on somewhere inside Daniel, a battle for his life, or what was left of it. If she took the Goa'uld genetic memory, or Daniel's ascended knowledge, they were all screwed. He needed a weapon. *Anything.*

Aris had a weapon. And he had a knife.

"Are you just going to stand there?" Jack said, turning on Aris, who was watching with a mix of rapt fascination and horror. "Don't you get it? Do you want that thing loose on your planet?"

Aris turned to look at him, and it was as if Jack's presence barely registered with him. "She can't really leave here," he said, his eyes narrowing as though he was struggling to make out Jack's face. "She's not real."

"She looks pretty damn real to me," Jack said.

Daniel let out a low moan, a sound that wasn't Sebek but all

Daniel. His entire body jerked, arms contracting in, palsied and curled to his body, hands rigid, legs bent at the knees. He fell backward, convulsing.

Jack willed himself forward, but he only managed a single step before he was on the ground, where he could use the floor to help him. He crawled, but the air was quicksand, and he was sinking. "Come on," he gasped, pinned by his own weight. He could sense that thing behind him, could hear her sickening, inaudible song, like pressure rising in his ears, like falling too fast from high altitude. Daniel turned his head, and when he met Jack's eyes, an agony of fear and despair stared out at Jack. White foam bubbled at the corner of his mouth. Daniel lifted a hand and smeared it away with his fingertips, looked at it and back at Jack. As clearly as if Daniel had said it out loud, Jack knew he was dying – the host, deteriorating, unable to withstand the pressure of that thing's attention.

"Don't," Jack whispered, unsure of who it was meant for. "You're killing him."

The thousand-pound weight on his chest lifted and his lungs filled with air, and he could move. He slumped to the ground, trying to get his bearings, but Sebek was up and moving, his eyes a flash of yellow determination, fixed on Lorelei's shifting shape. Jack sat up and twisted to look at Aris, who moved to put himself between Sebek and the wall.

"Now's your chance," Aris said, his blaster leveled at Daniel. He lifted the knife from its holster and tossed it to Jack.

In his hand, the knife was cold, and a trick of the light stained the edges red. Jack's grip on the hilt was sure, and he saw Daniel's pleading stare, heard his own promise to his friend echoing back to him from so long ago. He couldn't let Sebek give anything away. Not his own knowledge. Not Daniel's, either.

He couldn't let Sebek give Daniel away.

His eyes flicked to Aris, then to Sebek, and for a moment, they all stared at one another. Lorelei's vacant crooning had begun again, but she was *slithering* toward them now, although she was still there, against the wall, and the sensation was ants, bugs, a million spiders creeping over Jack's body. He planted his left foot on the ground, ready to shift his weight, and glanced up at Sebek, trying not to see Daniel there and unable to see anything else.

One quick cut, one twist, and it would be over and this would be ended. He wasn't close enough, but it was his only opportunity. All he needed was a little luck. Aris stepped back.

Jack lunged.

Sebek was stronger in Daniel's skin than Jack would ever have given him credit for. He grappled for the knife as his mocking smile disappeared behind his efforts. Jack bashed out a foot and caught Sebek's kneecap; Sebek barely paused as he struggled to keep Jack at bay. They danced across the room like broken marionettes, light playing over them. Over the rasping of his own breath, he could hear the sighing of metallic tendrils releasing Lorelei's physical form, one after another, as she disengaged from the wall. And there were two of her, then, one solid and real, the other like a ghost, an insistent yearning in Jack's head, in his mind's eye. As the last connections hissed free, the projected Lorelei flickered like a fading signal. But she stepped nearer and nearer – real or an illusion, he couldn't tell – and the sharp echo of her voice

*give up give up give up give up*

was blood filling Jack's ears and eyes, drowning all sound and sight. His hands slipped on Daniel's sweaty skin and Sebek pushed him, throwing him aside with some reserve of strength dredged up at a dear cost to Daniel. Jack caught his balance and turned to see Sebek hurl himself at Lorelei, the real one, grasping at her like a lifeline, twisting his hands against her parody of skin.

"You will be our host, and we will live forever in you," Sebek rumbled, and his mouth opened against her mouth, into her scream, her desire. His body stiffened, and Jack shuddered as the rustle of scales scraping together filled the room. Daniel's body tipped slowly backward, his hands sliding away from her face like a lover left behind, and he fell to the stone, fresh blood coating his parted lips and trickling from the corners of his mouth, over his chin. He gave a strangled cry and coughed. Jack stumbled to him, hunched his shoulders away from Lorelei as he knelt by Daniel and turned him onto his side. Daniel choked out a mouthful of blood. Jack didn't need to look to know that Sebek had left the premises. Daniel was going to die here, bleed to death from the back of his throat, torn open by the thing that could have saved him.

Lorelei's face was tilted up, and her soulless eyes were fixed on a point above them. She stretched out her arms, and when she spoke, her voice was amplified, a Goa'uld times ten. "Now we are nearly complete," she said, the sibilance of her voice an aural house of mirrors. Her repulsive joy made Jack's skin crawl.

Daniel reached up a hand to his throat, then gripped Jack's arm. He choked out another mouthful of blood, but, miraculously, it appeared to be less than before. "Daniel," Jack said, and was rewarded by a quick nod. He grabbed the back of Daniel's t-shirt and pulled him across the ground, away from Lorelei. Then he turned his rage on Aris. "What's it going to take?"

By way of an answer, Aris pointed his weapon at Jack. "Take Jackson and go," he said, still watching Lorelei's ecstatic rapture.

"You still think this thing can be useful to you? Are you nuts?" Jack hissed. There was a part of him – the part interested in self-preservation and in getting Daniel the hell out of there – that wanted not to care, that wanted to leave Aris and that thing down there together. The other part of him, the part interested in keeping the galaxy safe from über-Goa'uld, was stronger. "Shoot it now, damn you! Or give me that thing and I'll do it."

"Don't make me tell you twice," Aris said, aiming the weapon directly at Daniel.

Lorelei turned then, and the pressure surged in Jack's brain again, the feeling of freefall. "There is more in you," she said, staring at Daniel. "Much more. You may give it to us now." She stretched out her hand toward Daniel, and Jack knew with awful clarity that Daniel had two things that might interest her – all his knowledge of Earth's defenses, and his ascended knowledge. Either way, she was going to leave him a husk, burned out, useless. Dead.

"Oh, hell no," Jack said. He hauled Daniel bodily to his feet and slung Daniel's right arm over his shoulder. The motion made Daniel retch, and he spat and choked out blood. Full-blown nausea, over-powering, and the stench of rotted flowers assaulted Jack, and he felt his own body weaken, even as he tried to support Daniel. He took a step toward the door, but his legs gave out and he pitched forward, falling half on top of Daniel. He was heavy again, sinking into the floor, and the sounds surrounding him were children screaming and worlds dying, and he wasn't responsible, he didn't want to know, he had to get moving and get them out of there.

"Sir!"

Carter's voice. Another bit of his imagination breaking free. He got a knee under him, forced his arms to lock and lift his body. He heard the sound of *zat* fire, and something like an unholy scream that shivered down his body.

"Sir!"

When he raised his head to disavow the phantom voice, he saw Carter crouched at the doorway, staring at him with urgent concern. If she was a hallucination, she wasn't the nice kind, all pristine and beautiful, because she looked like she'd rolled in ten tons of dirt before charging in like the cavalry. Teal'c was with her – no, not with her, coming toward Jack, loping across the room as if he couldn't feel the world sitting on top of his body. Jack fell back down to the ground, and rolled over onto his back.

"Teal'c," he gasped. "Get Daniel out of here."

"O'Neill," Teal'c said, pressing a *zat* into his hand.

The familiar shape of the weapon in his grip worked its own kind of magic, recalling a sense memory of his own that was a solid point of reference in the kaleidoscope of color and sound and the crushing weight of wanting and horror. Jack rolled onto his shoulder and then up onto his knees. Aris was still there, between him and the creature. His blaster was still aimed at Daniel, but he turned slowly – everything seemed to move so slowly – and aimed the gun at Sebek-Lorelei instead.

"Get out or give up," Aris said to them.

*Give up, give up, give up*, the monster sang in Jack's head, only now her thin voice, the keen blade of ominous yearning, was weighted down by the symbiote's arrogance. Jack could feel it bearing down on his chest, cracking ribs, breaking skin. But he could also feel Daniel shuddering as he curled against Jack's legs.

"Get him out of here," he told Teal'c again, and this time Teal'c stood and began untangling Daniel so Teal'c could lift him. "Carter," Jack called. "Monster." He pointed with his *zat*.

"Sir," she answered steadily from behind him. "It's a machine. Some kind of cyborg."

Jack was about to point out how much that didn't make a difference, but, like the *zat* in his hand, her voice seemed to have the power not only to ground him but to shape the sense of the place. The rib-cracking weight receded, like the monster was pausing to suck in a deep breath before the next attack. In that moment, the room changed again, the next layer of illusion swept away by Carter's words. The writhing tentacles and tendrils that laced the walls rippled and resolved into regular patterns, the straight lines and sharp angles of circuitry, panels tricked out with flashing lights, status screens. It was so shockingly mundane that a laugh ripped from Jack's mouth.

But one look at the cyborg, at the new Sebek, was enough to bring the weight down on him again. The beautiful mermaid was gone. There was still a creature with them, still vaguely female, still humanoid, still wearing a skin of glass scales, but this thing was a parody, a nightmare. Her body was emaciated: tendons – or whatever passed for them – roped around her limbs, the mirrored skin stretched taut over a sharp-edged frame so that the face was skull-like, the full-lips that had come so close to kissing Daniel thinned and stretched like a slash in tight canvas, the mouth toothless, sunken under the blades of angled cheekbones. The eyes were enormous, bug-like, reflecting the room, inverted, distended, a world seen through a fever dream. The body was waspish and fleshless. The arms were too long, ending in multi-jointed fingers like the legs of a spider, all of them – he couldn't count them – restlessly moving, reaching out. They scrambled and skittered across Jack's brain. He knew absolutely that the touch of those fingers on his head would tear him to shreds from the inside out. What he'd felt before, when she'd reached out to him through her apparition, would be nothing compared to what the touch of her real hand could do.

He raised the *zat* and fired. Light flared across her glass body, swirled and arced, and her whining scream climbed up and up until he was sure it would slice him like wire across a throat. He squeezed his eyes shut and focused on the hardness of the floor against his knees. The ground lurched, and he had to put a hand out to catch himself, grinding his teeth against the stab of pain in his finger, but he held onto the *zat*.

When he opened his eyes, Sebek was still there, unharmed. The creature's gashed mouth was wider, smiling, and then wider still, laughing. There was nothing inside but darkness.

Aris had shifted his blaster to him, but then, after a second's hesitation, he aimed it back at Sebek. Jack wasn't sure whom he was protecting from whom. The expression on Aris's face told him that Aris wasn't sure, either.

"It will kill you and you'll have nothing," Jack said, amazed at how even his own voice was, that it carried through the surging, leaping light in his head.

"Not your concern. Get out or give up," Aris repeated, but his own voice was brittle, faltering. He was falling into the blackness of that open mouth. The blaster wavered, swung on Jack again.

"We have your son," Teal'c said.

Aris went still.

Behind him, Sebek continued toward them on spindly legs, one shuffling step at a time bringing him closer. Daniel was over by the door, next to Carter, a huddle of pain at her feet. Coming back toward Jack, Teal'c strode across the floor as though it weren't quicksilver and coals and slithering. He lowered the staff weapon and fired, over and over. After the first shot, he went down on one knee, and his face was a grimacing mask of determination. The percussion of the blasts ricocheted and rolled around the room, echoes like fists pounding on Jack's skull.

The light that erupted from Sebek was palpable, shoved against them, threatened to bowl them over, and the high-pitched wail drew its razor-edge through Jack's brain again. And again, the ground lurched under him. And again, when the flare settled, Sebek was unharmed and laughing.

Teal'c growled.

Aris blinked at him as though none of it had just happened or had happened in a dream he was waking from. "My son," he said tonelessly.

"This thing gets out and your son's good as dead." Jack got one boot under himself, pushed up. He was on his feet. He wanted to run to her – to *it* – he *wanted* it. He wanted to *give up, give up, give up.* From the corner of his eye, he could see Daniel crawling toward it, on his belly. Carter stepped up and blocked his path and the sound of miserable desperation that Daniel made was a cold hand closing around Jack's ribs.

Aris's gaze stuttered across Jack toward Daniel. Then he looked over his shoulder at Sebek. The blaster faltered again, recovered, then fell.

Beyond him, Sebek was a scintillation of color against patterned walls – circuitry, the monster's brain – framed by a black starburst scar, the mark left by Aris's blaster shot when he'd aimed it at Jack. A thin ribbon of memory slipped across Jack's mind: the monster weeping when that shot had hit home, the color of the place changing. Lifting his hand – it seemed to be far away, like it belonged to someone else – Jack pointed at the scar.

"Carter," he said. "See?"

She followed the line of his arm – her whole body turning slowly, too slowly, away from him toward the wall – and then looked back at him, blank, confused. Her head tilted a little to the side as if she were listening to something distracting. Her mouth fell open and her eyelids fluttered and closed. Daniel started moving forward again, going around her spread feet. Light rose up between Jack and the others like water flooding in. He wanted to say something. Daniel was crawling. Carter's head tilted the other way, dreamily. Teal'c was on one knee, motionless. Aris was unmoving, blaster at his side. Sebek smiled and came forward to meet Daniel. He was only meters away, talons reaching.

"*Major*!" Jack shouted, and Carter's head snapped up, her eyes on him, waiting for orders. He wanted to say something…something. His arm was still pointing, so he followed it himself, now, to the black burn on the wall. "The brain," he said.

Her head turned again.

She fumbled in her pocket. It took a long, long time, but finally she pulled out a grenade, held it toward him, the question clear.

The room wasn't that big. The blow-back would probably take them all out.

But Daniel was crawling and Sebek's fingers were reaching, inches now from Daniel's face. Sebek's mouth was open wide, black and empty and ready to swallow them all.

Jack met Carter's eyes and nodded.

The grenade collided with the wall, rebounded, spun like a top.

The explosion knocked him on his ass again. He could hear something, distant, beyond the ringing in his ears, a child crying, crying. Pitifully. And beyond that, even farther away, a voice roaring. Rage. His skin was being seared away by that voice, the vast, aching rawness of it. He tried to find his hands, his legs, but there was nothing, free-fall, not even wind, nothing but the child and the rage. Then the planet under him convulsed, heaved up like something huge was trying to surface under his back, its shoulders braced against bedrock, then dropped away beneath him, the beast collapsing with exhaustion, the whole weight of the mountain crashing down on top of it.

The darkness was terrifying and beautiful after so much light. He was falling. The world was ending. Jack closed his eyes.

# CHAPTER TWENTY

Sam wasn't entirely sure how she got the Colonel moving. It might have been when she smacked him on the face hard enough to make his head stop lolling to the left and loll to the right instead, or maybe it was the sound Daniel made, that gurgling groan and the blood that followed it, or maybe it was Teal'c's solemn, unruffled announcement that there was 'fire in the hole,' indicating the deployment of his own grenade. Whatever it was, the Colonel's feet were moving. Not in a terribly coordinated fashion, but – she wasn't afraid to admit now – it was better than she'd hoped for.

The howling chased them down the corridors. The Colonel leaned heavily on her as they stumbled after Teal'c, who had Daniel thrown over his shoulder. One of Daniel's hands swung back and forth with his steps. The Colonel kept his eyes on that hand, and that was fine. Whatever worked, so long as he kept going.

And they had to keep going because the collapse was chasing them too. The first grenade had taken out an entire wall, which exploded away from them, blasting the bulk of the debris into an adjoining chamber. Like everyone else, Sam had been thrown off of her feet. Her jacket had been burning and she'd rolled, coming up against Aris, who first kicked her away and then helped her beat out the flames. Everything was a jumble, the floor pitching and the sky falling. Frozen with its arms outstretched, obscene mouth gaping, the cyborg was a rigid line of agony. Daniel was sprawled at its feet, one hand wrapped around the thing's ankle. Teal'c had had to pry his fingers free.

And then the lights went out.

And then they were running.

Filling the corridors with a palpable darkness, the dust billowed out ahead of the destruction as the maze crumbled from its center, walls slumping inward, revealing the erratic blinking and flaring of the vast hidden network of the mainframe. The mountain was finally coming down, crumbling from above, where the processing plants were still exploding, and below, where their grenades had set off a chain reaction in the systems of the maze – and they were in the middle of it. So what else was new?

Sam forced herself not to look back, not to feel a moment's regret as the data – so much data – crackled and bled away. Over the rumbling of the collapse, she couldn't possibly hear the discharging static electricity in her hair, and it really couldn't have been those last wisps of knowledge sparking into nothingness, but she imagined she could feel all of it dissipating as the maze toppled in on itself. She did hear Aris panting as he came up beside her, looped the Colonel's other arm around his neck and helped her pick up the pace.

It wasn't as easy going out as it had been going in, when they'd been lured along by…that thing. Sam shuddered. Maybe because he felt it, the Colonel said something unintelligible. She didn't stop to ask for clarification. Not for the first time, she was grateful for Teal'c's keen eye and the fact that he had remembered to leave markers as they'd made the dash into the center of the maze, once the Colonel's had abruptly stopped. He followed them now, running his free hand over the marks at each corner before setting off again. A few paces away and he disappeared in the dust. Even Aris's flashlight did little more than show them thicker shadows in the drifting haze. Sam wished she had a bandanna to cover her mouth with.

The Colonel's breathing was uneven, but, as they got farther away from the cyborg, he seemed to gather a little more strength, finally pulling his arm from around Aris's shoulder and pushing away from Sam when Teal'c paused at a corner to get his bearings. Bending low, he braced his hands on his knees and coughed so hard Sam expected to see blood. When he straightened up, he reached out to steady himself against the wall, but snatched his hand back as if he'd been burned.

He mumbled something that sounded like "Sea monsters," and set off after Teal'c.

Sam decided to take his word for it.

At the vault entrance, they got lucky. The shield was down. After tossing a good-sized rock through the opening to make sure,

Sam led them into the chamber. The torches were doused and the same thick dust hung in the air, turning Aris's flashlight beam into a seemingly solid shaft as he angled it around the open space. They all held their breath and listened for any sign of danger before moving cautiously up toward the ramp. From beyond the chamber, they could hear muffled shouting, staff-fire and, after a long pause, an explosion that brought a patter of debris down on their heads.

Then they heard a small voice coming from the angle between the wall and the ramp.

"Father?"

The flashlight beam stabbed into the darkness, revealing Aadi, one hand held up to shield his eyes. In his other hand was a *zat*, aimed, stiff-armed, at them. Beside him, Hamel was lying on his side. When the light hit him, he made a move to rise, but slumped down again. Brenneka was laid out in front of them, hands folded on her breast.

"Here," Aris called, his voice strangely soft.

Aadi didn't move. The *zat* wavered a little, shifting toward Aris's voice. "Sebek?"

"Dead."

Again, a waver, but Aadi recovered. "The Nitori? Did they come?"

"No."

"No," Aadi repeated. "I hoped – Hamel said – maybe they'd come for her. But I knew they wouldn't." The *zat* fell to the floor with a clatter. As he stared, wide-eyed and vacant, into their light, Aadi began to cry.

Finally Aris moved. He crossed the space slowly, as if he were approaching a wounded animal, and settled down onto his knees beside his sister. He brushed the side of Aadi's face with the back of his fingers, then let the hand fall to Brenneka's hair, then her cheek, wiping the dust away with his thumb. After a moment, he leaned forward and touched his forehead to hers.

"Jaffa," Aadi managed. "I killed him." A shaky arm pointed up at the body sprawled across the ramp.

Aris nodded, silent approval.

Teal'c shifted Daniel's weight on his back, and the Colonel rested a hand on Sam's shoulder for a brief moment. The darkness and the dust seemed to settle into Sam chest. Blindly, she reached out and smoothed Daniel's hair away from his forehead, feeling the moist heat of his breath on her skin.

She had to clear her throat twice before she could find her voice. "We have to go."

As if to make her point, a low rumble rolled behind them and more dust belched from the mouth of the maze. The ground shifted under their feet, and the debris that clattered down was big enough and heavy enough to do damage. She shielded Daniel's head with her body as Aris did the same for Aadi and Hamel.

"Now's good," the Colonel agreed, his knuckles rubbing the top of his head where a chunk of the ceiling had landed on him, and then led the way toward the ramp. Taking the flash from his father, Aadi clambered up toward the tunnel opening and shone the light down on them. Sam detoured to help Hamel to his feet, while Aris got his arms under Brenneka's broken body and rose. Her head resting against his shoulder, her long hair falling away from her face, she could have been asleep. He met Sam's eyes as if daring her to object. She nodded and helped Hamel up the ramp.

The tunnel that led up toward the surface was blocked by a wall of rubble, but Sam turned left and headed down.

From behind her, the Colonel called, "Uh, isn't up thataway?"

"Better route, sir," Sam gasped, turning Hamel awkwardly at the entrance to the intersecting tunnel so she could see her CO. "If it hasn't collapsed, too." And wouldn't that be adding insult to injury, to survive all of this only to be buried alive. She thought of the cyborg raising its skeletal head to look at her with those cold, mechanical eyes. No way. She was not going to get stuck down here with *that*. Dead or not.

Hamel started to sink and she struggled to get a better grip on him. Aadi helped, taking the old man's other arm over his houlders. Sam craned her neck to peer down the narrow passage. Somewhere down there, a torch was burning.

As they made their way down the sloping tunnel, the dust seemed to clear a little and the air grew damper and heavy with the smell of water. That seemed to perk Hamel up a bit. He tilted his head back and to the side to watch where they were going with his one good eye. The other side of his face was a solid burn, black and flaking, that eye closed. Sam could smell cooked flesh.

"Almost there," she murmured under her breath, more like prayer than encouragement. It seemed farther than it had on the way in.

At the site of their first battle, Behn was lying where they'd left him, covered now in fallen rocks and drifts of sand that hid his face. Hamel paused and wobbled himself into a crouch to close Frey's eyes. Rebnet was slumped on his knees against the wall in the next tunnel, shot in the back.

"We'll come for you," Hamel whispered indistinctly. His burned lip gleamed with seeping blood.

They moved on into the last tunnel.

It was so quiet here, nothing but their own labored breathing, the scrape of their boots on stone, and now the unmistakable sound of sluicing water. At the point where this tunnel intersected with the short passage to the landing, Aadi stood on his toes to pull the torch out of its sconce, and they all paused in the wavering shadows while Sam and Colonel O'Neill slipped ahead, one on either side of the passage, hugging the walls.

Two Jaffa were sprawled at the edge of the water. They were both dead.

"So," the Colonel said in a low voice, barely audible over the steady rush of water. "We gonna swim?"

"No, sir," Sam answered and found herself smiling. She made her way to where the landing stopped at the tunnel wall and, hooking her hand into the anchor ring, leaned out over the water and around the corner. "Eche!" she called. Nothing but her own voice doubled back on itself. She called again, and finally the boat loomed into the light.

Eche stood at the bow, leaning all his weight into the rope so he could heave the boat forward, hand over hand. He was smiling and looking a little wild around the eyes. "I did—" he began, cutting himself off as his hands slipped and the boat skidded backward on the current. One-handed, the Colonel helped Sam guide the boat up to the landing. "They came, and I was hiding, and when they weren't looking I shot them," Eche went on in a whispering rush. He looked a little appalled when he caught sight of the bodies.

"Good," Hamel said from behind Sam. "You did good."

Eche nodded, but the wildness didn't fade much.

It took a fair amount of shuffling to get them all into the boat, Sam and Aadi staying until last to hold it steady. Eche hesitated and then held Aris's arm to brace him so he could step over the side to settle Brenneka into the stern. Then Aris and Eche hunched down on either side of her. The Colonel went next and got Daniel under the arms as Teal'c stood him unsteadily in the boat. The Colonel couldn't take the weight too well, though, and the two of them fell together, Daniel sprawled on top of him. There was some grumbling about too many walnut cookies and somebody having to go on a diet while Hamel clambered in after Teal'c, then Aadi, and finally Sam, who let the rope play out. The current caught the boat and they slipped into the tunnel, going twice as fast downstream as they'd come up.

Teal'c kept a guiding hand on the rope as they surged away from the mine and down under the city. Sam leaned her head back against his knee, looked up at the ceiling, and wondered what was going on up there. Something big had rallied most of the Jaffa out of the mine. She guessed they had Brenneka and the Order to thank for that. Aris sat in the stern beside his sister, one arm around her, the other thrown over Aadi's skinny shoulders. Pale tracks of tears showing through the dust on his cheeks, the boy stared blank-faced over Sam's head and at the guttering torch wedged in at the bow. Eche was reaching out to touch Hamel's burned face, but the old man swatted his hand away, then caught the kid's fingers, squeezed them tightly and didn't let them go. At Sam's knees on the other side of the boat, the Colonel slouched, his chin tucked in to his chest. Daniel was curled up under his steadying arm. In the torchlight and the oblique angle of Jack's flash, which was upended between spars on the floor, Daniel's neck and chin looked black with drying blood. When the Colonel coughed, covering his mouth with the back of his hand, Daniel stirred, rasped out something she couldn't hear, and the Colonel patted his shoulder. "Easy, easy," he said between coughs. "Almost home."

Sam could imagine that was true. At least, they'd come an awfully long way. They had to be close. It was only fair.

The boat coursed down the tunnel, and time seemed suspended. The walls that passed by on either side were the same liquid black, the water murmured and clapped against the boat, breath came and went, around and around. Sam was surprised to feel Teal'c's hand shaking her, waking her from a doze. They were getting there. Daniel was sitting up, still leaning on the Colonel, his eyes closed.

Colonel O'Neill, though, was watching her, angling his head to see around Eche who was helping Teal'c to slow their progress when the landing came into sight. "Good work, Major," the Colonel said simply.

Sam could only nod, and a smile ghosted across his drawn face.

"Okay, Daniel," he said, tapping the back of Daniel's head with his fist. "Nap time's over. Let's go."

When Daniel's eyes opened and then squinted, annoyed, into the torchlight, Sam found herself actually laughing a little, and at the same time feeling a bit watery with relief inside.

"What?" he mouthed. No sound came out at all. But the Colonel rapped his head again, and Daniel rubbed at it with the heel of his hand. "Ow," he said, and this time it was audible. Whiny and broken, but audible.

While the others crawled out of the boat, Colonel O'Neill felt around inside his jacket and pulled out Daniel's glasses. "Here," he said, handing them over.

Daniel put them on carefully, his hands shaking a little, and raised his head to peer at Sam. One of the lenses was a spider's web of cracks. He squeezed that eye shut. "Gee, thanks," he whispered, the slight curve of a grin softening the sarcasm a little.

With a grunt that might have been a rebuke but which came out more like a laugh, the Colonel pulled the glasses off of Daniel's face, poked his finger through the broken lens, shook the pieces out into the river, and reseated the glasses on Daniel's nose. "Better?"

The intact lens was opaque with torchlight, but Sam could see Daniel's other eye crinkle up. "Much," he said dryly.

"Good."

They were a little closer to home.

The Colonel held Daniel's elbow as they clambered out onto the landing, and Sam held the Colonel's when he slipped on the slick stone and almost tipped backward into the water. Teal'c and the others waited for them where the tunnel started to angle upward away from the river, but Aris and Aadi weren't with them. Aris's boots rang on the stone as he carried Brenneka toward the light of the chapel. After checking to make sure that Colonel O'Neill and Daniel seemed steady enough on their feet, Sam led the way, Hamel stumbling along between Teal'c and Eche.

Once they were back in the chapel, Aris carried Brenneka to the dais and laid her gently at its foot, then waved Hamel and Eche over. They spoke together for a few moments and, although Eche protested, they both remained behind as Aris came to join SG-1.

"So?" Colonel O'Neill asked.

Daniel was gaping upward at the wall of steel. His unsteady finger pointed as he took a step toward it, but he came up short against the Colonel's extended arm.

"Are you nuts?" the Colonel demanded.

Daniel closed his mouth and frowned as though he were seriously considering the question.

With a roll of the eyes, the Colonel turned back to Aris. "So?" he repeated.

Aris looked over his shoulder to where Eche was squatting in front of Hamel, dabbing at Hamel's face with a square of sterile gauze. Teal'c was watching. Beside Eche was a small stack of foil packets from Teal'c's pockets.

"They'll be safe here while I take you topside to get an idea of what's going on up there." Aadi moved closer to his father. "Yeah, you can come," Aris added, although he didn't look too happy about it. Sam knew how much luck he'd have getting Aadi to stay behind.

"And then?" she asked.

"Then I bury my sister." He walked away before they could say more.

Topside was seething. Their small quarter seemed mostly deserted when they slipped through the low door into the alley and then made their way to the tiny courtyard, but the unmistakable sounds of a riot came from the direction of the mine. Sam braced a hand on the gate and leaned back to look up at the Ancient tower. It rose unperturbed against the pink-edged grey of early morning clouds, but behind it death gliders cut through the sky in elegant arcs, swooping low to strafe the streets on the far side of the city, then shooting upward to hang at the top of their pendulum swings before falling back downward for another run. Sam counted five as she walked to the other end of the courtyard and stood next to the Colonel. Above the rooftops they could see the livid glow of a massive fire: the processing plants, still burning, she guessed. The Colonel's face was grim.

"Can't see squat from here," he muttered. Then louder, "We need a better vantage point. See if we can get to the 'gate."

Aris shouldered past them to lead the way. He stopped when he noticed that they weren't following, and he pointed ahead. "Come or not. But make up your mind. There's a revolution on, in case you hadn't noticed."

Sam spared half a thought on why the Colonel started moving then, why he would even consider following Aris, but there was no time for debate. He took Aris's lead, Daniel walking behind, Teal'c at his shoulder. Sam brought up the rear.

Aris led them away from the worst of the noise. At one of the broader alleyways, they were caught in the riptide of the crowd, half the people running away from the riots, half toward it. Teal'c gripped Daniel by the upper arm and guided him deftly across the intersection after Aris and Aadi, while Sam and the Colonel took their chances alone, getting bowled over more than once in the process. From there, the *ha'tak* was visible, and it was clear that the death gliders were concentrating their fire on the space around it, no doubt keeping back the crowds. They moved on, winding their way through the streets and alleys, past gangs of workers with shovels and picks and determined or crazed or desperate expressions, past huddles of children who hunched themselves into smaller knots or dispersed into the corners and crevices of the city. Under their feet, the Nitori swirled in glass and the mosaic faces of their people gazed upward at the empty sky. There was no lightning or whirlwind. There were six thousand slaves and a few hundred Jaffa, and a dead wannabe god, and another on his way.

She wondered how far away Yu was and what he would do when he arrived to find the mine collapsed and the city in full rebellion. Maybe this place was dismal and miserable and worthless enough that he would find no value in reclaiming it. Maybe he'd blast the mountains down on them. Sam couldn't help her gaze straying to the sky: she looked for a hint of lighting, a gust that could be a whirlwind. The people were on the road. Where were Ancients and their promises now?

After what seemed like endless turning and doubling back to get around crowds and noise, they emerged into the square in front of a squat, windowless bunker: the *roshna* stores. While the death gliders blasted holes in the mosaic walkways of the old city and toppled the remaining towers into the streets, the people dodged and ran and killed the Jaffa guards, overwhelming them with numbers and desperation. They came together in front of the wide doorway of the storehouse where the sturdy, belligerent bulk of Esa emerged from inside the bunker. He held his fists over his head, one closed around a staff weapon, the other clutching a bag full of phosphorescent blue packets. Esa shook his trophies at the sky and at the death gliders. The roar of the crowd's triumph made Sam cover her ears.

Aris skirted the edge of the riot, down another narrow passageway, up a long flight of stairs and then another, and finally out onto an open landing above the city. From there they could see plumes of smoke rising from the bunker where they'd been held, from the processing plants, and even from the blasted hulks of heavy equipment at the base of the *ha'tak*, although the ship itself didn't appear to have been breached. New layers of black dust and smoke hung low and choking over most of the city, wreathing the *ha'tak* and the Ancient tower. The death gliders made pass after pass around the mothership, protecting it for a god who was never going to return. Behind Sam on the landing, Aris's ship gleamed dully as the first rays of sunlight stabbed between the mountains.

"Yep," the Colonel said, gazing into the distance and the smoke. "That's a revolution, all right."

# CHAPTER TWENTY-ONE

Anarchy was good, Jack thought, as he fought the urge to sit down and pass out. His eyes were dry and burning from the fine ash and soot in the air. Overhead, death gliders continued their circular patterns over the city, laying down cover fire. Jack backed up instinctively, squinting into the sun to see if they had now become one of the many targets, but the ships soared by without nearing their position. "How many people do you have contributing to this little rebellion?" he asked, looking at Aadi.

The kid looked scared to death, but his father's hand on his shoulder made him taller, and he lifted his chin. "I don't know. Bren was the one who planned it. She always said there were many who would help, once they believed they could win."

"Looks like they believe it now," Jack said. He stared down at the destruction being wrought in the name of freedom. He'd seen it, been in the middle of it, what seemed like a thousand times, and the weariness in his body was the heaviest exhaustion he could ever remember. He shook it off and took a quick inventory. Carter looked dead on her feet, but she was alert. He could see it in her eyes, the burden of command and decision-making, still active in her quick, assessing glances. Teal'c had looked better, and Jack suspected he was going to hear that Teal'c had taken a few knocks of his own, but it wouldn't come up until Fraiser had her hands on him. Daniel was worst off. Jack didn't even want to look at the back of his throat. The idea of the wound there made his teeth clench. They had to get the hell off this world, and if they couldn't find a way in the middle of a full-fledged rebellion, they didn't deserve their hard-to-kill reputation any longer.

"Sir," Carter said. "Brenneka told me there are only a few thousand of her people left. They're no match for a mothership full of troops."

"Never underestimate my people, Major." Aris was watching the sky, and a calculated look, full of satisfaction, had come over his face. "This has been a long time coming."

"They're expecting you to bring weapons to their rescue," Carter said. The anger in her tone made Jack turn to look at her. She was shaking, not much, but enough that Jack could see it. Delayed shock, Jack guessed, but she knew he was watching her, and she got herself under control. She was a hell of a leader.

"They know by now it's not going to happen," Aris said, gesturing at the valley beneath them, which still trembled with aftershocks from the deep-ground collapse below. "But they're still fighting, aren't they?"

A stab of pain shot up through Jack's arm, direct from the abused fingers of his hand, but he ignored it. Beside him, Daniel had slumped at Teal'c's feet, but now he groaned and sat up, his eyes more focused than they had been since they'd left the library. Jack took a long, assessing look at him, at the way his body was shaking, and said to Aris, "We don't have time to stand around debating. Point us the way to the Stargate and we'll be out of your hair."

"We do not have our GDOs," Teal'c said.

Jack turned to look at Carter, whose expression caught his irritation and flung it right back. "We haven't exactly been in control of what equipment we had access to, sir."

"Well, we can gate to the alpha site," Jack said, but Aris was already shaking his head.

"You won't get through the Stargate," Aris said. "That's the only thing on this rock valuable enough to put a guard on."

"You could hide with us," Aadi offered quietly. He rested his fingers on Carter's sleeve. "I know our kin would be willing to shelter you here, for as long as it takes."

"Thank you, Aadi," she told him, curling her fingers over his. She gave him a small, genuine smile, not the kind that was PR. "But you have your own people to worry about, and we have injured."

Jack didn't especially like being lumped into that category, but her assessment was accurate.

"We could help care for them," Aadi said, returning Carter's smile. Under other circumstances, Jack would have been grateful for any help at all, but now, accepting it would involve staying. He was turning to Plan C, which involved going by any means necessary.

Aris angled his head up to look at the clouds. "Yu's coming. By then most of us will be in the mountains, if we have any luck at all. You can hide there as well as anywhere."

"Thanks, but we'll find our own way," Jack said. No more caves and tunnels. When he got home, he was going to sleep in the backyard and stay inside the mountain only long enough to get to nice, quiet, grassy worlds. He nudged Teal'c. "What are the odds we can steal one of those cargo ships?"

"About the same as getting to the Stargate," Aris answered, though he hadn't been asked. "You people aren't equipped."

Jack's annoyance flared again, fueled by his sense of urgency. "You have a better suggestion?"

Aris stroked his son's hair, once, twice. Aadi looked up at him, and Jack saw a spark of adoration in the boy's eyes. So he didn't hate his father, after all. Like most teenagers, he'd only thought he did. "A trade," Aris said. "A fair bargain."

"Really," Jack said, his eyes narrowed. "Maybe you've noticed we don't have anything to trade with?"

Aris held up his free hand, warding off Jack's skepticism. "My word is good on over two thousand planets, Colonel. I didn't get that kind of reputation by cheating my trading partners."

"Whatever," Jack said. He'd already run out of both patience and time, and if Aris was playing some kind of game, he wasn't in the mood. He hadn't completely made up his mind to leave Aris alive when they ditched his planet. "Get to the point."

"You gave me this," Aris said, resting his hands on his son's shoulders. He glanced over at Teal'c, then at Sam, and nodded. Jack had a strong sense of déjà vu. "I'll give you my ship."

"Just like that?" Carter asked. Jack was happy to hear that she was as skeptical as he was. He'd trained her well, clearly. "How do we know it's not a trick?"

"Major Carter, I could already have shot you where you stand. I could have killed you all. Yet here you are." Aris regarded them all with an amused expression, as though they were simple to even have asked the question.

"So you're not being generous, then," Jack said. Aris met his eyes for a long moment.

"Hardly. What would be in it for me?"

"Perhaps you and your son should come with us," Teal'c said, making the question sound like an imperative. Jack shot him a look, but Teal'c studiously ignored him. The last thing Jack wanted was Aris Boch in his way. He wanted Aris Boch on his side even less.

"I'm afraid not. Chances are you won't make it off this planet, and I have other concerns now." Aadi pressed back against Aris, who dropped an arm over his chest to pull him close. "You'd better hurry. Don't forget, Yu is on his way."

"Yu, Yu, Yu," Jack muttered. He'd put that issue on the back burner and let it boil dry. It was like he'd left half his brain down there in that cave of a library.

"Your race's resistance to the Goa'uld…if we could isolate the source of it, think of the benefits to all the races enslaved by them." Carter leaned forward to lend emphasis to her persuasion. Aris looked diffidently at her. "I thought it was the *roshna*," she went on, "but Brenneka told me so much about the Nitori. It might be genetic. Your people could help humans all over the galaxy, if we could just—"

"If I would leave my people to help yours," Aris said. "Not going to happen, Major. Come back and visit us sometime. If we're still here, we'll be happy to help you with your little science project." He moved his hand to his blaster. "My son and I have plans for the Goa'uld."

"Those plans wouldn't include going back down to that vault, would they?" Jack asked. The thought made his skin crawl, and the look on Daniel's face told him he didn't like the idea much, either.

Aris's smile was completely not reassuring. "Not your problem, Colonel. Now get off my planet before I have to shoot you."

"Password," Daniel croaked, and Jack looked down at him, concerned by the way saying even one word made him choke and gasp.

"*Barokna*," Aris said, in answer to the question.

Daniel raised his eyebrows, and Jack asked what he was probably thinking. "The same as the old ship?"

"No reason to change what works," Aris said. He stepped back, pulling Aadi with him. "Here's hoping you're as good a pilot as I am, Colonel. Though I doubt it."

"Here's hoping you manage to live past sunset," Jack said. For Aadi's sake, he left the sarcasm out of it, though he was pretty sure Aris heard it anyway. The twisted smile on Aris's face confirmed it.

"My people are resourceful, Colonel. And so am I." Already Aris was backing away from them, but Aadi pulled away, stared at Carter for a moment and then Teal'c, as if he wanted to come to them.

"Thank you, Aadi," Teal'c said, and inclined his head. Carter smiled again.

"Aadi," Aris said, a tone of command in his voice. The boy's eyes turned glassy with unshed tears, but he nodded his head at Teal'c and retreated to his father's side.

Jack stared up at the ship behind them. With any luck, he might still remember how to fly her. "Let's get the hell out of here," he said, helping Teal'c pull Daniel to his feet.

The password worked like a charm, and once they were all aboard, Teal'c slid smoothly into the pilot's seat, displacing Jack without so much as a request for permission. Jack had some vague thoughts about protesting, but the sharp twinges from his finger stabbed the idea of that right out of his head. Fondling that bug-eye of a control was not going to be easy, so he sat down to play navigator and contented himself with watching the black, disgusting landscape fall away beneath them as they climbed along the rock face and out of the valley.

Behind his shoulder, Carter leaned closer and sucked in a breath at the sight of dead rebels and Jaffa scattered in the streets.

"Better to die free," Teal'c said, in what was always his last word on the subject. No need for Jack to say he agreed. They all did, though it was a damn waste to have to wipe out half a planet's people to get to it.

"Carter," Jack said. "Find us someplace to go. Someplace close, with a 'gate." Daniel was curled up against the wall behind him, and for all Jack knew he could be bleeding to death. Nothing they could do about it but hurry.

"Yes, sir," she said. The pressure on the back of his chair eased when she straightened and went to the center console. A moment later she said, "Sir, there's a *ha'tak* headed straight for this planet. It'll enter orbit in less than three minutes."

"It is undoubtedly Yu's *ha'tak*," Teal'c said, maneuvering them through the last fading blue of planetary atmosphere and out into the yawning darkness of space. Jack scanned the star field. Death gliders and cargo ships swarmed around them. They fit in perfectly.

"Let's just ignore it and get out of here," Jack said. "They won't notice us."

"Sir," Carter said, and before she even said another word he'd heard the entire argument in her tone. "From orbit, that mothership can wipe out entire cities. The revolution will be over before it's even begun."

"They expected it, Carter." Jack swiveled in the seat to face her. "They knew he was coming."

"No, Aris knew. And he knew he couldn't stop Yu. Especially not without a ship." She met his gaze steadily.

"Oh, come on," Jack said, annoyed. "Don't make this out to be a sob story for these people. After what he did to us?"

"There are more lives at stake here than that of Aris Boch," Teal'c said, though he wasn't looking at Jack. "We gave those who assisted us our assurance we would aid them in winning their freedom. Now we have abandoned them to lose it again."

"You know how this game is played, Teal'c," Jack said.

He swung back around. Now the mothership had come into view, a faint speck ahead, but growing. In the foreground was a black shadow that blocked out the stars. A second *ha'tak* already in orbit. As it began to rotate, the central pyramid became a narrow wedge of light.

"I know only that we made a promise in order to secure your freedom," Teal'c said, and now he did turn his head so Jack could see the look of determination on his face.

Jack sighed. "We don't have any weapons. What the hell are we supposed to do, ring over and take them on one by one? Look at us," he said, gesturing widely to include all his walking wounded.

"This vessel is heavily armed," Teal'c said.

"I thought cargo ships didn't carry weapons," Carter said.

"In general, they do not. However, this one does."

"Why wouldn't it?" Jack muttered. "Considering who owned it last."

"Sir," Carter said, pointing at the mothership that was now looming beyond the nearer one. Teal'c maneuvered around to get a closer look. The ship slowed, then assumed orbit.

"It is moving into position to bombard the surface of the planet," Teal'c said. "If we are to act, we must act quickly."

"Can we even do enough damage to make this worthwhile?" Jack asked.

Teal'c glanced back at Daniel, obviously weighing 'worthwhile' with 'promised', and nodded once. "I believe we can."

Jack looked at Carter, whose silence gave agreement. Then he raised his hand, capitulating. "Do it. But make it good, Teal'c. I want to be home in time for dinner."

That tiny ghost of a smile that passed for a grin appeared, then Teal'c gave all his concentration to finding a point of vulnerability on the nearer ship. Both *ha'taks* glowed on the view screen in front of them.

"They have not raised their shields," Teal'c said. "They do not expect attack from other ships."

"Well, at least there's that," Jack said, and leaned back to watch the show. Nothing else to do now but play it out.

# CHAPTER TWENTY-TWO

"SG-one-niner, do you copy?" Jacob boosted the signal and adjusted the orbit of the cargo ship. Most of his attention was taken up by the approaching *ha'tak*, which he'd been watching with growing dismay. His ship was cloaked, not that it mattered; his *tel'tak* was indistinguishable from the other Goa'uld vessels drifting in orbit. The arrival of a second mothership here couldn't be a good sign, not with Sebek's *ha'tak* already on the planet, and this second one rotating into firing position, batteries aimed at the planet's surface. Chatter from the ship in orbit told him that the newcomer belonged to Yu, and Yu was undoubtedly on board. Chatter from the ground told him the remaining city on the planet was in the throes of some sort of rebellion, which meant that, if SG-1 was really down there, they had either caused it or were trapped in it.

With the signal boosters on his ship, Jacob was pretty sure he should've been able to get through to them by now, if they had access to their radios. It was a gamble, but he had nothing else to go on.

He got up and stretched, restless, frustrated. There wasn't much left for him to do here. Either they'd hear him, or they wouldn't; either they were in the middle of chaos, or they were already dead. It could be they'd never come to this planet at all, but there was a part of Jacob that wasn't ready to admit it could be true. It would mean he had no leads, no way to find Sam. This option was better than no option at all.

The display of the planet's surface showed plumes of smoke rising into the atmosphere, circling up from large explosions below.

*If there is a way to escape, they will find it,* Selmak reminded him, ever practical. Jacob was having trouble believing it at that moment, and although he knew Selmak was troubled by his pessimism, he reached for the radio yet again.

"I could put the ship down and take a look around down there," he said, only to be met with Selmak's violent objection.

*You are Tok'ra. In the eyes of half the galaxy, you are no better than a Goa'uld. These people have risen against their masters. Do you wish to kill us both?*

With a sigh, Jacob said, "SG-one-niner, come in. SG-1, do you read me? This is Jacob Carter."

As before, there was nothing but silence. Jacob stared at the ceiling. He'd have to keep hailing. They'd have no idea he was there.

The ship's automatic beacon squawked at him, the proximity warning triggered by the nearest ship. He leaned forward to get a better view. This wasn't exactly a fine specimen of a mothership, by any stretch. A vast section of the outer ring was actually open to vacuum. Maybe it explained why Yu had come to mop up the planet himself. Jacob was vectoring his cargo ship away when a *tel'tak* disengaged from the traffic around the *ha'tak* and blasted across Jacob's bow, laying a heavy pattern of fire against the underbelly of the *ha'tak,* where many of the vital systems were. Then the *tel'tak* swooped around in an elegant turn to finish with a volley of shots directly into the open decks of the ring. The results were immediate and spectacular. Debris blossomed silently as the *ha'tak* started to yaw, the outer ring breaking up, separating in jagged sections. The mothership started to spin away, propelled by the force of the explosions, irreparably disabled.

Jacob double-timed it out of there and looped back above the plane of destruction to watch as Yu's ship changed course in an attempt to avoid the expanding cloud of debris. Too slow, the mothership couldn't avoid a section of the destroyed outer ring that collided with it in a glancing blow, raking and skipping along its underside before tumbling away. The explosions that erupted from the impact proved that Yu's shields weren't up, and, Jacob hoped, with that damage, they wouldn't be. The mystery *tel'tak* emerged from behind one of the largest drifting sections, squeezing between it and the scarred angle of the *ha'tak's* damaged central pyramid, and headed for Yu's mothership.

"Son of a bitch," Jacob breathed. There was a wordless stirring inside him. Selmak agreed.

The *tel'tak* rose up, gracefully slipping past two death gliders that turned to challenge it, and circled around to the sloped side facing the planet. A moment later, the ship's navigational array was reduced to spark and cinder. Precision shooting, Jacob noticed, and precision flying. This was no local native who'd managed to grab a ship and take the fight to the air.

This was someone who knew how to fly.

The *ha'tak* returned fire, striking the ship's thrusters and sending the little craft spinning for a moment before the pilot righted her, and then ducked to evade the gliders giving chase. Jacob leaned forward and switched the com signal over.

"Unidentified vessel, do you read me? This is Jacob Carter. Come in."

A moment's silence, and then, behind a burst of static, a familiar voice: "Jacob? Jacob, what the hell are you doing here?"

Jacob grinned, and Selmak mirrored his elation. "Jack! I could ask you the same question. Is Sam there with you?"

"I'm here, Dad." At the sound of her voice, the tension Jacob had been carrying released, like a knot unwinding from the base of his spine, and he took a deep breath. "Your timing couldn't be better," Sam said.

"We've got damage, Jacob." Jack was all business. "And we've got wounded."

"Stand by to ring over. I'll de-cloak."

"No, wait," Jack said. There was a period of silence, then Jack came back online. "Teal'c's going to ram this thing right down Yu's throat. Can you grab us out of here in time?"

"You bet."

He watched Teal'c take out one of the gliders, then lined up behind him until the second glider had been blown out of space. Teal'c had probably never met a death glider he hadn't dreamed of destroying. Jacob matched their speed and got into position below the other ship. It was a tricky maneuver, and he immediately ceded control to Selmak, who had the experience to get it right the first and only chance they'd have.

"Stand by," Selmak told them, and then Jacob was up and moving, toward the ring controls. A press of a few buttons and the rings activated. No time to spare to make sure he had them all. He caught sight of people within the rings and ran back to the pilot's seat to cloak and move away.

The *tel'tak* above accelerated suddenly as the autopilot kicked in, headed straight for the command bridge of Yu's ship. Selmak handed Jacob back control as he sped away, putting safe distance between them and the imminent collision.

Jack's hand landed on his shoulder and squeezed hard. "I don't know how you knew we were here, but I'm damned glad you showed up," he said, and Jacob grinned.

"You should be glad. I saved your ass. What the hell were you thinking, attacking a mothership?"

"It was his idea," Jack said, jerking a thumb at Teal'c, who was claiming the navigator's seat as his own. "Thinks he's invincible."

"Unlike the rest of us," Sam said. She leaned forward to kiss Jacob's cheek. He raised an arm and hugged her, pulling her closer.

"It's good to see you, kid," he said softly, taking in the dirt and blood all over her. She shook her head, answering his unspoken question.

"You too," she said, with a smile that told him she knew exactly why he was here.

"Carter," Jack said, calling her attention forward and Jacob's with it. The *tel'tak*-turned-missile slammed into Yu's ship, creating a spectacular light show that died within moments, only to reveal Yu's ship mostly intact, although there was a satisfyingly ugly scar on the pyramid below the command decks. Still, he'd hoped for better. "Crap," Jack said.

"Considerable damage has been done," Teal'c reported. "All weapons systems are non-operational. Yu's shields are down."

"He'll retreat now," Jacob said.

"It's enough to give them a fighting chance, sir," Sam said.

"Well, that's nice," Jack said, and his sarcasm alone told Jacob there was a long story behind it. "Glad we were there to help." Jack crouched behind Daniel, who was unconscious on the floor. His face and arms were covered in fresh and dried blood. "I think it's time we took care of our own now."

"The closest planet is Relos," Jacob said, and Jack's head snapped up. The score he planned to settle was written all over his face, but Daniel stirred, and Jacob could see Jack setting that account aside for now. "I have a GDO. We can gate in from there. George'll be anxious to see you."

"It'll be good to be home," Sam said, taking Jacob's hand.

# CHAPTER TWENTY-THREE

Janet glanced up from her charts and slipped off her stool to meet Sam in the doorway of the infirmary. Her smile was bright, but her eyes were dulled with fatigue. She'd spent the night clucking over them, as the Colonel would put it, running tests and doing meticulous examinations of all their wounds, asking questions and patting each one of her wayward SG-1 gently with warm, firm hands in that way that was somehow both admonition and comfort. She took it personally when they came back broken.

"Right on time," she said to Sam and nodded her toward a bed on the other side of Teal'c's.

Teal'c's eyes followed Sam as if he were in prison and pleading for a jailbreak, but he followed orders and stayed in bed, resting, aiming his eyes again at the ceiling when she shrugged helplessly at him. Sam grinned, even though that pulled at the bruises on the side of her face. It was the good kind of pain.

The Colonel wasn't in bed; he'd claimed the only chair in the room, at the head of Daniel's bed, and had tipped it back precariously on two legs, using the wall behind him for support. He was still in surgical scrubs and slippers, which probably were his only concession to medical protocol, and Sam was sure he and Janet had argued about that, too. His hands were laced over his stomach, and his eyes were closed. Sam was amazed he could sleep that way and not break his neck.

Daniel was awake, though, and sitting up in bed in the circle of lamplight, the lamp angled so that the Colonel's face was in shadow. Across Daniel's lap lay a heavy, battered book, open to the middle. His head was bowed, his gaze intent on the text, and his brow furrowed. The fingers of his left hand rubbed his throat absently.

Janet flicked her penlight into Sam's eyes. "Any blurred vision? Dizziness? Ringing in the ears?"

The list of questions went on, and Sam answered them mechanically as she watched Daniel over Janet's shoulder. When Janet paused to probe Sam's black eye again, Sam took the opportunity to ask in a half-whisper, "How are they?" She could feel the Colonel's attention turn their way, even though he didn't move at all. Daniel kept poring over the book, oblivious.

Janet followed her gaze and then looked back at her, taking a moment to grasp the ends of the stethoscope around her neck, as if considering how much to tell and how much to tell by not telling. "*Physically*," she began, pausing to let the question of psychological wellbeing hang like a question mark between them, "they're not in bad shape. Daniel's mouth is pretty cut up from the symbiote's exit, but his throat is in better shape than I expected." She shrugged with her face. "I'm sure the Goa'uld—" Her eyebrows raised with the question.

"Sebek."

"—Sebek – wasn't concerned with being gentle when he left, but all Goa'uld secrete enzymes to aid with host transfer and…well, we don't really know how exactly, but the enzymes do the trick, regardless. At least they closed the wound well enough for healing to begin, and Daniel's body will do the rest." She looked at Daniel again, a half-smile dimpling her cheek. "Lucky for him. He might have bled to death otherwise."

"What about the protein marker?"

Janet shook her head. "No, nothing. Not even trace amounts of naquadah. It may be because the symbiote was having trouble with the blending. He won't be operating any ribbon devices, if that's what you're wondering."

Sam didn't bother hiding her uncomfortable response to that image. The legs of the Colonel's chair cracked down onto the concrete with a sharp *clank*. He was leaning forward, elbows on his knees, hands clasped between them, his head bowed. Daniel dragged himself out of his book to touch him on the shoulder, and he sat back again, slumped for a moment, then pulled himself up straighter to make a show of looking at Daniel's book.

Teal'c gave up contemplating the lighting fixtures and gazed at Sam instead. As she slid off of her bed, he pushed himself up on his elbows. Janet helped Sam stuff an extra pillow behind his head and raise the bed so he could sit upright.

"Aren't you supposed to be resting, Carter?" the Colonel asked without looking at her. He made as if to turn the page of Daniel's book, but Daniel flattened his hand against it, refusing.

"I'm rested, sir. Just checking in with Janet." She tucked her fingers into her pockets and came to lean her hip on the rail of Daniel's bed.

The Colonel made another attempt at turning the page, and this time Daniel slapped his fingers. "Hey, commanding officer here," the Colonel protested, shaking the sting out of his hand. Daniel snorted. O'Neill rolled his eyes. "Civilians." Sam's smile offered no sympathy, but the Colonel graciously overlooked the insubordination, asking, "You eat?"

She nodded. "Meatloaf."

"Ah. Jell-o?"

She made a face. "Green."

"Bastards."

"Yes, sir."

"Our Jell-o was red," Teal'c added, smugly.

Sam grinned at him before turning to aim her chin at Daniel's book. "What's this?" She angled her head so that she could see the picture more or less right-side-up. It was a row of eyeless stone faces against a backdrop of long, wind-bowed grasses, and, at the upper margin, a sliver of ocean, a turbulent sky.

The Colonel tapped one of the faces with his knuckles, his little finger in its splint held up delicately to ward off Daniel. "Easter Island," he answered. "Daniel's obsessing."

"Ah." Of course he was. Sam didn't divulge the fact that she'd spent most of her 'resting' time poring over databases trying to find something equivalent to the technology they'd found in that mountain, something that could scour thoughts from a subject's head, record and communicate them to others. The Tok'ra memory recall devices seemed to function on a similar principle and were maybe some nth generation adaptation of technology scavenged in the distant past, but they used nowhere near the same level of destructive invasiveness. She wondered if that aspect was part of the nominal operation of the library system, or if it had been the result of some kind of malfunction. The former option was pretty creepy to contemplate, and she was glad that, whoever they were, the library builders seemed to be long gone.

"Did you know that those statues on Easter Island had eyes?" the Colonel was saying. "Big, blank, white eyes." This time, Daniel let him page back and angle the book up a bit so she could see an example. The effect was chillingly familiar. She suppressed a shudder, and ran her hands over her arms to soothe the sudden pricking of gooseflesh.

"Yeah, my reaction exactly." He flipped back to the centerfold.

"Do you believe that these people are descendants of those who built the library, Daniel Jackson?" Teal'c was leaning on one elbow so that he could see the book over the Colonel's head.

In answer, Daniel shook his head slowly. "No," he said, but it came out as a wisp of voice. He winced and swallowed carefully, his tongue running across the inside of his cheek. The Colonel leaned back and snagged a cup of ice chips from the table beside him, waited while Daniel shook a few into his mouth, and then put it back again. Daniel was quiet while the ice melted, his fingers tracing the outline of the stern stone face. "But they met them," he finished finally.

"Too bad for them," the Colonel observed flatly.

"Maybe—" Daniel began and paused to accept another offering of ice chips, this time twisting the cup into a fold of blanket by his side. "Maybe the memories of their ancestors were in there somewhere, in the walls."

The Colonel sat back in his chair and rolled his head, left and right. Sam could actually hear the crackle in his neck. "Gone now," he concluded, and wasn't at all upset about that, it seemed.

"Yeah. I guess so." Daniel looked about as disappointed as Sam would expect, but there was a faint tremor of relief in his voice.

"And no snake is running around with all that stuff either, or sucking people's brains out of their heads." The Colonel punched Daniel lightly on the shoulder with his good hand. "Consolation prize."

Daniel nodded, but he still looked pained.

Sam contemplated the figures in the photograph. "Seems strange, though, to put up monuments to something like that. If it was so terrible." Her eyes met Daniel's long enough to see that 'terrible' didn't come close, and she looked away. The Colonel's face betrayed nothing.

Teal'c grunted his agreement but added, "Perhaps it was a reminder, so that they would not be tempted to greet them again."

Sam thought of that ribbon knotted under her ribs, the way it had dragged her forward, how much she'd *wanted* whatever was at the other end of it. Her fingers kneaded her sternum restlessly as if she could untangle that tether. She caught herself, closed her hand into a fist and let it drop to bounce a few times on the top of the bed rail.

"Smart folks," the Colonel said and tipped his chair back to look wistfully up at the ceiling. "In other news, I'm bored enough to eat Jell-o. Even green."

Sam straightened. "Yes, sir." Somehow it seemed like a tremendous relief to go on a quest for something as mundane as Jell-o. "Anything else?"

"I have some journals I need—"

"Shut up, Daniel," the Colonel ordered.

"Or," Daniel amended with as sidelong glance at him. "A chessboard."

"Cards."

"Or cards."

"Or, Major…" Colonel O'Neill's chair clanked down again. He leaned forward to scope out the room and the fierce doctor filling out charts at her desk by the door. "You could stage a jailbreak. You're good at that. So Teal'c says." He raised his eyebrows hopefully at her. "We could find steaks."

A plan was already taking shape in Sam's head when there was a pointed 'ahem' from the corner and Janet impaled them each in turn with a glare.

Sam looked from Janet to her CO. "Yeah, sir, but those were only Jaffa."

"Wuss," he muttered and sat back glumly.

Teal'c also leaned back against his pillows and resumed his perusal of the ceiling. Sam grinned at his quiet, "Indeed."

No matter how hard he tried, Daniel wasn't able to look at his reflection.

He washed his hands without casting his eyes up to the mirror over the sink, because he was afraid of what might be there, or might be missing. He knew it was irrational in the extreme, but that made no difference at all.

There was no one to tell, no one who might understand. At least, no one on whom he wanted to inflict the pain of remembering what being taken as a host was like. Sam had endured Jolinar's memories for so long now that he was sure she could happily live the rest of her life without ever thinking of Jolinar again. Jack...well, he was a closed book on the subject of blending. It had happened to him twice now, and he'd never wanted to talk about any aspect of it. Daniel felt awkward, knowing they shared that horror and couldn't speak of it. That left Dr. MacKenzie, the program shrink, and Daniel had nothing to say to him. Some things needed to be dealt with privately.

He gripped the edges of the sink, overcome with a feeling of vertigo so strong he could barely stand upright.

His throat was still sore. When he thought about why, nausea built in the pit of his stomach and bile welled up, ready to spill over. With an effort, he controlled his retching until the urge to vomit had passed. He splashed water on his face, cool enough to take the sting of sweat away, and toweled off slowly. Eventually, he was going to have to get some sleep, but not yet. There was work to do; his sketches of the glyphs from Atropos were scattered across the desk and worktables of his office. He could make the work last all night, and many nights to come.

By the time he'd wandered back down the deserted corridor – even the diehard workaholics were home by two in the morning – Jack was sitting in Daniel's office, swiveling slowly around in Daniel's desk chair and stopping once each revolution to glance at the sketches. He looked up when Daniel came in and nodded to him.

"Hey."

"Hey," Daniel replied, gathering up the piles of sketches as he crossed the office.

"It's 0230," Jack said, watching him.

"Yep." Daniel kept his eyes on his own hands. "Which begs the question: why are you still here?"

"Mission report's due at 0800," Jack said. "They don't write themselves, you know."

"Believe me, I know." He'd finished up his own frustratingly vague report around midnight. Once in a while, Daniel had secretly thought that if Jack could outsource writing all his own reports, he'd probably do it in a heartbeat. It would have saved Jack from many late nights hunched over a keyboard, procrastinating by interrupting various members of his team who were trying to write their own late reports.

Daniel went to the desk and began straightening up the messy stacks of paper and sketches. Stray pieces fluttered from the pile. Jack caught one crinkled bit before it hit the ground. "I would've thought you'd be sick of staring at these," Jack said, turning the paper right side up, then upside down again, before handing it back to Daniel.

"I wanted to draw out as many of the glyphs as I could," Daniel said. "Before I forget it all."

"Sometimes forgetting's not a bad thing," Jack said. He fished a couple of pencils out of Daniel's desk drawer and began toying with them.

"There's not that much left to forget," Daniel said. He set down his stack of sketches, then leaned back against the counter and folded his arms over his chest. "I don't remember any of the things I was trying to pry out of Sebek. Most of the trip down into the library is fuzzy, too. It's like…it's like I can almost get to it. But not quite." He stared at the naked fluorescent lights overhead for a moment. "It feels like it did when I first descended. There are pieces missing, and I can't reach them. I don't know where to find them."

"Then stop looking." Tap, tap. Jack rapped the pencils together in an uneven rhythm.

Daniel shook his head. "That's fine for you. But I hate this...
this..." He held a hand up to his head and made a hooking motion.
"These gaps in my brain."

"Listen, Daniel. Some things aren't meant to be remembered."
The pencils stilled. "Shifu knew it. Oma must've known it. Who
really wants to know what a snake thinks?" The grimace of disgust on Jack's face said it all. He was perfectly content to leave
some things buried as far down in his subconscious as they could be
shoved, and that was fine for him, but the desire to access knowledge
– Sebek's knowledge, the library, even his own ascended memories
– was a compulsion for Daniel. Jack didn't understand.

*Compulsion.* The thought sent a shiver of memory down Daniel's
spine. That was one thing he wouldn't mind forgetting, but he didn't
have the choice of which memories he could touch and examine
and which were hidden from him now. He couldn't articulate any of
this to Jack, though, so he picked up one of his sketches and traced
the figure with his finger. "I've been comparing this to the *rongo
rongo* on Easter Island. Looking for connections. Patterns. Maybe
there are remnants of that technology somewhere else. It could be
important, if we found it and learned to use it."

"Maybe you'll find something," The way Jack said it suggested
other unspoken words behind it: *There's nothing there, Daniel.
Forget it.*

For a moment, Daniel's finger continued around the curving
edges of the small figure, following a cold trail. Around and around,
slower, and then he stopped. "Maybe."

"Memory is tricky." Jack dropped the pencils on the desk and
stood up. Hands shoved in his pockets, he said, "The way I see it,
it's a good thing you have those gaps."

Daniel met Jack's eyes. They'd known each other for a long
time; Jack didn't need to spell it out. The knowledge he was missing was what could have been acquired and used by the thing in
that library – worst case, he could have been the instrument to harm
or kill millions. A shiver gathered at the base of his spine, curving
through him. He took a deep breath, let it out, and the chill in his
skin dissipated.

Although Daniel hadn't said anything, Jack nodded, as if in response to his unspoken agreement. "Go home, Daniel. Get some sleep."

"Jack." Daniel's voice stopped Jack in the doorway. The harsh light sharpened the lines of fatigue on Jack's face. "Are you able to forget?"

"Forget what?" Jack smiled briefly at Daniel as he rounded the corner and headed home. Which, Daniel had to admit, sounded like a good idea. He was ready for some uninterrupted sleep. There were mirrors everywhere in his new house, but he could avoid those until he was ready to recognize himself in them. Maybe it wouldn't take as long as he'd feared.

# SNEAK PREVIEW

# STARGATE ATLANTIS: THE CHOSEN

"Heads!" Aiden Ford announced, his boyish features alight with triumph. "Victory is mine."

Teyla's brow creased. "What have you won, Lieutenant?"

"The last brownie." Pocketing the coin, Ford grabbed the desired treat and plunked it onto his tray. Stackhouse walked away with slumped shoulders.

"We still have brownies?" John Sheppard's eyebrows shot up as he settled into a seat at the nearest table.

"That was the last one."

"Damn."

"Yeah."

"Please tell me the defenders of our fine city aren't spending their time mourning the lack of desserts." Rodney McKay announced his arrival with a characteristic scoff.

After the waking nightmare that had been the storm and the concurrent Genii assault on Atlantis, John thought they'd all gained a new sense of ownership, for lack of a better term, of this place. It *was* their home, damn it. They'd paid for it in every way imaginable. Right now, just being able to sit here and argue about dessert was enough to provoke a sensation of deep relief. It was normal, and normalcy had been in short supply from day one.

"You're getting on *our* cases about provisions?" Ford looked indignantly across the table at Rodney. "After your little one-man melodrama with the coffee?"

"Do I need to explain the debilitating neurological effects of caffeine withdrawal again?" the scientist fired back.

"No," John cut in, glancing over at their Athosian teammate. "Teyla, little mystified by this overdose of Earthly idiosyncrasy?"

Teyla looked grateful that someone had brought her back into the conversation. "I am still pondering this 'coin toss' Lieutenant Ford spoke of. It is a contest of some kind?"

Ford withdrew a coin from his pocket. "We generally use them as currency, but sometimes we use them to make a choice by tossing it in the air, and assigning a decision to whichever side lands face up."

"Would it not be more beneficial to weigh the positive and negative aspects of each option, rather than make a choice at random?"

"Well, yeah, but there are times when both options seem equally right, so you leave it to chance, fate."

"I see." Her tone suggested that she didn't. With long fingers, she plucked the medallion from the Lieutenant's hand and studied it. "The design is intricate."

"That's the symbol of my Marine division." Ford pointed to the crest. "There's a tradition that says if someone catches you without your unit coin with you, you have to buy them a drink."

"A drink?" Teyla shot him a curious look.

"Of alcohol, preferably," John elaborated, reaching for his glass of water. "But if there are any stills cropping up around here, Lieutenant, I don't want to know, because I'd have to put the responsible parties in my weekly report. And you know I like to keep those as short as humanly possible."

Ford's expression froze somewhere between a knowing grin and feigned innocence. A second or two passed before he opted for a change of subject. "You got a challenge coin, Major?"

"What? You thought it was just a Marine tradition?" John reached into his back pocket, withdrew a scratched silver coin, and handed it to his second in command.

"Special ops. Cool," said Ford, reading the designator. "Bet you've got some hardcore stories to tell, huh, sir?"

On second thought, maybe that hadn't been such a bright idea.

"Stories, yes – stories to tell, not so much."

"Because you can't say? Or because you don't want to?" The young man's expression betrayed his naïveté.

"Little of column A, little of column B." For John, part of the allure of the Pegasus Galaxy had been the fact that, here, his record wasn't nearly as remarkable – and not in a good way, either – as it was on Earth. He'd been happy to let the Marines believe that he was nothing more than a throttle-jockey, rank not-withstanding. His days of relative anonymity on that front were probably over, thanks to his star turn during the Genii attack. Now, there could be no denying his... What was the proper euphemism? Breadth of experience? The trail of dead Genii in his wake during the storm had seen to that.

Then there'd been the unrelenting *thud* of bodies striking the gate shield, one after another, until a rational person could no longer keep count.

Deliberately shoving that thought aside, John grabbed something that passed for a French fry off Rodney's tray before changing the subject. "I used that to decide whether to come along on this little road trip."

"To *Atlantis*? You flipped a *coin*?"

John shrugged, choosing not to complicate the issue with details. Rodney, of all people, nodded understanding and pulled something from inside his jacket. "I keep a Loonie around for just such contingencies." He held it out to Teyla, pointing to the bird on the dollar's face. "This is legal currency in my home country, as opposed to whatever those two are carrying around."

Behind a tall glass of Athosian fruit juice, Ford was hiding a smirk.

The Canadian scientist made a great show of turning to him in mock curiosity. "I presume you have some brilliant play on words to share? Because, gosh, I've never heard a Loonie joke before."

"No, nothing." Ford made a valiant attempt to resist the urge to make a wisecrack, but ultimately failed. "It's just... Is that a Loonie in your pocket, or are you just happy—?"

John groaned and lightly smacked the back of the Marine's head. "A wide-open shot like that, and that's the best you can do? Not only are you banned from naming things, you're relieved of mocking duty."

"Yes, hilarious, Lieutenant. Did I miss your thirteenth birthday last week?" Rodney glared across the table at them both, but then his attention was diverted by a minor commotion. A huddle of three engineers, expressions running the gamut from irritatingly determined to determinedly irritated, strode into the mess hall.

"This oughta be good," John muttered to Ford.

As the trio neared the team's table, their back-and-forth chatter became audible. "I'm telling you, it wasn't the power surge. It was—"

"Yes, yes, we know. Something else. Helpful suggestion, that."

"Dr McKay," the female member of the gang began. "We've run into a problem with the life-support systems."

Regarding the three-person squad with mild interest, Rodney grabbed the last of his fries before John could sneak any more off the plate. "A little clarification goes a long way, people."

"The storm caused a lot of damage."

The remark had fallen casually from the engineer's lips. Damage. That was one way to put it. John cast a surreptitious glance at Rodney.

The scientist's face didn't overtly change, but he tugged unconsciously at the sleeve over his bandaged arm, legacy of a Genii-style interrogation. "As usual, I'm impressed by the collective talent this group has for understatement," he grumbled.

That sounded enough like Rodney's normal self for John's concern to fade somewhat. Normal was good. Hell, even fake normalcy was worth something, because eventually they'd start to believe it.

"Right," replied the engineer. "Well, with the city's help we were able to restore primary life-support power shortly after the storm. Problem is, there are facets of the system that the city doesn't consider crucial. Potable water is critical, for instance, but waste disposal apparently isn't. Hence, a few days' worth of waste, even with a group as small as ours, is beginning to strain the capacity of the storage tanks."

Of all the things that could cause problems on an intergalactic expedition, John had never considered the possibility of clogged toilets. Eat your heart out, Buck Rogers.

"And this relates to me in what way?" Rodney wanted to know.

"Kwesi thinks that—"

"Kwesi thinks that he can speak for himself, thank you," one of the engineers cut in, his gentle Ghanaian accent sharpened by annoyance. "It takes someone with the ATA gene to make much of this technology work, Doctor. We believe that if you could interface with the city systems, you might convince it to rearrange its priorities."

Rodney still looked nonplussed, but John imagined that he could see a glint of something new there. Pride, maybe. Rodney had successfully received the gene therapy, and there was something to be said for being one of the select few to have the magic touch.

That something wasn't always good, but it was something.

"As flattered as I am that you see my potential for a job in sanitation, the city seems to like the Major here better than me."

John's focus snapped fully into the conversation. He got the distinct impression that he'd just been volunteered for something. "Say what?"

"Well put, as always," Rodney muttered dryly.

"But you know the systems better than anyone, Doctor," countered the female engineer, whose name John still hadn't learned but whose skills at buttering up the boss were apparently topnotch.

"I suppose duty calls, then. I should have had overtime pay built into my contract." Rodney rose from the table. Mess hall tray clutched in his hands, he somehow managed to adopt an air of unwavering self-assurance. "Lead on."

The rest of the team followed, picking up their trays and carrying them to the cleanup area. Ford reached down to save his hard-won brownie and discovered it missing. He jerked his head up just in time to see Rodney pop the last bite into his mouth.

"Hey!"

"Don't disparage a man's national symbols or his coffee habits, Lieutenant." The astrophysicist's voice was entirely unapologetic.

John tried not to crack a grin at Ford's crestfallen look. This version of 'normal' felt a little forced. Still, it was a start.

**Continued in** *Stargate Atlantis: The Chosen*
**Available from 21 April 2006**

# STARGÅTE
## SG·1 ™

# STARGATE
# ATLÅNTIS ™

**Original novels based on
the hit TV shows,
STARGATE SG-1 and
STARGATE ATLANTIS**

**AVAILABLE NOW**

**For more information, visit
www.stargatenovels.com**

# STARGATE ATLANTIS: RELIQUARY

Series number: SGA-2

**by Martha Wells**
**Price: £6.99**
**ISBN: 0-9547343-7-8**
**Publication date: February 2006**

While exploring the unused sections of Atlantis, Major John Sheppard and Dr. Rodney McKay stumble on a recording device that contains a new stargate address. The address leads them to a world with a mysterious ruined city that may be part of an Ancient repository of knowledge...

**Order your copy directly from the publisher today by going to www.stargatenovels.com or send a cheque or money order (currency: GB Pounds) made payable to "Fandemonium" to: Stargate Novels, Fandemonium Books, PO Box 795A, Surbiton KT5 8YB, United Kingdom.**

<u>Price</u>
**UK orders: £8.30 (£6.99 + £1.31 P&P)**
**Rest of the World orders: £9.70 (£6.99 + £2.71 P&P).**

Or check your local bookshop – available on special order if they are out of stock (quote the ISBN number listed above).

# STARGATE ATLANTIS: RISING

**by Sally Malcolm**
**Price: £6.99**
**ISBN: 0-9547343-5-1**

Series number: SGA-1

Following the discovery of an Ancient out-post buried deep in the Antarctic ice sheet, Stargate Command sends a new team of explorers through the Stargate to the distant Pegasus galaxy.

Emerging in an abandoned Ancient city, the team quickly confirms that they have found the Lost City of Atlantis. But, submerged beneath the sea on an alien planet, the city is in danger of catastrophic flooding unless it is raised to the surface. Things go from bad to worse when the team must confront a new enemy known as the Wraith who are bent on destroying Atlantis.

Stargate Atlantis is the exciting new spin-off of the hit TV show, Stargate SG-1. Based on the script of the pilot episode, *Rising* is a must-read for all fans and includes deleted scenes and dialog not seen on TV – with photos from the pilot episode.

**Order your copy directly from the publisher today by going to www.stargatenovels.com or send a cheque or money order (currency: GB Pounds) made payable to "Fandemonium" to: Stargate Novels, Fandemonium Books, PO Box 795A, Surbiton KT5 8YB, United Kingdom.**

<u>Price</u>
**UK orders: £8.30 (£6.99 + £1.31 P&P)**
**Rest of the World orders: £9.70 (£6.99 + £2.71 P&P).**

Or check your local bookshop – available on special order if they are out of stock (quote the ISBN number listed above).

# THE COST OF HONOR

**Part two of two parts**

**by Sally Malcolm**
**Price: £6.99**
**ISBN: 0-9547343-4-3**

In the action-packed sequel to *A Matter of Honor*, SG-1 embark on a desperate mission to save SG-10 from the edge of a black hole. But the price of heroism may be more than they can pay...

Returning to Stargate Command, Colonel Jack O'Neill and his team find more has changed in their absence than they had expected. Nonetheless, O'Neill is determined to face the consequences of their unauthorized activities, only to discover the penalty is far worse than anything he could have imagined.

With the fate of Colonel O'Neill and Major Samantha Carter unknown, and the very survival of the SGC threatened, Dr. Daniel Jackson and Teal'c mount a rescue mission to free their team-mates and reclaim the SGC. Yet returning to the Kinahhi homeworld, they learn a startling truth about its ancient foe. And uncover a horrifying secret...

**Order your copy directly from the publisher today by going to www.stargatenovels.com or send a cheque or money order (currency: GB Pounds) made payable to "Fandemonium" to: Stargate Novels, Fandemonium Books, PO Box 795A, Surbiton KT5 8YB, United Kingdom.**

**Price**
UK orders: £8.30 (£6.99 + £1.31 P&P)
South Africa, Australia and New Zealand orders: £9.70 (£6.99 + £2.71 P&P). Not available outside these territories.

Or check your local bookshop – available on special order if they are out of stock (quote the ISBN number listed above).

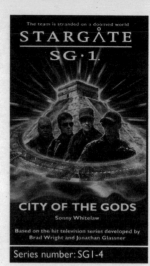

The team is stranded on a doomed world

STARGATE
SG·1

CITY OF THE GODS
Sonny Whitelaw

Based on the hit television series developed by
Brad Wright and Jonathan Glassner

Series number: SG1-4

# CITY OF THE GODS

### by Sonny Whitelaw
### Price: £5.99
### ISBN: 0-9547343-3-5

When a Crystal Skull is discovered beneath the Pyramid of the Sun in Mexico, it ignites a cataclysmic chain of events that maroons SG-1 on a dying world.

Xalótcan is a brutal society, steeped in death and sacrifice, where the bloody gods of the Aztecs demand tribute from a fearful and superstitious population. But that's the least of Colonel Jack O'Neill's problems. With Xalótcan on the brink of catastrophe, Dr. Daniel Jackson insists that O'Neill must fulfil an ancient prophesy and lead its people to salvation. But with the world tearing itself apart, can anyone survive?

As fear and despair plunge Xalótcan into chaos, SG-1 find themselves with ringside seats at the end of the world…

• Special section: Excerpts from Dr. Daniel Jackson's mission journal.

**Order your copy directly from the publisher today by going to www.stargatenovels.com or send a cheque or money order (currency: GB Pounds) made payable to "Fandemonium" to: Stargate Novels, Fandemonium Books, PO Box 795A, Surbiton KT5 8YB, United Kingdom.**

<u>Price</u>
**UK orders: £7.30 (£5.99 + £1.31 P&P)**
**South Africa, Australia and New Zealand orders: £8.70 (£5.99 + £2.71 P&P). Not available outside these territories.**

Or check your local bookshop – available on special order if they are out of stock (quote the ISBN number listed above).

# A MATTER OF HONOR

**Part one of two parts**

**by Sally Malcolm**
**Price: £5.99**
**ISBN: 0-9547343-2-7**

O'Neill faces a nightmare from his past

**STARGÅTE**
**SG·1.**

**A MATTER OF HONOR**
Book One
Sally Malcolm
Based on the hit television series developed by
Brad Wright and Jonathan Glassner

Series number: SG1-3

Five years after Major Henry Boyd and his team, SG-10, were trapped on the edge of a black hole, Colonel Jack O'Neill discovers a device that could bring them home.

But it's owned by the Kinahhi, an advanced and paranoid people, besieged by a ruthless foe. Unwilling to share the technology, the Kinahhi are pursuing their own agenda in the negotiations with Earth's diplomatic delegation. Maneuvering through a maze of tyranny, terrorism and deceit, Dr. Daniel Jackson, Major Samantha Carter and Teal'c unravel a startling truth – a revelation that throws the team into chaos and forces O'Neill to face a nightmare he is determined to forget.

Resolved to rescue Boyd, O'Neill marches back into the hell he swore never to revisit. Only this time, he's taking SG-1 with him…

**Order your copy directly from the publisher today by going to www.stargatenovels.com or send a cheque or money order (currency: GB Pounds) made payable to "Fandemonium" to: Stargate Novels, Fandemonium Books, PO Box 795A, Surbiton KT5 8YB, United Kingdom.**

## Price
UK orders: £7.30 (£5.99 + £1.31 P&P)
South Africa, Australia and New Zealand orders: £8.70 (£5.99 + £2.71 P&P). Not available outside these territories.

Or check your local bookshop – available on special order if they are out of stock (quote the ISBN number listed above).

# SACRIFICE MOON

**By Julie Fortune**
**Price: £5.99**
**ISBN: 0-9547343-1-9**

*Sacrifice Moon* follows the newly commissioned SG-1 on their first mission through the Stargate.

Their destination is Chalcis, a peaceful society at the heart of the Helos Confederacy of planets. But Chalcis harbors a dark secret, one that pitches SG-1 into a world of bloody chaos, betrayal and madness. Battling to escape the living nightmare, Dr. Daniel Jackson and Captain Samantha Carter soon begin to realize that more than their lives are at stake. They are fighting for their very souls.

But while Colonel Jack O'Neill and Teal'c struggle to keep the team together, Daniel is hatching a desperate plan that will test SG-1's fledgling bonds of trust and friendship to the limit…

The team battles an ancient enemy

STARGÅTE
SG·1

TRIAL BY FIRE
Sabine C. Bauer

Based on the hit television series developed by
Brad Wright and Jonathan Glassner

Series number: SG1-1

# TRIAL BY FIRE

### By Sabine C. Bauer
### Price: £5.99
### ISBN: 0-9547343-0-0

*Trial by Fire*, **the first in the new series of Stargate SG-1 novels**, follows the team as they embark on a mission to Tyros, an ancient society teetering on the brink of war.

A pious people, the Tyreans are devoted to the Canaanite deity, Meleq. When their spiritual leader is savagely murdered during a mission of peace, they beg SG-1 for help against their sworn enemies, the Phrygians.

Initially reluctant to get involved, the team has no choice when Colonel Jack O'Neill is abducted. O'Neill soon discovers his only hope of escape is to join the ruthless Phrygians – if he can survive their barbaric initiation rite.

As Major Samantha Carter, Dr. Daniel Jackson and Teal'c race to his rescue, they find themselves embroiled in a war of shifting allegiances, where truth has many shades and nothing is as it seems.

And, unbeknownst to them all, an old enemy is hiding in the shadows…

**Order your copy directly from the publisher today** by going to **www.stargatenovels.com** or send a cheque or money order (currency: GB Pounds) made payable to "Fandemonium" to: **Stargate Novels, Fandemonium Books, PO Box 795A, Surbiton KT5 8YB, United Kingdom.**

#### Price
**UK orders: £7.30 (£5.99 + £1.31 P&P)**
**South Africa, Australia and New Zealand orders: £8.70 (£5.99 + £2.71 P&P). Not available outside these territories.**

Or check your local bookshop – available on special order if they are out of stock (quote the ISBN number listed above).